Intertwined

Also by Jennifer Slattery

Beyond I Do

When Dawn Breaks

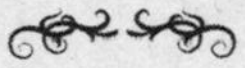

Intertwined

A CONTEMPORARY ROMANCE NOVEL

JENNIFER SLATTERY

BIRMINGHAM, ALABAMA

New Hope® Publishers
PO Box 12065
Birmingham, AL 35202-2065
NewHopePublishers.com
New Hope Publishers is a division of WMU®.

This novel is a work of fiction, and all storylines, plot threads, and characters arose solely from the author's imagination. Any similarities between events, people, and places are purely coincidental. Though the author gleaned information from numerous medical and mental health professionals while researching and writing this novel, she is responsible for any errors within.

Library of Congress Cataloging-in-Publication Data

Slattery, Jennifer, 1974-
Intertwined : a contemporary romance novel / Jennifer Slattery.
pages cm
ISBN 978-1-59669-443-9 (sc)
1. Christian fiction. 2. Love stories. I. Title.
PS3619.L3755I58 2015
813›.6--dc23
2015024858

ISBN-10: 1-59669-443-2
ISBN-13: 978-1-59669-443-9

N154121 • 1015 • 2M1

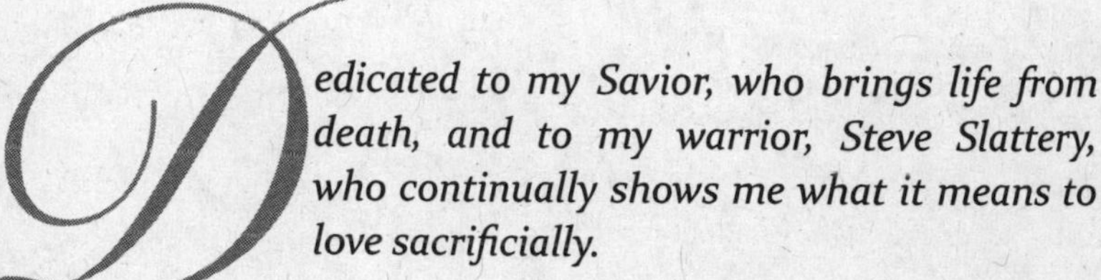

Dedicated to my Savior, who brings life from death, and to my warrior, Steve Slattery, who continually shows me what it means to love sacrificially.

Acknowledgements

First to my sweet, faithful *husband*, who I've affectionately called "Warrior" ever since he donated his kidney to a teenager he had never met (until the week before surgery): you inspire me. Thank you for always supporting my dreams and continually pointing me to Christ. I love doing life and serving Christ with you.

To all the professionals who shared their immense knowledge with me: *Ami Carr Koelliker*, thank you so much for helping me understand the medical processes and procedures involved in organ donation, for reviewing various plot threads for accuracy, and for combing through this story numerous times in order to ensure the utmost authenticity. This novel would not exist if not for you! Thank you also to *Francine Buda-Dardon,* MSLP, from Acuity Counseling Professionals in Papillion, Nebraska, for taking the time to review this story for accuracy in regard to all mental health issues touched on within. To insurance agent *Leon Van Burkam,* thank you for helping me understand all the ins and outs of insurance claims and payouts.

I especially want to thank my amazing, wise, and godly editor *Joyce Dinkins* for her continual guidance, support, prayers, and encouragement. You are such a blessing—major understatement! Thank you so much for all you do, and to your brilliant team as well. As always, thank you to everyone at New Hope® Publishers for allowing me to be part of the New Hope family. Your commitment to Christ, the gospel, and His mission inspires me, and I pray God richly blesses your ministry and continues to expand your reach.

And finally, a big shout out to all my faithful critique partners who had the courage to tell me like it is and the patience to brainstorm new ideas and threads with me, even if that meant you'd have to sift through the manuscript yet another time. *Kathleen Freeman, Laura Hodges Pool,* and *Tanya Eavenson,* thank you for standing by me from first draft to twelfth—or maybe that's the twenty-seventh!

Chapter 1

Tammy pulled into her garage and stared at the entrance door to her home with a heavy sigh. Most likely, her husband Brody was asleep. Or zoned out watching television.

Completely oblivious to their rapidly decaying marriage.

She paused to read the verse taped to her dashboard:

"*Love is patient, love is kind. It does not envy . . . it is not easily angered . . .*"

A similar verse was tacked to the door leading into the house, and another one stuck to her bathroom mirror.

They weren't helping. Nothing was. No matter how hard she tried, how fervently she prayed.

With a heavy heart, she glanced back at her two sleeping kids. Tylan's chest rose and fell, his small lips slightly ajar. Beside him, Becky's strawberry-blonde head leaned against the window, her bangs splayed across her forehead. Such precious little angels.

She reached back and squeezed her daughter's knee. "Hey, sweet girl, we're home."

Becky stirred before opening droopy eyes. She glanced around, yawned, and then got out, shuffling forward in a semialert state.

Tammy moved to the rear passenger side of the car to retrieve her sleeping son. The buzz of cicadas filled the thick Missouri air, ushering forth memories of lazy summer evenings. Back when she and Brody were still in love. Was it too late to rekindle their romance? To begin again?

As if to answer, the door to the kitchen creaked open, and Brody appeared.

"Hey, Dad." Becky stopped in front of him as if waiting for a response.

"Hey." Brody stepped aside to let her pass.

No, *How was your day or hello hug?* When had he become so cold, so uncaring? Swallowing past an unsettled stomach, Tammy offered him what she hoped to be a welcoming smile. "Hi."

He nodded, stepping into the garage and continuing to the car. "I've got Tylan."

She studied his face. The normal edge was replaced by dull eyes and a slackened mouth. "Rough day?"

He held her gaze for a moment, causing the knot in her gut to twist tighter. "We'll talk later."

Nothing good ever followed those words, but whatever it was, they'd get through it.

Right?

Her pulse quickened as she followed her husband, carrying a sleeping Tylan, down the hall and into his bedroom. Crossing the room in three long strides, he laid the child on his comforter, decorated with the Royals' logo. He stirred, and his eyes fluttered open, before closing once again. A slight smile emerged as he rolled on his side.

Tammy unfolded a quilt on the foot of his bed and spread it over him, tucking the edge around his shoulder. She brushed a kiss against his temple. "Good night, sweet boy."

Behind her, Brody's footsteps receded.

She exited Tylan's room and paused in the dimly lit hall to brace herself against an impeding argument. Brody's words replayed through her brain. *"We'll talk later."*

Whatever he had to say, she would respond with love.

The floorboards creaked as she continued down the hall. She popped her head into Becky's room to say goodnight before entering the dark living room. Brody sat with his back to her, in his favorite chair—one she and the kids bought him several Christmases ago.

Not wanting to see her husband's loveless eyes, she kept the lights off.

She sank into the corner of the couch across from him, drawing up her knees and hugging them. Brody stared at his hands, twisted his wedding ring. Silence stretched between them.

She broke it first. "I'm sorry I'm late. Did you get my message?"

He raised his head, nodded.

"Look, if you're mad about—"

"I'm leaving."

Her breath caught. "What?"

He inhaled then let it out slowly. "I'm sorry. This isn't working."

"What do you mean it's not working? Marriage isn't a vacuum or blender you toss out when there's a glitch. Listen, I know things have been—"

"Dead. Our marriage is dead, Tammy."

She closed her eyes and massaged her forehead. "So let's fix it. With God's help—" *Lord, give me strength.*

"I'm in love with someone else. We're getting a place."

Tammy froze, bile seeping up her throat as a sharp pain seared her heart.

"I'm sorry." His eyes softened. "I never meant for this to happen."

"You're sorry?" Hot blood coursed through her, turning her stomach. "You're sorry? Don't give me that garbage. You're sorry for spilling soda or forgetting to pick up the clothes at the dry cleaners, not for . . . not for . . . How could you?"

He stood and raised his hand. "Calm down."

"Don't you dare." The verse taped on her steering wheel flashed through her mind with little effect. "After twelve years! Twelve years of dirty underwear and socks thrown on the floor. Twelve years of packing your lunch, going to your work parties, wiping your whiskers out of the bathroom sink." Tears pricked her eyes as she struggled to control her breathing. Lifting her chin, she leveled her gaze at her husband. "Think about what you're doing. For the kids' sake."

"Mom? Dad?" Becky's voice quivered as her big, blue eyes looked from one parent to the other.

"Oh, baby." Tammy's torso caved inward, a dull ache stabbing at her throat. How could Brody do this? "Everything's okay." Her voice shook. "Go back to bed. I'll be there in a minute."

Standing, she waited until Becky's footfalls had faded then turned to her, her legs threatening to give way. "Don't, Brody. Don't throw it all away."

He exhaled and shook his head. "It's over, Tammy."

Chapter 2
Three years later

Nick Zimmerman sat on the couch, a warm Mountain Dew in his hand. He looked from the clock to the television screen then back to the clock. His ex-wife was late—as usual—and the boys had school tomorrow, but at least he was actually getting his court-ordered visitation . . . for once. A full week and a half this time, which might prove long enough to undo the damage Marianne caused with how often she openly badmouthed him.

He'd filed for joint custody. It was going to cost him, lead to a long, bitter fight, but what else could he do? His boys needed a dad. Nick knew the sting of growing up without a father and refused to let his boys experience that same loss.

He fingered the military dog chain dangling from his neck, thinking of his dad—a man he'd never met, one who'd died a hero fighting for his country.

A vehicle approached and idled outside. Flicking off the television, Nick sucked in a calming breath and uncoiled his fists. Starting the visit with an argument wouldn't help. He clenched his jaw to hold his angry words at bay and walked to the front door.

Outside, a vibrant sunset of reds and purples stretched across the Missouri skyline, promising a beautiful day tomorrow. The idea gave Nick hope, a hope he'd focus on during his conversation with Marianne, one that, based on history, could turn stormy in a flash.

Leaning against the doorframe, he waited while his boys spilled from the car and gathered their things.

Marianne's boyfriend's convertible was parked along the curb. The top was down, and the silver paint looked freshly waxed. Wade, who lived with Marianne and the kids, stood near the rear bumper, acting like a step-in dad.

Gear unloaded, Wade dragged their suitcase up the walk, Marianne at his side. The boys trudged behind like they were heading to detention.

There was a time, not so long ago, when they would run to greet Nick each day he returned from work. How quickly things changed.

This week, he planned to change things back.

"Marianne." He gave a slight nod before turning to her boyfriend. "Wade." Extending a hand, he tried not to smirk at Wade's Miami playboy appearance, spiked hairdo and all. A deeply tanned Marianne stood beside him, thick, blond highlights streaked through her hair.

Nick looked past her to offer his sons an encouraging smile. "Hi, boys."

Payton scowled, his thirteen-year-old frame tense. Jeremy, Payton's seven-year-old brother, frowned and stared at the ground. His thin shoulders slumped.

Wade deposited the boys' suitcase near his feet. "How are things in the restaurant business?" He slid his arm behind Marianne's back.

A tendon in Nick's jaw twitched. "People keep eating."

Marianne ushered the boys forward. "You two, tell your father hello."

"Hey." Payton shoved his hands in his pockets.

Jeremy rolled the toe of his shoe over a pebble. "Hi."

"You two ready to work on your swinging arms?" Nick fist-nudged Payton's shoulder. The teen's scowl deepened. "I was thinking maybe we could visit the batting cages sometime this week. Whatdya' say?"

Payton shrugged, but Jeremy's head bobbed up, eyes bright.

Nick's heart warmed. A few hours of slow-pitch followed by generous scoops of ice cream, and the boys would be back to goofing off and playing pranks.

He faced Marianne. "You got numbers for me — in case you don't have cell phone service, and I need to reach you?"

She nodded and rummaged through a gold bag nearly the size of the boys' suitcase.

While she continued her lengthy search, Nick stepped aside and motioned the boys in. "There's ice cream in the fridge."

Both heads snapped up, Jeremy's cheeky grin flashing missing teeth. Nick chuckled as his youngest bolted for the door.

"Wait a minute!" Marianne caught Jeremy by the wrist. "Aren't you going to say good-bye to your momma?" Pulling him close, she kissed his cheek, leaving a splotch of maroon lipstick. "Remember, I'll call you on Wednesday at seven." She shot Nick a pointed glare. "You feed them way too much junk food." She crossed her arms. "But hey, if you want them jumping off the walls right before bedtime, what do I care?"

He rubbed the back of his neck. "The number, Marianne?"

"Right." She plunged her arm back into her purse and pulled out a wad of folded documents. "Remember, we'll be in the Caribbean. Roaming fees will be unreal." She flipped through the pages sheet by sheet. "If there's an emergency, and you can't reach my cell . . ." She scrunched up her face and chewed on her bottom lip, as if deciphering hieroglyphics. "Well, one of these numbers will work. I'm sure you won't need them anyway." With a flick of her wrist, she handed over the papers.

Nick flipped through the documents. An itinerary, a map of a bunch of islands, a cruise brochure that provided more information on menu choices than who to call in a crisis. Real helpful, but like she said, he wouldn't need them anyway.

She snapped her purse closed and smoothed a lock of hair from her face. "I'll call on Wednesday and Saturday to check on the boys." Her expression hardened. "Please have them close by."

Right. Like she did when he tried to call? He got the answering machine every time. They probably wouldn't be here now if not for her cruise and Marianne's need for childcare. What he wouldn't give to see things flipped. Except he was better than that. Besides, God would make things right, eventually. Had to.

Nick wouldn't lose his boys.

Not without a fight.

Marianne spouted a few more warnings and instructions—like he'd never parented before. He let her rant. It was what she did. In ten minutes, she'd be on her merry way, unloading on Wade.

When she finished, Nick offered a stiff nod, wished them well on their trip, and slipped inside. He found the boys in the living room, halfway through their ice cream. Jeremy had a chocolate ring around his mouth. Payton had located the remote and was flipping through the channels.

Nick sat beside him. "So, what all do you want to do this week?"

Payton shrugged.

Nick grabbed a stack of museum brochures from the coffee table. He handed them over. "I picked these up yesterday. Thought maybe we could—"

"Lame." Payton dropped them onto the seat cushions beside him.

"—visit the air and space museum in Greenwood." Nick suppressed a sigh and leaned against the back of the couch.

Help me out, Lord. Show me how to reestablish our bonds.

Or at least help us get through this visit without a blowup.

He thought of the court case and the long custody battle that lay ahead.

Did the boys even want to live here? Because right now, it seemed they wanted nothing to do with him.

For the next three hours, he watched Payton play video games and Jeremy turn the living room into an army fort, waiting—praying—for an open door. Every time Nick attempted a conversation, Payton scowled, shrugged him off, or worse, ignored him completely. And poor Jeremy seemed torn between the two of them, his sad eyes looking from one face to the other before the boy lost himself in make-believe once again.

Darkness settled around the house, the steady hum of distant traffic growing lighter as other Oak Blossom residents settled in for the night. Whatever connection Nick had hoped for would have to wait until tomorrow.

"How can one boy make such a mess in such a short period of time?" Forcing a nervous chuckle, he flicked off the television and stood. Two sheets draped the coffee table while every book he owned—including phone books—formed an archway entrance.

He nudged Jeremy's shoulder. "Time to clean up, champ."

Jeremy moaned. "But I'm not even tired." The red rims around his eyes said otherwise. "Ten more minutes?"

"Nope. It's late, and I don't want any grumps for our first full day together." He grabbed one of Jeremy's socks lying on the floor and tucked it in the boy's tennis shoe. When Jeremy didn't move, Nick grabbed his elbow and urged him to his feet. His son jerked away.

Nick turned to Payton. "How about you head up to brush your teeth?"

"You're kidding, right?"

Nick crossed his arms.

"Whatever." Payton tossed the remote on the coffee table and bolted from the room.

Jeremy, on the other hand, fisted his hands and scrunched his face. "You can't make me."

Great. Not even a day into the visit and they were already gearing up for their first battle. "Yes, I can. And unless you want to be grounded from all electronics for the next week and a half, I suggest you obey."

"Mom never grounds us." He cocked his head in a comical Marianne imitation, right down to the protruding bottom lip.

"Really?" Eyebrow raised, Nick hid his laugh with a cough. "Then this'll be a new experience for you."

After a brief, nonverbal standoff, Jeremy complied with a huff.

Next step, move from battles to bonding, preferably before their Spring Break ended. Which, since today was Wednesday, gave him eleven days. Although it was much more time than Nick had spent with them in quite a while, it wasn't nearly enough.

Cross-legged on the floor, Jeremy hunched forward, plunking Legos into a box one by one. "How come Payton doesn't have to help?"

"Because he didn't make the mess. But I'll help." Nick started gathering the plastic pieces. "Hand me that, will you?" He pointed to the Lego container.

Jeremy grabbed an old yearbook instead and opened it on his lap. "You in here, Dad?"

Nick glanced at the clock. The boy really needed to get to bed.

But more than that, the two of them needed a connection. Moving to the couch, he motioned Jeremy over. "Bring that here so you can see what a stud your old man used to be."

Jeremy grinned and jumped to his feet. He scooched beside Nick, their shoulders almost touching. Sliding the book between them, he began flipping the pages.

Jeremy's forehead crinkled as he studied the pictures. "Why are these guys wearing tights?"

Nick laughed. "Those are wrestlers, and that's what they wore back then."

"Weird! I'm glad I'm not a wrestler. What about you, Dad? Where's your picture?"

"A few pages over." He started to thumb to the baseball section, then stopped.

"What?" Jeremy grabbed the book and turned it toward him. He grinned. "Is that you with the shaggy hair and flaps hanging from your shirt?"

"Stylin', huh?"

Memories rushing back, Nick stared at the image of his former best friend, Tammy Yorkshire, standing beside a younger version of himself. Incredibly beautiful, her long, blonde hair framed her peachy complexion. He'd always been captivated by her crystal blue eyes, and that night, they'd shone even brighter than normal. She wore a flowing lilac dress and black tennis shoes, the dress a concession to her mother's nagging and the shoes in case she and the gang decided to ditch the dance for something more exciting like garbage tipping.

He smiled, thinking back to their "pact." Neither would turn cheesy, wear perfume or cologne, or waste hours on sappy phone conversations.

Things were so simple back then.

"Who's that?" Jeremy stabbed Tammy's picture with his index finger.

"An old friend." One he hadn't seen since his junior year of high school.

Chapter 3

With the mouse hovering over the Send key, Tammy paused to pray for the recipient of her message. After three years of fighting to live, young Jimmy Williams was now looking forward to college, to marriage, and all those other monumental moments.

But did he know Jesus, the Giver of life? Hopefully her verse, added at the end of her email, would stir his heart. Though ultimately, that was God's job. Hers was to obey and to share His truth, a truth that brought hope out of the darkest of circumstances. Her role as an organ procurement coordinator placed her in the perfect position to help do just that.

She hit Send, closed her laptop, and slid it into her computer bag. Smiling, she gazed through her office window. Such a lovely, sunny afternoon, and she had the rest of the day off. Maybe she and the kids could go for a bike ride before dinner.

The distinct click of her boss's footsteps approaching caused Tammy's neck muscles to tense. The woman was born with a scowl, and grace wasn't part of her disposition. Disciplinary measures, however, were—especially those aimed at Tammy.

Straightening, Tammy smoothed a stray lock of hair behind her ears and focused on her open door. A moment later, Ellen appeared, lips compressed so tight they practically disappeared.

Her pencil-thin eyebrows pinched together. "I need to speak to you. In my office."

Tammy nodded and stood.

Ellen turned on her heel, her sharp footfalls echoing down the hall.

Tammy rubbed her temples. If this job weren't so important, she'd quit.

Breathing deep, she dropped her phone into her back pocket and slipped out. She plodded down the hall and into Ellen's office.

Ellen looked up, her expression firm. "Close the door."

Tammy did, lingering near the entrance for a moment. Swallowing, she crossed the room and settled into the leather chair across from her boss. "Is something wrong?"

Ellen raised folded hands to her mouth and rubbed her upper lip with her knuckle. She studied Tammy as if attempting to search her brain. Or annihilate it.

"I just got off the phone with Dr. Bolton, the chief of physicians's relations at Children's Memorial."

Tammy held her breath.

"Dr. Prague has filed a complaint."

Tammy's face burned. With a nod, she cleared her throat. "I should have handled the situation better. We had a twelve-year-old — "

Ellen raised her hand. "I don't care what the circumstances were. What I want to know is, did you tell him," she glanced at a paper in front of her, "and I quote, 'I would think you'd be interested in saving lives, Doctor, not filling beds'?"

"I apologized immediately. It was a stressful night. The hospital was understaffed and . . . irritable. As I started to say, we had a twelve-year-old potential donor, but we were waiting for the family to arrive in order to gain consent. Dr. Prague said he needed the bed. I explained to him how many lives could be saved if he would wait. He grew frustrated and . . . unpleasant."

She paused and flattened her hands on her thighs. "I should've taken a moment to regroup, but I didn't. I spoke harshly and immediately regretted it. I apologized. I realize my response was inappropriate and unprofessional. It won't happen again."

"I seem to remember hearing that exact phrase not long ago when you were unable to meet with a donor family due to . . ." She looked back at her papers. "Childcare issues."

"That was two and a half years ago, ma'am, and I found someone to take the call for me."

"There have been other issues." She closed the file and folded her hands on top of it. "Is it true you recited a Bible verse before offering the customary moment of silence?"

"Well, yes, but that's—"

"And two months ago, your insistence on praying with the Jung family led to quite an emotional upheaval."

So that's what this was about. What it had always been about. Ellen hated anything to do with Christianity. Tammy included. "Mrs. Jung asked me to pray with her, ma'am."

"And when Mr. Jung, the donor's grandfather, grew agitated? Did you consider his feelings as well?"

Tammy breathed deeply and exhaled slowly. "I was trying to bring comfort and hope to a grieving wife."

"You're an organ donor procurement coordinator, Ms. Kuhn, not Mother Theresa. Your job is to recover organs, not proselytize. Remember that." She leaned forward. "Because contrary to what you may believe, you are not indispensible."

"I know you want to see them, Mom." With the phone pressed between his ear and shoulder, Nick poured a cup of coffee. "And I want to help make that happen. How about if you come here? You could spend the weekend."

Nick's mom sighed. "We're launching our Summer at the Leir next week, and my boss has us all pulling extra hours." She worked at a local art gallery, and with all the debt her new husband brought into the marriage, probably needed every penny of overtime she could get.

"What if we plan something for this summer? The boys and I can come down, spend a week."

"Marianne will fight you on that."

"This summer, I promise. We'll go to Lake of the Ozarks, do some tubing. Maybe rent some jet skis."

"There should be a law against what Marianne's doing, turning your boys against everyone like that—cutting off the entire family."

There probably was, but attempting to do anything about that would only mean more lawyers' fees—at $200 an hour. Faced with contempt charges, she'd act nice for a month, or week, then revert to her poisonous tactics.

Gaining full custody was the only answer.

While Mom continued to vent, Nick made the boys' lunch, per Marianne's instructions. Ham and cheese for Payton. Peanut butter and jelly for Jeremy, each ingredient packed in different containers so they didn't touch. Bagel wrapped separately, so it wouldn't get soggy, a plastic knife to spread everything. Sure, he could have pushed back on this one, tell Jeremy he needed to eat what Nick gave him, but he'd learned to pick his battles. Right now, how his boys chose to eat their food wasn't high on the list.

Footsteps and angry voices clamored down the stairs. "Where'd you put my DS?"

"I didn't have it."

"Quit lying."

"I'm not!"

"Whatever."

Nick chuckled. Some things never changed. "Listen, Mom, I've gotta go. Can I call you tonight?"

"Sure, Sweetie. We'll figure something out."

Returning the phone to his pocket, he faced his boys, skin-stretching smile in place. "You hungry?"

With a shrug, they slumped into opposing chairs at the kitchen table. Payton wore his usual frown while Jeremy rested his chin in his hands. His pudgy cheeks bunched beneath his eyes.

"What'll it be?" Nick pulled various breakfast items from the cupboard. "We've got bagels, granola bars, and oatmeal."

Jeremy grimaced. "Mom always makes eggs and sausage."

Right. Looked like Nick needed to return to the store. Or start a food war. "Sorry, kiddo, but this is all I've got." Although there was still ice cream. *No. That'd be bad. Very unfatherly.* "But maybe . . ." He sifted through leftovers in the fridge. Not much and everything else needed to be cooked first. "How about crackers and peanut butter?"

Payton rolled his eyes.

Jeremy flung his spine against his seat back and crossed his arms. "I want to go home."

Nick returned to the table, leaned forward, and looked his boys in the eyes. "Listen, guys, I know I may not do things the way you're used to. I know you miss your mom, but I'm doing my best. Can you . . . can't we . . ." Where was the father's manual when he needed one? Gazing toward the ceiling, he fingered his dad's dog tags, wondering what it would've been like to have him around, to learn from him, learn what it means to be a dad.

He clamped a hand on each of his boy's shoulders. "Let's make the best of it, all right? Who knows, you might even have some fun."

Jeremy huffed. Payton's scowl wavered. Progress. Now if Nick could find a way to inch their gloomy expressions into a smile. A stack of graham crackers and a handful of raisins helped. While Jeremy turned his breakfast into an art project, Nick readied their backpacks by the door.

A memory of Payton's first day of school surfaced. Standing on the stoop, wearing his favorite superhero T-shirt, his eyes had danced. *"Will you walk with me and Mom to the bus stop, Daddy?"*

"Of course, bud."

What Nick wouldn't give for a do-over. *Lord, please show me how to reach Payton's heart. Restore our relationship.*

"Dad, look. It's a monster." Grinning, Jeremy held up a cracker slathered in peanut butter and raisins.

Nick laughed and ruffled the boy's hair. "You're quite the artist." He shot Payton a wink, and for once, getting a smile in return.

By the time they headed out the door fifteen minutes later, Jeremy had even laughed at two of Nick's jokes.

The mirth fizzled when they reached the end of his driveway where Payton stopped. "You're seriously not going to walk us, are you?"

Nick kept walking. "Won't kill you. I promise. But don't worry, I'll try not to mortify you. And I won't go past the bus stop."

Jeremy's school was a fifteen-minute bus ride from Nick's neighborhood, stops included. Payton's was a mile walk east—and the primary reason Nick bought his house. He'd had a crazy fantasy that he and Marianne could share custody.

The naivety of the newly divorced.

Outside, his neighbor Howie lugged his garbage can to the curb. "Morning."

Nick waved. "Hey, Howie."

He smiled at the boys. "Fellas, good to see you."

They glanced up before staring at the ground again. A single dad himself, Howie gave Nick a conspiratorial nod—one that said, "I'm with ya, man." Sauntering over, he met Nick and the boys on the curb. "So, you guys are coming to the barbecue tomorrow night, aren't ya'?"

Nick studied the boys' faces, the slight smile on Jeremy's, the absence of a frown on Payton's. They didn't seem vehemently opposed to the idea. "We'll see what we've got going on." Most of the neighbor children would probably be there. Hanging out with other kids would help loosen the boys up. Maybe even motivate them to come back.

"You know Rhonda's planning on coming, right?" Howie wiggled an eyebrow.

Nick shook his head, shooting his neighbor a warning glare. The boys didn't need to hear Howie's philosophy on women and dating. Nor was Nick looking to spend time with the neighborhood flirt.

"I'll talk to you later."

Howie chuckled. "I'll be here."

Nick laid a hand on each of his sons' shoulders. Payton flinched and jerked away. Nick sighed and dropped his hand.

One step at a time. They'd soften up eventually, hopefully by the end of their visit. And if not, maybe one day they'd look back on this time, remember Nick's efforts. Know he loved them at least.

When they reached the bus stop, Rhonda and her daughter were already there. Rhonda's hair looked like it'd been sprayed with rubber cement, her lashes thick with black mascara. She wore white Capris and strappy sandals; her daughter, ribboned braids.

"Nick." She slung her leather tote over her shoulder and held out her hand, palm down, like a nineteenth century debutante. "How nice to see you." Red lipstick smeared a front tooth.

Ignoring her fingers, Nick fought a grimace and flashed a smile instead. "Good morning." He nodded at Rhonda's daughter who presented a mirror image of her mother, from her pouty, glossed lips to her fluttering eyelashes.

"So, boys," Rhonda angled her head and contorted her face in what she probably thought was a coy expression but merely stretched the thick pencil marks in her eyebrows. "You ready for spring break? Only two more days, right?"

The boys shrugged. Payton pulled out his cell phone, loaded with games, while Jeremy bounced from one foot to the other.

"A little crabby this morning, are we?" She shot Nick a wink and dug into her purse. "I'm guessing a couple of kiddos woke up on the wrong side of their beds. We really need to get the kids together sometime."

Saying no would be rude, but anything else would only fuel Rhonda's advances, so instead, Nick offered a slight smile and turned to his sons. "Two days before spring break, huh?" He nudged Payton's arm. "Anything special you want to do next week?"

Jeremy's face brightened, looking from Nick to Payton, who gave a slight shrug. Just then, the bus arrived, filling the air with diesel fumes.

Payton fist-bumped his brother. "See ya, twerp."

The moment the doors swung open, Jeremy clamored up the steps. Nick reached out to rustle the child's hair but missed. "Have a great day, bud."

The doors swung shut.

Searching for a safe conversation starter, Nick turned back to Payton, but the teen had taken off down the sidewalk.

In an effort to ward off further interaction with Rhonda, Nick focused on his cell. Scrolling through his contacts, he hurried toward his house. Heels clicked steadily behind him, their rhythm doubling his. He quickened his step and looked for someone to speed dial.

The clicking picked up and soon was accompanied by heavy breathing. "Nick?"

He raised a finger, still going through his contacts. He rounded the corner, his driveway in sight, but still fifty feet away. Where were nosy neighbors when he needed them most? Howie was the only one out, and he appeared deeply engaged in unclogging his lawn mower. Not helpful.

He didn't want to be rude, but he was *not* going to date this woman. Or meet her at a park, or sample her brownies. He refused to lead her on in anyway.

He lengthened his stride. So did she, reaching him at the mailbox.

There was a snapping noise, followed by a flash of color as Rhonda flew forward. "Oh!" She landed with her limbs stretched out, face planted in the grass. Items spilled from her purse—antiwrinkle goop, a prescription bottle, and hemorrhoid cream. A major too-much-information moment.

Nick rushed to her side. "Need help?"

Grass stains splotched her knees and strands of hair draped over her face and stuck to her lipstick. A few tangled in her lashes. When she swiped them away, she left a trail of red goop on her cheek.

"I'm fine, but thank you." She straightened, mascara-clumped eyelashes fluttering so fast they looked ready to take flight. The color in her cheeks matched the lipstick smeared across her face.

Poor woman. A bit of humbling did everyone good, but no one deserved total mortification. Squatting, he reached for her purse, ready to help.

"No!" She bolted forward, scrambling for her items like kids for parade candy. Then, kneeling in front of her mess, she inhaled and lifted her chin. "Thank you, but I know how busy you are." She swept her belongings aside, out of his view.

Nick knew better than to mess with a woman's personal products. "If you're sure."

"I'm fine." She waved him off with one hand while the other continued to gather her things.

Not wanting to embarrass her further, he turned to leave, casting one last glance over his shoulder. Before he made it to the end of his walk, she'd stuffed everything back in her purse and was hobbling home.

A low laugh caught Nick's attention, and he turned to see Howie watching Rhonda. Shaking his head, he ambled over. "Still fighting her off, huh?"

Nick shrugged. "She's just bored."

"You know there is one way to avoid her for good."

"What's that?"

"Get a girlfriend."

"Not happening, my friend. I've had enough relationship drama to last three lifetimes."

Chapter 4

Halfway through Wednesday night's Bible study, Tammy's phone vibrated. She checked the number and frowned. Ellen. Gathering her things, she eyed the pew on either side of her. People occupied both ends, heads bowed in prayer. So much for her stealthy escape.

Maneuvering around knees and feet, she apologized her way to the aisle. More than a few heads turned.

"Sorry," Tammy mouthed. "Gotta go." She held up her phone, clearing the end of the pew.

Slipping into the foyer, she pulled up her missed calls. She was about to return her boss's call when Constance, an older woman with short, silver hair, emerged from the bathroom. The two nearly collided.

Tammy stepped back. "Oh, excuse me."

Constance frowned, her round-rimmed glasses balanced precariously on the tip of her pointed nose. "Leaving so soon, dear?"

"I'm afraid so." Explaining the reason for her departure wouldn't help. It'd only instigate another argument as to why Tammy needed to quit her job. Which Constance had made clear she believed was the cause of Tammy's failed marriage, not her husband's infidelity.

An act that, according to Matthew 19:9, gave her biblical grounds for divorce, not that she'd sought it. No, she'd tried everything to hold on to their marriage. Begged Brody to go to counseling, met with her pastor, prayed for reconciliation. But her ex wanted none of it. He'd given his heart to someone else. Three years later, the sting of his betrayal still hurt.

She started to step around Constance.

"I've been meaning to give you something." The woman eyed an accent table pushed against the wall. "Wait a moment." She grabbed a pink card adorned with a satin ribbon and handed it over. It was an invitation to the women's tea, "*Focusing Your Heart on Home*."

Why? Because she thought Tammy was failing as a mom or because she was in charge of distributing the invites?

Constance regarded her with a raised eyebrow. "You are coming, right?"

"I'll have to check my schedule." Still maintaining a stiff smile, her upper lip twitched. "Thanks."

The woman's eyes softened, and she touched Tammy's arm. "How are you?" Her bony fingers felt like ice. "I heard . . ." She pursed her lips, shook her head.

What exactly had landed on this woman's gossip radar? That Brody had changed girlfriends? Again? That Becky had gotten in trouble for flirting with boys during youth group? That Tylan had knocked down the blinds in his Sunday school class? When he hurled an eraser across the room during the Bible lesson?

She didn't want to know. "I'm sorry, I'd love to chat, but," she shifted, looking to the stairwell, "I've gotta go."

The woman's lips flattened, forming tiny lines around her mouth. "Surely you're not going to work now. So late?"

Tammy fought to keep the bite from her tone. "I don't know. I haven't taken the call yet."

"What about your children?"

"I've got a great nanny. But I appreciate your concern." Her phone vibrated again, and she raised it. "Sorry."

"Of course. If you need anything, please don't hesitate to ask."

"Thanks."

Descending the stairs, she phoned Ellen. Her boss answered on the first ring, and she didn't sound happy. "Where are you?"

"Church."

"I need you to go to St. Theresa's. They've got a twenty-eight-year-old female who was admitted for seizures. She passed earlier this evening and has been declared brain dead. She was a registered donor."

"Do we have any history on her?"

"It appears she may have had some sort of infection, but it's hard to get the full story over the phone. I need you to go in."

"Okay." Tammy slid her phone in her back pocket and checked her watch. Looked like she wouldn't be getting much sleep tonight —again. But she could always nap while the kids were in school.

Continuing downstairs, she shot Joni, her babysitter, a text. *Got a call. Meet me at the house, please.*

Tammy's phone chimed. *On my way.*

She texted back: *Appreciate you!*

Rounding the corner, she dashed out of the way as a throng of kids raced toward the drinking fountain. Others clogged the hallway, pelting one another with crumpled snack bags.

Weaving through bouncing, shrieking kids, she reached the youth room with minimal injury—only one elbow to the rib and one crunched toe.

Vanessa, Tammy's best friend, stood near the sound system chatting with Reed, another youth worker. Becky, Tammy's thirteen-year-old daughter, flirted with a group of high school boys.

Sighing, Tammy rubbed her temples. *Again?*

When had Becky become so boy crazy? No wonder Tammy landed on everyone's prayer list.

Abran, one of the kids from the church's bus ministry, approached with a crooked grin. "Hey, Mrs. Kuhn! Where you off to?" He nudged her shoulder with a closed fist. "Did somebody keel over tonight, or somethin'?"

Tammy chuckled and raised an eyebrow in mock disapproval. "You realize you have a morbid fascination with death, right?"

Grinning, he tapped his temple, chestnut eyes sparkling beneath a Chicago Bulls cap. "Inquiring minds, you know."

Smiling and shaking her head, she watched him meander away, pants sagging. *Teenagers.*

"Seems you found an in with the youth."

She turned to see Vanessa standing beside her, clutching a heavy tote in one hand and a box of saltines in the other.

"One of the perks of being an organ procurement coordinator, I suppose."

Vanessa's eyes softened. "You okay? You look a bit . . . bug-eyed."

"Do I?" Tammy laughed. "Just cramming for time, like usual."

"If you need anything . . ."

"Joni's on her way, but thanks."

"Call me."

Tammy nodded, knowing if she didn't, Vanessa would be phoning her by the week's end—not to prod or pester, but to be a friend.

It took fifteen minutes for Tammy to gather her kids and get home. As expected, when she arrived, Joni was waiting for her. She was dressed in her PJs and carried an overnight bag.

Leaving the car running, Tammy jumped out to kiss her kids good-bye. "You two be good." She grabbed Tylan's shoulders and turned him to face her. "No games tonight, promise? Go straight to sleep." She shot Becky a warning look. "And no dragging your feet in the morning."

The kids mumbled their assent, and Tammy slipped back behind the driver's seat. She paused with the door open. "Thanks, Joni. You're priceless, you know that, right?"

"I try." She gave a weak smile, her eyes void of their usual sparkle.

"Is something wrong?"

She didn't respond right away. "You go. We can talk about it when you get home."

That couldn't be good. It'd taken Tammy almost two years to find Joni, and she was amazing. A college student studying child development, she had been such an answer to prayer. After two years of dealing with flaky babysitters, she couldn't go through that process again. Ellen's grace-meter was maxed out.

Without reliable childcare, Tammy would lose her job.

Chapter 5

Tammy found Nurse Lebbie in room 345 talking with Dr. Swenson, St. Theresa's intensivist. A woman with curly blonde hair and sunken eyes lay in the bed. Her head drooped to one side, and her skin looked ashen. Three IV bags dangled on the pole behind her. The chair beside her bed was empty.

Did she not have family? A husband, sister, friend? No one should have to endure sickness alone. Waiting in the doorway, Tammy offered a silent prayer—for comfort, mercy, and God's love to surround the woman.

Dr. Swenson tucked his chart under his arm. "Let me know when the lab results come back." He set his jaw and exited the room.

Nurse Lebbie turned to Tammy. "Hello. Can I help you?"

"I'm Tammy Kuhn with Heartland Donation Services." She smiled and extended her hand. "We talked on the phone earlier."

"Uh, huh."

"Can you take a moment to look at Ms. James's lab work with me? I have some questions."

The woman pursed her lips, her gaze shooting toward the hall, most likely thinking of all the other places she needed to be. With a heavy sigh, she glanced at her watch. "Yes. Sure. Fine."

She power walked out of the room and to the nurses' station. Tammy scurried along behind. At the counter, she waited for Nurse Lebbie to pull up the donor's chart.

She clicked on the lab results first. Most were normal, but the donor's white blood cell count was extremely high, indicating an infection.

Tammy frowned. "Can I see the patient's history, please?"

The nurse nodded and pulled up a consult report from an infectious disease doctor. Tammy leaned in. The patient had been treated with Zosyn, a high-powered antibiotic. "Can I see the other consult notes, please?"

Nurse Lebbie complied.

Tammy studied the screen. The patient had experienced a number of neurological abnormalities within the past two months—poor coordination, dementia, an abnormal EEG reading.

Odd. Tammy needed to speak with the woman's doctors.

After spending the next hour talking with various physicians, she called her administrator.

Ellen answered immediately. "Hey, what did you find out?"

"It's not good. Although they can't make a determinant diagnosis until an autopsy's been performed, the doctors believe she may have had mad cow disease." An infection no transplant center would want to deal with.

Ellen let out a long breath. "Okay." She paused. "Call a few of the aggressive centers—Nebraska, New York, maybe Chicago."

"Will do."

But no one wanted to take the chance of infecting their already critically ill patients with compromised organs. The risk was just too high. Tammy's heart ached to know lives couldn't be saved from this woman's death, but there was nothing more she could do. Except pray for the family and hope—trust—God would bring good from this tragedy.

Sliding her cell back into her pocket, she headed home.

She pulled into her neighborhood shortly after twelve thirty a.m. A crescent moon shimmered through a layer of smoky clouds, stars twinkling against a velvet backdrop. She eased into her garage and cut the engine. Her eyes felt like they'd been doused in vinegar; her rubbery muscles ached for bed.

Grabbing her tote filled with her laptop and organ donation release forms, she got out and shuffled inside. She dropped her belongings at the door.

The kitchen light was on, the day's mail waiting for her on the counter. Tammy paused to sift through it. Three bills—her mortgage note among them. A flyer for a summer baseball camp—one Tylan would love to go to, if she could afford it. Except with 170,000 miles on her car, it was nearing its last leg, and her air conditioning unit had seen better days. Chewing her lip, she estimated the total of her upcoming bills and compared it to her paycheck. Close, but unless gas prices took a major dip, not likely.

Maybe if she took him to the batting cage, tossed the ball around with him a few times . . . Who was she kidding? The boy needed his dad. Speaking of . . . her gaze landed on a letter bearing Brody's signature block lettering.

Her stomach tightened, heat climbing her neck. She pulled out the correspondence and spread it on the counter.

She shook her head. A formal business letter? Her ex had printed the date and his address in the top right hand corner. And according to the CC added at the end, he'd sent copies to both of their attorneys. As if expecting a fight. She thought of a similar correspondence sent last summer asking to take the kids to Disneyland, to which she'd conceded, only to have him cancel two weeks prior. To make matters worse, she'd been the one who had to break it to them. Tears pricked her eyes as the memory of Tylan and Becky's sad faces.

Breathing deep, she read the letter:

I have two weeks' vacation scheduled for the first week of August. We plan to go to Hawaii, and I'd like the kids to join us.

The man couldn't remember to show up for a scheduled visitation on time. How could she possibly trust him to care for the kids an ocean away? Not that it mattered, since he'd cancel anyway.

Exhaling, she slipped the letter back into the envelope, folded it, and tucked it in her back pocket. She didn't want the kids to see it. Not until she'd had time to process.

She returned to her mail pile. A gold envelope poked out from the bottom of the stack. She pulled it out and read the elegant writing—Oak Park Alumni Association. She ran her finger under the envelope flap and slipped out a gold embossed card. An invitation to her high school class reunion.

Would Nick Zimmerman be there? The thought quickened her pulse.

He was probably happily married and had forgotten about Tammy long ago.

She tore the invite into small pieces and threw them away.

Sleep beckoned.

Heading toward her bedroom, she passed the den and caught a glimpse of Joni, sitting on the couch.

"Hey." Tammy dropped her keys into a glass bowl. "I'm surprised you're still up. Is everything okay?"

Joni stared at her folded hands.

Tammy's gut knotted at the strained expression on her sitter's face. Her gaze shot to the hall. "The kids okay?"

"They're fine. I . . ." Joni picked at her thumbnail cuticle. "I need to talk to you about something."

Their previous conversation flashed through Tammy's mind. "*We can talk about it when you get home.*" She checked the time on the DVR. "Sure. Just give me a minute to check on Tylan and Becky."

Joni nodded.

She slipped down the hall and into Tylan's room. Her son lay on his back, the blankets tangled around his feet. She kissed his forehead, so smooth and soft, and ran her hand across his cheek.

Father, watch over my sweet boy. Keep him safe.

After untangling his blankets and tucking them under his chin, she headed to Becky's room. Soft music poured from the sleeping teen's cell, still clutched in her hand. Her laptop sat opened on a stool positioned beside her bed.

Rolling her eyes, Tammy closed the computer and placed it securely on Becky's desk, then eased the phone from her grip.

Becky mumbled, and her lashes fluttered before closing again.

Smiling, Tammy kissed Becky's cheek. "Good-night, sweet girl." Slipping from the room, she closed the door behind her.

She found Joni in the same position she'd left her, shoulders hunched.

Tammy sat beside her. "Is everything okay?"

The girl shook her head. "My mother's not doing well."

"Oh, sweetie, I'm sorry." Tammy placed her hand over Joni's and squeezed. "She started her chemotherapy?"

Joni nodded. "She's very tired, and . . . I'm worried she's getting depressed. That she'll give up." She sniffed and dabbed at her nose with a wadded tissue. "She needs me."

"Absolutely."

"She doesn't have anyone else. I know it's short notice, but I really need to help her out." A tear slid down her face. "I'm so sorry."

"Your mother is lucky to have you." She wrapped an arm around Joni's shoulder. "I understand." Joni's mom was ill—perhaps even terminal. Of course she'd need Joni with her. "Is there anything I can do?"

"I don't think so, but thanks."

"Let's pray." Tammy hugged the girl closer. "Lord, please be with Joni's mother, give her strength and peace. May they sense Your presence, and if it's Your will, provide healing." She held her for a moment longer, then released the girl to look in her eyes. "Keep me posted?"

Again, Joni nodded, more tears flowing. Placing a protective arm over the young woman's shoulder, Tammy walked her to the door. The full weight of the day's events—so much sickness, so much death—settled upon her as she watched Joni leave.

As the door clicked closed, an unsettling thought rose to the surface. Who would watch her kids? Finding reliable childcare in the best scenarios was hard enough. Her job—with its late-night calls and long shifts—made it near impossible.

What now, Lord?

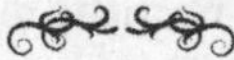

The next morning, Tammy slipped out of bed a minute before her alarm was set to go off. A dull ache spread through her, her muscles tight. Spending the night stressing over her childcare situation hadn't done her any favors.

I need coffee.

Shrugging into her robe, she plodded across the room, then paused, her gaze landing on her opened closet. The bar where Brody's suits once hung remained empty, the shoe rack below bare.

Would the sting of his abandonment ever go away? Her pastor always said God hated divorce—*"What God has joined let no man tear asunder."* Now she knew why. The act shattered families. If only she had it to do over, she would've talked him into counseling years ago. It was too late now.

Cinching her belt tighter around her waist, she trudged into to the kitchen and started a pot of coffee.

Once brewed, she grabbed a steaming mug, her Bible, and a notepad filled with names and numbers of potential sitters. Inhaling the steam rising from her cup, she shuffled into the living room and nestled into the corner of the couch.

It was too early to call anyone now. She'd wait until after she got the kids off to school.

What if she had to quit her job? Would she—could she—find another?

She laid her Bible on her lap and opened the front flap to a worn photo tucked inside. It was of her first college roommate, a girl who had suffered from cystic fibrosis. Although she managed to function—go to school, keep a job—she'd already been pretty sick when Tammy met her. Midway through their sophomore year, she was placed on the transplant list. She died waiting for an organ. Even worse, she'd never known Jesus. Tammy had always meant to share the gospel with her, but had lost her nerve every time. Even now, the guilt of her cowardice ate at her. The girl was dying, and Tammy had been too afraid to tell her about the greatest gift of all—salvation. And then it was too late. They whisked her off to a hospital near her hometown. She'd passed two months later.

Tammy switched majors the next semester and vowed never to waste such precious time again. Because life didn't always offer second chances.

A lump lodged in her throat as she slid the photo back in her Bible. She closed it and returned it to her end table. She couldn't quit. Her job was too important.

God had gotten her through worse messes than this.

She wrapped both hands around her cup and inhaled. The tension began to seep from her neck and shoulders.

She glanced at the clock. 5:10. Time to put her drama aside and focus on bigger problems, like giving hope to grieving families.

She opened her laptop resting on the coffee table and logged into Heartland Donation Services. While waiting for the program to open, she grabbed her phone. Three new messages. The first came from the charge nurse at St. Mary's. After listening to the voicemail, Tammy returned the call.

"St. Mary's, Joyce Lundquist speaking, how may I help you?"

"Good morning. It's Tammy with Heartland Donation Services. I'm calling about Mr. Chesney."

"He's Pam's patient. Would you like me to page her?"

"Yes, please."

She sipped her coffee as elevator music filled the line. Footsteps shuffled on the thick carpet. She glanced up to see a groggy Tylan approaching, and opened wide her free arm. Clutching his stuffed dinosaur, he wiggled onto the couch and snuggled in beside her, his head tucked under her chin.

The elevator music ended with a click. "Hello, this is Pam."

Tammy repeated her greeting. "How is Mr. Chesney doing today?" Still holding Tylan, she positioned her phone between her shoulder and ear to free her other hand for note taking.

"He arrived maybe thirty minutes ago. The family's on their way, and the doctor's at his bedside now."

"Any pupil reaction?"

"No."

"Does he breathe over a ventilator?"

"Yes."

She continued asking routine questions, jotting the answers on a notepad. What was his pulse, blood pressure, had his labs come back? The nurse's responses made no sense.

Tammy sat straighter. "His white blood count is 532? That has to be an error."

"Uh-uh."

"Wow. Do you have any history on him?"

"I'll get more information when the family arrives."

Tylan wiggled, tickling Tammy's side with his elbow, nearly producing a giggle. She covered by clearing her throat. "Do you know the plan for him? Are they talking surgery or brain death testing?"

"I'll ask the doctor."

The elevator music returned, and Tammy gave Tylan a squeeze. "As soon as I'm done, I'll make butterfly pancakes. How does that sound?"

He nodded, licking his bottom lip. "Can I help?"

Always her little helper. Sure, that would stretch a ten-minute task into thirty, splattered pancake mix and all. But his toothy grin and dimpled cheeks made it all worth it.

She pressed a kiss to his forehead. "I'd love for you to help me."

A Skype box pulled up on the bottom right of her screen alerting her that her mom had come online. A pop-up message followed.

Mom: Good morning. How are you doing?

Tammy: Morning. You're up early.

Mom: How are the kids?

Tammy: Sleepy.

Mom: Becky texted me last night.

Tammy: That's nice.

Mom: What's going on with your babysitter?

Tammy: Everything's fine.

Mom: That's not the impression Becky gave me. You've had three sitters in two years.

Tammy raised her hand over her keyboard, then dropped them in her lap.

Mom: That's not good for the kids. They need stability. Come home.

Tammy sighed. This had become a frequent conversation—since her divorce.

Tammy: I can't uproot the kids—move them so far from their father. You know that.

Not that he appeared to have any interest in them, but that was his choice, not hers. Besides, she'd never sell the house, not without a hefty loss.

Mom: Dad and I are coming for a visit.

Tammy stared at the screen, her fingers suddenly frozen. It wasn't that she didn't love her parents, nor that she didn't want to see them, but she had way too much going on to play host.

Tammy: I appreciate that, but now's not a good time.

Mom: Of course it is. You need a sitter, and we need time with our grandkids.

The nurse returned to the line. "They're taking him to the OR as soon as the surgeon arrives."

Tammy: We'll talk about this later. Gotta go.

She closed out the text box before her mom could press further, then returned to her phone conversation. "Thanks, Pam. I'll check back with you in a few hours. Contact me if anything changes."

She made a few more calls—closed out a patient and received a new one—then set her phone on the coffee table.

"Okay, muffin." She bopped Tylan on the nose. "I need to wake that sleepy-head sister of yours—"

"Then we'll make pancakes?"

"Then we'll make pancakes." She took one last sip of her coffee, then stood.

A door creaked, followed by soft footsteps. Her daughter emerged a moment later with tangled hair and droopy eyes. "Grandma and Grandpa are coming?"

Tammy frowned. "No. Why would you think that?"

Becky lifted her phone. "Grandma texted me. She said Grandpa's not lecturing at the university next quarter. He's got the entire summer off. Isn't that awesome?"

Like all three months? Wonderful.

Chapter 6

Tammy sat on her back porch swing, a tub of chocolate ice cream in her lap and phone in hand. The neighbor kids—three, all under the age of five—chased bubbles in the adjacent yard. They squealed and laughed, their cheeks rosy, damp hair plastered around their faces. Oh, the gift of ignorance.

And huge quantities of mint chocolate chip ice cream.

The kids' mother, a petite lady in her midthirties, knelt in front of an immaculate flowerbed. Would she be up for babysitting? With that many mouths to feed, maybe she'd welcome the extra money.

Not likely. She drove a luxury car and paid for lawn service.

Tammy focused again on her phone. Her mom had left a string of texts. Apparently, Becky had filled her in on the latest drama. Her highly exaggerated version, no doubt. Tammy was tempted to set ground rules: *No talking about our personal lives*. Except the last thing she wanted to do was encourage her teen to keep secrets, regardless of the reason.

She'd just have to deal with it, and her overly anxious parents. Find a way to convince them that, contrary to whatever Becky said, their family unit was not falling apart.

Although Tammy was getting close.

Kneading her forehead, she called the youth pastor. She got his voicemail.

"Hi, Leon. It's Tammy. I wondered if you might have the number of that girl looking for a summer job?" And hopefully a spring one as well. "Call me back when you get a chance."

Or sooner.

She hung up and grabbed the church directory. Maybe one of the ladies from the college ministry would be able to help out. But would they be willing to stay overnight?

She tried Judith Campbell first. "Hi, this is Mrs. Kuhn from Ozark Community Church."

"Mrs. Kuhn . . . hi." Judith's voice sounded like she'd just woken up.

"Listen . . . I wondered, do you babysit?"

"Um, I used to. When I was in high school."

"Oh. I see."

"Did you need something?"

"I, uh . . . No. I'm sorry to have bothered you." Tammy hung up, then stared at her phone screen, her ice cream melting.

The gate screeched open, then clanked shut. Footsteps followed.

Vanessa stepped onto the porch wearing a peach sundress and strappy sandals. Her long blonde hair was pulled back in a low ponytail. "Whoa! This must be serious."

"Double chocolate serious."

"And sure to be followed by an obscene amount of aerobics, right?" Vanessa plopped onto the swing.

"Exactly." Tammy raised a spoonful to her mouth, then dropped it back in the container.

"So . . . what's with the massive dose of comfort food?" Using her feet, Vanessa gave the swing a push. "What'd Brody do now?"

"Nothing. And I mean absolutely nothing." That was a conversation for another day. "But this isn't about him." She swirled her spoon through a lump of chocolate. "Joni quit."

"Oh . . . What are you going to do?"

Tammy shrugged. "Invest in Häagen Dazs?" Lifting the church directory, she read the list of names. A few she'd circled. Then crossed off. "And take out an ad."

The swing hinges creaked beneath them.

She watched a glob of chocolate slip down the outside of the tub. "You know how long it took me to find Joni? Two years of dealing with irresponsible babysitters who never showed or arrived late. Two years of Ellen's tirades, threatening to fire me. If I mess up one more time, she might actually follow through."

Vanessa squeezed Tammy's knee. "You know you can always count on me, right?"

Leaning her head against the swing back, Tammy watched a puff of clouds rapidly swallow the sun.

Vanessa nudged her. "I'm here. Let me help."

Tammy rested her head on her friend's shoulder. "What would I do without you?"

"Gain an exorbitant amount of weight." Vanessa flashed a grin. "And it's my duty to keep that from happening, even if I have to eat this entire tub by myself." She grabbed the ice cream and stood, looking into the container. "Give me a minute." She shot Tammy a wink and traipsed toward the sliding glass door, returning a moment later with a heaping bowl of ice cream, the tub gone. "See?" Plopping back onto the swing, she raised her bowl with a grin. "Problem solved."

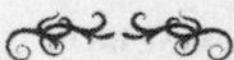

Nick tucked the phone between his ear and shoulder to pull items out of the fridge. "I'm taking the week off. Left Chef Rictor in charge." And barring any major catastrophes or wait staff drama, business at the Flaming Mesquite would continue as normal.

"Good for you." His mom paused. "How are things going?"

"Minus the occasional eye roll and body flail?" Nick chuckled.

"Sounds familiar."

"Come on. I wasn't that bad." Not before his stepdad entered the picture, anyway.

"How's your custody case going?"

"Slow. But the judge finally ordered a court evaluation."

"It's about time. Maybe now the judge will finally understand what a psycho she is."

"Doubt it." Nick sighed. "You know how deceptive Marianne is. She'll have the psychiatrist believing she's the next June Cleaver."

"Hang in there. The truth will come out eventually. It always does."

Before or after Marianne poisoned his boys against him?

He looked at the clock. Howie's neighborhood barbecue started in less than a half hour and Nick didn't want to be late. Most of the neighborhood kids would be there. If the boys made friends, had fun, they might be enticed to visit Nick more often. "Listen, Mom, can I call you back? We've got plans tonight."

Moving to the den, he paused to watch the boys play their "Manic Monsters Mania" video game. Jeremy sat with his legs extended, the end of the couch cushions hitting him midcalf. Payton sat beside him, wearing a slight smile.

Thank You, Lord, for this moment, this visit.

Nick strolled into the room and leaned against the back of the couch. "All right, my little gamers, set your weapons aside. Time to head across the street, get us some of Howie's hot-diggidy-dogs to go with our beans."

Clutching the game console remote with both hands, Payton continued to watch the screen. "That guy's weird. Can't you go without us?"

"Howie's a little . . . unique, but he's harmless. Besides, all the other neighbor kids will be there. You'll have fun, promise. And if not, we can always leave. Come on."

After minimal cajoling, the three headed across the street. Nick lugged a steaming slow cooker. Jeremy carried his baseball and mitt, and Payton a hand-held game system, along with three games.

Howie's gate hung open and "Welcome to the Jungle" by Guns N' Roses drifted from the backyard. The scent of charbroiled beef filled the air, making Nick's mouth water.

On the lawn, three teens close to Payton's age tossed a football back and forth. A few younger kids trailed behind, asking to join in.

Nick elbowed Payton and jerked his head in the boys' direction. "Bet they could use a couple more players."

Jeremy and Payton stopped and watched the boys. Nick nudged them again. "Go on."

His sons exchanged glances, and Payton shrugged.

Jeremy grinned. He shoved his ball and mitt at Nick, who, fighting not to drop everything shoved his way, sandwiched the items between his sides and arms respectively. Payton balanced his things on top of the slow cooker.

"Wait a minute!" Nick widened his stance, feeling like a pack mule.

Howie sauntered over. "Let me give you a hand." He grabbed everything but the slow cooker. "Glad you could make it. You'll be happy to know your gal-pal Rhonda isn't here."

Nick surveyed the area and smiled. It seemed God had provided two miracles today—an afternoon filled with more laughter than scowls and the promise of a pleasant evening without having to dodge the neighborhood flirt.

Nick was wrong about the latter. At a seven-thirty Rhonda showed up wearing a slinky little number and smelling like gardenias. Or stale soap, if there was such a thing. She immediately cornered Nick.

His phone rang not a moment too soon. "Excuse me." He raised a finger and stepped away. Chef Rictor's number flashed on the screen. Not a good sign. "Hey. What's up?"

"Well . . . Let me start by saying things are contained."

"Contained? What's contained?"

"The fire."

"What!" Nick paced between his chair and the table.

"We were slammed, had a lot of orders coming in and out." Rictor spoke quickly.

"Just tell me."

"A grease fire."

"How much damage?"

"Well . . ." He gave a nervous laugh. "I imagine it could've been worse. The fire marshal's checking things out. He'd like to talk with you. Ask you questions."

"Where's everyone now?"

"Thanks to Helen's freak-out . . . The customers bolted when she ran out of the kitchen shrieking, 'Fire!' The rest of the crew kept their heads for the most part. Well, until Helen started hacking and clutching at her throat like she'd suffered major lung damage. Figured it'd be best to send everyone home after that, before anyone got sue-happy."

Rolling Hills
LIBRARY

Date: 8/24/2017 12:35pm
Member: 22003000257897

Title	Author	Due
[LARGE PRINT] Giant Geor	Nasser, Dave	9/7
ILL BOOK - INTERTWINES		9/12

Total items currently out: 2.

Wow! In 2017, you have saved $789.

Check out our library events at our NEW
web site <www.rhcl.org>
Call (816) 232-5479 or log in to the
catalog to renew items if you need more time.
OR TEXT MSG "renew all" to (816) 287-9828

Rolling Hills
LIBRARY

Date: 8/24/2017 12:35pm
Member : 22003000257897

Title	Author	Due
[LARGE PRINT] Giant Geor	Nesser, Dave	9/7
ILL BOOK - INTERTWINES		9/12

Total items currently out: 2

Wow! In 2017, you have saved $789.

Check out our library events at our NEW web site <www.rhcl.org>

Call (816) 232-5479 or log in to the catalog to renew items if you need more time.

OR TEXT MSG "renew all" to (816) 287-9828

Great. Was she setting the stage for a workers' comp claim? "I'll be there in a minute." He scanned the yard. Where were the boys?

Rhonda approached, penciled brows furrowed. "Is everything all right?"

"Something I gotta take care of at the restaurant." He peered into the sliding glass door. Two couples sat on the couch munching hot wings. No boys. He turned back to Rhonda. "You seen Payton and Jeremy?"

She shrugged. "They might be out front with the other kids, playing football or something."

"Okay. Thanks." Nick started to leave, but Rhonda touched his arm.

"I can keep an eye on them." She fiddled with her necklace.

"I appreciate it . . ." He searched the yard one more time. Old man Johnson, the neighbor at the end of the cul-de-sac, sat in front of the fire pit wearing a straw hat. His wife sat beside him, her silver hair glimmering beneath the tiki lights. Two other couples Nick didn't recognize gathered around a wrought-iron table.

Howie drew near, frowning. "Something wrong?"

Nick shook his head. "We gotta go. There's been a . . . my restaurant caught fire."

"Whoa." Howie's eyes widened. "The boys can hang out here."

Nick raked a hand through his hair. "I don't know. Marianne would flip."

"She'd rather you take them to a fire?" Howie snorted. "That's a court case waiting to happen."

Nick closed his eyes, rubbed them. Legally, Payton was old enough to do the sitting, but Nick couldn't leave the boys unattended. Not with the upcoming custody hearing. Marianne would freak out if he brought them to the restaurant, though, claiming he'd placed them in danger. There was no winning with her.

He glanced past Howie at the other couples gathered in groups of fours and sixes. Responsible, trustworthy adults. Most of them parents. He'd only be gone long enough to survey the damage, make a few calls if necessary.

Bev, an empty nester, sat near a forsaken flowerbed, sipping what appeared to be iced tea. Nick turned to Rhonda. "Thank you for the offer, but . . . Uh, can you excuse me?" After offering a parting smile, Nick approached Bev.

"Hey, there."

"Hi. Have a seat." She motioned to a chair beside her.

"I've gotta go, but thanks." He shoved his hands in his pockets. "I got a call from one of my employees down at the restaurant. There's a . . . problem, and I need to head down there. I could bring the boys, but . . ." He sighed. "Payton's old enough to manage himself, to watch his brother, too, but knowing their mom . . . I really don't need to give her any ammunition."

"I totally understand, and I'd be happy to keep my eye out."

Just like Bev. She didn't even make him ask. "Thanks. I'll be back as soon as possible."

"Take as long as you need."

"I owe you."

"Be careful how many IOUs you toss out." The skin around her eyes crinkled. "I've got a roof and gutters in dire need of repair."

"Thanks, Bev. You've got my number, right?"

"Yep." She raised her phone, then shooed him away. "Go. We'll be fine."

Nick waved good-bye to everyone, apologized to Howie, and darted out front to find his boys. Bev emerged a moment later. Dianne, a lady from an adjacent cul-de-sac, joined her, and the two sat in Howie's front porch swing.

The boys and a handful of other kids spread throughout the yard, tossing a football between them. The ball spiraled across the street, and two of the teens raced after it, shoving each other out of the way. Jeremy stood on the sidewalk, a bit too close to the road.

"Hey." Nick motioned his boys over.

Payton huffed. "What?"

Nick gripped Jeremy's shoulder. "Not so close to the street, okay?" When Jeremy didn't respond, he gave a gentle squeeze. "Okay?"

His son rolled his eyes. "Fine."

Nick turned to Payton. "And watch your brother. I've gotta head to the restaurant for a minute. If you boys need anything, find Bev." He jerked his head toward her. She waved.

He slipped into his car. Queasiness nibbled at his gut, but he swallowed against it. He'd be gone only a few moments, and his boys were in good hands.

Chapter 7

Driving away, Nick watched his boys through the rearview mirror. Adrenaline pricked his nerves. Was it because of the fire or from leaving them? Maybe he should turn around.

He shook his head and veered right onto Pine Road. Since when had he become the helicopter parent?

Five minutes from the restaurant, his cell rang.

Howie's name flashed on the screen, and Nick's pulse quickened.

He pulled into a nearby lot to answer. "Hey. What's going on?"

"There's been an accident."

Nick gripped the phone tighter. "What kind of accident?"

"It's Payton. He's been hit by a car. The ambulance is on the way."

Ambulance? He whirled around, his right wheel jumping the curb. *Lord, no! Not my son. Not Payton.*

Moments later he was back at Howie's. People were huddled together in the street, their backs to him.

No.

Bile stung his throat as he cut the engine and jumped out. Everyone stared at him, faces solemn. Two knelt.

Heaving for air as his heart thrashed against his ribcage, Nick bounded over, staring at his son's leg—all that was visible through the throng. "Payton!" He pushed through everyone and gasped, falling to his knees.

No. Not my son. Please, Lord.

Payton lay on the ground, head sideways. Blood pooled beneath him and trickled from his nose and mouth. With a guttural cry, Nick lunged forward, ready to scoop the boy up, but strong arms held him back.

"Don't move him."

"Get off me!" Nick ground his teeth and fought to jerk free, but the hands held fast. His skin twisted and burned beneath their grip. Someone else grabbed his right shoulder and a gentle hand touched his left.

Rhonda moved into his line of vision, kneeling to eye level. Tears filled her eyes. "The ambulance is on the way."

Nick sucked in a gasp, then another. He needed to calm down. Think. Pray. "Where's Jeremy?" Muscles twitching, he searched the crowd for signs of his youngest. He stood a few feet away, torso caved inward, enveloped in Bev's arms.

Tears streamed down Bev's face as she stared into Nick's eyes. "I'm so sorry. I was—we were—I should have been watching him more closely."

Shut up. Just shut up.

He turned back to his oldest son, the sound of approaching sirens pounding his ear drums. He watched, dazed, as EMTs spilled from the ambulance. Lights flashed, and a police car followed close behind.

Lord, no! God! I'll do anything. Please, don't take my son!

Men wearing navy uniforms pulled a stretcher from the ambulance. Another stepped forward and motioned for everyone to move back.

Nick rose on numb legs and stumbled backward. Voices merged together, swirling through a thick haze.

"Driver?"

"The car came barreling out of nowhere."

"A blue Ford."

"No, it was a Honda, two door."

"Iowa plates, maybe Indiana."

The EMTs lifted Payton onto a stretcher, his limp hand hanging over the side. Nick's stomach revolted at the puddle of blood seeping into the asphalt. So much blood. Too much. Scampering after the stretcher, stomach convulsing, he climbed inside the ambulance.

This is my fault. Why'd I leave? I should've been here.

Oh, Payton, I'm so sorry. So very sorry.

His phone chimed but he barely heard it.

Reaching trembling fingers to touch his son's hand, Nick leaned forward and sucked back sobs. "Hold on, buddy. You hear me? Hold on."

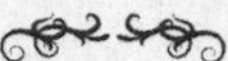

Tammy sat on Vanessa's couch, Tylan nestled between them. Becky occupied the recliner, on her phone, as usual. The scent of popcorn and hot chocolate permeated the air. Tylan giggled at a *Tom and Jerry* rerun. Even Becky seemed amused, or at least not utterly annoyed.

Tammy glanced at her watch. Brody was supposed to pick the kids up for his scheduled weekend visit three hours ago. Once again, he'd pulled a no-call, no-show. Good thing she hadn't mentioned anything about his visit to the kids. Instead, she'd whisked them off to Vanessa's for some junk food and giggles.

Vanessa laid her hand on Tammy's knee. "Sorry, T. I know this must break your heart." She gazed at Becky, who, frowning, texted furiously on her phone. "But they'll be okay. They've got you. And me."

Tammy offered a weak smile. She grabbed a throw pillow, hugged it to her chest, and rested her chin on the edge. "Thanks for giving up your Friday."

Vanessa shrugged. "Wasn't much of a sacrifice. It's not like men are beating down my door."

"Oh, I don't know about that. I can think of a few men who seem interested."

"Whatever." She grabbed a handful of popcorn. "You find anyone to watch the kids tomorrow night?"

"I keep telling you, I don't need a sitter!" Becky glared at Tammy. "I'm thirteen years old. All my friends' parents let them stay home. Shauna even babysits for other people."

Tammy lowered an eyebrow. "And watches R-rated television all hours of the night." Not to mention the fact that the girl had cycled through four boyfriends this year. Allowing teenagers to spend long hours alone wasn't Tammy's idea of effective parenting. "Besides, I doubt she's allowed to babysit overnight."

"What's the big deal? Tylan and I will be sleeping anyway."

Tammy raised her hand, palm out. "Conversation over." Ignoring Becky's glare, she turned back to Vanessa. "In answer to your question, I called a couple women from the college group. No bites yet. Not from anyone I can afford, anyway. I had no idea sitters charged so much."

"I told you, I'm here. Let me help you."

Tammy sighed. "Once in a while is fine, but you've got a life to live, dates to go on."

"Enough already." Vanessa grabbed a throw pillow and raised it in a hurl position. She lowered it when Tammy's cell rang.

A jolt of electricity shot up her spine, causing her muscles to clench. Brody, saying he was on his way and apologizing for being late?

She and Vanessa exchanged glances. Inhaling, Tammy wiggled her phone from her back pocket and looked at the screen.

Hanna, from Heartland Donation Services.

Not tonight.

Closing her eyes and pinching the bridge of her nose, Tammy answered. "Hello."

"I need you to go to St. Paul's Children's Hospital. They're preparing to do brain death testing on Emily Compton, and we need to do a clinical assessment."

"Where's Heather?"

"At Reynolds Memorial."

"Nory?"

"Down with the flu."

Tammy suppressed a moan and was about to say no when Vanessa touched her elbow, her eyes launching a conversation Tammy couldn't follow. "Listen, can I call you back in a minute?"

"One minute." There was an edge to Hanna's voice.

Tammy hung up and turned to her friend. "What's with the gyrating eyebrows?"

"Go. I'll watch the kids."

"I appreciate it, V, but I don't want to take advantage of you. Besides, it's my night off."

"We're friends, Tammy. Seriously, would it hurt to accept help once in a while? Go. This might be your opportunity to get back on your boss's good side."

Or at the very least, to avoid aggravating the woman further.

"Besides, I could use the company." Vanessa's face softened as her gaze drifted to Tylan. "Seriously, go. This is important. You're saving lives."

And hopefully, her job.

Chapter 8

Car idling, Tammy paused in the near-empty ER parking lot to prepare her heart for what she was about to encounter—family members facing quite possibly the darkest moment in their lives.

Lord, give me the words, the patience, this donor family needs. But more than that, give me the opportunity to speak words of life. To show that there is hope even in death. Please watch over my kids while I'm gone. And thank You, Lord, for Vanessa.

She slid out of the car and a cool, moist breeze swept over her. Dark shadows of the night pressed in on the streetlights dotting the pavement, a blanket of storm clouds swallowing the stars. The faint scent of motor oil wafted from the asphalt.

Loaded down with her computer tote, donor forms, and rolling medicine bag, she strode across the lot, into the hospital, and straight for the ICU. A couple, perhaps in their midforties, sat in a small lobby to the right. The woman hunched forward with her head in her hands, torso trembling. The man bent over her, rubbing her back. He glanced up, bloodshot eyes locking on Tammy's, holding her gaze.

Turning away, she approached the double doors and pushed the intercom button. "Tammy Kuhn with Heartland Donation Services."

A loud buzz sounded, followed by the click of a lock releasing. The scent of antiseptic swept over her as she entered the unit. Down the hall an orderly pushed an empty hospital bed. A pack of doctors passed by, talking about March Madness. Dr. Tailor was among them.

Keeping her gaze lowered to avoid his snaky eyes, Tammy strode down the hall to the nurses' station to drop off her things.

A tall nurse with black hair sat behind one of the computers.

"Hello." Tammy smiled. "I'm Tammy Kuhn with Heartland Donation Services." She indicated her name badge. "May I please speak with the charge nurse?"

"That's me, Hillary Green." Standing, she extended her hand.

"I'm here for Emily Compton. Can you take a moment to go over her information with me?"

"Yeah, sure." She sat, indicting for Tammy to take the chair beside her. Swiveling to face the computer screen, she shifted her head from one shoulder to the next, a loud crack sounding each time. "She came in two days ago with head trauma."

After relaying all pertinent patient information and answering Tammy's questions, the woman flicked her head toward the hallway. "Room 437. The patient's mother is with her now. Follow me. I'll introduce you to her mom."

"Thank you."

They continued down the hall, the soft scud of Tammy's shoes loud despite the peripheral noise. She paused outside Emily's door, the steady beeping of the heart monitor matching the pace of her pulse.

Tammy lingered in the doorway, watching the patient's mother sitting beside the bed. The poor woman. Tammy couldn't take the woman's pain away, but she could help her find hope. This was her calling, the reason she'd been created. She loved her kids, too, but she couldn't keep pushing them off on Vanessa.

Lord, please don't make me choose.

Nick paced the private waiting room, eyes burning. Friends and family filled the cushioned chairs. Some stared at their hands. A couple huddled in prayer. Others sat on the edge of their seats watching the door. Nick's stepdad stood against the far wall, ankles crossed, cell phone in hand. The man wasn't thrilled to be here. Nick's mom must have urged him to make the three-hour drive.

Nick looked at Jeremy, enveloped in his grandmother's arms. The child stared back with wide eyes, chin puckered.

Nick grabbed his phone. He needed to call Marianne, tell her. A wave of nausea swept over him, nearly doubling him over.

No, Lord. Don't take my son.

Her voicemail answered.

"It's Nick. There's been a . . ." He swallowed. "There's been an accident. Call me." He hung up and sent her a text and an email, then turned to his mom. "I've got some papers at home with Marianne's cruise information. Think you could . . . ?"

She jumped up, her gaze shooting to her husband before returning to Nick. "Absolutely." She turned to Jeremy who remained in his seat, face downcast. "How about we take you home, get you to bed?"

"No!" He balled his fists. "I want my brother."

"Shh . . ." Nick reached for his son when the door clicked open. He whirled around, locking eyes with the nurse. "How is he?"

The woman's gaze swept the room before returning to him. "We're going to do a CT scan to look for internal injuries. They're going to check his brain, spinal cord, chest, abdomen, and pelvis."

"Okay. Then what?"

"After we perform the tests, someone will talk to you about what comes next."

"But he's going to be all right?"

"They're trying to stabilize him." Her eyes softened as she looked at Jeremy. She turned to Nick. "Is there anything I can do for you?"

His fingers dug into the cushioned armrest. "Just take care of my son. Please."

She held his gaze for a moment, nodded, and slipped out.

Nick resumed pacing. His focus shifted from the closed door in front of him to his watch, then back to the door.

What's taking so long? What if Payton doesn't make it? My buddy! Lord God, don't take him from me.

Images flashed through his mind in rapid succession—of Payton as a toddler, his first day of school, his first T-ball game. Of the day Marianne stood in the hall, suitcases stacked by the door, young Jeremy in her arms, Payton hunched beside her.

Trembling hands lay limp at his sides.

A Bible sat on an end table. He picked it up and flipped it open, but his raging mind refused to focus. He closed the book and set it down.

Forty-five minutes later, the door opened again and a tall man with round glasses emerged.

Nick lunged from his seat. "How is he?"

"I'm Dr. Shefsky. Your son's scan showed signs of increased intracranial pressure." The doctor's Adam's apple bobbed down then up. "I need consent for a craniotomy and to possibly evacuate any bleeding in the brain. While he's in the OR, Dr. Fryar will repair his orthopedic injuries."

Nick swallowed, his throat dry. "What are his chances?"

"I really can't give you any indication at this point." Compassion filled his eyes. "It will depend how he does after the surgery, but we're hopeful."

That's not an answer.

The others gathered around, standing like a protective shield. Someone touched Nick's shoulder, and the faint scent of his mother's perfume filled his nose.

The doctor glanced around before returning Nick's gaze. "Although we are optimistic, cerebral herniation could lead to brain death or irreversible coma." He glanced from one face to the next. "We will keep you informed." He left, easing the door closed behind him.

Nick's mom came toward him, arms outstretched. "Honey— "

He stepped back, hands raised, palms out.

Jeremy stood, staring at Nick with wide, teary eyes. "He's going to be fine, isn't he, Dad?"

Nick touched the boy's head, tried to draw him close, but Jeremy resisted. "God's bigger than this. You believe that, don't you?"

Jeremy's brow furrowed.

Someone offered prayer, and Nick had a vague awareness of people gathering close, of hands on his shoulders, of someone reaching out to his son. But their voices were muffled in his fogged mind.

Why'd I leave? If only I had stayed, told the boys to go inside. Why?

As the night wore on, his friends thinned. Rhonda left first, then Howie, until only family remained. Jeremy sat on Nick's lap, cheek resting against Nick's chest.

His mom stood and touched Nick's shoulder. "How about I go get those papers now?"

He looked up. "What papers?"

"The contact number for the cruise line. And I'll take Jeremy home, let him get some rest."

Breathing deep, Nick nodded. "Thanks, Mom. I'll call you when I know something."

Tammy glanced at Mrs. Compton one last time before slipping from the private room. Peace settled into her heavy heart as she headed for the nurses' station. The death of a loved one was painful, but at least donation allowed families to find hope during their time of loss. To see life come out of death. And like she'd told Mrs. Compton when they'd prayed together, because Emily trusted in Jesus, the good-bye was really an "until we meet again."

If only she could say the same for all her donors.

Melissa, a petite nurse with short, spiral curls, closed her file and swiveled her chair to face Tammy. "How'd it go?"

"Okay. It's amazing how cathartic the donor questions can be. They give family members a chance to talk about their loved ones. It helps them grieve."

"It's so sad, losing her only child like that."

"I can't even imagine what that would feel like. But she did seem comforted to know good will come out of her daughter's tragic death."

"Speaking of kids, how are yours?"

"Sleeping." Tammy smiled. "You?"

Melissa shrugged. "You know how it is with teenagers. I'm the big, bad prison warden who takes extreme pleasure in ruining my children's lives." She laughed.

"It's our job, right?" She tried to fight a yawn but failed. One of these nights she needed to catch a full eight hours of sleep. Or twelve with an extended midday nap.

She turned to Melissa who was entering information into the computer system. "Have a great night."

"You're heading home, then?"

"After I hit the cafeteria for some brain-jolting caffeine. Can I get you anything?"

"A day off?" Melissa gave a crooked smile. "No, I'm good. Enjoy." She glanced down the hallway. "Although, I have a feeling you'll be back. You heard about the hit-and-run victim, right?"

Tammy shook her head.

"A thirteen-year-old male ran into the street to get a football. He's in critical condition. The dad's pretty broken up."

"Very sad." Tammy glanced at the monitor and the long list of patients, many her children's age. Some would return to live normal lives, others would soon breathe their last.

She thought again of her kids, asleep at home. "I better go." She rose, stretched. "See ya."

The bold colors, neon lights, and geometric shapes of the hospital cafeteria gave it a Pablo-Picasso-meets-the-twenty-fifth-century feel.

Two women, one older, maybe seventy, with silver hair, and the other who appeared to be in her mid-thirties, sat along the far wall beneath a green-framed television set. A dark-haired man with broad shoulders occupied the far corner.

The rich aroma of roasted coffee filled her nostrils.

Java or chocolate?

Both.

Brody always berated her for drinking coffee late at night. Why he cared, she never understood.

Obviously, he hadn't, otherwise he wouldn't have been sleeping around.

Swallowing a familiar surge of bitterness, she closed her gritty eyes and rubbed her face. After three years, it shouldn't bother her anymore. But it did, no matter how hard she fought against it.

Forcing her muscles to uncoil, she approached the drink station. She purchased a tall mocha and breathed in the soothing steam.

She sat near the doorway, wrapped both hands around her cup. *Lord, don't let my anger get in the way of Your love flowing through me. Help me to be sensitive to the needs and pain all around me.*

Chair legs screeched on the linoleum, and she glanced up. A familiar pair of blue eyes stared back at her.

The air left her lungs as she tried to make sense of the image of the man standing a few tables away.

"Nick?" She stood.

Gray speckled his black hair, and faint lines fanned from his eyes. His features had hardened, giving him a strong, rugged look. "Tammy." He stared at her for a long moment, his expression unreadable.

"You here for someone?"

"My son." His voice cracked, and he looked away, staring past her for a few seconds before making eye contact once again. "You work here?" He glanced at the name badge attached to her belt. "Organ Procurement Coordinator?"

She nodded, studied his face. "You want to talk?"

His eyes flooded with tears, and he shook his head. "I better get back. My son needs me."

He turned to leave, but she touched his arm. "Wait. Can I call you? To see how you're doing? How he's doing?"

After a long moment, he offered a slow nod and fished his wallet from his back pocket. He dug out a business card and handed it over. The Flaming Mesquite was printed across the top in maroon letters.

His grandpa's old place? Was Nick the owner now?

She rummaged through her tote bag and pulled out a business card. "Here's my number. Call me. If you need anything."

He studied it, a tendon in his jaw twitching, before tucking it into his back pocket. "Thank you."

Then he walked away, just like he had twenty years ago.

Chapter 9

Coffee burned like battery acid in Nick's stomach. Legs wooden, he plodded back to the private waiting room and checked his watch. Almost 10 p.m. Payton would be in surgery for another six hours, maybe more.

Six hours of not knowing whether his son would live or die.

Breathing deeply, Nick settled into a cushioned chair. His eyes felt heavy. His muscles, once charged with adrenaline, now felt limp. But he wouldn't sleep. Couldn't. Not until he knew.

He pulled Tammy's business card from his back pocket. *Organ Procurement Coordinator.* Was this a coincidence, or had God brought her here for a reason? The doctor had mentioned possible internal bleeding. Would Jeremy need a heart or lung transplant? Or was God merely providing a friend to help Nick through?

Leaning forward, he propped his elbows on his knees, head in his hands. He needed this terrible night to be over, for his son to return home, where he belonged.

His phone rang, and his pulse quickened as an image of a scowling Marianne came to mind. She'd make him pay. Somehow she'd find a way to use this against him, to try to strip him of his parental rights.

Maybe he deserved it.

If only he'd taken the boys with him, none of this would've happened.

His cell chimed again, and he glanced at the number. He released a shuddered sigh. "Hey, Mom. How's Jeremy?"

"Lying on the couch watching cartoons. He said he couldn't sleep. I thought maybe the television could . . . How are you holding up?"

"You find the contact info for the cruise line?"

"I did." Papers rustled on the other end. "Ready?"

He searched for a pen and paper. Not finding any, he put the call on speakerphone and used his notepad app. "Go ahead." He typed in the phone numbers—four total along with Marianne's cabin number—while she talked.

"Thanks, Mom."

"Any news on Payton?"

"No. He's not out of surgery yet. I'll phone you in the morning."

He ended the conversation, then dialed the first number typed into his phone. A voice recording followed. Three calls later he reached a message service.

This wasn't information he should let a stranger deliver. He rubbed at a knot in the back of his neck. "Yes, I'm trying to get a hold of Marianne Hawke. It's an emergency. Please have her call her ex-husband . . . uh, Nick Zimmerman, immediately."

With his next call, he reached an automated answering service that provided instructions on how to contact private cabins.

His hand went slick around the phone.

It would've been so much easier had he hit a permanent, impenetrable roadblock. One that necessitated leaving a message.

With slumped shoulders, he dialed her cabin directly. It rang three times before connecting. A series of clanks and rustlings followed, as if someone had dropped the receiver. Soundscape music played in the background.

"Hello?" Marianne sounded breathless.

"It's Nick."

"Who else would be calling me in the middle of the night?" Her voice was raspy. "What is it? Where are the boys?"

A dull ache throbbed in the back of Nick's skull. He raked his hands through his hair and started to pace. "There's been an accident. Payton is—"

"What kind of accident?"

"If you would shut up for three seconds, I'd tell you." *Watch it.* This wasn't the time to start a fight. He clamped his mouth shut and took in a calming breath, exhaling slowly.

"Don't you tell me to shut up, Nick." She cursed, her tone reaching near hysterics.

"I'm at St. Paul's Children's Hospital."

Marianne's hysterics ramped back up. By the time he explained everything, she'd condemned him to hell and threatened to never let him see his kids again.

"He's in surgery." *And could use your prayers, not your threats.* "Good-bye."

Tammy pulled into Vanessa's driveway as the sun was poking over the horizon. Light glowed through the living room window, indicating her friend was already awake.

Cutting the engine, Tammy smiled. *My sweet friend, what would we do without you?*

She needed to find a sitter. One who could show up on short notice without demanding more money than Tammy had.

She'd take out an ad. Today.

Birds chirped as she strolled up the walk. The faint scent of bacon floated on the air, causing her stomach to rumble. Standing on the stoop, she rang Vanessa's doorbell and waited.

Her friend answered in a thick robe and fluffy slippers. "Hey, there, Miss Night Owl."

"Thanks for watching the kids, V. I owe you."

"My pleasure. Keeps me young. And . . ." She wiggled painted fingernails in the air, revealing multicolored stripes and polka-dots. "Stylish." She giggled and moved aside.

As Tammy suspected, Tylan was already up, stationed in front of the television. He was hunched over a plate of food and shoveled mouthfuls of pancake in his mouth. A milk mustache stretched above his top lip and syrup splotched his Spiderman pajamas.

"Hey, bud." Tammy stepped toward him. "Whatchya watching?" She started to sit, but Vanessa grabbed her wrist and pulled her forward.

"Oh, no you don't." She guided Tammy toward the master bedroom. "You need to sleep."

"But I—"

"Nope. I don't want to hear it." She pushed Tammy in with a "Nighty-night," and shut the door.

Tammy stared at the closed door until fatigue drew her to Vanessa's bed. If only she could remain there indefinitely.

Any chance You can solve my problems while I sleep, Lord?

Nestling beneath the sheets, she closed her eyes and let dreamland swallow her concerns.

Chapter 10

"Mr. Zimmerman?"

Nick stirred from his restless sleep and opened gritty eyes.

Seeing the neurosurgeon before him, he bolted to an upright position. The sudden movement sent a stab of pain shooting through his cramped neck.

His pulse quickened. "How's Payton?"

"He's out of surgery and in a medically-induced coma. His intracranial pressure is high. We've had a difficult time keeping it down. Right now it's running at 30-40."

"What's that mean?"

"Under twenty is good."

"Just tell me straight out, in English."

"His brain cells are getting damaged."

"Meaning he could turn into a vegetable?"

"As I told you before the surgery— "

Nick shook his head and flicked his hand. He didn't need another medical lesson. "What now?"

"We're going to give him another 24 hours to see how he does. He's in his room. You're welcome to see him."

Nick nodded.

The doctor crossed to the door and opened it, holding it for Nick. The two headed down the hall, past the nurses' station and numerous patient rooms, some with curtains drawn, others with doors closed. Nick glanced in one to see a bald kid propped up in bed, skin pale. A man and woman sat on either side of him, faces drawn. The woman's eyes were red and puffy.

Entering Payton's room, Nick's lungs constricted as an overwhelming sense of helplessness swept over him. The teen looked so small, so frail. Tubes and wires stretched from him to numerous monitors positioned behind him. Thick bandages covered his head. A ventilator tube protruded from his mouth, taped in place.

Nick moved to his son's bedside and grasped the railing. Struggling for air, he touched Payton's hand. A fierce desire to pick him up and hold him tight ripped through him.

Leaning close, he whispered, "You gotta be strong, buddy. You hear me? Don't leave me, Payton." His words caught. "Fight."

Saturday, Tammy woke to the steady blare of her alarm. She fumbled for the snooze button, knocking something from the end table to the floor. The morning sun poured through the blinds, flooding the room with light. Based on the blare of the television, the kids were already up. She rolled onto her side and pulled a pillow over her head.

How was Nick? Had his son made it through surgery? She rubbed her eyes, propped herself on her elbows, and squinted. 9:15. Maybe she should call him.

Would that be weird? Intrusive?

She slapped her palm to her forehead. Tylan had a game today. They had just over an hour to get ready, pick up Vanessa, and make it to Grainworth's Field.

After donning jeans and a sweatshirt, she grabbed her cell phone and dialed Vanessa's number. "Hi."

"Hey. I was thinking of calling you. What time do we need to leave today?"

"Are you sure you want to come? It looks like it might be cold." Springtime weather in the Midwest was crazy. It wasn't unusual for temperatures to rise to the high seventies then plunge to freezing a day later.

"And miss Tylan's pre-pre-pre-playoffs?"

Tammy laughed at Vanessa's impersonation of Tylan. He'd been talking about the game all week and had finagled Vanessa into coming—as usual. "I can be at your house in . . ." She shuffled to the door, cracked it open. Becky sat on the couch, dressed and ready to go. Tylan still wore pajamas, and a clump of hair protruded from the left side of his head. "Forty minutes."

"Perfect."

Tammy tucked her phone into her back pocket and crossed the room to kiss each of her kids on the forehead. Frowning, Becky pulled away and swiped at imaginary slobber.

"I forgot." Tammy peppered her oldest with kisses. "I've got cooties."

"Stop." Puckered lips fighting a smile, Becky flailed her arms and pushed Tammy away.

Laughing, Tammy turned to Tylan. "And you, young man, need to get your uniform on." She turned off the television and tossed Becky the remote. Her daughter knew the drill. As soon as Tylan left, she could turn the set back on.

Tylan stood. Brow furrowed, he glanced from the curtained window to Tammy. "Is Dad coming to my game?"

Her heart sank. She pulled him close and pressed her lips to his temple. "I hope so, little man."

Slumping forward, he looked at the floor.

Some men didn't deserve to be fathers.

She headed to the kitchen for a dose of caffeine her tense muscles didn't need, then returned to the living room. Becky had flicked the television back on and was watching one of those talent shows. The high-pitched squeal of a thirtysomething woman, dressed in neon green pants and an equally radioactive shirt, rippled through the speakers.

Tammy winced, a headache pressing at the base of her skull. "Can you turn that down, please? Better yet, change the channel."

Becky obeyed with an exaggerated eye roll. The scene switched from a hyperactive teen to a room full of them, all bouncing to loud, pulsating music.

Rubbing her temples, Tammy grabbed her Bible and settled into the corner of the couch.

Give me patience, Lord. And maybe even a quick nap this afternoon.

Tylan emerged from his room ten minutes later, dressed and lugging his duffel bag. He dropped it near the door, then peered through the glass panel, hands pressed against the pane. He turned around, eyes hopeful. "Can I call Dad?"

Tammy sensed Becky watching her, and the tension in the room instantly thickened. She pulled out her phone and studied the screen. No missed alerts. No new text message. "Sure. You can try. He might be busy." And here she was making excuses for him—like always—not because he deserved it. But her kids did.

Grabbing her phone, Tylan beamed. "Maybe he'll take us for pizza after?"

Tammy forced a smile. "Maybe."

She waited, studying Tylan's face, analyzing the inflexions of his voice, while he spoke to his dad. When he returned her phone, she released the breath she'd been holding and placed her hand on his back. "What'd he say?"

Tylan shrugged. "We'll see."

The bitterness returned with a vengeance, but for her son's sake, she shoved it aside. "You ready to knock it out of the park, slugger? Huh?"

Frowning, he gave a noncommittal nod. His lashes fluttered as if fighting tears.

She tickled his ribs until a smile emerged, continuing until giggles followed. "Huh? Huh? Huh? Show me those muscles."

He flexed his arms with a half-grimace, half grin.

She squeezed his nonexistent bicep. "Impressive. The Lightning Bolts won't know what hit them. You ready?"

He nodded, the glimmer back in his eyes.

Tammy led both kids out into the bright morning sunshine. Tylan chattered about how fast he was going to run, how many fly balls he'd catch, and how he planned to hit his first homerun. Becky lagged behind, texting.

They pulled up to Vanessa's ten minutes later, reaching the field well before game time.

But not early enough, apparently. Spectators filled the hillside and crowded the stands. Tammy made a quick scan for Brody, her stomach knotting when her gaze landed on a tall man with dark, curly hair. He turned around, and she exhaled. Wasn't him.

Lugging the cooler, Tammy followed her kids down the hill, Vanessa at her side.

Upon seeing his coach and teammates, Tylan took off.

"Good luck, slugger!" She called after him.

She stretched a blanket across a vacant patch of grass beneath an old oak tree and plunked down. Vanessa joined her, but Becky took off in search of Mackenzie, a friend from school who had a brother on Tylan's team.

Tammy pulled two Cokes from the cooler and handed one to her friend. "You're never going to believe who I saw last night."

Taking her drink, Vanessa gave her a sideways glance. "Who? Nurse Psycho? "

Tammy chuckled. "No, thank goodness." She fiddled with the pop top. "Nick."

"What?" Vanessa's eyes widened. "*The* Nick?"

Tammy nodded.

"Wow. How'd that happen? Where?"

"At St. Paul's, in the cafeteria."

Vanessa looked at her for a long moment. "You still got feelings for him?"

Tammy huffed. "No." She picked at a thread in the blanket. "But I do feel bad for him. He's facing a difficult situation."

"You can't tell me about it, can you?"

"Nope. HIPPA laws, you know."

"Wow." Vanessa tucked her feet under her. "Out of all the hospitals you could have gone to, out of all the times, and you end up at St. Paul's the same night he does?" She shook her head. "It always amazes me how God surrounds us with friends and loved ones when we need them most."

Tammy shrugged. "I'm not sure how much comfort I provided. We're not exactly besties anymore. It's been decades."

"Never underestimate the power of a friendly face and a kind smile." She sipped her Coke. "So, you gonna call him?"

Tammy ran a finger around the rim of her can and shrugged. "I gave him my number. In case he needed anything." She'd also told Ellen she wanted to take the call, if Nick's son died.

"Uh, Tammy . . ." Vanessa tapped her on the shoulder.

"Yeah?" She turned to look and nearly dropped her drink. Brody strolled down the hill, grinning. A blonde with glasses, wearing a shin-length skirt covered in flowers, accompanied him.

Vanessa shoulder bumped her. "You okay?"

Tammy inhaled and wiped sweaty hands on her pant legs. "Yep."

Brody approached with an arm draped around his new girlfriend. The stench of musky cologne mixed with rose perfume emanated from them. "Tammy, Vanessa."

Tammy set her can down and stood slowly. Her legs felt like flimsy cardboard. "Brody."

"Dad."

She turned at the sound of Becky's voice. Her daughter walked toward him, a hint of a smile emerging, although the skin around her eyes remained taut. Her gaze flicked to Tammy before returning to her dad.

"Pumpkin." He enveloped Becky in a hug, then held her at arms' length. "Beautiful as ever." With an exaggerated scowl, he scanned the area like a poised leopard guarding his young. "I should've brought my baseball bat to keep those pesky boys away."

Becky rolled her eyes, although her smile widened slightly. "Are you taking us to Minsky's after the game?"

Tammy stiffened. *Don't you dare break her heart, Brody.*

He gave their daughter a sideways hug, watching Tammy. "I'd love to, princess, but . . ." He looked at his date, who appeared to be sending Morse code. "I can't. Not today."

Becky pushed away from him and crossed her arms. "So you lied then. Again."

Brody frowned. "No. I said we'd talk about it. How about tomorrow? Then we can have the whole day. We'll do pizza, maybe get a movie, rent some video games. Whatdya say?"

Tammy stepped forward and spoke between clenched teeth. "Their raincheck bank is full."

Brody's eyes narrowed. "Not now, Tammy."

She snorted. "You're—" Glancing at Becky, she clamped her mouth shut. *Pathetic.*

"I don't have time for this." He turned to Becky with a close-lipped smile. "I'll call you this afternoon. We'll work something out."

Becky's face fell, sending adrenaline shooting through Tammy's veins. She opened her mouth, ready to explode, but Vanessa gripped her arm and pulled her back.

"What do you say we get something to eat?" Vanessa's voice was firm.

Tammy fisted her hands, her molars grinding together. Making a scene wouldn't help. But high doses of sugar might.

"Food. Right." She touched Becky's shoulder. "Come on, sweetie. I bet they have Fudgsicles."

"See you, peanut." Brody flashed a stupid grin. "We'll be sitting over there." He pointed to an empty section of grass a few feet from the playground. "Come find us, okay?"

Why? So he could hurt Becky more?

But what could Tammy do? Legally, he had a right to see his kids.

Whether he wanted to or not.

An image of Nick, sitting beside Payton's hospital bed, flashed through Tammy's mind. While he cried out to God, begging for more time with his son, Tammy's ex wasted the time he had with his.

Chapter 11

Sunday morning, Tammy pressed the phone to one ear and her palm to the other. "Hold on, Mother. I can't hear you." Cupping the mouthpiece, she whirled around.

Tylan barreled through the room growling, claws bared, chasing an imaginary monster.

She grabbed his arm, stopping him in mid-lunge. "Can you please find something quieter to do?" No more Tangy-loops for breakfast. Or dinner. Or afternoon snacks. In fact, no more sugar period.

He stared at her as if she'd asked him to find the cure for cancer. Then he hunched over, lowering his voice, and resumed his march.

"He's so annoying." Sitting in the recliner, Becky rolled her eyes. "Can I go to Robin's after church?"

"We'll talk about that later." Tammy returned to her phone conversation. "Sorry, Mom. You know how it is. The minute I get on the phone, the kids go crazy." She migrated to her bedroom and closed the door. "Listen, I hate to cut this short, but I've got about ten minutes."

"Honey, you're going to run yourself ragged."

Tammy rubbed her temples, preparing herself for the imminent, "I worry about you" lecture.

"I really wish you'd find something else. I don't like the idea of you driving all over the place all hours of the night."

There it was, soon to be followed by the "for the sake of your children" plug. She tried to remind herself that her mom meant well, that she spoke out of love, but Tammy couldn't help but feel condemned. Like she was failing as a parent.

"Tylan and Becky are only young once, you know. And with Becky nearing high school . . . Do you have any idea what kind of garbage teenagers face nowadays? It's amazing more of them don't—"

"We're doing fine, Mom." Okay, perhaps fine was a stretch, but her chaotic home life had nothing to do with her job. Yet. "Can I call you back af—"

"I know you don't like to hear this, dear, but you know I'm right. You've got to think of the kids."

"I appreciate your concern, but we're good."

"You need help, and no one will care for your children like family. Think about what I said."

"About moving in with you and Dad? We've discussed this." Along with all the reasons that wouldn't work, her and the kids jammed in her parents' basement was a major one. "Besides, I'm a grown woman. I can handle this."

"Hold on. Your father wants to talk to you."

"No, Mom. Don't put—"

There was a rustling noise followed by her father's signature loud breathing. "Muffin, how are you doing?"

"Hi, Daddy."

"Listen, I know how much you value your independence, and you've given it a good effort."

Good effort? What did that mean? That she'd tried to manage her life but failed, so now they needed to step in and save her?

She rested against the dresser, listening as her father prattled on about the tanking economy, the challenges of single parenting, and the pitfalls of her job. Her mom's voice peaked in the background, coaching him.

"I hear you."

Hiding her impatience, she leaned into the mirror to inspect the faint lines fanning from her eyes. Face powder had settled into the creases. Beautiful. Holding the phone between her ear and shoulder, she grabbed her compact to smooth out the wrinkles. She stopped when her gaze landed on Nick's business card.

It lay on her dresser next to her jewelry box. She dropped her compact and picked up the card. She ran her finger along the edge.

Nick Zimmerman. After all this time. How was he doing? How was his son? She needed to call him this afternoon.

"Listen, Dad, can we talk later?"

"Your mother and I will be there this afternoon."

"What?" She nearly dropped the phone. "I . . . uh . . . I appreciate the offer, but now's not a good time. How about we plan something for this summer?"

"We'll see you this afternoon, princess. Love you."

The line clicked.

Tammy closed her eyes and pinched the bridge of her nose.

Sitting at Payton's bedside, Nick's mind felt thick, his ears dull. Hospital staff merged in and out, checking the machines and making notes on clipboards.

A nurse popped in, turned on the television, and flicked through the channels. "You like history? Sports?"

Nick shrugged.

"Well, here you go." She set the remote on the bedside table. "Press the call button if you need anything."

After she left, Nick pulled his phone from his back pocket. He'd turned it off around midnight, after Marianne's fifth call. There was no sense trying to talk to the woman when she was hysteric. He'd only say something he'd regret.

A knock sounded. He glanced up to see Chef Rictor standing in the doorway, eyes soft, brow wrinkled. His frown lengthened when he glanced from Payton to Nick. "Hey. Mind if I come in?"

Nick shrugged.

Rictor grabbed a chair from the corner of the room and dragged it over. "Where's Jeremy?"

"With my mom."

Rictor nodded. "The police canvassed your neighborhood, asked everyone a bunch of questions. They'll get the guy who did this."

Nick's stomach revolted as the memory of that night came rushing back. Everyone gathered in the street. The sound of the screaming sirens, of muffled voices. Of the paramedics lifting his son onto the stretcher.

But the image that stuck out most was seeing his sons playing football as he drove away. If only he'd never left.

Nick shifted. "The fire?"

Rictor nodded. "I followed that disaster plan you made. Well, for the most part, once I remembered it. Took a bunch of pictures." He pulled a memory card chip from his pocket and handed it over. "You need this for your insurance claim, right?"

"Yeah, and probably some before photos too." Which he'd never finished taking. Closing his eyes, Nick rubbed his face. The Flaming Mesquite was the last thing he cared about right now, but letting it fail wouldn't pay his high deductible. Or child support.

Had he purchased loss coverage? If not, this fire would tank his business and cost his employees their jobs.

Would end his custody battle. Lawyers didn't work on IOUs.

He could lose both sons.

His eyes blurred as he stared at Payton, all the responsibilities leaving him paralyzed.

Rictor placed a hand on Nick's shoulder. "Sorry, man. This is rough. Real rough."

Silence stretched between them for ten minutes, maybe longer, before Rictor spoke again. "You been here since Friday?"

"Yeah."

"You need to take a break, man. Check on Jeremy." He paused. "How's he doing?"

Nick stared at his hands, fighting back tears. "Don't know." Rictor was right. The hospital staff had said the same thing. But what if he left and something happened?

"Listen, if you need anything . . ." Rictor stood.

Nick nodded.

What I need is my son.

Tammy's phone vibrated all during church service, numbers flashing on her screen faster than sparks from an electrical wire. Half she didn't recognize. The others came from both of her brothers and two of her aunts. A cousin she hadn't spoken to in five years left her a text: *Your mother's very worried. Let her help you.*

Mom! Had the woman sent out a press release? "*Cell phone intervention, starting during church service. Whoever wears her down first wins a prize.*"

Tammy tried to focus on the sermon, but the words didn't resonate. She turned to the bulletin while an emotional war raged in her soul.

Are you there, God? Because I could sure use some of that peace that surpasses understanding right about now.

And a reliable sitter.

The service concluded with one last song and the pastor dismissed everyone with an invitation to return that night for the monthly business meeting. Clutching her Bible to her chest, Tammy stared at the end of the pew to avoid eye contact. A chipper, *God bless you*, would only send her over the edge.

Hallelujah, praise the Lord, my life's a mess, and my mom's driving me insane. How was your week?

Unfortunately, she got trapped behind a family of four halfway down the aisle—right beside the row Constance waited to leave.

"Good morning, dear." The woman's lips stretched into a close-mouthed smile. "How've you been holding up?"

"Good, thank you. Catching up on my sleep." She stepped aside, adding a manageable distance between herself and the woman. Next, she needed to find a way to deflect the focus of the conversation. "How are you? Has your son returned from Hong Kong?"

Constance's eyes lit up. "July 10th. You'll have to stop by. I'm hosting a welcome home reception." She pulled a handmade invitation from her purse and handed it over.

"Thank you."

"I almost forgot." She opened the front cover of her Bible and pulled out a business card.

Tammy took the card and blinked. *Good Shepherd Family Counseling Services.*

"The therapist, Mr. Turner, is a friend of mine. A good Christian man. A praying man." She squeezed Tammy's hand. "Never be ashamed to ask for help, dear."

Help for what exactly?

Heat crept up Tammy's neck, her gaze shooting to the numerous empathetic faces turned her way. She opened her mouth, hoping words would follow—Sunday morning words, that is. None came. "Thank you." She checked her watch. "Oh, my. Look at the time. I better pick up the kiddos." She dashed out, not slowing until she reached the bottom of the stairwell.

Maneuvering around chattering women, laughing men, and giggling children, she made it to Tylan's classroom in time to see him dive over a craft table. He landed in a tangle of chairs, socked feet in the air.

"Tylan Kuhn!" She stomped in. Offering his teacher, Mrs. Wilson, an apologetic smile, she tugged him to his feet. "Where are your shoes?"

He shrugged and wiggled out of her grasp.

Tammy shook her head. "What has gotten into you?" His shoes lay in the corner amidst a pile of blocks and overturned plastic cups. She grabbed them and tossed them his way. "And put your shoes on."

Hearing a deep-throated chuckle, she glanced up.

Jenson strolled over, smiling. Dark hair framed strong features; his teal golf shirt accentuated his tan. "Kids. Can't sell them, can't trade them. What're you gonna do?"

"Invest in deadbolts and duct tape?" Tammy laughed and watched Tylan fight with his laces. "How've you been?"

He propped a foot on a chair. "I'm good. Staying busy." His brows dropped. "How about you?"

She studied his face. "Fine, thanks." When his expression didn't change, she asked, "What's going on, Jenson? Why the sudden concern?"

"I got an email from Elder Johnson. I guess Glenda called him this morning."

She blinked, mouth agape. "She what?" How in the—? *Mom.*

Aching to grab her phone, she forced a stiff smile and shook her head. "Parents. You can't sell them . . ."

"You all right, then?"

She shrugged. "My mom's blowing things way out of proportion. We've hit a bit of a . . . hiccup. Babysitting issues. Nothing I haven't handled before." Although each time, her boss Ellen grew less patient. One more call-in could cost Tammy her job.

And her credit.

And quite possibly, her home.

She needed to find a good sitter.

Joni had been great. She made sure Becky studied and talked with her about purity. She helped calm Tylan down. As much as he could be calmed. But sitters like Joni, who acted more like moms than childcare providers, were hard to find. And expensive.

"Well . . ." Jenson pulled out a business card and handed it over. "I normally handle commercial properties, but I'm familiar with the residential market. If you need to talk, to explore your options."

More evidence of Mom's "move Tammy" campaign. She inched backward, eyeing the exit. "Thank you." She took the card and turned to Tylan, lowering her voice to ward off any protests. "Let's track down your sister."

They found her near the soda machines, surrounded by a group of kids. "Becky, let's go."

"Just a minute, Mom."

"Now."

Her head throbbed as they made their way out of the church and across the lot, Becky and Tylan's protests falling on deaf ears. As soon as she slid behind the steering wheel, she pulled out her cell phone and called her mother.

"Hello, dear. How was church?"

"Don't give me that. You called Glenda, didn't you?"

"Now, don't get upset. We're a body, and God wants us to call upon one another, speak truth to one another—"

"Mom, this isn't your church anymore."

"Oh, honey, the body of Christ extends beyond those four walls."

Tammy sighed and kneaded her forehead. Her mom meant well. And in a week, maybe two, Tammy would be grateful for her love. But today, she needed time to decompress. “Mom, I appreciate what you’re trying to do here, but brownies and hugs won’t fix this one. I need to deal with this on my own.”

“No, what you need is a big ol’ hug followed by a clear course of action.” She paused. “Look at that! Tammy Lynn, you never told me your neighbor Mrs. Greenland was pregnant! How cute she looks! We should bake her something.”

“What? Mom, where are you?”

“At your house, dear, like I told you.”

Chapter 12

Tammy rounded the corner, and her eyes widened. *You've got to be kidding me.* Her parents' RV—all forty feet of it—sat in her driveway.

"Yay," Tylan squealed. "Nana and Poppa."

Becky glanced up from her permanent appendage—her phone. "Are we going camping?"

"No." *Please tell me this is a pit stop.*

Dad stood near her garage door, shielding his eyes and peering at the gutters. He'd have a ladder out by the end of the day.

A few feet away, Mom fiddled with a flowerbed on the porch. A soft-sided cooler rested against the siding next to a paper grocery bag. Filled with what? Feel-better cupcakes?

Tammy's grip tightened around the steering wheel as she eased to the curb and cut the engine.

Upon seeing her, Mom strolled over, grinning and waving. The kids tumbled out. Becky ran to Nana, Tylan to Poppa. Tammy shuffled along behind them, working her stiff face into a smile.

Okay. So, she'd have company. For an extended period, apparently. Could be fun. Good for Tylan and Becky. Maybe God knew they needed some extra snuggles and kisses.

Tammy approached Mom first and gave her a sideways hug. "Hey. How are you?"

"Oh, sweet pea." Mom opened her arms wide and wrapped them around Tammy, her hand pressing against the back of Tammy's head. The familiar scent of almond-cherry lotion swept over her, triggering the threat of tears.

Don't fall apart now. And whatever you do, don't show signs of weakness. That'd trigger Mom's hovering instincts faster than a flame to kerosene.

Inhaling, she blinked and pulled away. She turned to Dad. "Good to see you." Despite the sixty-plus temperature, he wore his favorite shorts—teal Bermudas with pink palm trees—topped with a faded Seahawks T-shirt. A lopsided straw hat covered his bald head.

"Been too long, huh? How's my favorite daughter?" He engulfed her in what was more of a headlock than a hug.

"I'm your only daughter." The youngest of three, the others boys, and hence the reason both parents treated her like a princess in need of rescue. She'd spent her entire life trying to prove otherwise. Any progress she'd made had been shattered by her divorce.

Dad gripped her shoulders and studied her face, his eyes soft. "How you doing?" He stared at her for a moment.

"I'm good."

He continued to stare at her, his mouth quivering as if he didn't believe her and was searching for something to say.

Wanting to alleviate his papa-bear turmoil, Tammy soft-punched him in the gut, then looped her arm through his. "How was your trip to the Rocky Mountains?" They strolled up the walk, Mom and the kids following.

"Too much hiking for this old man." Shaking his head, he lumbered up the porch steps, favoring his right leg.

Behind them, Tylan chattered about Saturday's little league game while Becky fired a zillion questions in rapid succession. Mom responded to both of them with ease, alternating from praises to "I don't see why not."

Tammy's cell rang. Great Grandmother Lotus's number flashed across the screen. She rolled her eyes. "Mom, how many people have you contacted?"

"Unlock the door, will you, dear?" Mom touched her elbow. "I've got perishables in there." She motioned toward the cooler.

Mom and Dad hovered over the welcome mat while Tylan rang the doorbell incessantly.

Tammy dug in her purse for her keys and engaged the lock. She opened the door and froze, her gaze sweeping across the cluttered living room. The kids' cereal bowls sat on the coffee table, Tylan's blanket on the couch. Shoes—like eight pairs—lay scattered across the floor, along with a pair of grass-stained socks. "I . . . uh, I haven't had a chance to clean up yet." She glanced over her shoulder, catching Mom's hint of a frown.

"Don't you worry about a thing." Mom patted her on the shoulder, then scooped up her bags with a grunt. "That's what I'm here for. To manage the house while you rest, which is exactly what you need, rest. And time to reevaluate." She wiggled past Tammy and headed to the kitchen while Dad and the kids migrated to the living room.

Reevaluate? Translation—concede to their wishes, which included quitting her job, selling her home, ripping her kids out of the schools they knew and loved, and moving them three hundred miles from their father and into a 700-square-foot, musty basement. Not happening, no matter how long and hard they nagged her.

Cupboards banged in the kitchen. Following the sound, Tammy found Mom digging through spices and bowls. Large quantities of food would soon follow. The one bright spot in her otherwise frustrating Sunday.

Tammy moved to the archway. "Dad, can I get you something to drink?"

He waved her off and bopped Tylan on the head with a pillow. This initiated war, and soon shrieks and squeals filled the house. Tammy smiled. Annoying or not, this would be good. Their house could use more laughter, and the slight scent of Arthricream. At least her babysitting dilemma was solved. For now.

She crossed the kitchen and started to help Mom unload. "So, how long are you staying?"

"As long as you need, darling."

Needed for what? To change her mind or find childcare? But there was no sense initiating the debate. The subject would arise soon enough.

Mom pulled a freezer bag filled with raw meat from the cooler. She held it up, inspected it, and then set it on the counter.

"What's with the spiced beef?"

"Lunch."

"I've got thawed chicken in the fridge."

Mother shrugged and continued pulling items from her cooler—a green bean mixture in a lidded baking pan, spices, a bag of red potatoes, and cooking wine.

Tammy reached for a paring knife, but her mother smacked her hand. "Uh-uh. You relax, dear. Would you like a cup of tea?"

"No." Tammy leaned against the counter. "It's been three years, Mom, and we haven't died yet."

"I know, dear, and I know how hard you've tried to stand on your own, but there's no shame in asking for help."

"Speaking of." Tammy crossed her arms. "Thanks for enlisting my church elders in your 'Save Tammy' campaign."

Mom sucked in a deep breath and pressed steepled hands to her lips. "Let me get lunch going, then we'll talk."

That was one conversation she wasn't looking forward to.

Three hours and two lectures later, Tammy rubbed her temples and glanced at the clock on the microwave.

Sitting at the kitchen table beside her, Dad reached over and rubbed her back. "Listen to your mother. It's for the best. For you and the kids."

Mom nodded. "Maybe you could even go back to school. Change careers, find one with more reasonable hours."

"You and Dad have given me a lot to think about."

Mother smiled and patted her hand. "Good."

If she avoided the conversation long enough, would they give up?

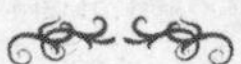

Nick sat at Payton's bedside, the steady beep of the machines thudding in his brain. He stood and moved to the window, staring mindlessly at the endless stream of cars on the streets below. People pumping gas, buying and gorging on fast food, fighting with their kids.

Footsteps clicked behind him. He turned to see Melissa, one of the nurses, holding a food tray.

"Hungry?" She glanced at the bedside table where another tray sat, barely touched.

Nick shook his head, staring at the handmade sign propped against an unopened milk carton. Jeremy had brought it that morning. Poor kid. Nick's mom said the boy had barely slept the night before, plagued by one nightmare after another. If Payton didn't pull through . . . A sharp pain stabbed at his chest, stealing his breath.

"Can I get you anything else?" the nurse asked.

He shook his head again. No sense telling her he wasn't hungry.

She replaced one tray with the other, watched him for a moment longer, then left.

He stared at the food, his stomach alternating between cramps and convulsions. A peanut butter and jelly sandwich lay beside apple slices. Unable to stomach solids, he grabbed the pint of orange juice instead.

Returning to the window, he caught a glimpse of himself in the mirror. Dark shadows hung below his dull eyes, his skin ashen beneath course whiskers. Taking a swig of juice, he glanced at the travel bag his mother had brought. Eventually he'd need to shower, change, brush his teeth.

Check on the restaurant.

He pulled his phone from his back pocket to dial Chef Rictor. A missed call flashed on the screen. An unfamiliar number with a Woodland Pines area code. He played the message.

"Hi. It's Tammy. I . . . Call me back."

He paused with his finger over her return number. He wasn't in the mood for a social call or to field questions asking how he was doing. He called the restaurant instead.

After four rings, Nick started to hang up when Chef Rictor's voice came on.

"Hello? Er . . . I mean"—he cleared his throat—"thank you for calling the Flaming Mesquite, home of the best steaks south of the river. May I help you?"

"Hey, Rictor, it's Nick."

"Oh. Any news?"

"No. The doctors said Payton could come out of his coma at any time or he could . . ." He swallowed past a lump in his throat. "Or he could remain in his current state, indefinitely." He looked back toward his son, staring at the squiggly lines stretched across the EEG machine. "How are things there?"

"The fire marshal came out, did a thorough inspection."

"They find the cause of the fire?"

"The deep fryer's high-limit switch failed."

Nick closed his dreary eyes, trying to process through a thick fog of fatigue. He really needed to go down and survey the damage for himself, get a repair crew out there. "Did it spread past the hood and duct system?"

"A little, but not much, thanks to our meticulous cleaning. The guy said it could've been worse—used the opportunity to lecture us on fire prevention."

"What's the damage?""Minus the swamp caused by the sprinkler system?" Rictor gave a hollow chuckle.

Nick leaned against the wall, still watching his son. How much could Rictor handle? "Could you get some people out there, gather a few estimates for me?"

"I don't know, bro. The marshal said you'd need to get some kind of renovation permits and construction applications. Would the city let me do that? Maybe you could give me power of attorney or something."

Nick rubbed the back of his neck. "No. I'll take care of it."

"I don't mean to sound forward, but . . ." Rictor paused. "Do you got the capital to make it through this?"

Translation—will I still have a job once this is over?

Nick wasn't the only one with bills to pay. He sighed, his breath reverberating in the mouthpiece. "We'll figure it out."

Fire damage was just the beginning. Each day the restaurant stayed closed, he lost more money. And with mounting medical bills, he didn't have a dime to spare.

"Yeah, that'd be good. The crew's getting nervous, talking about unemployment and all that garbage. I told them not to worry—that you had our backs."

"Thanks, Rictor. I'll call you later." Tucking his phone back into his pocket, he sank into the chair.

Lord, give me strength because I'm about to break.

Chapter 13

Tammy stretched and rolled on her side. Birds chirped outside her bedroom window, the morning sun slanting through cracked blinds. Bunching the pillows under her head, she smiled and closed her eyes. She hadn't felt this rested in weeks.

Except today was Monday.

She bolted upright and checked her clock. Nine thirty.

Ugh. Her alarm never went off. The kids would be late for school. And had probably already torn the house apart. A lovely start to her week.

Shucking the blankets, she sprang out of bed and slipped on her bathrobe. She paused at the door and cocked her head. A steady hum drifted from the living room and pounding came from somewhere beyond. She sighed.

Mom and Dad.

Squaring her shoulders, she smoothed her tangled hair behind her ears and emerged with what she hoped resembled a smile. Her mother stood with her back to Tammy, running a vacuum across the same patch of carpet. Her cleaning bucket filled with sprays, rags, and polish, sat on the end table.

Tammy turned toward the sound of clanking metal and shook her head.

Dad, what are you doing?

Propped against the outside glass of her living room window stood an old rusted ladder. All that showed of her dad were his stained tennis shoes and hairy legs, from ankle to wrinkled knees. While he worked, blobs of decaying leaves plunked to the porch.

That explains the pounding.

Propping her hands on her hips, she glanced around the immaculate living room. "Where're the kids?"

Mom continued to vacuum, head bobbing as she belted out an old hymn.

Tammy approached and tapped her shoulder.

She squealed and whirled around, eyes wide before crinkling into a smile. She flicked off the vacuum. "Good morning, sweet pea." She planted a slobbery kiss to her check. "You sleep well?"

"Too well. Where are Becky and Tylan?"

"At school." She said it matter-of-factly, as if this was to be expected, like it'd been her responsibility to see them off.

There was another loud clank and a yell. Tammy turned to see her gutter dangling, brown gook splattered across the window.

Mom turned and cupped her hands around her mouth. "Wilbert, you be careful!"

Dad lumbered down the ladder, shirt dusted with decaying leaf matter. He flashed a grin and a thumbs up sign.

Shaking her head, her mom turned back to Tammy. "I told him to call someone, but no. Had to do it himself, the old penny-pincher."

Tammy tensed. *I'm not a child in need of rescue.* "I appreciate the help, but . . ." She glanced at a stack of laundry on the couch, her folded underwear on top. "How long have you been up, anyway?"

Mom gave a flick of her hand. "Since five, maybe five thirty. You hungry?"

"Not really." She glanced from her mother to her bedroom. "Did you turn off my alarm?"

Mom smiled. "I knew you needed the rest. Now," she crossed the room and pulled a Bible from her book bag, "how about you have some sweet time with Jesus while I cook you up some eggs and sausage?"

Grown woman, here. Thirty-eight years old. "I've got my own Bible, and like I said, I'm not hungry."

Her mother frowned, staring at her for a long moment before closing the distance between them. She grabbed Tammy's hands. "I worried this might happen."

Tammy sighed. "What's that?"

"You're depressed."

"What?" Tammy snorted. "I'm *not* depressed."

"Of course you are." Releasing her hands, Mom wrapped her in a hug. "But that's why we're here. For as long as you need. In fact . . ." She returned to her tote bag and pulled out a thin book with a gray cover. "I picked this up for you."

Battling Depression: A Step-by-Step Guide.

There was another clank, followed by more cascading leaf splatter, as the rest of the gutter came crashing down.

"Mom, listen . . ."

"Yes, dear?"

She studied at her mother for a long moment then huffed. "Never mind." It wasn't worth breaking Mom's heart. So Tammy would wake to the sound of vacuum cleaners and falling gutters. And the extra sleep had been nice.

"I need a bath." Choosing a moment of self-imposed isolation over much needed coffee, Tammy shuffled back into her bedroom. She headed straight for the master bath with its Jacuzzi jets and fragrant oils. She soaked until her skin shriveled.

After wrapping a towel around herself, she trudged back to her room and plopped onto the bed. She scooted back until her spine rested against the headboard, grabbed a pillow, and hugged it to her chest.

How long can I stay in here?

She really had nothing pertinent to do.

Her phone rang.

She glanced at the number. Brody. So he'd finally taken the time to call her back.

"Hey." She rose to a sitting position and leaned against her headboard. "I was calling about Friday. What time are you picking the kids up?"

There was an extended pause. "This Friday?"

"Yes, Brody. It's your weekend, remember?" Seriously, when had he turned into the absent-minded father? Didn't he *want* to spend time with them? Come to think of it, he'd never fought her on custody.

Brody sighed. "Sorry. It's been crazy at work, and I guess I got my dates mixed up. But this weekend's good. What time?"

"They get out of school at three."

"Yeah, okay. I'll be there."

The line went dead. If he bailed one more time . . .

Her kids needed a dad.

There was a soft rap on the door, and a moment later, it creaked open, and Mom poked her head inside.

"Hey there." She stepped forward, holding a steaming plate in one hand a glass of orange juice in the other.

Tammy wrapped her towel tighter around herself. "Mom! I'm naked."

"Then I suggest you get dressed." Mom laughed and deposited the food on the end table, plunking onto the edge of the bed. "How long are you planning on hiding out in your bedroom?"

"Um . . . Till three?" She gave a wry smile, not sure whether to be amused or irritated.

"You know what you need, dear?"

"A deadbolt?"

Her mom chuckled. "No, a day at the spa." She stood and straightened a few things on the nightstand. "Now hurry up. The day is wasting away."

Nick eased into his garage and let the engine idle. Silence pressed down on him, the midmorning sun lengthening the shadows in the garage. He sat frozen, his hand on the gearshift. Payton needed him. He could wake at any moment, scared, disoriented.

But Jeremy needed him too.

Marianne was trying to book a flight home from her next port city. After that, Nick would be lucky to see Jeremy at all.

Unless the judge granted him custody.

He cut the engine and stepped out, his legs rubbery. Opening the door, he blinked in the bright kitchen light. Muffins, scones, and other baked goods cluttered the counter, and a stack of mail sat next to the sink.

"Nick, is that you?" His mom emerged wearing sweats, her hair pulled in a loose ponytail. Bags shadowed red-rimmed eyes. Her husband followed half a step behind.

She hugged Nick, then pulled away, holding him at arm's length. "Any news?"

He shook his head and glanced around. "Where's Jeremy?"

She angled her head toward the den where Mario raced across the television screen in time to the faint theme music.

Inhaling, Nick approached his son and rounded the couch. Jeremy sat with shoulders slumped, eyes wilted, video remote in his hand.

"Hey, bud." Nick sat beside him. "How you doing?"

Jeremy shrugged, focused on the screen.

Nick watched him for a moment, longing to draw the boy close. But his son's clenched jaw and plunging brow line told him not to push. Instead, he grabbed the second game controller. "Mind if I join you?"

Jeremy shrugged again and gave him a sideways glance.

After the first game, Jeremy's scowl eased into a slight frown.

"Can I read you something?" Nick grabbed a Bible from the coffee table and flipped to Psalms 121. "Reading the Bible always helps me when I'm scared." He flipped to his favorite passage. "'*I lift up my eyes to the mountains—where does my help come from? My help comes from the* L*ORD*, *the Maker of heaven and earth*.'" He closed the Bible and laid it in his lap. "You remember when we used to try to count the stars?"

Jeremy nodded. "And find monsters and lions and bears."

Nick smiled. "That's right."

"You remember what I told you?" Nick asked.

Jeremy nodded, his face crumpling. "God named them?"

"Every star. And the God who made and named the stars knows your name also. He knows Payton's name too. Loves Payton even more than you and I do."

Mom joined them on the couch, sitting on Jeremy's other side and slipping her arm behind his back.

Jeremy's chin puckered. "Is God gonna take Payton to heaven?"

Tears burned Nick's eyes but he blinked them back. "I don't know, buddy. I hope not." He lifted Jeremy's chin so the child looked into his eyes. "And that's what we gotta hold on to—hope. We've got to trust in Jesus, okay?"

Jeremy nodded, a tear sliding down his cheek. Sitting between Mom and his son, Nick's pulse quickened as an urge to return to the hospital gripped him.

He'd give Jeremy five more minutes. Just five more.

His muscles, limp and numb, sank into the seat cushions. He tried to focus on the video game playing on the screen, but the colors blurred. His eyes were so heavy. Jeremy curled into Nick's chest, warm and soft and smelling like mint shampoo.

So very tired.

Nick's head drooped forward and a thick cloak of sleep overtook him.

"Nick? Nick?"

He jerked awake, pulse ignited.

Mom stood before him, face pale, eyes wide.

Fighting panic, he wiggled out from under a sleeping Jeremy and lurched to his feet. "What is it? Is everything okay?"

"It's the hospital." She held out the phone.

Bile flooded his throat as he grabbed the receiver. "Hello?" He struggled to breathe. "This is Nick Zimmerman."

"Mr. Zimmerman, this is Melissa Feigan at St. Paul's."

"Yes?"

"Your son's condition has deteriorated. I need you to return to the hospital."

No. His legs buckled and he gripped the back of the couch for support. "What does this mean? Another surgery?"

"The doctor would like to talk with you."

"I'm on my way." He dropped the phone.

"What is it?" His mom stood in the hallway, hand on her throat.

"I need to go back to the hospital." He moved for the door.

She grabbed his wrist. "Wait. I'll come."

"Dad?"

Nick spun around to find his youngest staring at him with wide, teary eyes.

"What's wrong?" the boy's voice trembled. "Is Payton okay?"

Nick's heart wrenched. *Help us, Lord: Please help us!* He dropped on one knee to look Jeremy in the eye. Grabbing his shoulders, Nick fought to keep his voice steady. "I'm going to see him now. Everything's going . . ." He looked at Mom and swallowed. *Everything will be okay, right Lord?*

"You go." She pushed him toward the door. "We'll meet you there."

The doctor's words swam through his mind as he stumbled into the garage and to his car. *"Herniation could lead to brain death or an irreversible coma."*

When he arrived at the hospital, he found Payton's room crowded with medical personnel. The hospital chaplain stood a few feet away. Adrenaline shot through Nick.

The staff looked at him with solemn expressions.

He hurried to Payton's bedside, staring from the machines to the steady rise and fall of his son's chest. Gripping the railing, he exhaled.

Payton was alive.

They could get through this. He grabbed his son's hand and leaned closer. "You can make it, bud. Hold on. You hear me? Hold on."

Someone touched Nick's shoulder. He looked up to see the nurse standing beside him. "Mr. Zimmerman, let's go to a quiet room where we can talk about your son's condition." She spoke softly.

He studied her expression for a hint of hope. Moist eyes stared back at him.

"I . . . But he . . ." Nick exhaled, struggling to focus. "Okay." Standing on stiff legs, he cast one last glance at his son before following her out of the room and down the hall.

They passed an orderly pushing a gurney, triggering images of the night they brought Payton in. Nick felt an urge to whirl back around, race into Payton's room. But what could he do? Instead, he followed the nurse into a private waiting room

The nurse faced him. "The doctor should be here any moment."

"What is it? Is something wrong?"

"The doctor will want to speak to you himself."

They sat in awkward silence for what felt like forever but was probably only five minutes. Then the doctor arrived, his eyes blood shot, dark shadows beneath them. He sat across from Nick. "As you know, your son's condition took a turn for the worse, and it appears he herniated."

"So what now? Another surgery?"

"We plan to do brain death testing." He paused, his expression softening, as if pained by the conversation. "Do you remember when I explained herniation to you?"

Nick nodded, feeling numb. Like his brain wouldn't work.

"Do you understand what it means?"

"I want to see my son." He bolted from the room, the nurse's footfalls following close behind.

Nick hurried to Payton's bedside, his pulse pounding against his eardrums. He gingerly picked up the teen's hand. Emerging calluses, earned through hours of baseball practice, felt rough beneath his fingers.

Payton wanted to be the next Mickey Mantle. Could've done it, too, given time. Nick would've done everything he could to help him. Heavy, rhythmic footfalls fell behind him, followed by the scent of hand sanitizer. He turned to face the doctor who stood a few feet from the doorway.

"Mr. Zimmerman, I'll be testing Payton's reflexes now to see if there is brain activity. We will also do a cerebral blood flow study to determine if there is blood flow to the brain."

No! No! No!

"Daddy?"

Nick glanced up to see Jeremy standing in the doorway, his grandmother beside him.

His gut wrenched. He crossed the room and wrapped an arm around the boy's frail shoulders. The boy didn't need to see this.

Jeremy looked around, his eyes growing wider. "What are they doing?" His chin puckered when he looked at his brother.

"They're running some tests, son." Nick and his mom exchanged glances. Motioning for her to follow, he guided Jeremy into the hallway. "You hungry?"

Jeremy shook his head, craning his neck to look back into the hospital room.

Mom stepped in. "Sure you are. Come on. Let's see if we can find us some chocolate chip cookies." Holding Jeremy's shoulders, she ushered him forward.

Jeremy glanced back, eyes moist. "You coming, Dad?"

"How about you bring me something?"

"Payton too?"

Tears stung his eyes. "Sure, bud."

This can't be happening. Lord, save my son.

Chapter 14

Tammy stopped at the nurses' station to calm her heart and gather her thoughts.

Melissa sat on the other side of the counter entering patient records into the system. She closed her file and studied Tammy. "You all right?"

Tammy shrugged. "Doing better than Mr. Zimmerman." *After all these years, why now, Lord? What can I possibly say that could provide any comfort?* She'd prayed with countless families, spoke Scripture, even shared the gospel when the opportunity arose. But this was different. This was Nick.

"This never gets easier, does it?"

She shook her head. "The family's in the quiet room?"

Melissa nodded. "The dad— "

"Nick."

Melissa raised an eyebrow.

Her cheeks heated. "I mean, Mr. Zimmerman."

"Right, Mr. Zimmerman mentioned trying to contact the mom."

According to Tammy's notes, the mom was on a cruise. Tammy had the woman's cell phone, but reception at sea could be iffy. "Do we have an additional contact number for her?"

"I've got her private cabin number, but that won't help now." Melissa grabbed another file and flipped it open. "Last we spoke, she said they were docked at a port city. I believe she's trying to catch a flight on standby. I imagine she could arrive any minute."

"Or not, depending on the size of the airport and how many flights they run. Did she say where she was trying to fly out of?"

"No. She was pretty upset. And she sounded . . . like she'd been drinking."

"Lovely." Trying to explain brain death and organ donation to grieving family members was tough enough without adding alcohol into the mix . . . and Nick.

Dr. Johnson rounded the corner, stethoscope hanging from his neck. He flashed a toothy grin. "Can't get enough of us, huh?"

"Something like that." Tammy checked her watch. "Have you seen Dr. Shefsky?" They couldn't keep Nick and his family waiting. Delayed communication led to distrust.

Dr. Johnson glanced down the hall. "He was here a minute ago. You're here for the Zimmerman kid, huh?"

She nodded.

"Sad case." The doctor frowned.

"What do you mean?"

"Guess this was the first time the dad had seen his son in months. For more than a few hours, anyway."

"Why's that?"

"Disgruntled ex-wife? I don't know. I only caught bits and pieces in passing—including the end of a phone conversation that left Dad rubbing the back of his neck like he wanted to tear the skin right off. The woman was screaming so loud, I could hear her through the phone." He shook his head.

So, the mother was drunk, upset, and possibly mentally unstable. Then again, grief could make people do and say things they normally wouldn't.

Dr. Johnson drummed his fingers on the counter, a crooked smile emerging. "You and that cute friend of yours are signed up for the Alpine Hill Run, right?"

Smiling, Tammy shook her head. "She's not interested, Dr. Johnson."

"That's only because she doesn't know me yet. That's why I need your help. Flexing my manliness during arguably the most grueling run in Woodland Pines wouldn't hurt either."

"Sorry to disappoint, but we're not participating this year."

"Come on. We need you. You're not going to let FMC show us up, are you?"

Tammy shrugged.

"Shoulda known you'd bail on us."

She crossed her arms. "Manipulation tactics don't work on me. But nice try."

Doctor Johnson turned to Melissa.

She shook her head. "Me neither, although a juicy steak dinner—or three—might help." Chuckling, she grabbed a file and stood. "But don't you worry. I'll be there bright and early to cheer you on—via Facebook."

The doctor rolled his eyes and strolled toward a patient's room with a blinking call light. He passed Dr. Shefsky who approached the nurses' station.

Tammy grabbed her tote and stood. "Looks like I'm up."

"Good luck," Melissa said.

Luck? This wasn't a casino. "Not luck. More like a divine appointment."

"Appointment for what? Like with a kidney?"

Melissa wouldn't understand. She was too busy traipsing all the roads she thought led to heaven.

Did Nick know Jesus? Probably not, considering all the religious jokes he made in high school. But death had a way of changing things, of initiating spiritual conversations.

Is that why You brought me here, Lord? To share the gospel with him? And to show me my life isn't as bad as it could be? An image of Becky and Tylan came to mind. She couldn't imaging losing either of them. She shuddered and hugged herself.

Stopping a few feet in front of Tammy, Dr. Shefsky cleared his throat. "Are you ready, Mrs. Kuhn?"

"Yes, of course."

The two walked toward the quiet room, then paused outside the door.

She tucked her hair behind her ears and wiped sweaty hands on her pant legs. The doctor entered, and with a deep breath, she followed.

Nick and his mom sat on the couch, his son between them. His mom had aged considerably, her once peachy complexion now ashen, her hair streaked with gray. Arlene, Heartland's family coordinator, and the hospital chaplain sat across from them. Looking up, she gave a knowing nod. Tammy would be the one to do the talking.

"Tammy, Nick said you were working here." His mom dabbed her eye with a tissue. "It's been a long time."

"Yes, it has." A sharp pain stabbed at the back of her throat as Tammy looked at the young boy sitting between them. Dark, wavy hair, long, straight nose, and dark lashes—he was a younger Nick, only thinner. More willowy.

With fallen faces and sorrowful eyes, the family looked from Dr. Shefsky to Tammy. When her gaze met Nick's, her heart clenched at his hollowed expression—as if the life had been ripped from him.

Oh, Nick, I'm so sorry.

She longed to go to him, to hold his hand, comfort him. But they didn't have the relationship for that. Not anymore. At least he had his mother.

The doctor stepped forward. "It appears you all have met Mrs. Tammy Kuhn. She's with Heartland Donation Services, and she—"

"I know why she's here." A tendon in Nick's jaw twitched. "My son's dead, isn't he?"

Tammy and the doctor exchanged glances.

The doctor nodded, his Adam's apple dipping. "Your son has been declared brain dead by brain death criteria. Mrs. Kuhn will explain what that means along with your options." He paused, his face unreadable, and Tammy knew he was fighting to keep his emotions in check, to remain calm and professional. "She will be able to answer any questions you may have." With a brisk nod, he stood and strolled from the room. The door thudded closed behind him.

Nick puffed air through tight lips. He stared at his hands, rubbing at his thumb knuckle with his other thumb.

"Let's talk about what this means." Tammy sat in the chair across from Nick and his mom, hands folded in her lap. "Do you have any questions about brain death? What it is, how it's determined?"

"I'm not stupid." Nick continued to rub his thumb knuckle. "Payton's . . . Payton's . . ." He swallowed, blinked, caving inward as if he could crumble at any moment.

"Dad?" Nick's younger son's voice squeaked out. "What is she talking about?"

Nick swiped at his tears with the back of his forearm. Then, as if inhaling strength, he straightened and draped his arm over the young boy's shoulders. "Your brother didn't make it, bud. But we know where Payton's going—where he's at."

What did that mean? Was Nick a Christian? She longed to think so, but many believed in an afterlife. Not everyone accepted Jesus as the only way to heaven.

"Can I see him?"

Sniffling, Nick's mom lifted Jeremy's chin. "Your brother's dancing with the angels, sweetie."

Jeremy nodded, his chin quivering. How much did the child understand?

Watching the young boy—only a year or so older than Tylan—trembling in his grandmother's arms, Tammy fought back tears.

"This is all my fault." Nick's bloodshot eyes locked on hers. "I should've been there—shouldn't have—" He dropped his head in his hands. Still holding her grandson, his mother rubbed Nick's back. At her touch, he lost it, deep-throated sobs wrenching through him.

Tammy suppressed a sob of her own. *Lord, help him. Comfort him. Give me words of hope and healing.*

"Would you like to pray?" the chaplain asked.

Nick gave a slow, almost indiscernible nod. He pulled his son close, and his mom inched closer, wrapping her arms around both of them and resting her forehead on Nick's shoulder.

Tammy bowed her head as the chaplain prayed for the family to find comfort and strength in God. Silently, she offered her own prayer—for mercy and strength, and that God's Holy Spirit would envelope Nick and his family.

When the prayer concluded, Nick inhaled a shuddered breath, drying his tears on his shirtsleeve. Tammy grabbed a box of tissues and handed them over.

"Thanks." He blew his nose.

Oh, Nick.

He lifted his chin, the familiar twitch returning to his jaw. She'd seen it at least a hundred times, always when his world was starting to crumble, and he was fighting for strength.

"You want to talk to us about donating his organs, right?" he asked.

She nodded. "That's an option."

Jeremy turned teary eyes toward his father. "What's that mean?"

Nick stared at his son, his upper lip twitching as if struggling for words. Tammy waited. He would let her know if he preferred to have the boy leave.

"Your brother's . . . dead." Nick's voice cracked. "Nothing's going to change that, but maybe . . ." His face hardened and he stretched his hands flat, then balled them into fists.

It was an internal battle she witnessed often—the one between wanting to help someone else and wanting to cling to the loved one who had passed.

"Your brother could help save someone's life." He looked at Tammy. "Isn't that right? If we donate his organs, someone else's boy might be able to live?"

"Your son's . . ." She looked at Jeremy. "Brother's organs could save numerous lives." Tammy explained donation in more detail. She pulled the necessary forms from her tote. "Do you believe your son would have wanted to be a donor?"

"Of course." Nick's mom twisted her tissue, tugging at the end. "He was such a caring little boy. Always bringing me shiny rocks and other treasures. I . . . never . . . even . . . got . . ." Sobs choked her words. "to . . . see . . . him."

Nick dropped his head into his hands again, his torso shaking, which triggered tears in his son.

Tammy gave him a minute. "Would you like to take a break?"

He didn't answer for some time. When he did, his voice was husky. "No. I'm okay. I want to do this. Need to do this."

"How do you feel about donation, Nick?"

"Least some good can come out of this. But you need to talk to their mother. She has custody. I just . . ." He shook his head, fresh tears springing to his eyes. He pulled his cell from his back pocket and tossed it on the coffee table with a thud.

Someone knocked on the door and eased it open. Melissa stood with her hand on the knob, face tense. "The mother's here—"

A slender woman with long brown hair and more bling than the local jewelry store barged in, shouting accusations. A tall man wearing a pink polo and white slacks trailed behind her.

Marianne Hawke?

The chaplain jumped to his feet.

Tammy prayed for peace and wisdom, then stepped forward with her hand extended. "Good afternoon. I'm Tammy Kuhn—"

The woman whirled around, glaring at Nick, fisted hands trembling at her sides. "Let go of my son."

Nick's eyes narrowed. "He's my son too."

"If you think for a moment that I'm letting my child go home with you, you're crazy."

"Now's not the time for drama, Marianne." Nick's mother engulfed her son and grandson in a protective embrace.

"Drama?" Red blotches sprang out on the woman's neck. "Don't you dare talk to me about drama. It's because of your son we're here." Spittle flew from her mouth. "Some father."

Nick flinched, which only seemed to fuel Marianne's anger, initiating a slew of accusations and verbal condemnation.

Tammy stared from one to the next, her mind spinning through training files in search of the best response. "How about if we . . . Let's take a step back for a minute. Give yourselves time to process."

Marianne cursed and grabbed her son's arm, giving it a tug. "Come on."

Jetting her chin, the grandmother held tight to the boy. "If you want to leave, go ahead. But the boy's staying with his father."

"Some father," Marianne spat.

"Stop it." Nick released Jeremy and stood, glaring from Marianne to his mother before looking at his now trembling son. Chest heaving, the child swiped at his tear-streaked face.

The chaplain stepped forward. "Ms. Hawke, please."

Marianne's breath came in quick bursts, her face flushed. "Jeremy, do as I say! I'm taking you home. Now." She grabbed her son again and pulled him to his feet. The man who'd accompanied her stood beside her, face pale and eyes wide, arms dangling. Apparently Marianne's hysteria intimidated him too.

Clutching Jeremy to her chest, Marianne glared at Nick. "How much are they paying you?"

He blinked. "What are you talking about?"

"Ms. Hawke," Arlene's voice rose above the emotional due, calm but authoritative, "how about if we take a break and talk later?"

"There's nothing to talk about." She whirled around to face Tammy. "I know exactly what this little meeting is about. You want my son's body parts. And you!" She stabbed a finger at Nick. "This is all your fault."

Nick's mom sprang to her feet. "That's uncalled—"

"Stay out of this, Vicky." Marianne's hands fisted, her eyes fiery.

This initiated a screaming match, both women hurling barbed words and accusations while Jeremy covered his ears, eyes closed. Tammy had seen a lot of family anger, here in this room—when loved ones passed, emotions ran raw and tensions high—but few fights were as vicious as this. It was clear these women had a history of bitterness between them.

"Enough." Nick raised his arms, palms out, gaze steely. "Payton's gone. Acting hateful won't bring him back." His voice quivered. "But we can help someone else."

Marianne's face contorted into an ugly scowl. "The man who killed his son wants to play the hero now?"

"I'm out of here." Nick stomped toward the door, then stopped. He returned and knelt in front of Jeremy. "I love you. You know that, right?"

Jeremy nodded. Tears streamed down his face.

"Leave him alone." Marianne's voice shook. "You've done enough."

Nick stood slowly, swiveled his head to look at Marianne, his eyes cold. "You're a piece of work." Then he left.

"Wait." His mom scurried after him, leaving Tammy and the rest of the hospital staff to try and calm Marianne down.

Tammy glanced at the time on her phone. The doctor wouldn't want to tie up a much-needed hospital bed with a brain dead patient who may or may not be a donor. She sighed and massaged the back of her neck. With one word, Marianne had the ability to save up to eight lives. Eight critically ill patients desperately praying for an organ, many who might not live to wait for another donor.

Chapter 15

Nick stormed down the hall toward the elevator.

Hurried footsteps followed behind him.

"Nick, son." His mom grabbed his arm as he rounded the corner. "Honey, wait."

He turned, her crestfallen face and teary eyes stabbing at his heart. So much pain and nothing he could do about it.

"She's just upset. She'll calm down. She always does."

He shook his head, stared past her at a woman in scrubs pushing a gurney. The wheels creaked on the linoleum. "I need this, Mom. I need to see something good come from this. To see some kind of purpose." *To know God's still here*. "Donation is the only way I know how to make sense of Payton's death."

Mom took his hand in hers. "Let's pray."

"I can't. Not now." He released a heavy breath. "It wasn't enough to lose one son. Now Marianne's going to steal the other one from me as well."

"She won't do that."

"She will and you know it."

"So don't let her."

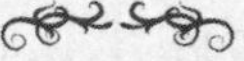

Tammy stood in the center of the room, staring at the closed door. She longed to go to Nick, to comfort him, pray with him, but her job was here. So instead, she focused on the task at hand, praying she wouldn't do or say anything to trigger another emotional eruption.

Still simmering in a rage that could only come from deep grief, Marianne stood a few feet away. Her male companion held her by the shoulders, speaking softly to her. Tammy couldn't hear him, but whatever he said, it appeared to be helping. Within a few minutes, Marianne's stature visibly relaxed, and she crumpled in his arms.

Tammy waited to speak until the woman looked her way. "I know this is hard. Painful. I'm so sorry for your loss. Would you like to sit and talk about this?"

Marianne sniffed and wiped her eyes. She nodded. "I'm sorry for my outburst. You must think I'm . . ."

"I think you're a mother mourning the loss of her son."

Marianne nodded and leaned into her boyfriend as if drawing strength from his presence.

How long had she and Nick been married, and who walked away first?

A crazy thought and absolutely none of her business.

"Would you like me to say a prayer?" the chaplain asked.

Marianne's face hardened. "It's too late for that." She crossed her arms. "What now?"

Before Tammy and Arlene could discuss donation further, they needed to make sure Marianne had come to terms with Payton's death. That could take time. For some, years. "Do you understand Payton's condition?"

Marianne's chin quivered as she glanced from one person to the next. Tears spilled over her lashes and streaked her face with mascara. "The nurse said his brain died." She shook as sobs wretched through her. "My sweet boy."

Tammy noticed Marianne's pale complexion, the tremor in her hands. "Do you need a moment?"

Marianne snorted. "What I *need* is my son." She clutched a hand to her neck, and her legs buckled. Her boyfriend caught her under her arms and guided her toward the sofa. He sat beside her and pulled her close.

Marianne's sobs turned to whimpers. Slipping from her boyfriend's embrace, she dried her puffy eyes and smoothed the hair from her face. With a shuddered breath, she folded her hands in her lap and straightened.

Her gaze swept from one staff member to the next before landing on Tammy. "Can I go see him? Say good-bye one more time?"

"Of course."

Marianne's boyfriend helped her stand and guided her and Jeremy out. Tammy and the others followed a half step behind.

Upon reaching Payton's room, Marianne froze. "Out! Get out!"

Tammy glanced past her. Nick and his mom sat shoulder to shoulder at Payton's bedside. Nick held Payton's limp hand. His other arm draped over his crying mother. He lifted his head slowly, turned it, stared as if not seeing.

Marianne charged toward him. "I said out!"

Tammy scurried after her. "Ms. Hawke, please calm down."

Marianne spun around. "I want to see my son. Can't you give me that? Get him out of here!" Her arm shook as she pointed at Nick.

Footsteps approached, and soon the room crowded with personnel. Nick stood amidst them all, unmoving, with slumped shoulders, staring at Payton.

He shifted teary eyes toward Tammy, held her gaze. A sob caught in her throat, stealing her breath. *Oh, Nicky!*

He turned to his ex-wife, his face void of expression, and raised his hands. "Relax. I'm leaving."

Staff parted as he trudged to the door.

Tammy followed him out, lingering in the hallway. There was a time he would've turned to her when in pain. And she to him, sitting silently by his side plucking blades of grass or watching clouds slip across the sky.

But that was long ago. Too long.

After taking a moment to regain composure, she returned to Payton's room. The chaplain prayed—a prayer about plans beyond our understanding. Marianne and Jeremy said their good-byes, then Arlene led everyone back to the quiet room.

Arlene guided Marianne to the couch, then sat across from her. "Tell me about your son."

While Arlene initiated the donation conversation, Tammy worried about Nick. Losing a child was hard enough. But assuming the blame? Worse, hearing it blurted out by your angry ex-wife? Tammy could understand Marianne's reaction on a rational level. Intense grief triggered intense anger, and people needed someone to blame. To Marianne, Nick was the perfect target. But that didn't make the situation any easier. Or right.

Tammy returned her focus to the conversation.

"He was always such a sweet boy." Marianne dabbed her nose with a tissue. "Loved trying to find four-leaf clovers. He never did, although he tried to convince me he had. He tore the leaves in half, making six out of three. Then he'd run in, grinning, to give it to me." She stiffened and dabbed at her eyes with a tissue. "He'd always tell me to make a wish—for anything I wanted."

Arlene pulled a form from her bag. "Today you have the opportunity for Payton to continue his legacy of kindness through organ donation."

Marianne stared at her hands.

Tammy leaned forward. "Although there is nothing more we can do for Payton, through donation, he can help save the lives of other children." She explained the process, choosing her words carefully so as not to guilt Marianne into a decision. "Do you have any questions?"

Marianne looked at her boyfriend. He placed his hand over hers and kissed her forehead.

"Would you like a moment to think about this?" Tammy hoped for consent, not only for those on the waitlist, but for Marianne and Nick's sake too. Of all her years as an organ procurement coordinator, she'd never met a remorseful donor. She had, however, witnessed great anguish from those who decided against donation. Those who, once the grief cleared, mourned not only the loss of their loved one, but the death of a stranger as well. It was a heavy burden to carry.

Marianne stared at the wadded tissues in her hands. "By donating his organs, Payton can save up to eight lives?"

Tammy nodded.

"Okay. He would've wanted that."

Tammy exhaled. Thanks to Marianne's kindness, at least something good would come out of this tragedy.

Chapter 16

Tammy pulled into the church parking lot behind the bus. Feeling tense after yet another round of "discussions" with her parents, she paused to pray, to focus her thoughts not on the craziness that had become her home but instead, the God who brought beauty out of chaos.

She glanced at her phone in the car console. Maybe she should call her parents to apologize, or at least explain her rapid departure. She really shouldn't have left like she had—right before dinner, whisking her kids out the door with popsicles and potato chips. But if she'd waited one more moment, she would've lost it.

She really needed an extra dose of patience.

She unfastened her seat belt and swiveled to face the kids. Oh, no. Tylan was a sticky mess. Popsicle juice stains circled his mouth and splattered onto his once white T-shirt. Now it looked more like a tie-dye.

Beside him, Becky primped in front of a pocket mirror, her heavily made-up face scrunched into a scowl.

"When did you—? How did—?" Tammy grabbed a package of tissues from her purse and threw them toward her daughter. "Never mind. Wipe that gunk off."

"But Mom."

"Now."

Becky harrumphed and swiped a tissue across her mouth, leaving a smudge of red on her cheek. Maybe it would've been better if Tammy had left them at home.

No. They needed church, now more than ever.

"Come on. Let's get you guys cleaned up." She slid out and moved to Tylan's door.

"Tammy, good to see you this evening."

She turned to see Constance approach, lugging a tote in one arm and a tray of cookies in the other. Large sunglasses dangled on the tip of her nose, the low-lying sun reflecting off the lenses.

"Good evening, Constance." Her voice came out flat. "How are you?"

The woman's face tightened as her gaze swept from Tammy to the car window. "The question is, how are you?" She squeezed Tammy's hand. "I can't imagine trying to raise kids alone. That must be quite difficult. For all of you."

"Yes, well." Tammy looked around, searching for a polite way to end the conversation. "I better get these kiddos inside. You know how Mrs. Langton appreciates punctuality."

Turning her back to Constance, she opened the rear car door, hoping the woman would find someone else to pester. No such luck. Dressed in a long, jean skirt and floral blouse, Constance hovered behind Tammy's shoulder, her onion breath fumigating the air.

Tylan had already unfastened his seatbelt and was reaching toward his Popsicle stick, which lay on the floor in a puddle of goo.

"Uh-uh." Tammy grabbed his wrist. "Leave that there."

"But it melted." He flung himself against the back of the seat, kicking up bare feet.

Mouth gaping, she stared at his dirt-covered toes. "Where are your shoes?"

He gave a lopsided smile and shrugged. "Oops."

She took a deep breath and searched the interior of the car, finding an old tennis shoe and one of Becky's flip flops—a pink one with rhinestones. That would create more of a stir than Tylan's bare feet.

"Come on. Let's get you two to the bathroom where I can hose you both down." Ignoring Constance's raised eyebrows, she helped Tylan out. That's when she noticed Becky's rather sparse and slightly retro apparel. The evening kept getting better. "Those shorts are way too short. I thought I told you to throw them out?"

Becky looked down at her legs. "I forgot."

Tammy sighed. "We'll talk later."

She didn't have to look to envision Constance's pinched face and condemning eyes. The woman's kids had probably gone through childhood in bubble-wrap, primly dressed and perfectly groomed. Well, some people lived in the real world where kids got dirty and splattered themselves with high-fructose corn syrup.

Heads turned as she led Tylan through the hall to the bathroom. Becky tried to drift away but Tammy grabbed her wrist. "Uh-uh. You're coming with me. To wash that garbage off your face."

By the time they finished and Tammy dropped a wet and stained Tylan into his classroom, Mrs. Langton had already launched into her lesson.

With a soft smile, she started to approach, but Tammy ducked out with a wave. She wasn't in the mood for sympathy or public prayer chains.

More heads turned when she slipped into the sanctuary. Unfortunately, the study was on intimacy and building hedges around a marriage, only adding to her insecurity.

The rest of the evening dragged on. She tried to listen to the message, but her mind refused to settle. The previous events—Brody's betrayal, her parents' meddling, Nick's brokenness, Marianne's accusations—all swirled together, spiking her pulse.

Why, Lord? Why me?

No answer.

After the closing prayer, she quickly gathered her things. If she was lucky, maybe she could slip out unnoticed.

And return home to hovering parents.

On second thought, she'd sit a while longer.

A warm hand landed on her shoulder. "Hey."

She startled and glanced up to see Jenson standing beside her.

"How you been?" He smiled, his green eyes soft and warm. He was dressed in tan slacks and a coral, button down shirt.

"Keeping one foot in front of the other."

"Did you get my phone message?"

Instinctively, she touched the side pocket of her purse. "I'm not sure. I'm a bit overloaded in the voicemail department." With the gazillion advisory calls her mom had initiated of late, Tammy only checked messages from numbers she recognized. Jenson's wasn't one of them. Although always kind, he'd been more of Brody's friend than hers. Which was why his attention seemed odd.

"I see." His smile wavered.

"Did you need something?"

"I was calling to ask . . ." He gave a nervous cough. "I had extra tickets to the ballgame and wondered if you and the kids wanted to go. I know how much Tylan loves baseball."

"Oh." Tammy straightened. "That was thoughtful. Thanks for thinking of us."

He shrugged. "Maybe next time." He held her gaze for a moment, as if wanting to say more.

Awkward silence ensued. She shifted and gazed past him. Most everyone had filed out, although a group of four occupied the back pew, heads bowed. Constance and her Bible study huddled to the right of the entryway.

Jenson lingered, blocking the aisle.

Tammy glanced at her watch. "I'd love to chat, but I better get the kiddos."

"Right." He moved aside, still watching her.

With a parting nod, she stepped out of the pew. "Have a good night." She continued to the foyer. Unfortunately, he followed.

He accompanied her to the hall, clogged with teenagers.

Tammy trudging ahead, dodging kids along the way.

He waited near the door while she gathered her son. She apologized profusely for the torn paper mess beneath his chair. "I'll help clean up."

Mrs. Langton flicked her hand. "No worries." She strolled over with a wide smile. "I've been meaning to call you. You know, we've got a parenting class coming up. I'm pretty excited about it. Peaceful Parenting—Making Your House a Home. We start this Saturday. It should be a wonderful time for us ladies to connect, swap stories, and of course, eat chocolate." She laughed. "I can get you a flier."

Heat seared Tammy's face. "I . . . Sounds interesting." She grabbed Tylan's wrist and pulled him to her. "I'll call you."

Though she knew—or at least hoped—Mrs. Langton had invited all parents, Tammy couldn't help but feel inadequate. Judged.

Chapter 17

Dark clouds advanced across the sky, engulfing the cemetery in a blanket of gloom. Stepping from her car, Tammy watched the mourners gathered around Payton's gravesite. Some trembled, crying, others stood stiff, looking straight ahead. Nick stared at the ground. His muscular arms hung limp at his sides.

Tears pricked her eyes. She and Nick had been through a lot together. First year of high school, first dance—which neither of them danced at. She helped celebrate his first varsity win. Tutored him through chemistry.

Almost gave him her first kiss.

Only to have her heart shattered less than a week later.

Why did she always pick the leaving kind?

Relaxing her grip on the steering wheel, she released a heavy sigh. Regardless of their past—as painful as it may be—Nick needed her now.

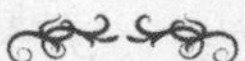

Nick stared at the closed coffin, a deep emptiness threatening to swallow him. He felt numb, his head clogged, as if his thoughts moved through sludge. One question raged, over and over. *Why?*

But he knew the answer. Because he'd driven away when everything in him told him to stay.

Pastor Tim stood at Nick's side as a man in a navy suit presided over the service. There'd be no verses, no comforting prayers, thanks to Marianne. She'd undone everything he'd arranged. Probably would've banned him from the service, if not for fear of legal retaliation. Like he had the money to pay more legal fees.

"Those who knew Payton well say he lived life to the fullest, seized every day." The man made a fist as if giving a motivational speech and not a eulogy. "That is how we'll remember him. Let's celebrate the life Payton lived. The example he set."

Across from him, Marianne dabbed at her eyes beneath a black lace veil. Wade stood on her right, Jeremy on her left, the three huddled together. The boy raised teary eyes to Nick, his face blotchy and red. Nick's knees nearly buckled, his lungs fighting for air.

Oh, Jeremy, I'm so sorry. Please forgive me.

But he didn't deserve forgiveness. It should be him in that coffin, not Payton.

Mom squeezed his hand, her fingers cold.

Marianne's family—parents, siblings, aunts, and uncles—lined the gravesite. A few cast sympathetic glances his way. The rest glared.

Tears lodged in his throat, burned his eyes. His thoughts drifted in and out, the present merging with the past. Payton's toothy smile flashed through his mind.

Footsteps approached, and Nick saw a pair of black leather shoes stop in front of him. Then someone put a shovel in his hand, and he moved his feet forward. Standing over the open gravesite, his stomach soured. He heaved in air. He couldn't move.

This can't be real. Not Payton. My buddy.

Dirt crumbled down the hole, splattering on the lacquered wood. And still he stood, his grip tightening around the wooden handle. Icy sweat dampened his palms, snaked down his back. Distress rose from Marianne's throng like a slow, moaning wind, their words nondescript in his muddled mind.

A hand landed on his shoulder and another on his back, the familiar scent of Pastor Tim's aftershave cutting through Nick's haze. Sobs wretched through him as the pastor slipped the shovel from his hands and handed it to Nick's mom.

Then it was over, and with a few murmured platitudes, everyone left. Tires crunched on the gravel. Engines hummed and faded, merging with the distant sound of traffic.

But still he stood, staring at the gravesite, wishing he was lying there instead.

"Nick?"

He turned to see Tammy standing beside a budding oak, her blonde hair stirring in the breeze.

Holding his gaze in her deep blue eyes, she stepped forward. She carried an envelope in one hand and cut lilies in the other. Kneeling, she placed the lilies on the ground, then, rising, handed him the card.

His hand brushed hers, lingered, the familiar touch soothing his raw emotions. Breathing deeply, he withdrew his hand and studied the envelope.

"Thanks for coming." He tore the envelope open.

A hand-written note was tucked inside. Eraser marks indicated numerous attempts.

Nick,

I'm sorry for your loss. May you draw comfort in knowing your son's legacy of giving will live on.

Below this, she listed five recipients; one a year younger than Payton had been, explaining which organs went to whom. Five people, two of them teens, who might have died had Nick—and Marianne—said no to donation. Tammy called Payton a hero.

A hero.

Nick's breath caught as the reality of Tammy's statement took hold. His Payton would continue to bless others long after his death.

She closed the letter with a verse: Psalm 34:18 *"The LORD is close to the brokenhearted and saves those who are crushed in spirit."*

His body shook as tears coursed through him. Tammy wrapped her arms around him, held him close, let him cry.

He sobbed until his throat was raw, his nostrils swollen. Then he pulled away and wiped his tears.

He pressed the dampened page to his chest, blotted it dry, then refolded it. "Thanks." He tucked it into his back pocket.

"I'll provide more information as I have it." A few strands of hair, stirred by the wind, clung to her glossy lips. She swept them away. "Can I call you later?"

He swallowed. Studied her face, her soft blue eyes that deepened depending on what she wore, her pink lips that had always held a smile—always made him smile. "Sure."

He longed for a friend, to hear someone tell him everything would be okay. That the intense pain threatening to pull him under would eventually end.

Chapter 18

Tammy followed her mom through the mall to Pinky's Treasure, a nail salon. Metal tiles covered the floor and white curtains pulled back with golden tassels draped from the ceiling. Instrumental music poured from hidden speakers, and the faint scent of cinnamon filled the air.

Tammy glanced from the sleek furniture to her Lavender Ladies bag loaded with lotions and bath oils—a gift from Mom. "This is too much."

Mom squeezed her hand. "I want you to feel like the beautiful woman you are. A treasure."

Tammy smiled as she thought of her own daughter and the incredible joy she received when they went out for Saturday afternoon dessert, just the two of them. Or when they sat on the living room floor, bare toed, with an assortment of polish spread between them. Few things blessed her heart like spending quality time with her kids.

She wrapped an arm around her mom's waist and squeezed. "Thanks. This has been nice."

"Like old times."

"But this one's on me, deal? You've spent enough today." She studied the prices listed above the counter. Ouch. But that was all right. It'd been a while since she and Mom had connected like this, just the two of them. With minimal lecturing or arguing.

"Nonsense. This is my treat," Mom grinned. "How often do I get to spoil my baby girl?"

Tammy's heart pricked. She needed to be more understanding, compassionate . . . cooperative. Not move-back-home cooperative, but less irritable. Empty nesting hadn't been easy for Mom. This visit was good. For both of them.

A woman with long burgundy hair and gold eye shadow, blush, and lipstick approached. "Can I help you?"

Mom stepped forward. "Yes, we'd like manicures and pedicures, please. With pretty flowers." Smile widening, she shoulder-bumped Tammy.

The woman nodded and led them past pedicure stations with leather recliners to a section of manicure tables near the back. Various colors of nail polish lined the wall. While waiting for her manicurist to show, Tammy scrolled through her emails. She clicked on one from Ellen. There was a mandatory grief-training class coming up.

Tammy's thoughts drifted to Nick and the image of him standing over his son's grave. How was he doing? Maybe she should pay him a visit. With the kids being gone this weekend . . .

No. He was probably overwhelmed with family and friends. She'd wait. Give him time to process. To grieve.

But she could send him a message.

She clicked on her texting icon and stared at her screen. What could she say?

Lord, give me the words—Your words.

"Good afternoon."

Tammy startled and turned to see a young lady standing beside her. "Hi." She dropped her phone on the table.

The woman set a bowl before her and placed a thick hand towel beside it. She plunged Tammy's hands in the water. It was warm, soothing, and held the faint scent of roses.

The woman motioned toward the rack of nail polish. "What color would you like?"

Tammy surveyed the row of colors along the wall.

"I chose fire red." Mom's eyes twinkled.

Tammy laughed. "Daring." She selected a muted pink, chatting with Mom while the manicurist rubbed scented lotions into their hands and forearms.

The tension of the week eased from Tammy's neck and

shoulders. How long had it been since she'd allowed herself to be pampered? She smiled at Mom. "We'll have to do this again sometime."

Mom nodded. "You know, if you moved to Dover, we could do this more often."

And for a brief moment, surrounded by soft fragrance and soothing music, Tammy almost considered it. No more scrambling to find a sitter. No more all night calls.

No more independence. No more Nick. Besides, she couldn't move the kids away from their friends, their church. Their dad.

She watched, without really watching, as the nail technician dried her hands and started painting her nails.

"You okay, sweet pea?"

She looked up to find her mom studying her.

"Just thinking."

Her phone chimed a text, preventing Mom from pressing further.

"Excuse me." Tammy slipped her hand away and wiggled her phone from her back pocket, smearing three nails.

Her manicurist grimaced.

The message was from Becky: *Where's Dad?*

Tammy checked the time on her screen, 3:05, and typed, *Give him a few more minutes.*

Growing tense, she set her cell on the table and extended her hands. With a frown, the manicurist grabbed the polish remover and went to work repairing Tammy's mess.

Five minutes later, her daughter sent another text, producing yet another frown—and an eye-roll—from the manicurist.

Tammy offered an apologetic smile, mouthed *sorry*, and picked up her phone.

Becky: *He's still not here.*

Tammy: *I'll call him.*

Unfortunately, she got his voicemail, which meant his phone was either off or dead.

"Brody, where are you? Please don't tell me you forgot to pick up the kids." She hung up and turned to the manicurist. "I'm sorry. I've got to go." She grabbed her purse and stood.

Mom sprang to her feet. "What happened?"

"Brody, that's what."

She paced while her mother paid then stormed out of the salon and through the mall. Of course they had parked at the furthest entrance. Becky texted three more times before they made it to the parking lot, each message more agitated than before. Tammy gritted her teeth and lengthened her stride. The irresponsible, selfish . . .

Mom scurried along beside her. "I always said that man was trouble. Remember? I told you— "

"Yes, Mom, I remember. You told me not to marry him. That I'd regret it. You were right, okay? Can we please not talk about this anymore?"

Her mom's lips flattened. She shook her head. "Avoiding the situation won't help, that's for sure."

Tammy rolled her eyes and quickened her step.

Her mother matched her stride-for-stride, her breath coming out in short bursts. "You know this isn't healthy for the kids. More than that, it isn't safe. What if you hadn't been around? He's irresponsible, Tammy. Surely you don't think— "

Tammy spun around, nerves firing so fast it felt like her muscles were ready to convulse. "And what would you have me do? Get fined for contempt? Grab my kids and go on the run?"

"Move to Dover. Brody can hardly carve out the time to pick the kids up from school. He won't mess with an hour and half drive, and you know it."

Tammy stared at her, her warring thoughts arrested as Mom's words took hold.

Could it really be that easy? Just up and move?

Intentionally rob her kids of their father?

Her stomach soured. Had it really come to that? Besides, that'd only make things worse. If—when—Brody did show, he'd whisk the kids back to Oak Park Blossoms, making it even harder for her to clean up after him.

They continued out of the mall and across the lot in silence, Tammy's mom's wooden soles scraping on the pavement. When they reached Tammy's car, her phone chimed again.

The number for Tylan's school flashed across the screen.

"Hello, this is Tammy Kuhn."

"This is Mrs. Sharpe from Pioneer Elementary. We have your son here."

Tammy checked the clock on her phone. 3:15. "I'm so sorry. His Dad—I'm on my way."

She yanked her car door open and slid behind the wheel, her temperature rising. She shot Becky a text. *I'm going to Tylan's school now and will pick you up after. Sorry!*

Her kids would be crushed.

Of course, Mom used the drive to remind Tammy of her need for support and community.

Tammy rounded the corner. "I've got Vanessa."

"And I'm so grateful for that, but she's not enough. You and the kids need family. Besides, Vanessa can't be there all the time, and with your schedule . . . You know, our hospital's hiring ICU nurses. That'd be the perfect job for you. You'd still be ministering to others, saving lives." She patted Tammy's knee. "Pray about it."

Tammy sighed. "Okay, Mom. I'll pray."

Mom nodded with a smile, shifting her focus to the side window. "Oh, my, look at that. They've turned old Mrs. Harlington's place into a cute little café. We should go there some time."

"Mm, hm." Nearing the school, Tammy slowed.

Brody's car, sleek and shiny, was parked along the curb in the bus zone.

"How nice of him to show up," she mumbled.

As she eased her car behind his, he and Tylan strolled out of the school, hand in hand, both grinning. Angling her torso to stare out the window, Mom huffed.

Tammy touched her arm. "Let me handle this. Please?"

Mom frowned, her mouth twitching as if struggling for the right words—or perhaps fighting the wrong ones. After a moment, she breathed deep and nodded. "Of course, dear. I'll wait right here."

Tammy met Brody at the curb. "You're late."

"I'm sorry. I really am. I got caught up in a meeting."

She crossed her arms. "Tylan, why don't you wait for your dad in his car?"

The boy nodded and climbed into the backseat.

She waited until the door closed to continue. "You couldn't call?"

"My phone died."

"Unbelievable." Tammy shook her head. "These are your kids. Be the parent."

Brody shook his head with a condescending smile—as if she were behaving irrationally—and got into his car. The engine roared to life.

Tammy's hands clenched into fists.

Lord, hold Tylan close. Please don't let Brody break his heart. Not again.

Jaw clenched, she returned to her car to watch Brody pull away. The callus, irresponsible—the man was destroying their children.

And there was nothing she could do about it.

A verse swept through her mind like a fragrant breeze: *But you, God, see the trouble of the afflicted; you consider their grief and take it in hand. The victims commit themselves to you; you are the helper of the fatherless.*

Fatherless. That was exactly what her kids were. Oh, Brody might have shared his DNA, but that was it.

God had taken care of her and the kids so far. Although their earthly father had failed them—continued to fail them, their heavenly Father never would.

She needed to remember that.

Arms folded, Nick leaned against the kitchen counter. His mom stood across from him, unable to hold his gaze while her brute of a husband hovered at her side. He wanted to leave. Mom wanted to stay. Not that Nick expected any different. They had a life, jobs to return to.

Mom scanned the cluttered room with its untouched baked goods and unopened sympathy cards. "Are you sure you'll be okay?"

"I'll be fine." Nick looked at his stepdad.

Keys in hand, Roger cleared his throat. Mom cast him a sideways glance, her chest rising and falling with her deep inhalation.

She grabbed her purse, clutched it to her chest. "All right, then. If you need anything." Deep wrinkles stretched across her forehead.

Nick stepped forward and hugged her. "I'll be fine. I could use some time alone. To think." That was the last thing he needed. Silence ate at him, lured his mind down dark pits of self-loathing, caused him to relive that terrible night again and again.

Roger shifted.

Mom looked from him to Nick, her eyes moist. She nodded.

Nick followed them to the door, said a few more good-byes. He leaned against the doorframe as they slipped into their car and drove away.

Then he was left in an empty house haunted by memories.

He paused at the accent table to stare at the two handprint impressions made when his sons were infants. Pain stabbed at his chest as he raised a trembling hand and pressed the tips of his fingers into the tiny indentations. So small.

Memories of Payton as a toddler rushed forward, threatening to overtake him. Of Payton's pudgy hand wrapped around Nick's index finger, of him scooting around the kitchen in his walker, spitting mashed peas all over Nick.

My buddy.

He grabbed the keepsake and clutched it to his chest. Marianne had initiated the project, pre-divorce. Nick had gone rounds in order to keep it—keep any mementos of his boys. In the end, he walked away with a handful of photos and the imprint. He'd purchased a camera the next week. After that, he snapped pictures obsessively during each visitation. Had a whole drawer full now, but so few of when the boys were little.

If only there was a way to go back in time. If only he'd been a Christian when he and Marianne said their vows. They'd be together now . . . and Payton would still be here.

His life was plagued by "if-onlys."

A snippet of a verse came to mind, *"Forget the former things; do not dwell on the past."*

His jaw clenched. He wasn't in the mood for verses or words of encouragement. Wasn't in the mood for anything. It was like life suddenly ceased, except that he remained, entrenched in a thick darkness that seeped into his soul. He longed to give into it, to allow every cohesive thought to slip into nothingness, but insanity didn't pay child support. Didn't win custody battles, either.

No. He had to keep moving forward. Keep fighting. Jeremy needed him.

He called his lawyer. The secretary answered.

"Hey, Linda, it's Nick Zimmerman. Is Mr. Cooper in?"

"He's with a client right now. Can I have him call you back?"

"Sure. He's got my number."

Nick ended the call and returned his phone to his back pocket. He recalled the next part of the Bible verse. *"Forget the former things . . . See, I am doing a new thing!"*

Chapter 19

Nick and Chef Rictor sat across the table from two insurance agents who acted more like police investigators than claims officers. Mr. Thompson, a wiry man with sunken eyes, handled claims made on the property's exterior. Mr. Borland, a tall guy with a shiny, bald head and pock marks on his nose and cheeks, handled everything related to the restaurant's interior.

They were nothing like those smiling, slogan-slinging agents seen on television commercials. More like hardened FBI agents who tried to intimidate suspects into confessing to heinous crimes.

Mr. Borland flipped the page on his notebook. A scowl pulled his thick brows together and shadowed his dark eyes. He folded his hands on the table and looked at Nick. "Why did you wait so long to file a claim?"

Nick shifted beneath the man's intense gaze. "My son . . ." His voice wavered. He cleared his throat. "Was hit by a car that night and taken to the ICU. He . . . died a short time later."

Mr. Borland's frown deepened. "I'll need to see some sort of verification."

Nick's temperature spiked. Did this man get paid extra for being obnoxious? "Like a death certificate?"

Rictor snorted. "You gotta be kidding me. This guy's a victim here, and you're treating him like a con man."

"Just doing our jobs, sir." Mr. Borland focused on Nick. "Do you owe anyone money, Mr. Zimmerman?"

"No." He shoved his financial records across the table. "Here. Dig all you want. I've got nothing to hide." What if they didn't believe him? Found some way to get out of paying his claim? "This was an unfortunate accident. You read the report made by the fire marshal, right? He investigated everything, declared it an accidental fire due to a sensor malfunction."

"Relax, Mr. Zimmerman. Like I said, we're merely doing our jobs." He turned his attention to Rictor. "What about you?"

"What about me?"

"Owe anyone money?"

"Look, man, I'm a chef. Been working here since I was in high school, first as a dishwasher, then prep cook, now kitchen manager."

"You're what, sixty-two? What's your retirement package like?"

"You tell me. You've got the paper work right there."

Mr. Borland eyed Rictor like a pit bull itching for a fight. He jotted a few notes on his legal pad, then returned to Nick's financials. "Your accountant . . ." He flipped back a few pages, checked his notes, then glanced at Nick's ledger. "How long has he been handling your finances?"

A muscle in Nick's bicep twitched. "If you're looking for a conspiracy, you're wasting your time." Time he didn't have. Each day the restaurant remained closed, he lost more money.

"Answer the question, Mr. Zimmerman."

"Mr. Rowle from Merchant Accounting has been handling our accounts for as long as I've been here." And at least twenty years before that. Many of Nick's employees, the accountant included, had been grandfathered in, like a package deal. Having served his grandfather for decades, then his aunt for seven years after, they made Nick's transition to ownership relatively smooth. More than that, they provided an instant support system. "He's with a reputable firm."

Mr. Borland flipped the page, his finger tracing the text. It stopped midway, and he raised an eyebrow. "What's Safe Haven Ministries?" He marked the page, then flipped backwards, adding more notes.

Truth be told, Nick had no idea. It was part of the purchase deal. "I'll have to ask my accountant, but it was something my grandfather set up. I imagine it's a nonprofit he donated to. My grandfather was a generous man."

The agents exchanged glances, and Mr. Borland made more notes on his legal pad.

Nick wiped sweaty hands on his pant legs. Why did these guys have to make everything seem so sordid? Maybe that was their tactic. Grill someone and make them jump through so many hoops they eventually gave up.

The interrogation lasted forty-five minutes, covering everything from how much Nick paid in child support to whether or not he had a life insurance policy on his son. With each question, his frustration grew until he feared he might not be able to contain himself any longer. The meeting concluded not a moment too soon.

Mr. Borland tucked his things into his briefcase, grabbed his camera, and stood. "We'll need to see the burn site now."

Nick led them to the kitchen. He and Rictor waited in the doorway while the men took pictures, checked equipment, and fired off more questions. By the time they finished, Nick had a raging headache.

If they denied his claim—or delayed the payoff—he could go bankrupt.

Rictor looked at him, questions brimming in his sad eyes.

Nick had no answers.

Tammy sat in Heartland Donation Services conference room, resisting the urge to check her watch. It was their first meeting in almost a month. Which meant, it would drag on as they reviewed four weeks' worth of cases and whatever else Ellen wanted to discuss.

Tammy arched her spine. Her neck and back muscles felt like flash-frozen taffy—stretched, then tightened into painful knots. Having her parents camp out at her place didn't help. Especially since her Dad usually chose the living room couch over the guest room bed. Worse, he snored louder than a bear, but her kids loved having their grandparents around. The extra hugs and accolades would do them good.

Averting her thoughts from the chaos at home, she focused on the meeting. Hanna, Tammy's co-worker, and Ellen were discussing a case involving a thirty-year-old female donor.

Ellen checked her notes. "Did the hospital stick with the plan prior to talking with the family?"

"Well," Regina, one of Heartland's social workers, leaned forward. "The nurse was very helpful. She was willing to include me as part of the team, but the doctor mentioned donation when he told the family the patient was brain dead."

There was a chain reaction of mumbles and sighs.

"Wonderful." Tina, a newbie from Central Kansas, rolled her eyes. "That only makes our job harder."

Despite all the increased education and awareness, there was still a prevailing myth that donation trumped patient care. However unfounded, doctors coupling donation with brain death proclamations only fueled the erroneous beliefs.

The room quieted when Ellen narrowed her gaze on Regina. "What's your communication level been like with the hospital staff?"

Regina frowned. "I asked him prior to going into the family meeting to include me but not to mention donation."

Ellen shifted her focus to Yvonne, the coordinator of hospital relations.

Yvonne tidied already straight papers in front of her. "I've met with Dr. Jossey before. Twice. He said he wouldn't mention donation next time. I guess I need to have another meeting with him."

Ellen's lips flattened. "Apparently."

They moved to the next case, which happened to be Peg's—a woman who could turn a five minute discussion into an hour-long dissertation. Stifling a yawn, Tammy gazed from the clock to the window.

She blinked.

You've got to be kidding me.

Her mother rode—on Tammy's bike—through the parking lot, wearing a backpack and a floppy hat with a large paisley bow tied around the brim. Nearing the window, she flashed a toothy smile and waved, her arm pumping it faster than a hummingbird's wings.

Midwave, her torso jerked right, and her bike wobbled, her face morphing into a panicked expression.

"Tammy?" Ellen's icy voice sliced through the room. "Is everything all right?"

Now that she was the focus of everyone's attention, heat flooded her face. "Yes, I— " She pushed away from the table. "Can you excuse me, please? I must attend to something."

The room grew silent as everyone watched Mom fight to get her bike over the curb and onto the sidewalk. She glanced up, smile returning, arm pumping once again. Balancing the bike between her legs and holding the handles with one hand, she raised her backpack with the other.

Tammy cringed to guess what was tucked inside. She hurried out to hopefully intercede before Mom felt the need to unveil the contents.

Stepping from the conference room, she closed the door on the soft chuckles and whispers behind her.

Mom met her in the lobby, face flushed. She smoothed sweaty strands of hair off her forehead, hat tucked under one arm, backpack slung over the other.

She enveloped Tammy in a breath-squelching hug. "How's my sweet pea?"

"Uh, fine." She stood with her arms slack at her sides, memories of her first day at junior high rushing back, adding mortification to mortification. If Mom produced her old Polaroid and started flashing, Tammy would lose it.

The plastic plates Mom pulled out of her backpack weren't much better. They looked like slices of watermelon, and she had cups to match. She set everything on a nearby end table, then glanced around. "Is this good, or would you rather eat somewhere else?"

"What's all this for?"

"Lunch, dear. Just like old times."

Tammy rubbed her face. The door behind her creaked open, and Ellen poked her head out. "Is everything all right?"

Tammy forced a smile. "Yes. I'll be there in a minute."

Ellen's eyebrows raised, her narrowed gaze shifting from Tammy to her mother. For a moment, Tammy feared she and her mom would become the afternoon attraction, but then Ellen slipped back into the conference room.

Exhaling, Tammy turned back to her mother. "Listen, I appreciate . . ." White lies were still lies. "I . . . Can I take a rain—" She clamped her mouth shut. "We're in a meeting."

Mom's face fell. "Oh. All right. Maybe later?"

"Sounds great."

"By the way, I brought something for you to look over. When you have time." She fished through her backpack and pulled out a stack of glossy college brochures. She handed them over. "I spoke with the admissions counselor from here." She pointed to a pamphlet entitled Stockhearth Online. "Registration is open now. And they have a lovely bachelor's of education program. The tuition's a bit high, but I think—"

"Mom, I'm not going back to school. I have a job. An important one." She tried to return the brochures, but Mom raised her hand.

"Keep them. Pray about it." Her eyes softened. "I know how much you love your job, but look at the signs, dear. First Brody, then your childcare problems. God's closing doors. You know what that means, right?"

"He's teaching me perseverance?"

"No. He's got another door opening wide for you somewhere else."

"In Dover, right?"

Mom gave a soft smile. "You never know. As I told you last night, this is an important decision, one with long-term consequences. You've got a lot more to consider."

"Yeah? And what's that?"

"Your kids."

Chapter 20

Nick entered the dim restaurant. The scent of smoke lingered in the air. The mid-morning sun pushed through the dining room windows, casting long beams on the old wood flooring.

The steakhouse, a brick building located on the fringe of the Historic Market, had been in his family for three generations. His great-great-grandfather on his father's side, a miner by trade, had purchased the building from an old printing press. He'd kept the original flooring and left the historic brick and ductwork exposed.

The property should've gone to Nick's dad, had he been alive. Nick's grandpa willed it to Nick's aunt instead. She tried to keep it going for seven years—almost ran it in the ground. She finally put it up for sale five years ago. Not wanting to see his granddad's legacy lost, Nick made an offer, then spent the next three years resurrecting the place.

Only to have all his hard work go up in smoke. Literally.

With a heavy sigh, he flicked on the switch, flooding the restaurant with light. As he walked past the empty tables made from recycled wood, memories flashed through his mind. Of him as a kid, slurping chocolate milk shakes, watching his grandfather make his rounds. Then later, him as a teenager, wiping tables with a bleach-doused rag. Shortly after that, sipping his last soda before Mom whisked him away to Oregon.

That was the year he moved away without telling Tammy good-bye. Something he always regretted, not that he'd had any choice.

It was also the last time he saw his grandfather. He should've spent more time with him—more time here. Except it always made

Mom so upset. Anyone on Dad's side did. He guessed after Dad's death, it was too painful. Triggered too many memories.

The thick stench of burned grease intensified as he entered the kitchen. Patches of the walls and ceiling were stained black. Everything else was a soggy mess thanks to his sprinkler system. His gut knotted as he tried to calculate all the damages. Like he knew anything about construction—except that this building was old and would probably need some major restructuring. He wouldn't know the total, nor the amount awarded by his insurance, until the agency finished their evaluations.

The biggest question: How much would they give him for loss of business and when? Enough to keep the place afloat? Even then, his deductible would near level him. What if he didn't have enough capital to carry him through this? After four generations, Grandpa's restaurant could go under, destroying his legacy and leaving his employees without jobs.

Like Chef Rictor, a man who was more of a mentor than a kitchen manager. A dear friend, and in many ways, a fill-in dad.

Nick left the kitchen and headed to his office to begin gathering all the material his adjuster would need. But all he wanted to do was go to bed. And never get up.

He shouldn't have left that night. He knew something wasn't right. Why hadn't he listened to his gut?

Sitting behind his grandfather's desk, he pulled his wallet from his back pocket. He'd folded the card Tammy gave him and tucked it behind Payton's school photo. The boy wore a crisp white shirt, his hair slicked to the side. His eyes sparkled, his mouth curved in that mischievous grin that suggested a crazy idea simmered in his brain.

Gone. Dead. At least, because of Payton, five others got a chance to live.

That didn't take away Nick's searing pain, but it provided a thread of hope.

There was a faint knock, and he glanced up to see Rictor standing in the office doorway dressed in jeans and a T-shirt. His unshaved face and disheveled hair matched Nick's.

He motioned him in. "Thanks for coming."

"Hey." Rictor glanced around the cluttered office. "How you holding up?"

He fingered Tammy's card.

Rictor approached the desk and studied Nick for a long moment before sitting.

Nick closed his wallet and tucked it back into his pocket. "I contacted a public adjuster to walk me through all the insurance stuff. He's already been out here to assess the damage."

"Yeah? What's your coverage like?"

He shrugged. "I need to gather information, list everything I lost, get more before photos." He had half a dozen, most of the exterior. Only one of the kitchen. "Then he'll have to review my coverage and determine the replacement cost."

"All for a fee, I imagine."

"Ten percent of money paid on my claim. But . . ." He swept his hand over the papers scattered across his desk. "It's worth it to avoid all the headache. You remember if my grandfather took any pictures?"

"For cataloging purposes? Doubt it. He was pretty laid back."

Venturing on careless, but the man had one thing going for him, at least in this instance—he was a packrat.

"You checked the files?"

"Yeah." Nick glanced at three tattered boxes on the corner of his desk waiting for him to go through. "Found these on a shelf. Full of old newspaper clippings, a few photos. Of people more than anything else."

Rictor lifted the lid. "You mind?"

"Be my guest."

He reached inside, sifted through some papers, and chuckled. "I'll be." He pulled out a photo. "Crazy Jane, and looking ready to pop to boot." He showed Nick an image of a bleached-blond. "Haven't thought of Crazy Jane in ages. Wonder how she's doing. You probably don't remember her, do ya?"

Nick studied the picture, shook his head.

"She worked for your grandpa, back in the day. Full of drama, she was, always coming in with a new man on her arm. Gotta a kick out of you, though. She often brought you candy or whatnot. 'Course, your momma had a fit. Like you could catch Jane's loose living through osmosis or something. Always did wonder why your grandpa kept her on. Guess it was his nature, huh? Always reaching out to the lost causes. Did you know he prayed over his staff every day? Prayed over you, too."

Nick remembered. There'd been many a time he and Mom had stopped by and caught Grandpa in prayer. As Nick got older, Grandpa invited him to join in. Best legacy the man could've left. One Nick always hoped to leave to his own children.

Pain stabbed at the back of his throat as his thoughts turned to Payton. At least the boy had known Jesus. Had accepted Christ the summer before at one of those neighborhood Bible camps. Though Nick would've liked to see his son show more fruit of his faith, to see him brought to youth group and church where he could grow, Nick was grateful to know his eternity was secure.

Rictor returned to the box, then froze, his gaze shooting to Nick. He withdrew his hand and closed the lid. "Not much in here, I 'spect."

An odd reaction. Maybe there was a picture of another waitress in there—one Rictor preferred Nick not know about. Not that he cared about twenty-year-old scandals.

He looked at the unpaid invoices cluttering his desk. The sales log from the restaurant's last night was curled beside an old manual typewriter. An inventory list lay beside it. Next to it was a clipboard with a long list of reservations that were never filled.

Hands on the armrests, Rictor leaned back and angled his head. "Helen's been lighting up my phone. She wants to know when she can return to work."

Nick rubbed his temple. If he didn't give his staff answers soon, they'd find employment elsewhere. Which would add yet one more issue for him to deal with—hiring and training new staff.

If the restaurant stayed open.

Maybe it was time he worked somewhere else. Where he could clock in, clock out, and leave the stress of management to someone else.

Rictor propped his elbows on his knees and rested his chin in his hands. A shadow fell over his dull eyes.

The man had a mortgage, a kid in college.

Breathing deeply, Nick pushed to his feet. "I'll take care of this."

Gloria, his hostess, came to the doorway, holding what looked to be a bundle of mail. With one hand fiddling with her necklace, she turned sad eyes to Nick.

He knew what was coming. The same thing he expected Rictor to say, as soon as financial needs overpowered his loyalties.

"Hi, Gloria." Nick drew closer, stopped a few feet away.

Her gaze wavered, as if it took great strength to meet his. "I . . ." She let out a puff of air, glanced between the two men before focusing on an empty chair along the far wall.

Nick turned to Rictor who'd already made it to his feet. "I'll call you later?"

"Yeah, sure." Rictor left, pausing in the hall to look back one last time.

Gloria sat in front of the desk and dropped her armload of paperwork on the surface. Her posture looked rigid, her expression tight. "I brought the mail."

Nick sat back down. "Thank you." A thick rubber band secured the stack of envelopes. Probably more bills. He'd look at them later.

"How are you holding up?" The maternal side of Gloria radiated from her eyes.

"Still breathing." Which struck him as ironic. Leaving Howie's that night had done more than kill his son. More than shred Nick's heart. It left his mom, Payton's mom, and Jeremy leveled. It was like a chain-reaction of devastation, hurting those Nick loved most. And it was all his fault.

Maybe he deserved this, but they didn't. Not even Marianne.

"I've been offered a job." The skin around her mouth sagged. "At my church. The pay's . . . not the best, but the hours are good."

What could he say? Don't go? Blow this opportunity—one she could very well need if the restaurant failed? Maybe this was God's way of tying up loose ends.

"I appreciate all your family has done for me."

Nick's grandfather had hired her over twenty years back. Nick was a teen when she came in, wide-eyed and stammering. Two months into an unwanted pregnancy, she was desperate for a job. Grandpa gave her more than employment. He started what became a close-knit family—a place of acceptance and safety—for Gloria and her daughter.

Chapter 21

Tammy manned the vacuum, earplugs in, her phone radio cranked high. She tried to focus on the lyrics, and not her mom's watchful eye. Both parents hovered.

She should be grateful. They loved her, would do anything for her. If only they could help from a distance. Like a four-hundred-mile distance.

Keeping the vacuum running, she cast Mom a sideways glance and switched to the hose attachment. Now seemed like the perfect time to suck up the dirt along the edge of the carpet. In fact, a thorough spring cleaning was in order. Anything to delay the inevitable.

Her phone vibrated. She pulled it out of her back pocket and gave the screen a cursory glance. Yet another unrecognized number. Someone else jumping on the save-Tammy bandwagon?

She hit ignore, counted to three, and glanced at Mom. Yep, her phone chimed. Apparently, the caller phoned her next. That would keep her occupied for a while.

Tammy flipped off the vacuum and tiptoed to her room, leaving the door ajar. Closed doors, apparently, were seen as open invitations. She grabbed Nick's business card off her dresser. How was he doing? Maybe she and the kids should stop by his restaurant for dinner. Except Mom and Dad would want to come, which would create a whole mess of problems. They hated Nick. Always had. Hated any male who'd showed the slightest interest in her—including Brody.

They'd been right about him.

No. That wasn't true. The problem hadn't been entirely Brody—except his infidelity. That one had been all him. But Tammy couldn't deny that their marriage had been in trouble long before she'd lost Brody's heart. Maybe if they'd gotten help, learned how to communicate rather than fight, things would've turned out differently. But there was nothing Tammy could do about that now.

Averting her thoughts, she pulled up Nick's number up on her phone, an odd fluttering filled her stomach. Sucking in a calming breath, she dialed.

"Hello?" His voice sounded flat.

"Hi. How are you doing?" Stupid question.

"Surviving." He paused. "Any more news on the recipients?"

"Not yet. But I'll let you know when I have any."

"Okay?"

Translation: *Why are you calling?*

She shouldn't have. Except the man needed a friend. Which was all this was about. Her reaching out to an old friend in need, nothing more. In fact, it'd be callus not to.

"I was thinking maybe . . ." She glanced at her bedside clock and stifled a sigh. Brilliant idea. Not so brilliant timing. The kids would be home any minute. But she was off tomorrow. "I . . . Are you . . . ? You want to meet for coffee?"

Gut-twisting silence ensued, and she immediately regretted her offer. Once again, she thought back to their near-kiss, followed by heartbreaking *nada*. She'd been a fool then, and she was acting like a fool now.

"Honestly?"

Tammy braced herself for the rejection. The knots in her stomach increased as the silence stretched on.

"I've got a lot of inventories to go through." Papers rustled in the background. "You're welcome to head here, to my restaurant."

Was she putting him out or offering much needed support? Everyone grieved differently. But isolation wouldn't help. She needed to go, even if only for a moment. "Yeah, sure. That sounds great. What time? I can meet you at the restaurant at eight thirty. If that works for you, I mean."

He paused again, reigniting Tammy's nerves. She felt like she was back in high school, except back then, Nick had been the one person who hadn't caused her stress. The one person she could be real around.

Obviously, things had changed.

"Eight thirty's fine." His tone carried no emotion, which probably meant he responded out of obligation.

The bus engine hummed outside the window, followed by the faint swoosh of airbrakes, providing the perfect end to an awkward conversation. "Listen, I gotta go."

She hung up and stared at her phone screen. After all these years, could it be she still loved him?

How could they be friends if her heart longed for more?

Shoving her thoughts and the conflicting emotions aside, she dashed out. Mom had already made it to the porch. Dad, sweaty and covered in grass clippings, left the lawnmower in the center of the yard. He joined Mom on the sidewalk. Tylan beamed, looking from one grandparent to the next.

"Hey, little man." Tammy met Tylan with a hug, resting her chin on the top of his sweaty head. "How was your day?"

Tylan shrugged. "Okay," then eased out of her embrace. Grin widening, he turned back to his grandparents. "Wanna see what I made at school today?" He pulled papers and art projects from his backpack.

"Oh, my!" Taking his brightly painted sheet of paper, Tammy's mom widened her eyes and pressed a hand over her mouth. "Look at this, Wilbert. Did you know your grandson was so talented?"

Dad grabbed Tylan in a headlock and ruffled his hair. "Of course. I always said the boy was a genius."

By now, Becky had arrived and soon joined in the chatter, going well beyond her normal one-to-three-word responses.

Watching the sweet interaction, Tammy smiled, her heart warming. Despite their hovering, nagging, and brochure flinging, it was good Mom and Dad were here.

On a short-term basis, of course.

She moved aside to allow the chattering pack inside. Trailing them into the kitchen, she caught the end of their conversation.

"Jenna's bringing caterpillar cupcakes." Tylan dropped his backpack on the floor and climbed into a chair at the table.

Becky sat across from him, chin propped in her hands. Tammy's mom dished cookies onto plates while her dad found a spot between both kids, hungry eyes locked on his wife. He paused salivating over the cookies long enough to toss out a few jokes, all insect-related.

"Wait until you see what we're bringing." With a wink to Tylan, Mom set four filled plates on the table.

Tammy lifted an eyebrow. "What are you guys talking about?"

"Didn't I tell you?" Mom's eyes sparkled. "The room coordinator called this morning, said they were short on volunteers. I signed up to help with Tylan's end-of-school party."

Tammy blinked. That was three weeks away. Surely they weren't planning on staying that long.

Mom smiled. "You're going to join me, right? It'll be fun."

Tammy rubbed her forehead, reminding herself of Mom's good intentions, of how much Becky and Tylan enjoyed having them here, of how much she needed them here—for childcare purposes.

Ouch. That was pretty selfish.

She mustered up enough self-control to offer a smile. "I'll have to check my schedule."

"You know," Dad spoke over a mouthful of cookie, crumbs tumbling from his mouth. "If you got a job at the Dover library, the schedule would be much more flexible. Then you wouldn't have to miss any of the kids' important events."

"Don't." Tammy raised her hand. Her mouth quivered, ready to release angry words swallowed down for much too long, when the doorbell rang. Shaking her head, she exited the kitchen and crossed to the front door.

She opened it to find a man standing before her. He wore a long-sleeved, collared shirt and held a leather briefcase. He extended his hand. "I'm Mr. Leroy with Residential Solutions. Are you Tammy Kuhn?"

Tammy gaped at him. She glanced behind him to his car, parked along her curb, then back to him.

Footsteps approached from behind, Dad's hairy arm protruding through her peripheral vision.

He and the man shook hands. "Mr. Leroy, thanks for coming."

Tammy fisted her hands, then slowly released them. She would not lose it in front of a stranger. She faced her father. "What's this about, Dad?"

"Remember that game plan we talked about?" He grabbed hold of Tammy's shoulders and stepped aside, pulling her with him. "Come in, Mr. Leroy."

Mom closed in with a cheeky smile. "Can I get you something to drink? Iced tea? Soda?"

"I'm fine, but thank you." The realtor followed Mom and Dad to the couch and set his portfolio on the coffee table. All three looked at her, eyebrows raised.

Mom patted the recliner beside her. "Sit, dear."

Tammy stared. Had she stumbled into some weird parental reality show? *Smile, you're on* Freaky Parents.

Mom pressed her knees together and faced Mr. Leroy. "You'll have to excuse my daughter." She cupped a hand around her mouth as if relaying a sordid secret. "She's under a great deal of stress."

Tammy stepped back to give herself space, only to run into the wall. Shaking her head, she pressed her fingertips to her temples.

Hold it together.

"Sweetie, are you all right?" Mom zeroed in, encircling Tammy's waist. Suffocating her. Mr. Leroy stood, wide-eyed, looking from one person to the next.

Tammy threw up her arms, pushing Mom away. "Excuse me."

She started to leave but Mom grabbed her hand. "Relax, dear. Take a few moments. We can do this whenever you're ready."

Tammy pulled away.

"What she needs is a game plan." Dad turned to Mr. Leroy. "Why don't you tell us about your services? How do you market your listings?"

Mr. Leroy stared at Tammy, mouth slack. "I . . . uh . . ."

Dad's phone rang. "Hello? Yes, thank you for calling back . . . It's a two-story, four bedroom, three bath, located in the sought after neighborhood of . . ."

Tammy gaped at him. "What are you doing?"

He shushed her. "Tomorrow? I'll ask her. Better yet, how about you talk to her yourself?" He handed over the phone, then glanced at Mr. Leroy. "No offense, but we thought it'd be best to interview a few realtors."

Tammy brought the phone to her ear. "Hello?"

"Good afternoon. This is Patrick Riggleman from Millennial Realty. When would be—?"

She hung up and dropped the phone onto the coffee table.

Dad grabbed it and stared at the receiver as if it held the secrets to unlocking a woman's brain. Secrets he could learn easily enough if he would only listen. But of course he wouldn't. He was too busy trying to fix everything. Only there wasn't a solution. Not this time, and Tammy wasn't a stupid kid they could surround and protect anymore.

Mom rushed to her side. "Honey, be rational about this. Let's discuss your options. Then you can make an informed decision." She nudged her toward the couch.

Tammy locked her knees. "Leave me be, please."

"It was good meeting you." Mr. Leroy pulled out a business card, extending it to Tammy. When she made no move to receive it, he returned it to his pocket. He raised a hand. "Ma'am," he dipped his head, "sir," and dashed out.

The parental barricade returned, Dad's coffee breath flooding her face as they loomed close. They started talking, their words merging together in a jumble of advice until Tammy's head pounded.

"Leave! Now!" She broke away from their stranglehold and widened the distance between them. Blood pulsated in her eardrums, drowning out all cohesive thought. Standing in the center of the room, she pointed a trembling finger to the door. "Just leave."

"But we're only— "

"Go." Tammy closed her eyes, fighting tears. "Please."

Chapter 22

A blaring horn sliced through the nightmare dancing on the edge of Nick's mind. It took a moment to orient himself—the dark office, the cluttered desk, the stench of melted plastic and charred wood.

Like a suffocating torrent, it all came rushing back, from Rictor's phone call to Payton's lifeless body. The images tortured him every time he closed his eyes. That was why he came to the restaurant. He had to stay awake, stay busy, otherwise the grief would plunge him into a pit too deep to crawl out of.

His Bible lay before him, opened to his favorite passage, Isaiah 43:2-3.

> *"When you pass through the waters, I will be with you; and when you pass through the rivers, they will not sweep over you. When you walk through the fire, you will not be burned; the flames will not set you ablaze. For I am the* Lord *your God, the Holy One of Israel, your Savior."*

God beckoned to him from within the pages, surrounded him. Only Nick didn't want comfort or protection. He wanted his son. No words, regardless how sacred, could bring Payton back.

He closed the Bible and pushed it to the far corner of his desk.

The box filled with newspaper clippings and old photos remained untouched. He needed to go through it eventually, find whatever before pictures he could.

But not today. Photographs of what had been would only deepen his loss.

Massaging his kinked neck, he plodded out of his office in search of coffee. The kitchen was a mess. All the food would have to be thrown out, every dish cleaned. Even the table linens, contaminated by an ashy film, had to be washed. He had a special fire-cleanup crew coming out later that week. They were expensive but necessary.

While the coffee brewed, he pulled out his phone and skimmed through his emails. Two from Mom, checking to see if he was okay. Half a dozen from church family. The pastor wanted to know how Nick was doing financially.

Ignoring the $30,000 plus worth of damages looming before him and the growing stack of medical bills back home, he replied, "I'll make it."

He didn't have a choice. Too many people were counting on him.

Tammy's stomach fluttered as she pulled into the Flaming Mesquite's parking lot. She glanced at her dashboard clock. Ten minutes early. Not wanting to appear anxious, she used the time to call Vanessa.

"Hey, girl. I saw you called."

"Hi. How are things on the home front? Your parents relax any?"

Tammy gave a nervous chuckle. "I sort of kicked them out."

Vanessa laughed. "Uh-huh."

"No, seriously. They're gone, and things are . . . weird." She filled Vanessa in on the events of the past couple days. "You know how they get."

"And how you get when you feel pushed."

She sighed. "I overreacted, I know. I just . . . I need to call them back to apologize." She grabbed her lip gloss from her purse and dabbed it on.

"What about . . . ?"

"The kids?" She was a terrible, ungrateful daughter, concerned more about how the fight would impact her childcare situation than the fact that she'd hurt her parents. Well, that wasn't true. She felt bad, truly. But if they'd stayed one day longer, things would've been much worse.

"Right."

"I've got an ad running in this week's paper. What about you? Did you need something?"

Vanessa paused. "I gotta head out of town for a two-week business trip."

"Oh."

"I'm sorry, Tam. The timing stinks, huh?"

"No." She tried to sound cheerful. "It's fine, really. I've got some nanny interviews set up for later this week. In the meantime, I can always call some of the ladies from church." Constance's condemning face came to mind, setting her nerves on edge.

"I'm meeting with the vice president of operations . . . to talk about a potential transfer."

"Oh."

Once again, she apologized. "They're cutting back at the Oak Park Blossoms branch."

Tammy needed Vanessa and not just for childcare. Their late night chats, ice cream gorges, and giggle-fests kept Tammy sane. That was selfish, of course. Vanessa had a life. "When will they make a final decision?"

"There's no telling. It's pretty hush-hush right now. Listen, you want to meet for coffee?"

The familiar stomach flutter emerged when she glanced toward Nick's restaurant. "I can't. I've got a . . . something I need to do."

"Care to share?"

"Not really. You go. And good luck with the job possibility. Truly." She ended the conversation then dropped her phone into her purse and stepped out of the car.

The restaurant was dark, the sun reflecting off the shadowed windows, creating a mirror-effect. A silver pickup occupied a spot near the entrance. A baseball team emblem decorated the back window, reminding her of Payton and the stories Marianne had shared during their meeting.

She shouldn't have come. Except she'd told him she'd stop by. She needed to honor that. He could always ask her to leave. Besides, she knew how to read people—it came with her job. If he gave any indication her visit was more of a burden than help, she'd go.

The front door was unlocked, the inside stale and humid, as if the air conditioning hadn't been run in some time.

"Nick?" She glanced about the shadowed interior. An odd smell permeated the air—a mixture between paper factory fumes and a campfire. "Nick?" She spoke a little louder, feeling like she'd stepped into a funeral parlor rather than a restaurant.

"Coming." His voice called from somewhere near the back, and a series of lights flicked on. He appeared a moment later, his clothes wrinkled, his face unshaven, hair unkempt. Dark shadows hung beneath dull eyes. "Hey."

"How're you holding up?"

He shrugged. "Life goes on, huh?" He snorted. "Least, that's what everyone always says, right? Life will go on. God has a purpose. Wounds heal."

She refused to feed him empty clichés, to pretend like she had the answers. "How's Jeremy?"

His face hardened. "Don't know. His mom won't let me talk to him."

"Oh, Nick." Her heart ached for him. What kind of mother would rob their kids of a dad?

She thought of her ex, of his numerous no-shows, of all the times Tylan scanned the ball field, hoping to find Brody in the bleachers.

Nick cleared his throat. "You want something to drink? Coffee? Soda?"

She glanced around, memories from the past resurfacing. Her gaze lingered on a back corner booth where she and Nick once sipped milkshakes and downed huge quantities of fries. His grandfather used to tease them something awful, suggesting they were more than friends. And each time, she looked at Nick, her heart racing as she tried to read his playful smile and dancing eyes.

Stop it. The man lost his son, and I'm obsessing over the past—

over an almost kiss—one that obviously meant nothing to him. We were a couple of hormonal, stupid kids.

Her face warmed when she realized Nick was still awaiting an answer. "Water would be great, thanks."

She followed him into the charred kitchen, images from the past colliding with the mess that lay before her.

"Are you all right?" Nick studied her.

With a weak smile, she nodded. "I'm fine, thank you." Just falling apart at the sight of a burned kitchen. "What happened?" How much tragedy could hit one man?

He raked a hand through his hair. "Grease fire. Started in the deep fryer, thanks to a faulty sensor. Got a general contractor coming to do repairs later this week."

Questions surged, but she suppressed them. It really wasn't her business.

"So." He pulled a glass from the shelf and inspected it with a frown. It looked grungy. He shook his head and moved to the sink, Tammy following, where he rinsed the glass off. Sooty water swirled to the drain. Once filled, he handed the glass to her, then motioned for her to follow him back to the dining area.

He paused near their old booth. She understood his hesitation. It was as if they were standing on a precipice between the present and the past, between a life filled with obscene amounts of chocolate and greasy food and the harsh reality of adulthood.

Nick set down the glass. "You wanna get out of here?"

"Sure."

She trailed him out of the restaurant and into the parking lot, the early morning sun reflecting off the pavement and stinging her tired eyes. She turned to his truck, expecting him to do the same, but he headed the other direction.

"Figured we'd go for a walk. If you don't mind."

"Sure." Nick had always needed movement, especially when he was upset. Back when they were kids, when his mom started acting strange, fearful he'd hit the gym hard.

They walked in silence for a while. Cars whizzed by, filling the air with exhaust.

Nick smiled as a pack of teens streamed out of a convenience store. "Remember Jimmy's Gas-n-Go?"

"Our favorite afterschool hangout."

"And mid-school escape." The skin around his eyes crinkled. "Let's get a soda."

"Sure. I could use a drink." *Déjà vu* swept over her as they wove through the parking lot and onto the curb. "I can't believe we never got caught — sneaking off campus as often as we did."

He held the door open, a mischievous grin emerging. "How else did they expect us to stay awake through Mr. Vandhelm's lectures? That candy kept me occupied through fourth period."

"And earned you a week's worth of detention, if memory serves." He'd used his Skittles as ammunition, pelting unsuspecting students on the back of the head, feigning innocence when they turned around, of course.

"Hey, Cliff started it." He led the way to the drink fountain. "Dared me." He grabbed an empty cup. "Dr. Pepper, right?"

She nodded, warmth spreading through her.

Someone bumped into her shoulder. She moved to allow a mom with two toddlers go by, then followed Nick to the cash register. Drinks purchased, he led the way around back to a rickety picnic table. Tammy sat and ran her hand across the peeling paint that covered the countless names etched underneath. A few poked out, black ink now faded in the wood grains.

Nick sat across from her. "It's been a long time."

"It has." She stirred the ice with her straw.

"Seems you've done good. Medical degree, decent job. Always knew you'd make something of yourself. Once your parents released the reins." He smiled. "You got kids?"

"Two. A six- and thirteen-year-old."

"Close to my boys' ages." His eyes clouded. "Hey, Tammy . . . about when we were kids. Maybe if I'd — "

She held up her hand. "No big deal." Lying didn't become her, but now wasn't the time to stir up the past.

Watching her over the top of his cup, he took a drink, then set it down and ran his finger along the rim. "You married?"

"Divorced."

"Sorry to hear that. Guess we shoulda stuck to our pact, huh? No mushy dating garbage."

She laughed. "We were wiser than our years." She studied him—same chiseled jaw, stark eyebrows, thick lips that once hovered near hers. Oh, how she'd loved him. "How about you? Did you go to KU?"

He shook his head. "Spent too many years spiraling." He gave a hollow laugh. "Didn't make it to back to school until my mid-twenties. Met my boys's mom." He exhaled and rubbed his neck. "That was a mess waiting to happen." He was silent for a moment. "Sure wish I'd found Jesus before we said our vows. Everything would've been different."

She traced a ringer along the rim of her cup. "When'd you become a Christian?"

"Two months five days after my divorce. Funny how it took losing everything to turn my eyes heavenward, huh?"

The more they talked, the more tumultuous her emotions became. It was as if time hadn't passed, and they were back at the old Gas-n-Go swapping stories and devising plans to radically change the world.

Don't do this, Tammy.

But with Brody gone and Vanessa leaving, she needed a friend. As long as they kept it at that, everything would be fine.

"I looked at some old photos the other day." Nick gave her a sideways glance.

"Oh, really? What of?"

"Big hair and high top shoes under a satin dress."

Warmth crept into her cheeks, and he chuckled.

She raised an eyebrow. "Are you really wanting to drudge up the past? Because I remember someone peeing on Smithville's football field. Twice."

"Hey, we were rivals."

"And trying to get Jordan to light his farts on fire."

He laughed. "Jordo! That kid had more gas than the Conoco station."

"We sure were a couple of stupid, crazy kids."

"The weirdest." He checked his watch and gulped the rest of his drink. "I should probably head back. I've got a general contractor coming out to give me some estimates." He stood and tossed his drink into a trashcan. "It was good talking to you." He paused, and his eyes softened. "I've missed you."

Her stomach flipped, and she chastised herself for it.

They were just friends. F. R. I. E. N. D. S.

Chapter 23

Sitting across from Mr. Clark, Nick read the list of repairs and estimated costs on the sheet given to him.

"As you can see, we need to gut the walls," Mr. Clark said.

"Because?"

"They're not up to code. I'm surprised the fire marshal didn't catch that. You'll also need to replace your structural supports with steel beams, and we need to add steel wrappings around the wood."

"How long will that take?"

Mr. Clark rubbed his chin. "Beams shouldn't take long. Maybe two weeks. I'll contact the sprinkler guy today. Should be able to get those installed first thing next week. Course, your biggest issue is going to be with the city—getting them to come and do all their inspections. Those guys sure can drag their feet."

"So I'm learning." He couldn't support this place much longer without funds coming in. Barring a miracle, he was going to lose Grandpa's restaurant. "When can you start?"

"First thing tomorrow."

"Perfect."

After the contractor left, Nick returned to his office to work on his loss-of-business claim. This was a biggie. Somehow he needed to prove how much he'd lost—would continue to lose—each day the restaurant stayed closed. And even then, the check could be a long time coming.

Shoving a thick stack of sales receipts, invoices, and payroll records aside, he turned to his grandpa's box. He pulled it close and ran his hand over the dusty lid. If Grandpa were here, he'd know what to do—where to get the money.

How to prevent the fire from starting in the first place.

Nick lifted the lid and sifted through old newspaper clippings. He chuckled at a picture of Gloria and Grandpa, clearly taken in the eighties. Grandpa wore his signature cowboy hat and thick red suspenders. Gloria resembled an eighties rock star with her big hair, glittery T-shirt, and hooped earrings. A bearded man wearing a splattered bib stood between them. He held one edge of a giant check while Grandpa held the other. The headline read: *Local restaurant hosts their inaugural charity rib-eating contest.*

Nick had witnessed a couple of those events. He participated in one. Ended up puking halfway through. He smiled at the memory. Maybe he needed to resurrect the tradition once he reopened. It'd be a good way to generate buzz.

He set the clipping down and sifted through other mementoes. Each item evoked a memory—of Grandpa with his deep-throated laugh, of Gloria's goofy attempts at mothering. None of which Mom appreciated. In fact, whenever Mom showed up, the tension escalated and everyone started acting stiff and awkward. Things got worse just before they moved Nick's junior year. He always hoped Mom and Grandpa could work things out—whatever it was. But they never did.

He picked up an old Polaroid and stared at the faded image of himself—at what, aged four?—his mom, and a broad-shouldered man in jeans and a T-shirt. Although the man looked vaguely familiar, a black ball cap with red lettering shadowed his whiskered face. Standing stiff as cardboard cutouts, no one in the photo appeared happy.

Was that Nick's dad? He flipped the picture over and read the date on the back. 1976. It couldn't have been. His dad died in the Vietnam War, and the last US troops were withdrawn in 1973, though a few specialists remained until the complete evacuation in 1975. A year before the photo.

Nick grabbed his dad's dog tags, dangling around his neck, and closed his hand around them.

If only the war had ended a few years earlier. Shaking his head, he turned his attention back to the photo.

Nick's mom wore her hair short. She looked thin, her pink sundress hanging limp from her frame. The man beside her held a beer bottle in one hand and a cigarette in the other.

Who was he? Did Nick know him? His gut said he did.

Nick's mom had never been the type to engage in casual relationships. Never had time for men at all, as far as he could remember, and certainly not so soon after his dad's death.

When had his father died exactly? Did Mom ever say? In the war, Nick knew that much. Beyond that, Mom remained close-mouthed. That had to be traumatic—terrifying. His dad shipped to Vietnam during her first trimester, turning Mom into a widow soon after.

He used to pester her for more information. How he longed to hear stories about his dad, to see photos, anything. But each time he'd broached the subject, she got agitated and prattled off some answer about how he'd died a hero. That was all Nick needed to know. Not that he blamed her. He knew what it was like to lose someone you loved, to feel the rip of loss every time you hear their name or a memory surfaced. Mom couldn't afford to break down. She'd had a kid to care for. And Grandpa. He'd lost his only son.

Setting the photo aside, Nick returned to Grandpa's box. A small manila envelope lay on the bottom, *Unit #375* printed on it. A key was tucked inside. To what? It must have been important for Grandpa to save it.

Nick closed his hand around the key, torn between two worlds—the past and the present. Both were riddled with pain and loss.

"Nick?" Rictor poked his head in. "There's a guy from Prime Beef and Poultry here to see you."

A vendor looking for Nick to place an order—which he'd need to do, considering all the contaminated supplies he had to throw out. Only problem, that took money. "I'll be there in a minute."

Rictor nodded and turned to leave.

"Hey, Ric?"

"Yeah?"

Nick held up the key. "I found this in Grandpa's keepsake box. Any idea what it's for?"

Squinting, Rictor crossed the room, his expression tightening as he drew near. "Uh . . ." Acting like a kid caught between the class cheater and the principal, he looked from Nick to the key, then back to Nick.

"There something I need to know?" Nick leaned forward. "You're not playing games with me, are you?"

Rictor sighed and sank into the chair across from the desk. "I imagine that's to your grandpa's storage unit."

"What storage unit?"

"Out near Stateline, I believe. On the Kansas-Missouri border."

"Is it still there?"

"I imagine so."

"But I thought I . . . Why didn't I know?"

"You'll need to ask your momma that one. And maybe Mr. Aspens."

Nick's accountant and the executor of Grandpa's will. "Be straight with me—is there something I need to know?"

Rictor studied him for a moment before shaking his head. "Sorry, man, but this isn't my can of worms to open."

Tammy stood and extended a hand. "Thank you for meeting with me, Ms. Pura."

The woman, a petite lady with short hair and a stocky build, stared back, unmoving. "When should I expect to hear back?"

Uh, never. "I have a few more interviews to do this afternoon." Four of fifteen left. Hopefully God had saved the best for last, otherwise Tammy was in trouble. "I'll let you know." Her phone vibrated in her back pocket. She pulled it out and checked the number. Mom, returning her call. She offered Ms. Pura an apologetic smile, "Excuse me," and answered. "Hi, Mom. Can I call you back?"

"Sure, honey. Is everything all right?"

"Yes, I just wanted to talk to you about . . ." Ms. Pura was watching her a bit too closely. "Will you be available this evening?"

"I'm sorry, but your father and I are going out to dinner with friends. How about I call you tomorrow?"

"Perfect." Tammy ended the conversation and faced Ms. Pura. "As I said, I have a few more applicants to interview, but I'll get back to you by the end of this week."

"I see." The woman's rear remained sunk in the couch cushions, and for a moment it appeared she wouldn't leave. But then she gathered her things and rose.

She paused to smooth her shin-length, lavender skirt. "I'll look forward to hearing from you. Remember, it's never too late to establish a predictable routine and train strong work ethics. Children love stability, you know."

Stability, yes. An obsessively long list of rules enforced by a woman who bore a freaky resemblance to serial child-killer Beverly Allitt? No.

Maintaining a stiff smile, Tammy walked Ms. Pura to the door and held it open.

The woman extended a hand, palm down. "It was great to meet you. Do call."

Tammy nodded. Hopefully, she'd get the woman's voicemail. Maybe a text would be better.

She checked her watch and grimaced. These "appointments" were stretching on longer than she'd anticipated. A Stephanie Morrison was set to arrive in five minutes, which gave Tammy just enough time to regroup—and down an obscene amount of caffeine.

Her thoughts spiraled as she watched the coffee percolate. This wasn't how she'd planned things—single parenting, struggling to find sitters.

Brody's words, tossed out three plus years ago, came rushing back. *"I'm in love with someone else. I want a divorce. Don't fight me on this, Tammy. It'll only get ugly."*

It got ugly anyway. Just once, in all his pushing for freedom, had he paused to consider how divorce would affect their kids?

Obviously not.

What if she didn't find a sitter? She'd have to quit her job. A wave of nausea swept over her. She raised a trembling hand, ready to hurl her cup, to shatter it against the wall—like Brody had shattered her life. With a deep breath, she lowered her arm and moved stiffly to the coffee pot.

She grabbed her phone and scrolled to Vanessa's number. Tammy needed some ice-cream-eating V time. Like a weekend's worth. Only those days wouldn't return for a while. If ever.

Lord, why? Why must You rip everything out from under me?

Only this wasn't God's fault. No, her and Brody had messed things up all by themselves. But at least she had Nick. At one time, he'd been her whole world, her closest friend.

Her greatest heartache. And now she was latching onto him . . . because she didn't have anyone else. Most likely, he was doing the same. That meant, it was only a matter of time before one of them got hurt—most likely her. She'd be wise to walk away now. Except he needed her.

Aaarrrgh!

She was being ridiculous, allowing one emotion to spiral into another. Which was why she absolutely didn't need more coffee. She poured herself a mug anyway and shuffled back into the living room to wait for her next appointment.

The moment she sat on the couch, the doorbell rang. With a sigh, she set her mug on the coffee table and shuffled to the door. She found Jenson standing on her stoop, dressed in a button-down shirt and slacks. He carried the faint scent of spicy citrus.

"Hi." Tammy held the door open, her body blocking the entryway.

"Hi. I . . . uh." He shifted, his confident smile faltering briefly before returning full force. "I wanted to check how you're doing. See if you needed any help. With anything."

"That's very thoughtful. I'd invite you in for a glass of tea, but I'm expecting someone."

His face fell. "Oh."

"I'm doing interviews. Trying to find a nanny."

"I see." The sparkle returned to his eyes. "Maybe next time." He lingered, turned, then faced her again. "How about tomorrow? Starbucks?"

Was he hitting on her or offering support as a brother-in-Christ? She didn't have the time or energy for either. "Can I call you?"

"Yeah, sure. Whenever you get a chance."

Slipping back inside, she peered through the glass panels flanking her door, watching him leave. Why Jenson's sudden appearance? Was God trying to tell her something? Why else would He bring a realtor to her doorstep?

Maybe she needed to seriously consider putting her house up for sale. Moving in with her parents . . . relaxing—regrouping—for a while.

She'd rather God make all her problems go away.

Tammy trudged back into the living room to wait for her next applicant. She arrived five minutes late. Unacceptable. In Tammy's line of work, grace and tardiness didn't merge. Not only could it cost Tammy her job; it could threaten a recipient's life.

"You must be Stephanie." Her cheek muscles cramped as she forced yet another smile.

The girl—who looked eighteen, nineteen tops—nodded. Clutching a sparkly handbag to her chest, she looked past Tammy and into the room. The corners of her lips tipped up as if on the verge of a smile. A good sign. Soft makeup, round features, casual attire—all indications of normalcy.

"Please, have a seat." Tammy motioned to the couch.

Stephanie obliged and pulled a portfolio from her tote. "I assumed you'd want references?"

"Please." Tammy accepted the binder with a raised eyebrow. A cover letter topped the stack. It said Stephanie loved children and hoped to pursue a career in early childhood education, which was her major. On the next page, she'd listed references, and although none were past employers, everyone spoke highly of her. Two professors called her conscientious and dependable. Nice.

Thank You, Lord.

Tammy's tight-lipped smile softened into a genuine one—one that came from intense relief. She asked a few more questions: Where was Stephanie from? What was her discipline philosophy?

Could she handle the odd hours? Tammy then explained the nature of her work, stressing the need for punctuality.

Stephanie's cheeks flushed. "I'm sorry I was late. There was an . . ." She swallowed and stared at her hands. After a deep breath, she looked back at Tammy. "There's no excuse. I apologize."

Trying to appear firm and authoritative, Tammy fought against an emerging grin. Yes, this girl would do quite nicely. "When can you start?"

Stephanie beamed. "Whenever you need me."

"Well, I'm off this week." She had taken personal leave, much to her boss' chagrin. But she needed to find childcare and, hopefully, get a handle on her mess of a life. She flipped open her day planner. "I'll need you for sure on the thirteenth, fourteenth, fifteenth, and eighteenth." She jotted down her schedule. "And you'll need to be on-call when I am."

Stephanie nodded and took the slip of paper.

After the girl left, Tammy collapsed on the couch and propped her feet on the coffee table. Problem solved.

As long as this sitter didn't bail on her.

Chapter 24

Nick eased into Secure Storage's parking lot and cut the engine. Grandpa's envelope lay in the console, the key tucked inside.

Miss you, Grandpa. Could sure use your help now. Your wisdom.

He gripped the steering wheel, reluctant to move.

Why was his gut churning? Obviously this storage unit held nothing of value, otherwise Grandpa would've left it in the will. Most likely Nick would find a bunch of old magazines, maybe some antique furniture.

And a photo album of his dad?

What would it have been like to have a father? Someone to teach him how to ride a bike or change the oil in his car?

Like he'd wanted to do with Payton, hoped to still able to do with Jeremy.

Don't let Marianne keep me from Jeremy, Lord. I've already lost one son. I won't survive the loss of another.

He got out, a stiff breeze carrying the faint scent of motor oil and fertilizer. He switched his key to his other hand and wiped a sweaty palm on his pant leg. Lengthening his stride, he squared his shoulders and crossed the lot.

A lanky woman with long, silver hair stood outside the box-like office smoking a cigarette. Frowning, she dropped her cigarette and ground it into the pavement before stepping inside.

A gust of cold air assaulted Nick as he followed her in. The place smelled like stale coffee and cheap air freshener.

She rounded the counter. "How can I help you?"

"I need to get into locker #375." He slid the key toward her.

"You got the security code to get past the gate?"

"No."

"What's the name?"

"Should be under Harris Zimmerman."

"That you?"

"No." Why the interrogation? This woman was acting like he wanted to break into a bank vault, not check out an old metal locker.

"Unit number?"

"375," he repeated.

She typed on the keyboard. "You Randall?"

"That was my dad."

"He send you?"

"He's dead."

"Who is?"

"Both of them."

She scrutinized him for a moment before returning to her computer screen. Her eyes shifted right to left, her teeth working her bottom lip. "Hmm . . . I got a note here says if a Randy Zimmerman shows up, to let him in, no questions asked."

Apparently no one updated her notes after Dad's death.

She cocked her head. "I wonder if that applies to you, too, being his son and all." Her scowl deepened. "You got ID?"

Nick nodded and plunked his driver's license on the counter. She inspected it as if looking for a fake.

He swallowed back a snort. *Yep, I created an alternate ID to break into some dead guy's storage locker.*

He reached for his cell phone. Maybe Mr. Aspens could help him out—give him the gate code or something. "Listen, if you need me to call—"

"Don't get your gander up." She slid his license back to him. "Come on."

He followed her out, waiting as she pulled another cigarette from a crumpled pack. Her wrinkled cheeks caved in as she took a drag. "Follow me."

Stepping over grease splotches and large cracks in the pavement, Nick trailed her through the gate to a row of metal storage units.

She stopped in front of one near the end. A rusted deadbolt secured the lock. Arms crossed, she moved aside, watching as he worked the lock. It unlatched with a click.

The woman started to leave, and Nick whirled around. "Wait. Who pays for this unit?"

She shrugged. "I'd have to look, but it's on an automatic payment plan."

"Thanks."

She left and Nick turned back to the unit. He opened the metal door with a screech, revealing a mess of old furniture and boxes. Cobwebs hung in the corners and draped over old lamps. Grandpa's wicker rocker peeked out from under a cherry headboard. Nick smiled, remembering Grandpa rocking on his porch, pine block in one hand, whittling knife in the other.

But other than the rocker and a few other random pieces of furniture, none of it looked familiar.

He moved to a stack of boxes to his right and lowered them on the ground one by one. The first contained a bunch of old records. The Beatles, The Rolling Stones, The Doors. He pulled out a Jimi Hendrix album and ran his hand along the faded cover. These could be sold for a pretty penny. He surveyed the other boxes piled around him. How much was all this worth? Enough to pay his insurance claim deductible or mounting medical bills?

Only problem, they didn't belong to him.

Or did they? Maybe this locker had gotten missed during the estate managing. He'd call Mr. Aspen when he returned to the restaurant. If anything, Nick would ask for the rocker and records. They were only catching dust, anyway.

Setting the albums aside, he moved to the next box. It was full of manila file folders, cloth-covered scrapbooks, and paper-wrapped picture frames. He sat on a rusted filing cabinet and pulled out a stack of files. Inside the first one he found a glossy brochure for Safe Haven Ministries, the charity Grandpa supported. Matthew 25:35 was printed on the bottom in elegant letters: *"For I was hungry, and you gave me something to eat, I was thirsty, and you gave me something to drink; I was a stranger, and you invited me in."*

There were other papers detailing the ministry's mission and policies, along with an invitation to a Christmas party dated 1984. Included was a Missouri address and phone number.

Why was Grandpa sending money to a ministry almost two hours away? Nick folded the paper and tucked it in his back pocket and put the rest away. He moved from file to file, skimming documents and old newspaper clippings.

Near the bottom, he found a leather photo album with yellowed pages. Pictures of a pudgy, green-eyed kid with black hair filled the first page. His heart pricked when he read the caption. Randall Everett Zimmerman, age four.

My dad.

The same smiling toddler appeared in the next page nestled on Grandpa's lap. His grandfather's eyes sparkled in a face free of wrinkles, his hair free of gray. A woman's hand rested on his shoulder. Grandma? Nick had never met her. She died of tuberculosis long before he came around, leaving Grandpa to parent their only child.

Nick shook his head. A legacy of single-parenting—first grandpa, then Mom, now him. Except in his case, he only had himself to blame.

He continued flipping the pages, soaking in every image and caption until, three-quarters of the way through, he stopped.

He blinked at a photo of a man in army fatigues, jaw covered with scruffy whiskers, eyes dull. He wore a black ball cap with red lettering. The image of the photo Nick found in Grandpa's keepsake box flashed through his mind, crisp and clear.

Dad?

It couldn't be. He was dead—had died before the war ended.

But pictures didn't lie, which meant, someone else had.

Chapter 25

At his desk, Nick laid the photo of his dad—the one he'd taken from the storage locker—next to the one from Grandpa's keepsake box. No doubt, it was the same man. He turned the images over, compared the dates printed on the back.

This made no sense. He needed to call his mom.

Unfortunately, his stepdad answered. "Hi. How are you holding up?"

Like the man cared. But it was the polite question, and Nick would give the polite response. That was the extent of their relationship, which suited Nick fine. "All right. Can I talk to Mom?"

"She's not here. I don't expect her to return until this afternoon."

"Have her call me, will you?" Nick hung up and leaned back in his chair, sifting through decades' worth of memories, grasping onto the smallest fragments. But when it came to his dad, everything got muddled.

Picking up the photos, he went in search of Rictor. He found him in the kitchen talking with the general contractor. The construction crew lingered a few feet away, their tools set aside. A section of the wall had been cut out, leaving exposed beams.

Nick approached the general contractor. "How's it going?"

The man swiped at his sweaty forehead with the back of his forearm. "Waiting on the building inspector. Can't close this wall up until he signs off."

Great. Between the feet-dragging insurance guys and equally slow city inspectors, Nick would be lucky to get this restaurant opened by the end of summer—his busiest season.

The general contractor hooked a thumb through his belt loop. "I know a guy, an expeditor, who can help you push things through."

"Is that legal?"

"'Course. He used to work for the county. Knows all the ins and outs, how those guys think. What holds things up and how to get 'er done."

"How much will that cost?"

The man shrugged. "Less than playing the waiting game, I imagine. But each job's different. Depends on how long this project takes. Tell you what. I'll give him a call, have him write up some figures."

Nick rubbed his face. "Yeah, okay." He turned to Rictor. "You got a minute?"

Rictor raised his eyebrows. "Sure."

Nick led Rictor into the dining area and to a booth along the far wall. Plunking down, he placed the photos side by side on the dusty table.

Rictor sat across from him, mouth grim, staring at the aged images—one crisp and clear, the other heavily shadowed. There was no mistaking it was the same man.

"How much do you know about my dad?"

Rictor shifted. He didn't respond right away. "A little, I suppose. Why?"

Scoffing, Nick shoved the shadowed image toward him. "What do you mean, why?" He flicked the picture over to reveal the faded date printed on the back. "1976." He punched the number with his finger. "The war was over."

Rictor inhaled and rested his chin on fisted hands.

Nick scowled. "Quit with the games, already. What's going on?"

"This isn't my place, bud. I think you need to talk to your mom."

"So that's how it is, huh?"

"I don't know, man. This really isn't—"

"Your can of worms. Right. Thanks for the help."

"Maybe you oughta talk with some of your grandpa's friends."

"You were his friend. Mine, too."

"Still am." Rictor thumbed his jaw. "You got a lot going on right now. Dealing with your son's death, the fire, reopening the restaurant."

"Don't patronize me." Nick stood, engaging Rictor in a stare off. Grabbing the photos, he stomped to his office and shut the door. What was Rictor hiding? And what about those automatic deductions written into Grandpa's will?

Nick pulled a ledger from the file and scrolled down until he got to a debit paid to Safe Haven Ministries. $300. Not a lot of money, but over time . . .

He called the ministry, got a prerecorded message, and hung up.

Was his dad still alive? After all these years of wishing, dreaming—after all the empty Father's Days, career days. Why would his mom, his grandpa, even Rictor, keep from him the one thing he longed for?

He pulled his wallet from his back pocket and slid the photos beneath Payton's. All he'd ever wanted was to have a dad, and be a dad. To give his kids what he'd never had.

He'd failed miserably on the latter. He refused to lose Jeremy, too.

Jutting his chin, he pulled out his phone and called Marianne. He got the machine.

"You know what to do." A long beep followed.

Uncoiling his fists, Nick fought to keep his tone even. "Marianne, pick up. I have a right to talk to my son." She and her boyfriend were probably standing right there, listening to his message, laughing. And there was nothing he could do about it.

Except call his lawyer. He hung up and dialed Mr. Cooper's office.

The secretary answered. "Cooper and Copland Family Law, how may I help you?"

"It's Nick." How often had he called this past month? Five times? Six? He'd know soon enough—when he got his bill. "Is Mr. Cooper in?"

"Can you hold, please?"

Piano music filled the line, followed by a click.

"Mr. Zimmerman, I planned to call you back later this week. How are you?"

Peachy. That's why he was taking up his $200 an hour, $100 a half hour, $3.3 dollars per minute, time. "Been better. Marianne's giving me grief again. Haven't seen or talked to Jeremy since . . ." His heart wrenched, and he swallowed past a lump in his throat. "She's back to playing the voicemail game. This is illegal, right? Parental alienation?"

"Parental alienation is very difficult to prove, but we can file contempt charges. I imagine if given the option of court fees or visitation, she'll choose the latter."

"We've done that. Or have you forgotten all the show cause hearings?"

"No, I haven't forgotten but—"

"I'm done making threats. They work for a while, but a month from now, she'll go right back to her manipulation tactics."

"I hear you." Apathy dulled his voice. "Unfortunately, these things can take time."

And time's money, right? Come to think of it, the guy had no reason to help him at all.

I'm being paranoid. I'm frustrated and angry and looking for someone to blame. Besides, Mr. Cooper was all he had.

He breathed deep. "How's my custody case coming? Do we have a new court date yet?"

"We do, although I expect them to request a postponement. Listen, Nick, I don't mean to discourage you, but I think we're better off going for joint. As a business owner—"

"What does that have to do with anything?"

"Her lawyer made a comment that indicates they plan to make what happened on the night of the fire an issue."

His teeth ground together. Just like Marianne, twisting and turning everything—even the death of their son—to her advantage.

"You think that'll affect my case?"

"I think she'll do whatever she can to drag things out and make you look bad."

And if the Flaming Mesquite went under, it'd weaken Nick's case even further. It was like climbing up a down escalator. For every step he tried to take, the thing kept dragging him backward.

He ended the call and dropped the phone onto his desk.

Lord, I need Your help. Rise up in my defense.

Chapter 26

Tammy jotted a few more numbers on her notepad, tore off the top sheet, and stuck it to the refrigerator. She checked the clock on the microwave, then entered the living room.

Stephanie, her new sitter, sat on the floor building Lego structures with Tylan. Becky lounged in a nearby armchair, remote control in one hand, phone in the other.

Was Tammy forgetting anything? "I left emergency numbers and instructions on the fridge." Instructions she'd already gone over verbally. "Like I said during the interview, I could be back in a few hours, or I could be at the hospital all night."

Stephanie nodded. "I'll set the alarm just in case. What time do they need to be at school tomorrow?"

"Thanks, Stephanie. Tylan catches the bus at seven thirty. Becky walks to school but needs to leave at the same time." She crossed the room and kissed Becky's forehead. "Ten more minutes of TV, then study for finals, got that?"

Becky rolled her eyes. "Fine."

Tammy moved to Tylan and lowered to his level. "I expect you to go to bed without a fuss. One glass of water and one trip to the bathroom. Got it?"

He focused on his Legos.

Tammy tickled his ribs. "Got it?" When he didn't respond, she tickled some more. "I know you hear me."

She and Stephanie exchanged knowing smiles.

Peace swept over Tammy as she left her house and strolled to her car. Her kids were in good hands.

Thank You, Lord.

Parked in Central Medical's parking garage thirty minutes later, she pulled out her cell phone and scrolled to her mother's number. She got her voicemail.

"Hey, Mom, Dad, it's me. Seems we're playing phone tag. I was just calling to see how you're doing." She swallowed. Why were those three little words so hard? "Look, I'm . . . I'm sorry for our . . . little spat." She exhaled. "Call me when you get a chance. Love you."

She hung up and started to put her phone away when she noticed a missed call alert. Nick. A smile tugged on her mouth.

Stepping out into the crisp evening air, she clicked return call.

"Hello?" His deep voice quickened her pulse.

"Hi, Nick." She wove her way through parked cars to the ICU entrance. "Thanks for returning my call."

"No problem. Do you have more news on the recipients?"

Her gut dropped. Way to elevate then dash his hopes. "No. I'm sorry. I was calling to see how you're doing." Passing the information kiosk, she waved to Dottie, a grandmotherly volunteer who always had a smile and a kind word.

"Honest answer or the politically correct one?" He paused. "You ever feel like you're trapped on a merry-go-round, wanting to jump off but not having anywhere to land or the wherewithal to let go?"

All the time, but this wasn't about her. "Sounds like you need me to bring you a sugar and caffeine-loaded Mountain Dew."

He chuckled. "That oughta relax me."

"Like a jolt of electricity to the brain. You know . . ." Her stomach knotted. This was a stupid idea . . . "You wanna meet somewhere for dinner tomorrow?"

"How about Medford's?"

"Perfect." Tylan would love eating at the old train depot turned restaurant. Oh. Tylan and Becky. "Uh . . . would you mind if I brought my kids?"

When silence ensued, she tensed. Did the mention of kids aggravate his sorrow? Had he gotten to see Jeremy yet?

"Yeah, sure," he said. "Of course."

Tammy exhaled. For all her training, she had no idea how to talk to a grieving parent, at least not when that parent was Nick. "Great. I'll meet you at seven."

"I'll be there."

Tammy hung up and slipped her phone into her back pocket. A woman she didn't recognize occupied the nurses' station. She glanced up as Tammy approached. "Can I help you?"

Tammy extended her hand. "I'm Tammy Kuhn from Heartland Donation Services." She read the woman's name badge. "I called earlier and talked with a nurse Kinzer. I'm here to speak with Mr. Carmichael's family." Heather, Heartland's social worker, had already spoken with the family, but apparently Mr. Carmichael's sister had a few questions.

"Room 236."

"Thank you."

Tammy continued down the hall. She paused outside the patient's doorway to review the donor's family's names. Mom, Sandra Howard; sister, Katrina White.

A young woman, most likely Katrina, sat at the patient's bedside, holding his hand and sniffling. Her shiny black hair was cropped at the chin, her frame small. She glanced up when Tammy entered and swiped at her bloodshot eyes.

Donning a smile, Tammy approached with her hand extended. "Are you Katrina White?"

Katrina nodded, and the two shook hands. She dabbed her eyes with a wadded tissue. "Mom's outside smoking a cigarette. This has been very difficult for her."

"I understand." Tammy pulled up a chair and sat beside Katrina. "I'm Tammy Kuhn from Heartland Donation Services. I was told you have some questions about the donation process?"

Katrina studied her for a moment before staring at her tightly clenched hands.

A quietness fell over the room, and Tammy's heart stirred as the presence of the Holy Spirit enveloped her.

This was more than an informative visit. God had arranged

a divine appointment, an opportunity for this woman to gain life through her brother's death.

Lord, give me the words. In Your perfect timing.

"I keep wondering if there was something I should've done. Travis and I went hiking last week. Halfway through, he started to get a headache, sick to his stomach. It was hot, and we were carrying heavy backpacks. I thought he was just getting overheated. Or dehydrated. I can't help but wonder if maybe I should've known something was wrong." She grabbed another tissue from the box on the bedside tray and folded it. "The last time he came for dinner, I served fried chicken and mashed potatoes with gravy. I should've—" Her voice cracked. "I should've been more alert."

Tammy shook her head. "He had bad hypertension. One of the arteries burst in his brain. There was nothing you could do."

The woman swiped at her tears, watching her brother. The machines buzzed and beeped behind him. Footsteps approached and faded in the hall, blips of passing conversation drifting into the room.

Katrina looked at her. "Do you believe in life after death?"

"I do." Tammy's heart pricked. This was what she loved most about her job—what made the late-night calls and long hours worth it. Saving physical lives was great, but nothing compared to seeing Christ bring spiritual life out of darkness.

"Travis made a lot of mistakes, back when he was young. Drinking and drugging. But he really turned his life around. He said he found Jesus." Her gaze intensified. "Do you think . . . ?" Breathing deep, she stared at her hands again.

"I *know* your brother is in heaven, with Jesus, because Jesus never turns anyone away who comes to Him."

Katrina's cell rang. She stared at it and then gave a loud sigh. "Excuse me." She answered. "Hello? Thanks for calling me back. Can you hold on please?" She looked at Tammy, "Thanks for talking with me," then returned to her phone conversation.

Tammy nodded and stood, disappointed their conversation was over. But God's timing was perfect, and He always finished what He started. She would trust Him to water whatever seed He'd planted in Katrina's heart.

She handed over her business card. "Call me if you need to talk. About anything."

Katrina studied the card before putting it in her back pocket.

Lord, keep this door open. Please.

Tammy helped the nurse unplug the bed and pack everything up while the respiratory therapist placed Travis on a different ventilator. They wheeled him out of the room and down the hall, Katrina following close behind.

When they reached the OR, Tammy turned to Katrina one last time. "If you need anything . . ."

Katrina nodded, fresh tears spilling over her lashes.

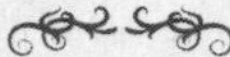

Tammy didn't arrive home until well past 3:00 a.m. Her feet throbbed after hours of standing. The familiar cloak of fatigue numbed her brain as the robust coffee she'd downed before leaving the hospital wore off. Had Joni been here, Tammy would've been guaranteed a full eight hours of sleep—or as much as she needed. But Stephanie? The girl was young, inexperienced.

Entering through the garage door, Tammy paused to listen to the strange noises emanating from the living room.

What in the world?

It almost sounded like shrieking. She dropped her keys on the counter and surveyed the cluttered area. Blackened crumbs scattered the counter and dirty dishes filled the sink. The scent of burnt toast lingered. A stark contrast to how Joni had always left things—dishes washed, counters cleaned, kids in pj's and tucked in bed.

Tammy found Stephanie asleep on the couch. The television was turned to one of those raunchy music video stations. Empty soda cans and an opened bag of potato chips lay on the coffee table, toys and pillows were scattered on the floor. Not exactly the way to start off a peaceful day, but at least she had childcare.

Heading to her bedroom, she caught a glimpse of Becky's backpack, zipped closed and propped against the wall. Right where she'd deposited it after school. That meant she hadn't studied for finals. Wonderful.

Yet another reason Tammy missed Joni. She needed more than a sitter. She needed a nanny. Someone who'd take an active interest in her kids.

Mom's words, spoken countless times over the past three years, resurfaced: *No one's going to care for your kids like you do.*

What should she do? Quit her job? Walk away from the chance of pointing women like Katrina to the hope that never disappoints?

Except like Mom said, things were different now. She had her kids to think about.

What if her ministry hurt them?

Chapter 27

Sitting behind his desk, Nick grabbed a sheet of paper for a fathers' rights support group he'd printed off the Internet. The guy who'd started it was fighting a custody battle himself, and according to the claims on his website, without the help of expensive legal aid.

Maybe Nick needed to set up a time to talk with the man, see how he did it. Although the website didn't mention whether he'd been successful or not.

A knock sounded on the door, and Rictor poked his head in. "You all right?"

Nick studied his employee. He was a good guy, had always been a faithful and true friend. Rictor would never hurt him—keep something from him, on purpose. So why was he being so evasive? "I'll make it."

"How long you planning on hiding out in this dungeon of yours? Don't you have a hot date tonight?"

Heat flooded Nick's face. "It's dinner with a friend. Nothing more."

"Uh-huh." Rictor drummed his fingers on the doorframe. "Because your face turns watermelon red whenever you hang with your buds, right?"

"Did you need something?"

"Yeah. The GC said his sprinkler guy's running behind. Got held up on another job."

"How behind?"

"Don't know. He said he'd call sometime next week."

Nick checked his watch and crossed the room. "Would you mind locking up after the repair crew leaves?"

"I'm all over it."

"Thanks."

Rictor clamped a hand on Nick's shoulder, his gaze intensifying. "That's what friends are for. Now get. Don't want to keep your lady friend waiting." He winked.

Nick rolled his eyes, fighting an emerging smile as his thoughts shifted to Tammy, who had been the only drop of sunshine in his otherwise murky life.

Nick searched the dim interior of Medford's lobby for Tammy. With all the bench seating taken, she waited near a window, framed by the evening sun. Her pink blouse, gathered at her narrowed waist, brought out the peach in her complexion.

A boy with carrot-toned hair and ruddy cheeks stood beside her, acting more fidgety than a caged squirrel. A teen girl with freckles and strawberry-blonde hair occupied her right. Hip shoved out, the girl alternated between staring at her phone and scanning the clogged lobby. She looked as enthused as a sleep-deprived sloth.

Straightening, Nick maneuvered through the throng of people to Tammy.

He glanced from her to each of her kids in turn. "Hey, guys".

Tammy placed one arm around her son's shoulder and the other around her daughter's waist. "These are my children, Tylan and Becky." She cast a sideways glance at her daughter. "This is Nick, a friend from high school."

"The donor guy?" Tylan regarded him with a wrinkled brow, the corners of his mouth dipping into a frown.

Tammy's cheeks flushed. "I . . . He . . ."

"It's all right." Nick turned to Tylan. "Yes, I'm the father of an organ donor." He pulled his wallet from his back pocket and flipped it open to a picture of Payton. "This is—was—my son. He was fourteen. Almost . . ." His voice caught. He swallowed. "Would've turned fourteen this August. He was quite the young man. A dynamo on the football and baseball field."

Awkward silence ensued.

Nick surveyed the restaurant. Nearly every table was occupied. Bussers hustled to clear and wipe those that weren't. The door swooshed open, and a party of five crammed into the already crowded lobby. People jostled out of the way, only there was nowhere for them to go. The thick, nose-burning smell of cheap perfume wafted from a group of bejeweled women standing a few feet away. They laughed and carried on as if everyone else wanted—needed—to be part of their conversation.

Nick kept his arms pinned to his sides to avoid stabbing someone with his elbows. He glanced at Tammy. "You put our names down?"

She nodded with a sheepish smile. "They said it'd be a thirty to forty-five minute wait."

Tylan groaned, and Becky rolled her eyes. Nick smiled, remembering similar responses from his boys. It was a bittersweet memory, one that warmed and wrenched his heart.

"You know . . ." Nick glanced toward the door, then back to Tammy. "There's a burger joint around the corner. Hungry Man's Grill. What do you say we blow out of here?"

Tylan's head snapped up, a toothy grin emerging. Even Becky perked up.

Tammy laughed. "Sure."

The moment the words left her mouth, both kids bolted toward the door.

Chuckling, Nick extended a hand. "After you."

Tammy's blue eyes sparkled, a soft smile playing on her rose-petal lips. His heart stirred, taking him by surprise. Did he still love her, or was this his grief talking? Most likely the latter, but even so, it was good to have a friend.

Chapter 28

Outside Medford's, Tylan dashed toward the parking lot, about to run in front of a car.

Tammy's heart lurched. "Tylan!"

Nick made a guttural cry and lunged in front of her. He seized her son by the wrist. Glancing from Tylan's wide-eyed expression to his white-knuckled hand, Nick blinked and released his grip. He trembled slightly, and the color had drained from his face. "I'm sorry. I . . ."

"No need to apologize." She grabbed Tylan's other arm and yanked him to the curb. "You could've been hit."

Nick followed with slumped shoulders, his eyes moist.

Poor Nick. She touched his elbow. "You all right?" She'd received more information on Payton's recipients today, included it in a letter tucked inside a card. That card sat in her purse, waiting. But now wasn't the time.

His torso rose and fell as if inhaling a fortifying breath. "I'm fine." He offered Tylan a weak smile. "Sorry if I roughed you up."

Thin lines stretched across Tylan's brow. With mouth pressed shut and hands fisted at his sides, he stared at Nick as if deciding between remorse and defiance.

Tammy lowered to her son's eye level and gripped his arms. "This is a parking lot. What are the rules?"

Pink flooded his cheeks. "No running," he mumbled.

She nodded and took his hand. He tried to tug away, but she tightened her grip and shot him a warning glare. Releasing a heavy sigh, he moaned and complied.

"Tammy?"

She turned to see Jenson approaching Medford's with two other businessmen, all in suits.

"Hi." Still gripping Tylan's sweaty hand, she pivoted and offered a smile.

Jenson's narrowed gaze swept over Nick before shifting back to Tammy. He said something to his colleagues. They nodded and headed toward the restaurant while he strolled toward her.

"Hello." A tendon in his jaw twitched as he turned to Nick with an extended hand. "I'm Jenson Poynter, a close friend of Tammy's. And you are?"

"Nick Zimmerman." He accepted Jenson's handshake.

Tammy noted Jenson's tight-lipped smile. He looked between the two. "You know one another how?"

"High school." Tammy released her death grip on Tylan and wrapped an arm around his shoulder instead. They stood awkwardly for a moment longer, couples strolling past them, Tylan fidgeting, until Becky released one of her characteristic diva-sighs.

"Can we go already? I'm starving."

"Me, too." Tylan poked his bottom lip out, dimples forming on his chin.

Tammy laughed and ran a hand across his sweaty head. "All right. I hear you." She smiled at Jenson, surprised to see his scowl had deepened. "I better feed the kiddos. It was good seeing you."

They said their good-byes, Tammy released her death-grip on Tylan, and she and Nick continued down the walk. Becky walking a few feet ahead of them.

A warm gust swept over her, tickling her nose with the faint scent of Nick's cologne. Citrusy with a hint of cedar.

She fingered the strap on her purse, thinking of the card tucked inside. Watching Nick from the corner of her eye, she prayed for God's comforting words, His perfect timing.

An old house converted into a fast-food joint, Hungry Man's sat in front of a long wooden fence separating East Street apartments from downtown Oak Park Blossoms. The building was a forest green, the paint peeling, the roof made from corrugated metal sheets. A handful of rusted tables and chairs dotted a circular patch of pavement, checkered pop-tents blocking out spheres of the setting sun.

A gentle breeze stirred, carrying the scent of greasy French fries and onion rings. A pack of teenagers sat against the brick wall, knees pulled up. The largest of them all, a muscular teen dressed in a white mesh tank, eyed Becky.

Tammy tensed. Nudging her daughter out of the kid's sight, she made her way to the sliding window cut into the aluminum siding.

Nick muscled in front of her, flashing a smile. "I got this."

She moved aside. "Thanks, Nick. I owe you."

She stole a glance at Becky, her momma bear simmering near the surface. For once, Becky didn't make fluttery eyes.

Nick shot Tylan a lopsided smile. "Extra onions and tomatoes, right?"

"No." Tylan bolted to the window. "Just a burger with ketchup. Nothing else." He rose on his toes, forearms planted on the counter, neck craned forward as if afraid the worker might miss his request.

Tammy smiled as Nick continued to rib her son, suggesting everything from shoofly pie to fries dipped in whale lard.

That one got a raised eyebrow from Tylan. "Do they really make those?"

Becky rolled her eyes, and Nick chuckled. "Maybe in Alaska. After we order, remind me to tell you about my time with the Eskimos."

"Really?" Tylan's eyes widened, as did Tammy's. That was one she wanted to hear. Apparently, so did Becky, because she looked up from her phone.

Bags of burgers in hand, Nick glanced around. "You know, there's a playground half a block from here." He pointed toward a well-trodden trail edging a wooden fence a few feet away. "What do you say?"

"Yay!" Tylan grinned.

Becky shrugged.

"Sounds good to me." Tammy grabbed the drink tray resting on the order counter. By the time she turned around, Tylan and Becky were already heading down the trail. "Hey. Wait for us." But either they didn't hear her or they pretended not to.

As Tammy and Nick continued, a playground came into view, an alcove of green surrounded by lush, towering trees. A splattering of kids clamored up the jungle gym.

Tammy and Nick sat at a shaded park bench nestled beneath a dogwood. Tylan and Becky sat across from them, and Nick distributed the burgers and fries.

He glanced at Tammy. "Shall we pray?"

She nodded, and everyone bowed their heads.

"Father, thank You for this food and for special friends. More than that, thank You for Your Son and the promise of eternal life." His voice grew husky, and he cleared his throat. "Because You gave Your Son for us, one day, I'll be able to see my son again." He paused, and Tammy heard him inhale a shuddered breath before closing with an amen.

The prayer had barely concluded before Tylan tore off his food wrapper and gulped his burger down. Watching Nick, Becky picked at hers, her expression unreadable.

Tammy tapped Becky's foot with her own. "You okay?"

She shrugged. "Not hungry, I guess."

Tammy observed her for a moment longer but didn't press. Most likely, Becky was just tired. Or bored, spending the evening with adults and all.

When finished, Tylan swiped at his mouth with the back of his hand. "Can I go play now?"

Tammy ruffled his hair. "Sure."

Grinning, Tylan sprang to his feet and ran toward the jungle gym. Becky trailed behind and settled into a swing, focused on her phone.

Turning to Nick, Tammy reached into her purse and pulled out her recipient information letter tucked into a Hallmark card. "I brought you something."

His expression sobered as he took the envelope. "You received more information on the recipients?"

She nodded, holding her breath as he slid the card out.

He read her carefully crafted words aloud. "The recipient of your son's liver was a fifteen-year-old male who had a cancerous tumor. He was on the waiting list for eleven months before receiving his life-saving transplant. He plans to try out for the football team next fall."

The list went on, revealing the details of five young lives—their conditions and how long they'd been listed. Two of them probably wouldn't have made it another week had Nick and Marianne said no to donation.

Tucking the letter back into the card, he looked up with moist eyes. "Thank you."

She squeezed his hand, nodded.

He gazed toward the park. "Kids are a gift. To be cherished; held tight to." His jaw clenched, his thick brows drawn. Then, as if shaking off his grief, he turned his crystal blue eyes toward her. "How you been? I can't imagine it's easy, being a single mom 'n all."

She shrugged and picked up a fallen flower. "I'm learning. Trying." She rubbed a silky petal between her fingers. "My kids need a dad. I just wish my ex would understand that. That he'd make Tylan and Becky more of a priority."

He nodded and placed his hand on her knee, sending a jolt of electricity through her. "I'm standing with you, Tam. Just like you stood beside me when . . ." His face clouded, his eyes searching hers.

Her heart stirred, then stilled. They were friends. Nothing more. And the man had just lost his son. Romance was the last thing on his mind.

Footsteps crunched behind them. Tammy turned to see a sweaty-faced Tylan standing behind her. "Will you push me on the merry-go-round? Please?"

"Sure." She started to stand but Nick placed a warm hand on her shoulder.

"You relax. Allow me." He turned to Tylan. "That okay with you?"

Tylan's grin widened, his head bobbing.

"But be forewarned, I work up a pretty fierce whirl." He shot Tammy a wink and followed her scampering son to the playground.

Spending time with her kids seemed to do Nick good, bring him comfort.

Becky sauntered over with a frown. Plopping down beside Tammy, she crossed her arms. "What're you doing?"

"What do you mean?"

"I'm thirteen, Mom. What's with you and that guy? Do you like him?"

Heat flooded Tammy's face, and she struggled to look her daughter in the eye. "Of course not. Not in that way. We're just friends."

Maybe saying that enough times would make it so, except her heart wasn't listening any more than it had twenty years ago.

Chapter 29

Nick pulled into his cul-de-sac as Howie was leaving. The man's face blanched, and he looked away. Like most of Nick's neighbors did. It was as if he carried an infectious disease—one transported by smiles and eye contact. But he didn't blame them. Death made people uncomfortable. Initiated questions many preferred not to deal with, and in Howie's case, maybe even a bit of guilt. The accident had happened on his property, and there were rumors that some of the boys had been drinking. Of course, Nick didn't blame the guy. He was too busy condemning himself. He'd tell him that if Howie quit dodging him long enough.

Nick eased into his garage, cut the engine, and stepped out into the warm spring air. A warm front had moved in. The weatherman predicted temperatures in the eighties all week. Perfect fishing weather, and there was nothing like an afternoon at the Chapa River to get Jeremy giggling. As long as Marianne quit the game-playing long enough for Nick to get a visit in.

Walking to his mailbox, he pulled his cell phone from his back pocket and dialed her number. It rang four times, each one sending muscle-constricting waves through him. If he was a swearing man . . .

But he wasn't. He was a praying man. Only prayers hadn't done much when Jeremy had been fighting for his life. Even so, prayers were all he had.

He was about to hang up when Marianne's terse voice came on. "You are becoming obsessive, Nick."

Clenching his fist, he spoke as calmly as he was able. "Maybe if you'd answer your phone once in a while—called me back even, I wouldn't have—"

"Maybe if you stopped with the legal threats—"

"They're not threats, Marianne. I have a right to see my son."

She sighed, her heavy breath reverberating across the line. "What do you want?"

"Like I said, to see my son."

"He's got baseball camp coming up. And his annual Boy Scout event. I'll check my schedule and get back to you."

"Uh-uh. Not good enough."

A tense pause followed, Nick's fingertips growing numb as his grip tightened on his phone. "I'll pick him up tomorrow."

"He's got a baseball game."

"So I'll take him. What time?"

"Why are you doing this, Nick?"

"Doing what? Being a dad? Seriously, what is it with you?"

"Do you really think Jeremy wants to spend time with the man who killed his big brother—his hero?"

The air expelled from Nick's lungs. An image of Payton lying on the pavement, blood seeping from his skull, ravished his thoughts.

"I gotta go."

The line went dead.

Nick had the vague awareness of footsteps approaching from behind, of the mailbox next to his creaking open, of the evasive scent of floral perfume.

Rhonda. The last person he wanted to see.

Fumbling for his mail, he hoped she would pull a Howie and opt for extreme avoidance.

"Hey, Nick?"

Fail. Shoving his swirling emotions aside, he turned to face her. "Rhonda." She wore a yellow hat with large polka dots.

"I'm really sorry . . . Payton was a good kid."

"Thanks." The two stood face-to-face, Rhonda choosing neither avoidance nor cheap platitudes. Of all his neighbors, she was the last one he expected to understand. Maybe he'd misjudged her.

"I better get inside." He raised his stack of mail.

She looked at him a moment longer, something oddly maternal radiating in her eyes, then nodded. "I understand. But if you need anything . . ."

He thanked her again, then turned toward his house. Inside, cool air rushed over him, soothing his frazzled nerves. He longed to sink into the couch, pickle his brain with huge quantities of liquor, and waste away his remaining miserable life with hours of television. But he couldn't lose it. He had child support and employees to pay.

Sitting, he spread his mail in front of him. More medical bills, two Visa statements—his restaurant account and personal—and a bunch of other garbage not worth opening. He'd started to sift through an anesthesiology bill when his phone rang.

Mom.

"Hey, thanks for calling me back." Nick sat straighter. "You got a minute?" Now probably wasn't the best time to bring up the past.

"Of course, honey. Are you all right?"

How would she respond to questions about his dad? But it'd been almost forty years. "Did you know Grandpa had—has—a storage locker?"

No response.

"Mom?"

"Yes, I remember. Nothing but old junk, I'm sure."

"I went out there. There's more than junk, Mom."

"You what?" Her voice sounded pinched, as if the words squeezed past tight vocal chords.

"Tell me about Dad. Is he . . .?" Nick swallowed. "Is he alive?"

"What are you talking about?"

"Tell me."

"Hold on a moment, son." There was a faint rustling. His mom was talking to his stepdad, but their words were muffled. "I'm fine, sweetie . . . okay." When Nick's mom returned, her tone was sugary. "Honey, I know you've got a lot on your mind. I wish I could say something to make things easier. You're having a tough time with Jeremy, aren't you?"

Stop with the psychoanalysis. "My relationship with Jeremy has nothing to do with this."

"Of course it does. How could it not?" She paused. "Listen, I hate to put you off, but can I call you later? Now's really not a good time."

Her default response. "When is, Mom?"

"We'll talk later. I love you."

The call ended with a soft click.

Was there any truth in what she'd said? Was his grief-stricken mind clinging to irrational fantasies long since buried? Fantasies of having a dad who'd step in and set everything right, who'd be Nick's source of strength when he felt ready to crumble?

No. He had the picture. Faded and shadowed as it was, that was the same man.

Tammy stood at the stove, flipping her second batch of pancakes. The first lay in the sink, burnt, next to blackened bacon. She glanced through the archway into the living room, and her heart sank. Dressed in his baseball uniform, Tylan sat on the couch staring out the window. His duffel bag filled with overnight gear—just in case—lay at his feet. Sitting beside him, Becky scowled, cell phone gripped in both hands.

Lord, don't let Brody bail. Not today.

It'd be easier if the man left for good, so her kids could mourn and move on, but that wasn't her call to make. Unfortunately.

She checked her phone for missed alerts. Nothing.

What if she moved? Would Brody still make an effort to see the kids, or would he simply slip out of their lives after a few sparsely placed phone calls?

A twinge of uneasiness arose as she thought of Katrina sitting at her brother's bedside. The woman teetered on the edge of eternity, poised for a leap of saving-faith. Tammy had encountered many such men and women over the years, had watched many cross from spiritual death to life. It was a thrill, a joy like none other.

It was what she'd been created to do.

Footsteps plodded into the kitchen, and chair legs scraped against tile as Tylan climbed up to the table. "I'm hungry. Can I have a Pop-Tart?"

Tammy smiled. "Breakfast is almost done, little man." Maybe if she focused on the task at hand instead of obsessing on "what-ifs" and "could've-beens," she'd actually finish before Brody arrived.

If he arrived.

Her teeth ground together as an image of him and his girlfriend surfaced.

Strangling the spatula in her sweaty hand, she stared out the window to the cloudless sky. They'd been married twelve years, and divorce had never even crossed her mind. Until it was rammed in her face.

With a sigh, she returned to her pancakes, slipping them onto a plate moments before scorching her second batch.

"It stinks in here." Becky entered the kitchen with a wrinkled nose. She crossed to the cupboard and pulled out a bowl. "I'll pass on the ashy breakfast, thanks."

"It's not ashy." Tammy dropped the steaming plateful in the center of the table. "Now sit and eat."

She needed to do this—something domestic and motherly. As if a warm breakfast and hugs could somehow insulate her children from the pain caused by their father.

Tammy's phone chimed, and the kitchen went silent. Brody.

A dead weight lodged in her stomach. "Hello?"

A television program played in the background. "Hey, I'm going to be a little late. I've got to run into the office to handle a few things—"

"How late?" She slipped from the kitchen so she wouldn't have to watch the disappointment play on her kids' faces.

"I'm not sure. An hour?"

Walking toward her bedroom, she lowered her voice. "You promised Tylan you'd come to his game."

"No, I told him I'd see what I could do. But don't get your hackles up. I'll be there. Listen, I've got to go. Tell the kids I'll see them at the park. Oh, and remind them to pack an overnight. We're heading to the lake tonight."

We're? So he was spending the night with his girlfriend and bringing the kids along. Great role model. No wonder Becky acted like such a flirt. She was receiving conflicting messages—Brody's live-for-the moment lifestyle, which he made seem so fun and exciting. While Tammy played the boring parent with rules and responsibilities—homework and Sunday school.

She grabbed a sun visor from her closet shelf, her gaze lingering on the empty space where Brody's clothes once hung. "Don't forget, they've got church tomorrow."

"They go twice a week. Missing one Sunday won't kill them."

"And taking them to service won't kill you."

"You're the one nagging me to spend more time with them. But it's got to be on your terms, is that it?"

She tensed, hateful words surging to her tongue. But that was what he wanted—to antagonize her into losing her cool. It was all a game to him, only she wasn't playing. "Whatever." She ended the call.

He probably wouldn't show anyway.

She returned to the kitchen to find both kids watching her closely.

"He's not coming, is he?" Becky glowered, and Tylan's face fell.

Tammy forced a smile and ruffled her son's hair. "He's just going to be late, that's all. And he . . ." Telling them about the lake would only get their hopes up.

Frowning, Tylan planted his elbows on the table and plunked his chin in his hands. "Can't I have a granola bar?"

She checked the clock. It was getting late. Batting practice started in thirty minutes. She didn't have time to deal with breakfast drama.

She crossed her arms. "Seriously, kids, they're pancakes. Humor me, okay?" The tension she'd worked so hard to repress all morning bubbled to the surface.

"But they're burnt." With a wrinkled lip, Becky flipped one over, revealing the dark brown bottom.

"They're not burnt. They're toasted." Tammy moved to the fridge and pulled out a jug of milk. When she poured it, a plume of sour-smelling air flooded her nostrils. She checked the expiration date and moaned. After dumping the contents, she hunted for syrup. Empty. Now what?

"Fine." She tossed both containers in the trash and whirled around. "Eat what you want." So much for sending her kids off in a cocoon of love.

Chapter 30

Nick pulled into Coulter Field's parking lot and made a visual sweep of the area. Baseball diamonds spanned in every direction. Kids in red occupied the south field, green the north, two shades of navy blue east and west.

He grabbed his camera and headed south. Parents filled the bleachers and lined the fields. Coolers, chairs, and blankets dotted the hillsides, children scampering between them.

Nick shaded his eyes to search for his son. He spotted Marianne first and tensed. She sat on the second row of the bleachers wearing a pink hat and large sunglasses. Her boyfriend sat beside her.

Training his eyes on the pavement, he strolled past them to the batting cage and linked his fingers through the chained fence. He surveyed the field, sensing Marianne's hateful eyes boring into the back of his head. Jeremy and three of his buddies stood in a patch of grass beside the dugout, warming up their throwing arms.

Nick wanted his son to know he had come. Whether the boy wanted him here or not, he needed to know his father cared. He whistled and waved. Heads turned, Jeremy's among them. The boy's face went slack, his gaze shooting from Nick to just beyond.

To Marianne.

Nick's jaw tensed. That hateful woman. She had that boy so freaked out, so fed with lies, he couldn't even acknowledge his father's presence without first checking with his mom. When Jeremy turned around without so much as a smile, Nick slumped his shoulders and stepped away.

He didn't blame the boy. Marianne had declared Nick the enemy and was, ultimately, forcing Jeremy to choose between parents. Interacting with Nick would be viewed as betrayal. Poor kid. If only there was some way Nick could make things easier on him. But until the whole custody deal played out, there was nothing Nick could do but show up.

Hopefully, that meant something.

He aimed his camera and took half a dozen shots, then meandered to the concession stands for drinks—soda for him, Gatorade for Jeremy.

"Nick?"

He turned to see Tammy coming down the walk dragging a cooler with one arm, a chair tucked under the other. Becky followed, staring at her phone. She stumbled over a crack in the sidewalk, color seeping into her cheeks.

"Hey." Nick strolled over, greeting them both. The wind stirred a stray lock of hair against Tammy's forehead, and he fought the urge to brush them away. "Your boy playing?"

She nodded and pointed to a pack of kids spread across a vacant patch of grass. "Manning first base today."

Nick raised an eyebrow. "Impressive."

"Yours?"

He nodded. "This is his first season." He swallowed, tears pricking his eyes. "Following his older brother's footsteps."

Tammy's smile faltered, and her eyes softened. "I'm sorry."

He shrugged and gazed toward the south field where his son was warming up. "Perfect day for a game, huh?"

Tammy gazed toward the cloudless sky and smiled. "Absolutely."

"Yay." Becky's eyes sparkled as she looked toward a group of people sitting along the edge of the field. "Mackenzie's here." She turned to Tammy. "Can I hang with her?"

"Go." Tammy shooed her off, then faced Nick. "Where are you sitting?"

"Haven't found a place yet."

"You up for company?"

His gaze fell on her pink lips—the lips he once came close to kissing. "That would be great." He slipped his hand over hers on the cooler handle, then gently nudged hers aside. "Let me get this."

He took her chair as well, and they strolled side by side along the edge of the field and up a gently sloping hill. They were able to see both of their sons' fields. While Tammy fished for sodas, Nick readied his camera.

"Oh." She slapped her forehead. "I totally forgot my camera. I guess I'll have to use my phone."

Nick smiled. "I'll share." His face turned quizzical. "What is it?"

"Seems strange . . . We've lived in adjacent towns all this time, our boys play in the same league— "

"Actually, this is Tylan's first year playing."

"Even so, seems odd we never ran into each other before . . ."

"That night in the hospital."

He nodded, then pulled at a blade of grass, gazing across the field as if deep in thought. Probably reliving that night and all that led up to it and had happened since. Tammy wished she knew of something to say to ease his pain, but before she could try, he changed the subject to a baseball game he'd played, back when they were kids.

The rest of the morning passed pleasantly, the summer sun shielded by white puffy clouds. They talked about old times, friends from school—where they were now and what they were doing—and a bunch of random stuff like where to find a great steak. Nick considered asking her to dinner, but he hoped Marianne would let him have Jeremy tonight. Possible but unlikely, considering that a date had been set for their custody hearing. And the judge had denied Marianne's request for an extension—finally.

Jeremy's team struck out and jogged to the outfield. They were down 6-0, and he still hadn't had a chance to bat. In the adjacent field, Tammy's son seemed to be doing better, boasting three base hits.

Tammy leaned back, legs outstretched. "How are things with your restaurant?"

"Okay, I guess." He plucked a blade of grass, twirled it between his fingers. "The insurance company's dragging their feet. They'll pay for all repairs, minus my deductible. But they're making me fight for everything else, like replacement costs, cleaning expenses, and loss of business. Then there's the city with all their inspections and forms."

"When are you hoping to open?"

"By the end of the month." Any later and he'd have to seriously consider filing for bankruptcy. Still might, if the insurance checks didn't start coming in. "How about you? Work going well?"

She sat up and hugged her knees. "Well, I found a sitter, so that's a major praise." She told him about her old one and a series of interesting nanny interviews that followed.

Chuckling, Nick shook his head when she got to someone named Ms. Pura. "Crazy." He sobered. "That must be tough, finding and juggling childcare."

"It is. But all I can do is trust God. Remind myself that He loves my kids even more than I do."

His heart ached as he thought of Payton lying in the hospital bed with tubes and wires attached. Why hadn't God protected him that night?

"You all right?"

He turned to see Tammy watching him, her eyes filled with compassion. "What were you saying?"

"So anyway, I ended up hiring a college kid. She's not as mature as I'd like. Watches some questionable television, hopefully once the kids are in bed. Tylan and Becky seem to like her, although Becky's not too thrilled with a sitter, period. Thinks she's old enough to man the home." Tammy shook her head. "That'd be bundled chaos."

"You know, they can always stay with me."

Tammy studied him for a long moment, then smiled. "That's sweet of you. I appreciate the offer, but . . ."

The crowd roared. Nick looked at the field in time to see players forming their "good game" line. Jeremy lost, which meant he had one more shot to make the playoffs. His next game would make or break his team.

Nick stood. "Guess that's it." He watched Jeremy shuffle back to the dugout. "I'm gonna see if I can give my boy an encouraging word or two."

Tammy rose. "Hold up. I'll come." Tylan's game was near over as well, and it appeared he'd been benched for the remainder of it. "I need to corral Becky anyway."

He helped her gather her things, once again insisting on carrying them for her. When they reached the bleachers, she hung back with a soft smile. "Call me?"

He nodded, reluctant to turn away. Sweet Tammy. He was so grateful for her friendship.

Nick turned to find Marianne watching him, her face pinched like she'd swallowed a slug.

Here we go. Breathing deeply, he squared his shoulders and approached with what he hoped resembled a smile but felt more like a grimace. "Marianne." He extended a hand to her boyfriend. "Wade."

Marianne slung her purse over her shoulder and stared past him. She started to move around him, but Nick blocked her. "I'd like to take Jeremy out for ice cream. Maybe a movie."

She shifted icy eyes back to Nick. "We've got plans."

Stretching his fingers to keep them from clenching into fists, he fought to stay calm. "I have a right to see my son."

"That's fine. But not today. Like I said, we've got plans."

"When?"

She sighed. "I don't know. Maybe tomorrow."

"Fine. Tomorrow, three o'clock."

She blinked, her mouth twitching as if searching for an excuse.

Nick never gave her the chance. Seeing Jeremy leave the dugout, he hurried to reach him before Marianne did.

But she lurched like a crazy woman and grabbed Jeremy by the arm. "Let's go. Where are your things?"

Jeremy looked at him, and Nick offered a smile. "Hey. You played good."

"Thanks." Jeremy looked down, probably to avoid his mother's glare. Nick rested his hand on his son's shoulder. "How you been?"

Jeremy shrugged.

"Tell your father good-bye, Jeremy." She adjusted her sunglasses. "We need to go."

His son glanced up, and Nick gave him a sideways squeeze. "I'll see you tomorrow." The boy tensed beneath his embrace. "Maybe we can go to the batting cages."

It took all of Nick's self-control to release Jeremy knowing Marianne would be spewing lies the moment she and the boy were out of hearing range.

When, Lord? When will things get better? When will You rise up to my defense?

A soft hand slipped into his, Tammy's perfume sweeping over him like a soothing balm. "I could really use a few ginormous scoops of ice cream. How about you?"

Nick stared after Jeremy before turning to Tammy. "Ice cream? Yeah, sure. Why not?"

Leaving Nick waiting for her on the bleachers, Tammy crossed the field to where Tylan gathered with his team. Coach Thorton stood near the drink jug, mopping sweat from his brow and chugging lemonade. He was talking to Mr. Williams, the pitcher's father, a man notorious for his complaints. The coach never played his son enough, never gave him enough hits at bat, put him in the wrong positions.

Tylan lingered on the outskirts of a pack of kids clamoring around Lisa, the team mom, as she handed out bags of chips and Ziplocs of orange slices. Spotting Tammy, he left his post and dashed over.

"Is Dad here?" He looked around, his face hovering between a smile and a frown.

Tammy's heart ached. She dropped to one knee and placed her hands on his shoulders. "His meeting ran late, sweetie." She assumed . . . considering he hadn't had the decency to call.

Tylan's head drooped forward.

"You up for ice cream?"

He shrugged.

"Double scoop waffle cone. With sprinkles. And maybe we can stop by the gaming store to pick out a new Xbox game on the way home. Whatdya say?"

"Okay."

Her phone chimed. She glanced at the number—work—and suppressed a groan. "Hold on, little man." She ruffled his hair then answered. "Hi, Hanna. What's up?"

"Midwest Hospital just received a potential donor. A thirty-five-year-old male, subarachnoid hemorrhage. Name's Quincy Long."

"Okay. I'll contact the hospital." She ended the call and faced Tylan. "Give me a minute?"

"Then we'll go to get ice cream?"

What could she say? The boy didn't need another letdown today. "I hope so."

Tylan plopped on the ground, cross-legged, elbows on his knees, chin propped on his fists. His thin eyebrows pinched together.

Tammy called the hospital and asked to speak to the nurse in charge of Mr. Long. But the nurse wasn't available, so she left a message. When she put her phone away, Tylan raised his head, hope glimmering in his eyes. "You gotta go to work?"

"Not yet." She searched the ballpark for Becky, then, not finding her, drew Tylan close in a sideways hug. "Come on, slugger. Let's go find your sister." She glanced behind her to find Nick watching her, elbows propped on the bleachers behind him. He smiled, causing her heart to skip a beat.

Draping an arm over Tylan's shoulders, she guided him to the sidewalk and past the concession stands. She found Becky with the Granges, standing in the shade of a sycamore tree. Wendy Grange was gathering food items, tossing some in a plastic bag, dropping others in an opened cooler, while her husband talked to their son a few paces away.

"Hi." Tammy smiled first at Wendy, then Becky.

Wendy straightened, crushing a soda can. "Hi, good to see you." She nudged Tylan's shoulder. "Good game?"

He shrugged, watching Mr. Grange and the father-son interaction play out before him.

Tammy wrapped a protective arm around her son. "They won."

"Way to go." Wendy raised her hand, and Tylan gave her a weak high-five.

Becky sauntered over. "Where's Dad?"

Heat flooded into Tammy's cheeks as all eyes turned to her. "We'll talk later, honey."

Becky's face hardened. "Why don't we talk now? Because if he's not coming—and he's not, right?"

"I said we'll talk." Offering a sheepish smile to Wendy, Tammy grabbed Becky's wrist and pulled her aside. Tylan followed. "He's running late, but I expect . . ." him not to show, or to pop by late this evening, snag the kids for an hour or two.

Becky rolled her eyes. "Like I said, he's not coming. You know, if you'd quit nagging him all the time, maybe he'd come around more."

Tammy tensed. "That's not fair or accurate." But Becky knew that. She was mad and looking for someone to lash out at, someone to blame. Tammy breathed deeply to keep her emotions and words in check. "We're going out for ice cream. How's that sound?"

Becky crossed her arms. "I'd rather go to Mackenzie's."

"Sorry, hon, but it's your dad's weekend."

"News flash—he's not here."

Tammy sighed and pinched her bottom lip between her thumb and index finger. She could make the kids wait all day on the off chance Brody might actually pull through. Or she could let Becky have some fun and, hopefully, forget about the visit entirely.

She glanced up to find the Granges standing in a clump, loaded down with their gear, watching her and Becky. "Did they invite you?"

"Yeah. To dinner and a movie."

"Fine. Go." Spending an afternoon with a functional family—seeing a healthy marriage—would do her daughter good.

After sharing parting words with Becky and the Granges, Tammy led Tylan back across the field. He quickened his pace when he saw Nick.

"Hey, bud." Nick stood and fist-bumped Tylan's shoulder. "That's some swing you got. Three base hits? Not too shabby."

Tylan gave a shy smile. "You saw me?"

Nick nodded. "Saw you drive the ball to the outfield like a pro."

The three walked to the parking lot, Tylan in the middle, chatting about his next game. By the time they reached the car, he'd moved from the playoffs to the pros, which, of course, he planned to play in one day.

"My dad's going to teach me how to throw a fast ball." His voice lowered to a near mumble. "Once I get my regular pitch down."

Tammy and Nick exchanged glances before he shot her son a wide grin.

"You know, I played a little ball back in the day. They called me Zipping Zimmerman on account of my smoking arm." He rotated his arm in a mock wind-up motion. "I can show you a few tricks after ice cream, if it's all right with your mom."

"Really?" Eyes wide, he looked at Tammy.

She laughed. "We'll see. I'm waiting for— " Her phone chimed, and she raised it. Nick nodded.

"Tammy Kuhn."

"This is Lori from Midwest Hospital returning your call."

"Yes, hello. Can you please provide information on Quincy Long?"

"Sure. Initially, in the emergency room, he was unresponsive, but now that he's in the ICU, he is slightly improved. He's waking up and following commands for us now."

"That's great news for that patient and his family." Tammy grinned and gave Tylan a thumbs-up sign. "Please let me know if anything changes in his condition." Tucking her phone in her back pocket, she strolled over to Tylan and pulled him close. "Looks like we've got the afternoon free, kiddo."

"Yay!" He bounced on the balls of his feet.

She turned to Nick. "How about if I meet you at Baskin-Robbins?"

"Sounds like a plan." Nick flashed a wave and sauntered to his truck a few rows down.

Tammy climbed into the car and sat, hand on the key, key in the ignition.

She was falling for Nick all over again and dragging her son along with her.

"Mom." Sitting behind her, Tylan tugged on the back of her seat. "Can we go already? I'm dying hot."

She smiled and patted his hand. "Sure, sweetie." She cranked the engine and a gust of hot air blasted her in the face. "You know . . ." She swiveled to face him. ". . . about Nick."

What? Be careful not to get too attached? Did she really want to teach Tylan that people, men especially, couldn't be trusted? That'd guarantee therapy, for sure.

"Seat belt, please." She turned back around and eased out of the parking lot.

Her cell phone chimed as she pulled up to the ice cream store. She glanced at the number. Of course. Brody.

Nick stood on the curb waiting for her. Raising a finger, she answered the phone. "Hello?"

"Where are you?"

She bristled at the bite in his tone. "What do you mean, where am I? Where *were* you? You missed your— " She caught a glimpse of Tylan's face in the rearview mirror and stopped.

Outside, Nick continued to wait at the curb. He moved aside as a pack of tweens bustled out.

Holding her hand over the mouthpiece, she turned to Tylan. "Why don't you go in and pick your flavor."

"Flavors? I get two scoops, right?"

Tammy nodded. "I'll be there in a minute." She waited until the door shut before resuming her conversation. "You missed your son's game, Brody. Again."

"Quit the melodramatics, Tammy. I make it to plenty of games—just last week, in fact. Or did you conveniently forget about that one?"

Tammy snorted. "Right. When you showed up for a few hours, then bailed. I remember."

"I don't have time for this. Are you going to let me see my kids or not?"

"Let you? Let you? You're unbelievable, you know that?" She leaned her head against the headrest and sucked in a calming breath. "Meet me at my house in an hour."

"Thirty minutes."

"An hour, Brody. I promised Tylan ice cream, and unlike you, I keep my promises."

Chapter 31

Tammy pulled to the curb outside the Grange's house, strangling the steering wheel. She was tempted to turn around, call Brody back and tell him it was too late. That they'd made other plans. He couldn't expect her and the kids to spend their time waiting for him to decide whether or not he wanted to show up.

But that was exactly what he expected, and Tammy sitting here, ready to pull Becky from her friend's place, fueled the problem.

She twisted in her seat to look at Tylan. "You stay here. I'll get your sister."

His head bobbed, his eyes glittering at the prospect of seeing his father. Traces of chocolate ice cream lined his grin. How long before Brody, with his no-show, lying, conniving attitude, snuffed Tylan's joy?

A jolt of adrenaline shot through her, igniting her nerves. *Lord, this isn't fair. They don't deserve this.*

After one last glance at her sweet boy, she slipped from the car and hurried up the flower-lined walk. The grass, a lush green, was cut and edged, not a weed in sight. Two spiral trees, perfectly groomed, flanked the front steps. Stained glass panels framed the mahogany door. A plaque with the words, "Home is Where Love Resides," hung above a brass knocker.

Straightening, Tammy rang the bell, then waited.

She rang again, and this time, approaching footsteps followed.

The door opened, and Mrs. Grange stood before her with a raised eyebrow. "Tammy. Is everything okay?"

"Yes, thank you. I need to pick Becky up a little early, is all. I tried to call, but she's not answering her phone."

Stepping aside, she motioned for Tammy to enter. "Come in, have a seat. I'll go round up the girls."

Tammy glanced behind her. "My son's in the car."

"Oh, all right."

Tammy waited on the stoop while Mrs. Grange disappeared down the hall. She returned a few moments later with a scowling Becky. Mackenzie followed, also frowning, although it appeared she was trying to hide it.

Becky crossed her arms. "I just got here."

"I know, sweetie. But your dad called."

"Yay for him."

Tammy blushed at the edge in her daughter's tone. "Let's go." This wasn't the time or place for a loser-dad or you-drove-him-to-it conversation. She never knew which direction Becky's frustrations would take. "We'll talk in the car."

But her daughter wasn't interested in talking. As soon as she got into the car, she yanked out her cell phone and began texting.

Brody was waiting in the driveway when they arrived home. He leaned against his vehicle, while his latest girlfriend primped in the passenger seat.

Tammy eased into the garage. She'd barely put the car in park before Tylan scampered out, slamming the door behind him. She and Becky exchanged glances, a mixture of emotions clouding her daughter's face, making her appear five years younger.

She squeezed Becky's knee. "Have fun."

Becky held her gaze and swallowed. Then, clutching her cell phone as if it were her lifeline, she got out and strolled across the yard. After pulling the kids' overnights from the trunk, Tammy followed. Each step heightened her tension level sent her rolling stomach into near convulsions. Her gaze shot to Brody's girlfriend like a paperclip to a magnet. Shiny blond hair free of gray, smooth complexion . . .

"Hey, how's my beautiful princess?" With one arm draped over Tylan's shoulder, Brody wrapped the other around Becky and kissed the top of her head. "You up for some fun and sun at the lake? I've got a roaring bonfire planned with enough s'mores to give you both a bellyache." He poked Tylan in the gut, producing a giggle.

Becky's stiff stance relaxed, and a hint of a smile emerged.

Tammy handed over the duffel bag packed with the kids' gear, her heart aching at the emotional war she knew raged within her daughter.

She gave each of her children a hug in turn, reluctant to let go. "Don't forget to say your prayers and read your Bibles. I packed them in your bags."

Becky gave her signature eye roll and mumbled her consent. Tylan nodded. Neither would remember, and Brody certainly wouldn't remind them. Tammy felt like she was sending them off to Babylon.

Lord, please watch over them. Protect their tender hearts.

After giving both kids enough hugs to insulate them from whatever emotional blows that were to come, Tammy shuffled inside.

She headed straight for the freezer, reached for a tub of ice cream then stopped. Her stomach was still digesting the double scoop, chocolate mint she'd eaten earlier. Carb-comfort out, she opted for housecleaning instead. Unfortunately, her fragmented mind led to fragmented cleaning and she flitted from one task to the next without accomplishing anything. After thirty minutes of tail-chasing, she turned on the television and sank onto the couch.

It didn't help. Her emotions were too wound.

Vanessa.

She muted the television and dialed her friend's number. The call went to voicemail. She called Mom next.

"Tammy, how are you? I got your message, dear." Voices rumbled in the background, a high-pitched laugh slicing through them. "Is everything going well? How are the kids?"

"With Brody."

"Oh. So he's back to playing dad now?"

"For this weekend, anyway." Muted laughter from at least four different people traversed across the line, her dad's grainy chuckle among them. "Is now a bad time?"

"We're in the middle of bridge club, but I always have time for you. Give me a minute to—"

"No, that's okay. I'll call you tomorrow."

"You know, we'd love to have you and the kids come for a visit. No nagging, no pestering, nothing but lots of home cooking and hugs and some cool evenings out on the old porch swing."

Tammy sank deeper into the cushions, envisioning herself sitting beneath the stars with an iced tea in hand, the kids surrounded by the predictable love of their grandparents. "That sounds wonderful. I'll look at my schedule. Enjoy your bridge club."

She dropped her phone on the cushion beside her and flicked through more channels—a police chase, news of a local shooting, some reality television show. Depressing. She grabbed her computer for some Facebook time, but the status updates in her newsfeed only added to her loneliness. Everyone was checking into restaurants, posting family photos, or getting ready to go out.

What was Nick doing? Was his house as quiet as hers? Maybe she should call him.

Or leave him alone.

If only she could control her emotions—or at the very least, decide how she felt about the man. Not that it'd matter. He was grieving the loss of his son, not looking for romance.

Her doorbell rang. She checked her clock. Who would come by now? An image of Jenson surfaced, giving her pause. Elder or not, the man had shown a bit too much concern lately. Enough to raise some uncomfortable questions. She shoved the thought aside and answered the door.

Vanessa stood on the stoop clutching two Burger Haven bags in one hand and a drink tray in the other. "Hey, I got your message. Was going to call you back. Figured I'd drop by instead."

The tension left Tammy's shoulders and tears sprang to her eyes.

Vanessa's brow furrowed. "What's wrong?"

Tammy followed Vanessa's gaze past her to the messy living room. The vacuum stood near the couch where Tammy'd left it, cord snaked across the room. A half-folded mound of laundry sat on an armchair, also where Tammy'd left it. A mop and broom were propped against the kitchen entry.

She motioned her friend in and closed the door behind her.

Vanessa set the food items on the coffee table next to a dust rag and can of Pledge. "Looks serious." She cocked her head. "Hmm . . . no screeching monsters or electric guitars. Where are the kids?" Sitting, she glanced from the pile of laundry to the vacuum. "Never mind. The better question is, where's the ice cream?"

Tammy groaned and placed her hand on her stomach. "I'm sugared out." She sat beside her and took one of the food bags, the scent of French fries wafting to her. "So, how was your trip?" She grabbed the fries and started munching.

Vanessa pulled out a wrapped burger. Staring at the shiny paper, she pulled it off bit by bit.

Vanessa's sudden fascination with fast-food wrapping provided answers enough. Tammy sighed and dropped her fries back in the bag. "When do you start?"

Vanessa set her burger aside. "Next week."

"That soon? What about your house? You're going to sell it, right?"

"I'll sign it over to the relocation company." Her eyes softened. "I'm sorry, Tam. I know the timing stinks."

Tammy shrugged. "Story of my life. First Brody, now you."

Her friend pulled back as if she'd been punched. "That wasn't fair."

Tammy slumped forward. "You're right, and I'm sorry." She forced a smile. "I'm happy for you, really. I'm just having a rotten day."

"Wanna talk about it?"

"What's there to talk about? Brody. That says it all, right?" She picked up Becky's *God's Girl* devotional from the coffee table, then let it drop. "Seriously, how am I supposed to raise godly kids when their father is the epitome of sin?"

Vanessa stared at Tammy, expression taut.

"What?"

She shrugged but her face didn't relax. "Just worried about you."

"I'll be fine. I'm a fighter, right?" She raised her fists in a mock boxer pose and tapped Vanessa's shoulder.

"Maybe it's time you quit fighting."

"What're you talking about?"

"This isn't your battle, Tammy. Let it go—your fears, anger, the bitterness that's consuming you. Trust God. He'll take care of this—your kids. I promise."

Pressing her lips closed to keep her anger in check, Tammy nodded.

Chapter 32

At his restaurant, Nick stood in the center of the kitchen, thumbs hooked through his belt loops. He glanced at the newly tiled wall behind the newly purchased stove. "Looks great." He stepped back to inspect the sprinkler heads above him.

Rictor did the same. "Nice work, fellas."

He and Nick walked the crew out, then lingered near the back entrance.

Rictor rested his shoulder against the doorframe. "So, we're all set, then?"

Nick nodded. "As soon as the health inspector gives us his seal of approval, which I hope happens any day now."

"Want me to place an ad with a few local radio stations?"

Nick rubbed the back of his neck. That'd cost a pretty penny, but he didn't have much choice. "Yeah, go ahead. And . . ." He pulled a business card from his back pocket and handed it over. "Give these guys a call."

Rictor read the card with a raised eyebrow. "A television commercial?" He let out a low whistle. "You got the capital for that, man?"

"Gotta do something." He needed a successful reopen followed by a steady stream of business. Sometimes it takes money to make money.

"Can't hurt, I suppose." Rictor tucked the card in his back pocket and ambled out, the heavy metal door clicking closed behind him.

With one last glance around, Nick turned off the kitchen lights and returned to his office. He crossed the room and sat at his desk, the two photos of his dad spread before him. Three boxes pulled from his grandpa's storage locker sat to the right of his feet, the contents spread out. There were old grade cards, a high school diploma, an English journal dated 1955, but no death certificate. Not that it would be a keepsake.

He picked up the brochure for Safe Haven Ministries, flipped it over. Holding his phone in one hand and the pamphlet in the other, he read the information printed on the back. *"A safe place where the less fortunate can come to find love, hope, and healing."* Rather vague.

Obviously, this organization had been important to Grandpa. Important enough that he'd made provisions to continue his donation after his death.

Nick dialed the number printed on the back.

A woman answered. "Good morning, Safe Haven Ministries. How may I help you?"

Nick cleared his throat. "Yes, I . . . What exactly do you do?"

"Excuse me?"

"Your ministry? What is it for?"

"Are you in need of assistance, sir?"

"What? No. Uh . . . What kind of assistance do you offer?"

"We provide for the physical, emotional, and spiritual needs of the local homeless community."

Nick's stomach churned as his gaze fell to the 1976 photo of his dad.

Was that why? Was his dad . . . ?

No. Of course not. The two weren't related. Grandpa was a generous man; that was all.

But it wouldn't hurt to check the place out.

Tammy pulled into the Flaming Mesquite's parking lot and cut the engine. She checked the time on her dash. 8:30 a.m. Becky was twenty minutes into Spanish class and Tylan was most likely headed to PE.

Her phone chimed. She glanced at the number. "Hi, Arlene."

"Hey, did you get that material I forwarded from the Davenport family?"

"Yeah. I have everything with me now."

"Great."

She flipped open her manila file one last time. A note written by the recipient's mother lay beneath a photograph. Tears pricked her eyes as she viewed the picture. Smiling faces crowded around fourteen-year-old Rustin Davenport, the recipient of Payton's liver. Propped in a raised bed, the teen wore a toothy smile. His blue eyes sparkled beneath his thick curly hair. Other teenagers leaned over him, facing the camera, some with their tongues stuck out, others with eyes crossed.

A girl with auburn hair held two fingers behind Rustin's head. His mom and dad stood on his right, Dad with an arm draped over Mom's shoulder, Mom touching her son's arm. Two teens standing on either side of the bed held the ends of a handmade banner signed with at least thirty names. In red ink they'd written, "Rustin Rocks Rhinos!" Below this, someone had drawn a lopsided picture of the animal.

Rhinos? Tammy laughed.

She removed the Xeroxed letter, all identifying information blacked out, then closed her file. She placed the file on the back seat and the letter in her tote. She looked at Nick's restaurant. The windows were dark, the front door closed. His car was parked a few feet away.

Her stomach fluttered as she neared the entrance.

Tammy Kuhn, what's your problem? You two are friends. Nothing more.

If she couldn't remember that, she needed to turn back around and let someone else take this case.

She reached for the door. Just as it swung open, startling her. She stepped back a moment before Nick barreled out.

His eyes widened. "Oh, excuse me." He studied her, although whether with amusement or irritation, she couldn't tell. "I was about to leave."

"Oh. I brought you . . ." Clutching her tote, she bit her lip. Maybe now wasn't the best time.

"I'm heading to Birch County. It's an hour and a half east, toward Topeka. Wanna come?"

Tammy's heart skipped. Except he was only being polite. Right? But when she looked into his eyes, the raw vulnerability displayed within them tugged at her. Wherever he was going stirred up something—something raw and painful. He'd need emotional support. "Sure."

Once inside his car, he engaged the engine and pulled a pair of sunglasses from the console. "I should probably tell you where we're going." Donning his glasses, he wiggled his wallet from his back pocket and flipped it open. "I found some pictures in an old box tucked high on a shelf in the restaurant." He handed them to her.

Manila folder resting securely in her lap, Tammy studied the photos. She pointed to the chubby-cheeked child. "That you?"

Nick nodded and tapped the image of a man in a ball cap. "And I'm pretty sure that's my dad."

Tammy stared at him, any cohesive words clogging her throat. "But I thought . . ."

"He died in the war? I know. But apparently," he picked up a photo and flipped it over, revealing a date on the back, "he didn't."

"So, what're you going to do? Try to find him?"

He raked his fingers through his hair, then shook his head. "No chance of that, after all these years. But I would like some answers. My mom's not giving me any. I hardly know my aunt, so I figured I'd do the next best thing."

"Which is?"

He grabbed a folded brochure from his other pocket. "Find out if this place," he held it up so she could see it, "a ministry my Grandpa seemed to care an awful lot about, knows anything." He glanced at the file in her lap. "Whatchya got there?"

Tammy looked into his eyes, warmth flooding through her. "Arlene received a letter from your son's liver recipient this morning." She handed it over. "They wanted you to have it."

Nick took it in trembling hands, opened it slowly. For a moment, he appeared to quit breathing; he sat so still. "Can we pray?"

"Sure."

He reached across the center console to grab her hand, his strong and warm over hers. Drawn to him more in this moment than any other in all their years, she watched him from the corner of her eye. So vulnerable yet immensely strong as he unveiled his heart to his Creator. And his words, spoken in a hoarse whisper peppered with unshed tears, stole her breath.

"Holy Father, what a precious gift You've given this boy—the gift of life. I believe You saved his life for a purpose. Lord, draw his heart to You, reveal to him Your gift of salvation."

When the prayer concluded, Tammy studied him, at a loss for words. What had happened to the Christian-mocking teen she once knew?

The same thing that had happened to her. He'd found Jesus.

And now, they'd found each other. Could God be in this? Stirring her heart, rekindling their old flame?

Dare she even hope for such a thing?

Chapter 33

Dark clouds invaded the sky, threatening rain. Nick followed his GPS past brick buildings with blue awnings and through the historic district. As he continued south, the quaint structures gave way to apartment complexes with barred windows and rusted fire escapes.

A man with tattoos covering his shaved head and neck stood on the street corner. Two other men—one in jeans without a shirt, the other wearing a T-shirt with the sleeves torn off—stood on either side. Chiseled faces set in a scowl, they watched Nick's car as it passed. Instinctively, he hit his door lock button.

He glanced at Tammy who watched a woman dressed in a tank top and cargo pants pour water for her dogs. A paper bag sat beside her, a raggedy blanket beneath her.

Nick's stomach tensed as he thought about Safe Haven, his grandpa's donation, and the pictures of his dad. There couldn't be a connection—at least not in the way he was thinking. There's no way Grandpa would've allowed his son to live like that.

Rounding the corner, Nick watched the men and women sitting on the sidewalk or on bus stop benches—people's mothers, fathers, sisters, daughters.

"Arriving at 345 Holmes, on your left," the GPS cut into his thoughts.

Slowing to an idle, he scanned the street on either side of him. To his right, a sagging chain link fence barricaded an auto-body parking lot. Men dressed in mesh tanks and torn jeans gathered near the shop entrance. Next to this, an empty lot. A handful of men and women, some wearing heavy coats despite the heat, others dressed provocatively, lined the sidewalk.

"I think that's the place." He pointed to a three-story brick building tinged a smoky gray. Trash littered the sidewalk, and a handful of men and women, milled around the front smoking cigarettes.

He glanced at Tammy. She sat ramrod straight, hands folded tightly in her lap, eyes ready to bug out of her head.

"You all right?"

She swallowed. Nodded. "I've just never . . . been to a place like this before." She rummaged inside her purse. After retrieving her phone and a small bottle of hand-sanitizer, she tucked her bag under her seat.

"You up for this?" Seeing the timidity flashing in her eyes ignited an urge to protect her, to shield her from the harsh realities displayed before them. "I can always drop you off at a coffee shop or something."

She shook her head. "No. This is my issue. Maybe God wants to teach me something."

"Okay. If you're sure." He looped around the building, finding a partially filled parking lot in the back.

It appeared to be a receiving area of some sort with a panel lift door flanked by a metal dumpster and large, plastic bins on wheels. Inside was a hoarder's dream: stacked boxes, bulging garbage bags, and bins filled to overflowing with clothes and other items.

"Here we are." Nick glanced around. "Although something tells me this isn't the entrance."

One of the workers, a man with a gray beard that reached midchest, glanced up and frowned. Setting his box down, he approached.

Nick lowered his window.

"You came in the wrong way." The man pointed a crooked finger, dirt caked around the nail and clogged in the folds of his knotted knuckle, to a sign a few feet away.

Nick smiled. "Sorry."

The man's thick eyebrows bunched over squinting eyes, as he surveyed Nick's car. "You here to drop off?"

"Actually . . ." Nick glanced at Tammy before returning the man's gaze. "We were hoping to come inside to maybe . . . talk with someone."

"About what?"

"About . . ." Nick cleared his throat. "A donation."

"Park over there." He pointed toward the far end of the lot.

Nick complied and, stepping out of the car, hung his glasses on his shirt collar. The man led them through the receiving area and down a narrow hall with numerous turns and closed doorways. After continuing up a cement stairwell, he deposited them in front of a glass-encased reception area.

A woman with dreadlocks shoved the security window open. "Can I help you?"

Nick shifted. "I, uh . . ." What? Wanted to nose around? Find out where all the money automatically withdrawn from his restaurant account went? He had every right, but that sounded cold. "I'm a donor, and I wondered . . ." He pulled his wallet from his back pocket and flipped it open. He produced the three photos—the one of him, his mom, and his dad; the one of his dad, much younger; and one of his grandpa—and set them on the counter. "Do you recognize these two men?"

She leaned forward and wrinkled her nose. "Nope." Leaning back, she crossed her arms.

Nick sighed and glanced around. A woman dressed in an oversized T-shirt mopped the tiled floor. Another sat on a bench holding an infant, an umbrella stroller in front of her. Across the way, a metal door stood closed, one of those security card swipes mounted beside it.

He turned back to the receptionist. "Is there anyone I can talk to? Maybe even get a tour of the facility?"

"Hold on, please." The woman grabbed a multiline telephone, pressed a button. "There's a donor here to see you." She hung up and swiveled her chair away from them and picked up a magazine.

Nick stepped back, looking from one closed door to the next. A click sounded, and a plump woman with black, chin-lengthed hair emerged.

"Good morning." She extended a hand with a smile that radiated from every part of her. "I'm Lois Pennington, director of Safe Haven Ministries."

"Nick Zimmerman, and this is Tammy Kuhn."

"What can I do for you?" Mrs. Pennington asked.

"I've—well, my restaurant has been donating to this ministry for going on thirty years."

"Thank you for your faithful generosity."

"It was more my grandfather's doing. He, or his estate executor, I'm not sure which, set everything up on automatic withdrawals."

"I see. Who was your grandfather?"

"Harris Zimmerman."

"Can't say that I know him, but doesn't mean much. I'm fairly new. Came on staff a few years ago."

Nick showed her his photos. "Do these men look familiar?"

She inspected the images and shook her head. "Not sure. Maybe, although I spend most of my time working with volunteers. I don't get out around the general population much. I can ask around if you'd like."

"Yeah, I would." He tapped the picture of his dad. "That's my father. I wondered if maybe . . . if . . ."

"If he ever stayed here?"

Nick swallowed. "If he had anything to do with my grandfather's donation."

"Let's ask bookkeeping. Maybe Peggy has more information on file."

Unfortunately, Peggy was out for the day and the woman filling in for her was new and only vaguely familiar with their computer system.

"Hmm . . ." Mrs. Pennington drummed her fingers on the counter. "Perhaps some of our staff will be able to point us in the right direction. 'Course, most of them are pretty green. We have a high turnover here, but I bet Miss Marsha can give you some information. Or at least direct you toward someone who can."

Nick and Tammy followed Mrs. Pennington to a large room with exposed venting and cement floors and walls. Men with shaggy hair and whiskered faces gathered around circular tables, some talking, others engaged in card games. A young man, clean-shaven with a cropped military cut, stood near a far corner, head bowed, hand clasped on another man's shoulder. Another staffer meandered through the tables pushing what appeared to be a juice cart. Although clean and well dressed, his face had a stoniness to it, his bony cheeks slightly sunken, suggesting he'd lived a hard life.

Mrs. Pennington caught Nick's gaze. "That's Mr. Agar. He came in as one of our general-pops, entered our rehab program, got his GED. After he completed our intern program, we hired him on as a full-time employee."

Nick raised an eyebrow, his perspective of the homeless suddenly challenged. "Impressive."

She smiled. "It's amazing what hope and love can do, my friend."

She glided across the room, pausing to say hello to residents along the way. Nick and Tammy followed, stopping in front of Mr. Agar.

Mrs. Pennington hugged the man. "You look well."

He gave a flicker of a smile.

"This is Mr. Zimmerman." She motioned to Nick. "He's trying to find someone."

Nick pulled his photographs from his back pocket and handed them to Mr. Agar. The man's brows shot up before his stony expression returned. "Whatdya want to know?"

Nick's mind went on full alert. "Do you recognize this man?"

Mr. Agar held Nick's gaze, a tendon working in his jaw. "Lots of men come in and out of these doors." Crevices deepened across his elongated forehead.

Nick pulled a business card from his back pocket. "If you think of anything . . . or see him." He handed the card over.

Mr. Agar took it in his thick fingers, studied it a long moment before giving a slow nod.

Mrs. Pennington flashed the man a smile. "Catch you later."

Following Mrs. Pennington out, Nick caught one of the male staffers—a wiry guy with black hair and a pug nose—watching him with an odd expression. The man seemed like he wanted to approach Nick, but then he turned and started conversing with someone else.

Nick and Tammy trailed Mrs. Pennington through the building, pausing to question various staff members along the way.

They must have talked with half a dozen people. Nick showed each one the photos, watching their faces for the slightest hint of recognition. Nothing. No one, it seemed, knew or remembered Nick's dad or grandpa. Mrs. Pennington made color-copies of the pictures, promising to contact him should information arise. Then she led them back to the reception area.

"I'm sorry I couldn't be of any more help," Mrs. Pennington said.

He shrugged. "Not sure what I was expecting."

With a few more parting words, she left, and not knowing how to make it back to the receiving area, he and Tammy exited through the mission entrance. Standing on the cement stairs, he put on his sunglasses and gazed down the sidewalk.

Tammy touched his arm. "You okay?"

"Sure. Probably time I give up the fantasy, anyway. My dad's gone. Either he's dead or he wants nothing to do with me." A heavy weight settled in his chest—the weight of hopes stirred, then shattered. "You hungry?"

She smiled. "Starving."

A burst of cold air swept over them as the door behind them opened. A boxy woman with gray hair approached.

Holding a lighter in her mouth, she tapped the end of a cigarette package against her palm. "You looking for Randy?" Deep wrinkles spider-webbed her face, and her lips caved inward over toothless gums.

Nick stepped forward, a surge of anticipation shooting through him. "Yeah, you know him?"

She shrugged and wrestled a cigarette from her pack. She lit it, breathing deep before releasing a plume of smoke. "Who's he to you?"

Nick hesitated. "My dad."

The woman's gaze swept the length of him. "I seen him around. Been a while, though. Going on four years, maybe more." She took another drag off her cigarette, exhaling through her crooked nose. "Last I heard he was headed to Branson to find Jesus."

Nick frowned. "Branson?"

She gave a chesty laugh that ended in a cough. "On account someone told him that's where Jesus lived. Anyway," the woman tossed her cigarette on the ground, "he'll be back. They save a room for him, you know." With that, she turned on her heel and headed inside.

Feet bolted to the ground, countless questions swarmed Nick's brain as he watched her leave. Nausea swept over him as he closed his hand around his dad's dog-tags. The warm metal pressed into his palm as the woman's words pricked his heart. He looked at Tammy. "Can he really be alive? Is he . . . is my dad insane?"

Chapter 34

Standing at the kitchen sink conquering last night's dishes, Tammy glanced at the clock. 7:45 a.m. and still no pattering feet coming for breakfast. Her kids were exhausted—as usual—after their overnight with Brody. According to Becky, she and Tylan had stayed up until well after midnight the night before. Watching television. Unsupervised. Tammy cringed, thinking of all the late-night talk shows and infomercials they had likely been exposed to.

She heaved a heavy sigh and wiped her hands on a towel. Swallowing back the surge of bitterness that soured her stomach and set her nerves on edge, she headed toward her kids' bedrooms.

Becky sat on her bed, shoulders slumped, her diary opened in front of her.

"Hey, there." Tammy crossed the room and sat beside her. "What's going on, sweetie?" She resisted the urge to glance at what her daughter had written.

Becky lifted downcast eyes and gave a slight, almost indiscernible nod.

"Tough visit?"

She shrugged. Chewing on her pinky nail, she looked at her journal. "Dad's not a Christian, is he?"

A lump lodged in Tammy's throat. "No."

"That's why he . . . they . . . act the way they do."

Adrenaline surged through Tammy. "Did something happen?"

"No. He and his girlfriend are just different, that's all. They act so happy, but they're really not. I can see it."

The air expelled from Tammy's lungs. After all this time, all her fears, all Brody's irresponsible and ungodly behavior . . . Becky's revelation could only come from one place. Tears sprang to Tammy's eyes as she remembered the angry, faithless thoughts that had swirled through her head only days before. *Thank You, Lord.*

"I remember how the two of you used to fight."

That they had. Over church, tithing, what television shows the kids should watch, whether or not they needed to read their Bible. Though their marriage had been rocky from the start, the moment she chose to follow Christ, the battle lines had been drawn.

Becky traced her finger along the threading in her comforter. "Can we pray for him?"

Tammy's stomach soured. Pray for him? The man who'd betrayed her, abandoned her to raise her kids alone, who treated his children like . . . like . . . Her heart wrenched as she studied Becky's sweet face, her soft eyes, filled with tears. *Oh, my baby girl.* How could she teach forgiveness and love if she couldn't model it herself?

But she couldn't go there. Not yet. Maybe not ever.

Wrapping an arm around Becky's shoulder, she pulled her close. "You pray."

Becky nodded and dipped her head, her hair tickling Tammy's neck, just like when she was little.

"God, please save my dad so he and I can be close. So . . . so . . . he can quit having so many girlfriends and being so sad inside."

A simple prayer, but one that cut deep into Tammy's soul. Becky was right. The only way Brody could change—the only way he would ever be the dad her kids needed—was if God got a hold of him. What he needed wasn't a change of attitude, but a change of heart.

Tears surfacing, she pulled her daughter close and kissed her temple. "I love you." Holding her at arm's length, she looked into her daughter's beautiful eyes. "When did you get so grown up on me?"

Becky pulled away, the independent teenager in her resurfacing. "Whatever." She rolled her eyes, a hint of a smile showing through.

She squeezed Becky and stood. "You ready for breakfast?"

Her daughter nodded, the sparkle returning to her eyes. "Yeah."

She squeezed Becky's hand then sauntered to the kitchen. Tylan was kneeling on the counter, an overflowing cereal bowl beside him. Flakes splattered the counter and dirtied the floor. Face scrunched and using both hands, he held a jug of milk over his bowl.

"Hold on, buddy." Tammy rushed to his side. "Let me help you."

He relinquished the milk and climbed down, grinding cornflakes as he went. Tammy would clean it later, once she got the kids off to school.

Breakfast served, she moved to the kids' backpacks to check their homework logs. Grabbing Becky's notebook, she cast her a sideways glance. "You ready for your biology final?"

Becky stared at her cereal bowl. "I . . . forgot to study."

And Brody forgot to remind her. Tammy grabbed her daughter's textbook and plopped it on the table and opened to the unit review. "How about you study while you eat. And at lunch."

Becky sighed, then nodded.

Next, Tammy moved to Tylan's backpack. He never had much homework, and even less at the end of the school year. But the kid had more fieldtrips and parties—

Oh, no. His end of school party. Was that . . . ?

She dug into his backpack and pulled up a handful of wadded papers stuffed in the bottom. Among them was a flyer for his end of school party, today's date printed across it. Wonderful.

Hands on hips, she faced Tylan. "What time is your school party?"

He beamed, milk dribbling down his chin. "All day. Well, except for music class, 'cause of mean Mrs. Broadman."

What exactly had Mom volunteered for? Probably a gamut of things, all highly complicated. She'd call her in a bit.

"Are you making oatmeal raisin cookies?" Tylan talked over a mouthful of food. "The ones with coconut and cinnamon? Those are my favorites!"

"No, sweetie. I'll probably just hit the grocery store."

His bottom lip poked out, and his shoulders hunched forward as if she'd just told him they'd be skipping Christmas. Was he worried what the other kids might think? Like maybe all the cool kids brought home-baked goods?

She sighed. "Fine."

Tylan's head snapped up, his cheeky grin returning. It really took very little to make him happy, and she was off for the day. In truth, it'd be fun to participate in his little shindig. Although hanging out with the other moms might prove more of a challenge. She'd never seemed to fit in with those ladies.

The low hum of a diesel engine approached followed by the swoosh of airbrakes. Tammy spun around and stared out the window. Grabbing Tylan's backpack, she dashed out to signal the bus.

Frowning, the driver shook his head but waited long enough for Tylan to scamper out of the house and onto the bus. Becky followed a moment later to begin her short walk to school.

As soon as they left, Tammy called her mom. "Hey, I've got a question for you."

"Good morning to you, too, dear." The *Wheel of Fortune* theme song played in the background. "How has your week been? Have you given more thought to coming for a visit? We have Dover Days coming up, with games, carnival rides, and all sorts of food booths. I know the kids would enjoy it."

"Listen, Mom, remember how you signed up to help with Tylan's party?"

"Oh! Oh, my. Let me grab my—"

"No." Tammy spoke fast, hoping to intercede before Mom made it to the garage. "I appreciate the sentiment, but there's no time. I'm calling to find out what you volunteered for."

"Games and snacks. I thought I'd make caterpillar cupcakes. Do you know what I'm talking about? You divide yellow cake batter into four bowls, and using food coloring, tint each one a different color. Then you bake them as normal. Make sure to preset your oven to . . ."

Tammy kneaded her forehead. Why did Mom feel the need to explain every detail?

"You know what? I'll text you a picture and some instructions."

"Thanks, Mom. And the game?"

"Creepy crawlers." She giggled. "Now, this is an outdoor game. It's not going to rain, is it? If it is, I thought they could play

Buggy-charades. You'll need several pillows and beach towels, spray bottles filled with water . . ."

By the time Mom finished, promising to send various Internet links and photos, Tammy had a raging headache. And she was running short of time. Luckily, she had all necessary supplies on hand. Except her towels were a sad state — sun-bleached and threadbare from too much chlorine. Oh, well. It was a kids' party, not a five-star affair.

An hour later, she pulled into Pioneer Elementary's parking lot, vehicle loaded. Rounding her car to the trunk, she popped the lid and surveyed her mound of clutter.

Of course, one plate of cookies had toppled. Although the plastic wrap kept them contained, they were now a crumbled mess. Grabbing what she could — she'd need to make a second trip for the rest — she scurried across the parking lot to check in at the receptionist's office.

Her phone chimed. She tensed. Not now. Except today was her off day, unless Heartland had been flooded by a slew of referrals. Which would be just Tammy's luck. She set her items down and pulled out her phone. Ugh. The call center's number showed on her screen.

"Hello." She glanced down the school hallway, decorated with drawings and paper cutouts shaped like balloons and flowers.

"Hi, Tammy, this is Courtney. I need you to go to Children's Medical Center."

"Everyone else is out, huh?" She checked her watch, calculating the time it would take her to pop into Tylan's classroom, make afterschool arrangements for both kids, and reach the hospital.

Courtney laughed. "Believe it or not, things are pretty slow today. Knock on wood."

"Great . . . Then why are you calling me?"

"What do you mean?"

"You know I'm off today, right?" Tammy turned at the sound of giggling voices. A group of kids — maybe six- or seven-years-old, bounded around the corner, carrying paper lunch sacs covered in paint and glitter. A tall blonde wearing a rainbow-colored dress led them.

"No you aren't."

"I am. Check the schedule." Tammy held the phone between her ear and shoulder to free her hands to find her pocket calendar—just to be sure. Not that she hadn't reviewed her schedule umpteen times this week—enough to have it memorized.

"I . . . uh . . . Hold on."

"Sure."

Courtney returned to the phone a moment later. "I'm sorry. I guess I was looking at the wrong day."

"No problem." Tammy's heart lifted, a smile tugging at the corners of her mouth. She'd have the morning, uninterrupted, with her son. *Thank You, Lord, for these small blessings.*

By the time she made it to Tylan's classroom, the party was already well underway. The children—Tylan among them—milled around the room, sheets of paper in their hands. The other moms gathered in a corner, talking and taking pictures.

Tammy set her goods among the other desserts—cookies made to look like monkeys, pretzel sticks dipped in chocolate and colorful candy bits, sandwiches cut into puzzle pieces.

Marcia Neilson approached with a gentle smile. "Oatmeal and raisin?" She inhaled. "Looks wonderful. How have you been? I haven't seen you in a while."

Kind Marcia, always ready to embrace the outcast. "I've been good, but . . ." Tammy glanced around the room. "Can you excuse me for a moment? I've got another load to bring in."

"I'll help you."

"No need. I'll be just a minute."

After a quick hello to Tylan and his teacher, Tammy dashed out for her other items.

When she returned, heads turned her way, unhappy expressions on more than a few little faces. Tylan sat at his desk, shoulders slumped, face so flushed it looked ready to catch fire. A picked at oatmeal cookie sat on a napkin in front of him.

"Ew!" A girl with red braids spat a mouthful of food onto her plate.

Tammy surveyed the room, noting a handful of puckered faces. Others snickered, whispering to one another. Everyone looked at her. One of the other moms, a tall, blond with flawless skin and hair, regarded her with a slight, almost sardonic smile and raised eyebrows—like Tammy'd entered a formal dinner party dressed in pajamas.

Trisha, a boxy woman with long brown hair approached with a smirk, cinnamon raisin cookie in hand. "Do tell me, what did you put in these?"

"I . . ." Did she forget the sugar or something? Add too much salt?

Frowning, she marched across the room, grabbed a cookie, and bit off a chunk. She swallowed past a gag.

What in the—?

Snickers rippled through the classroom.

Little Billy Hanson slapped his desk. "That's awesome." He turned to Tylan and raised his hand in a high-five invitation.

Forehead crinkled and face still slightly red, Tylan looked at Tammy before unenthusiastically returning Billy's high five.

The distinct taste of chili powder clung to her tongue as she swallowed her grotesque bite.

Then like a slow-motion replay, she envisioned herself, frustrated and rushed, grabbing various spices from her cupboard and dumping them into the bowl.

Heat crept up her neck as realization dawned.

She'd swapped the cinnamon for chili powder.

Chapter 35

"Don't lie to me. I'm done with the games." Nick pressed his flattened hands against the surface of Mom's kitchen table to keep from fisting them. "What happened to Dad?"

Mom's gaze stopped near Nick's nose. "It's complicated."

"Right." Images of homeless men swam through his mind. "My dad, insane, living in . . . God only knows. All this time, I could've done something—could've helped him." He shook his head. "How could you? He's my dad. My dad!"

A tear slid down Mom's face. She wiped it away. "We married young. We'd only known each other a few months when they drew his number for Vietnam. He asked me to marry him. Said we needed to get hitched before he shipped out." She grabbed a napkin and balled it in her hand. "I was so young. Stupid. Starry-eyed. We got married a week later—down at the city hall.

"After he came back, he started acting strange, and he only got stranger as time went on."

"Not so romantic anymore, huh? Your husband comes back broke and you move on. Cut all ties."

She shook her head, more tears spilling over her lashes and leaving streaks of mascara on her cheeks. "It wasn't like that. I tried." She spoke between sobs, dabbing her redlined eyes with her wadded napkin. "To make things work, but he'd get so agitated. He had nightmares something awful, then they started happening during the day. He saw things, talked to people that weren't there. I got scared." She looked Nick in the eye. "Then he started talking about running away and taking you with him."

“That’s why we moved?”

She nodded. “He was so messed up. In the head. I thought he’d forget about us soon enough, or move on. He was always going somewhere—to Vegas, Nashville, Oklahoma.” She straightened. “Your grandfather was pretty upset. Wanted to see you. He talked me into moving back.”

“And keeping your secret.” Nick’s stomach soured. Grandpa lying about his own son. Lying to Nick.

“I was so scared, Nick. So very scared. Scared your dad would show up and take you from me. Scared you’d . . . you’d . . .”

“What? Be like him?”

She shrugged. “I didn’t know what was wrong with him—how it’d affect you. I read an article on children of sociopaths—”

“He wasn’t sociopathic, Mom. If anything, he was schizophrenic. You could’ve gotten him help.”

“I tried. You have to believe I tried.”

“He returned, didn’t he? At the beginning of my junior year? That’s why you yanked me out of school and across the state.”

She stared at him a long time before nodding. “I saw him at one of your football games, filthy, his hair all matted, beard, too. His clothes . . . He looked like a . . . a . . . vagabond.”

“You should’ve told me.”

“Can’t you see? I was trying to protect you.” She reached for his hand, but he jerked it away. “What was I supposed to do? I just wanted it all to be over, so we could move on. Have a normal life.”

“Which was it, Mom? Were you protecting me or yourself?”

“There a problem?” A low voice halted their conversation.

He looked over his shoulder. His stepdad stood in the entryway, eyes narrowed.

Nick stood, his chair screeching behind him. “I’ve heard enough. Now, if it’s not too late, I’m going to find my dad. Let him know someone cares.”

Tammy stood in Vanessa’s living room, partially filled boxes and reams of packing paper scattered around her. Her kids were in the kitchen, Tylan playing a video game, Becky with her cell phone, both devouring a bag of Cheetos.

Tammy and Vanessa had been friends—connected at the hip, people used to say—since their freshman year at college. They roomed together their junior year and had been inseparable since, going so far as to find employment in the same town.

Vanessa was there when Tammy first learned of Brody's affair. V stood by her as she fought to hold onto her marriage, ate large quantities of ice cream with her when Brody turned ugly and demanded a divorce. Cried with her on all those fearful nights when the reality of single parenting took hold.

Now she was moving twelve hours away. No more girls' nights or Sunday afternoon jogs. No more popping by for a hug and word of encouragement. Now Tammy truly would be all alone.

Except she had Nick. Maybe. But although her heart stirred for him, she doubted he felt the same. He was grieving, looking for comfort. And in she walked. She sighed and sat on the floor to wrap a stack of picture frames.

"You okay?" Setting a glass figurine down, Vanessa stood and crossed the room. She sat beside her and rested her head on Tammy's shoulder. "Gonna miss you, T."

"Me, too."

They sat in silence for a while, Vanessa's arm enveloping Tammy's shoulder, their heads touching.

Then Vanessa pulled away to look her in the eye. "You're going to be okay, right? Because I can always tell Mr.— "

"No." Tammy gave a dull chuckle. "I'm fine. Really."

"How's your babysitter working out?"

She shrugged. "Okay. She's young. Not as mature as I'd like. Does the bare minimum. But you know what they say about beggars being choosers."

"And Nick?"

Tammy's stomach did a little flip. "How many times must I whack my head against the same wall before I turn the other way?"

"You love him."

"Oh, Vanessa, why must my heart be so foolish? Did I learn nothing with Brody?"

"Not everyone's a cheater."

"I know, but . . ." She breathed deep and shook her head. "It doesn't matter. He doesn't love me. Never did. Which is why I have no business dreaming of what-ifs. But what I can't figure out—how can we stay friends when my heart won't respect my boundaries?"

Chapter 36

Nick closed his office door and stood behind his desk. Despite his best efforts and most fervent prayers, he still hadn't been able to spend time with Jeremy. Marianne said the boy didn't want to see Nick, that he was too traumatized. Of course he was, but keeping him from those who loved him wouldn't help the child heal. The boy needed counseling.

He picked up his phone. He'd left two messages on Marianne's voice mail, reminding her he had a legal right to see his son. No return call. Least, not from his ex. Tammy, on the other hand, had sent a text, asking how he was holding up.

Tammy was such a faithful friend. And he needed her. Needed her son, too. Tylan could be the friend that would help ease Jeremy back into father-son visits.

Did that make Nick manipulative? Selfish? Or desperate?

Probably all of the above.

Except it was more than that. He loved her. Had when they were teens, and he couldn't deny, that love had grown.

Dropping into his chair, he set the phone down and released a gust of air through tight lips. *Lord, if You want me to walk away . . .* His heart wrenched. *Show me. But I feel like maybe this is from You. Tammy came back into my life—during my darkest hour—for a reason. I don't know what the reason is, but I won't close a door You opened.*

He grabbed his phone again and dialed her number.

"Good morning." A muffle of voices and clanking drifted across the line.

Nick straightened. "Are you in the middle of something?"

"A cinnamon cream latte." Tammy chuckled. "I'm at Java Jones."

"Sounds delicious."

"I can bring you one."

An offer he almost jumped at, except the health inspector—hopefully—was due to arrive within the hour. "I wish I could, but actually . . . are you busy Saturday?"

"Nope. You wanna grab a Dew at the Gas-n-Go?"

"I've got Jeremy for the day, and I hoped, I thought maybe he and Tylan would get along."

"Oh." Her tone fell flat. "Yeah, sure."

His gut pinched. He'd offended her. He shouldn't have asked. But it was too late to take his words back now. "I mean, if you're not doing anything. I figured maybe we could go to Pizza Reos, my treat."

"Yeah. That'll be fun. I'm glad you get to see Jeremy."

"Thanks to an upcoming custody hearing. I imagine I'll hear all about it when I go to pick him up."

"Good luck with that."

"Zim-man?" Rictor poked his head into Nick's office.

"Listen, Tammy, I gotta go. Call you later?"

"Sure."

He hung up, motioning Rictor inside.

"Looks like the city's trying to get back at you for all your nagging phone calls. Sent Mark-up Marty to inspect the place."

Nick groaned. Marty Breeden was notorious for logging a long list of infractions at every restaurant he inspected. The guy had a power complex. Got pleasure from seeing owners, already stressed by the struggling economy and increased push for lower prices, sweat.

But Nick had nothing to worry about. Thanks to the fire cleanup crew, his place had been cleaned from top to bottom, corner to corner. All food items had been tossed and fresh ingredients ordered. Ads had been placed in local papers and a television commercial shoot was scheduled for Friday. Everything was set for their grand reopening Monday—depending on Breeden's findings.

Nick stood and crossed the room.

"You got this, man."

"*We* got this." Nick clamped his hand on Rictor's shoulder before slipping into the hall.

Rictor followed him to the kitchen where Mr. Breeden stood in front of the cook-line, electronic tablet in hand. Frowning, he examined the counter stacked with clean dishes.

Nick approached with a forced smile and extended his hand. "Good morning, sir. Thank you for coming out." In a very untimely manner.

Breeden accepted Nick's handshake with a grunt, his burly eyebrows casting dark shadows over his charcoal eyes. He ran his hand over the holding equipment—which was of course turned off—then lifted the lid. With a pinched expression that reminded Nick of Jeremy after a dose of cough syrup, the man leaned forward and inspected each bin. Then, as if disappointed, he made a wide sweep of the area.

He checked the supply inlets, the newly installed sprinkler system, and spent a great deal of time at the dishwasher. Again, Nick wasn't concerned. The cleaning crew had scoured the place, left it better than new. In fact, if this guy found anything other than a minor infraction, Nick would suspect foul play.

Breeden stopped in front of the dry goods area, read labels, checked dates, ran his hand across the dustless counter.

For the next two and a half hours, he scoured each nook, tile, and thermometer, using every opportunity to launch into a lecture on proper food handling. By the time he finished, the man seemed thoroughly disturbed at the lack of critical violations he found.

"Thanks for coming." Nick walked him to the door, anxious to be rid of the guy.

Mr. Breeden surveyed the restaurant one more time before shooting Nick a scowl. "I'll be back." He narrowed his gaze on Nick for a full two seconds before leaving.

When the door clicked closed, Rictor punched Nick's shoulder. "Way to go, man. Grand Reopening, here we come. Now we just gotta fill this place, huh?" He grabbed a stack of mail on the hostess podium and handed it over. "Oh, I forgot to tell you. Some guy by the name of Sherman Easton called. Left a call back." He pointed to a slip of paper lying on top.

Nick stared at the number, the memory of when he'd first met the guy—a property investor—rushing back. It'd been four and a half years—six months after Nick bought the place—since he sent the guy and his purchase offer packing.

But now the bills were mounting—insurance claims that still hadn't been paid, medical bills, lawyer's fees. How easy it would be to take the cash and walk. He'd been holding on to this restaurant, poured his life into it, for the sake of his grandpa's legacy. But where was Grandpa when Nick's mom robbed him of his chance to have a dad?

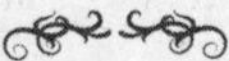

Night settled quietly over the house. A sleepy Tylan nestled under Tammy's arm, and a contented Becky curled in the corner of the couch as Tammy read aloud from her favorite book—*Hinds Feet on High Places*. It was an allegory about a woman named Much-Afraid and her journey to the mountain of God.

In their reading, Much-Afraid had just passed through "the shores of loneliness" only to be attacked by three of her enemies, personified as malicious relatives—Resentment, Bitterness, and Self-pity.

"That must have been hard," Becky said, "to hear Bitterness say all those things and not give in to the anger. But think of what would have happened if Much-Afraid had? If she'd listened to them and returned to the Valley of Humiliation, never having reached the High Places of God?" Becky dropped her gaze. "I wish life were like that."

"Like what, sweetie?"

"I wish our emotions—like anger and stuff—really were like people. Then we could just avoid them, or ignore them, or even walk away."

Tammy studied her daughter. "Is something wrong?"

Becky's eyes grew moist. "Why'd he leave, Mom? Why doesn't Dad want to be with us?" Her chin puckered. "I love him. I don't want to, but I do. And yet . . . I hate him at the same time." She stared at her hands, a tear sliding down her cheek. "I know that's wrong. The Bible says we should love. That if we don't love, we don't know God. But why does it have to hurt so bad? And how do I get rid of all this . . . anger I feel?"

Tammy pulled Becky close. "I don't know, sweetie. I don't know."

They sat like that for a long time, Becky nestled against Tammy's side, Tammy's chin resting on Becky's soft hair, Tylan quietly snoring.

I don't know how to do this, Lord. It's too hard. It hurts too much.

She thought of Nick, of his gentle smile and kind eyes. Of all the times they'd spent together, laughing, sharing some of their deepest fears, most humiliating secrets. To love again—to show her kids what a godly marriage looks like . . .

The kind she'd hoped to have with Brody.

What if she allowed herself to truly love Nick, truly trust him—what if her kids started to love and trust him—and he walked away?

Tylan's breathing deepened. His eyes roamed beneath closed lids, his smooth brows raised. The corners of his mouth twitched in what looked like the beginning of a smile. Tammy leaned over and kissed his forehead. "What are you dreaming of, sweet boy?" Most likely frog catching or something equally glamorous.

She glanced at the clock. 10:45, and well past both their bedtimes. Easing her arm out from under the children, she stood and turned to Becky. "It's getting late."

Becky frowned. "But I'm not tired, and I don't have school tomorrow."

Tammy's heart swelled. "This has been nice, hasn't it?" She ran her hand through Becky's soft curls then kissed her forehead. "Let's do it again soon." Turning back to Tylan, she slid her arms under him, bracing herself for his weight, and heaved. Nearly losing her balance, she bit back a giggle. A snickering Becky watched, eyebrows lifted.

Holding Tylan, his lanky legs dangling like anchors, his head dropped back, she wobbled from the room and down the hall. Her grip faltered. Fearing she'd drop him, she paused in his bedroom doorway to adjust her grip. A moment too late. As Tylan slid from her fingers, she bent her knees to catch him and landed on her rear.

Tylan jerked awake, still in her arms, her on the ground. With droopy eyes, he looked about, appearing to linger between reality and a dream world.

Tammy sat on the floor, laughter erupting. "My boy, I need to quit feeding you."

Footsteps shuffled toward her, Becky's soft laugh soon following. She shook her head. "You're so weird." She watched at Tammy and Tylan a moment longer before stepping around them and heading toward the bathroom.

"Love you, too." Tammy rested her chin on Tylan's head and closed her eyes. *Thank You for tonight, Lord. I needed this. We all did.*

With a contented sigh, she eased out from under Tylan then bent over him. She nudged his shoulder. "Hey, bud?"

He gave a soft moan, then rolled on his side, curling into a ball. Tammy knelt beside him and rubbed his back. "Sweetie?" She nudged again. "Come on. Let's get you to bed."

After a bit more nudging and back rubbing, Tylan awoke enough to shuffle into his room and flop onto his bed. Tammy grabbed a quilt and tucked it around him. She kissed his cheek. *Holy Father, watch over my son. Hold his heart in Your hands.* She thought of Brody, of his betrayal, of how often he let the kids down. Then she thought of Nick, of the deep pain he carried throughout his teen years, of what he dealt with now as he tried to find his dad. So much pain. Pain that could easily turn to hatred.

Were her kids headed for the same pain — the pain of not having a father?

Keep anger and bitterness far from them, Lord.

And from me. The thought came unbidden, like a jolt. The threat of tears followed. She shoved the thought and the emotions it evoked aside. With a deep breath, she strolled out.

In the living room, her cell phone chimed, eliciting a groan. Oh, well. At least she'd gotten a full evening with her kids. Personal need for sleep aside.

It rang again, and she hurried to answer it. Like she suspected, Hanna from the donation services call center.

"Hi, Tammy. I've got a twenty-four-year-old female, car accident with a subdural hematoma, heading to St. Francis Memorial. She's a registered donor."

"I'm on it." She ended the call, then scrolled to Stephanie's contact. Heading to the kitchen for a stale cup of coffee, she hit call send. It rang four times before going to voicemail.

Tammy's pulse increased. Why wasn't the girl answering her phone?

She sent a text then an email. *"I got called in. I need you to come watch the kids, please."*

While waiting for a response, Tammy dashed to her bedroom to trade her T-shirt and sweat pants for scrubs. Two minutes later, she was dressed and ready to go, and Stephanie still hadn't responded.

Tammy called again, hung up when voicemail came on, then called again. She tried four times, her tension level rising with each ring.

This was unacceptable.

Stephanie knew Tammy was on call tonight. She had explained, in explicit detail, the nature of her job and the need for her to be ready at a moment's notice. It was why Tammy paid what she did.

On her seventh call, Stephanie picked up. "Hello?" In the background music pulsated over the sound of laughter and voices.

"Where are you?" Tammy fought to keep her tone level.

"At a friend's."

"Why didn't you ans—?" As irritated as she was, there was no time for questions. "I need you to come over. Now."

Chanting spiked on the other end. Tammy held her breath and strained to catch the words. Her stomach rolled. "Are you at a party?" As if in answer, the noise level rose.

"Sorry. I can't hear you. Hold on. Let me go to the bathroom."

Tammy paced and checked the clock. She waited until the noise level abated. "Have you been drinking?"

Silence.

"Stephanie?"

"Just a beer or two, but no worries. I'll get a cab."

Tammy's grip tightened around the phone. "You've got to be kidding me. What in the—?" She slammed her mouth shut, biting back the words festering on her tongue. She spoke slowly. "You knew I was on call."

"But it's almost eleven. I assumed—"

"Unbelievable. I don't have time for this." Tammy hung up and resumed pacing. Now what? She glanced at the church directory on the coffee table and shook her head. She couldn't call anyone this late.

Her mom's voice sliced through her thoughts, taunting her. *"Then you wouldn't have to pawn your kids off on everyone else."*

Tammy sank into the couch. This wasn't working. No matter how hard she tried, how important her job, how many sitters she interviewed and lined up.

At this point, all she could do was call her co-worker, Nory. Tammy had covered for her a month ago when she got the flu. Hopefully, the woman would return the favor now.

Tammy dialed, knowing Nory would have her cell phone turned on and within reach.

She answered on the second ring. "Hello?"

"Hey, Nory, it's Tammy." She checked the clock on the DVR once again. She was running out of time.

"Hey. What's up?" Nory sounded cautious.

Tammy hated asking for help, or more accurately, shoving her responsibility on someone else. But what choice did she have? "Listen, I hate to do this, but . . . I'm in a bind." She explained her childcare issues. "If you could cover for me . . ."

Nory's breath reverberated across the line. She didn't speak right away, and when she did, her voice was dull. "Yeah, sure. Where'm I headed?"

Tammy exhaled, the tension seeping from her as she relayed the patient's information. "Thanks. I owe you one."

"No worries. I'm sure I'll be looking to cash in soon."

Tammy dropped her phone on the seat cushion beside her and rubbed her face.

She needed to find a new babysitter. Again.

Maybe Mom was right. She couldn't do this on her own anymore. If she moved to Dover, close to her parents, her childcare issues would be solved—for good.

But what about Nick?

Chapter 37

Nick stood at the rear wait station and surveyed the sparsely populated dining room. Mr. and Mrs. Wilkins sat in their usual corner booth sharing a Chinese chicken salad. Both drank water and asked for frequent refills of their breadbasket. Two women studied their menu in a window booth, and a handful of businessmen occupied a round table in the bar. Mrs. Jedlicka and her friends, all retirees who met for lunch once a week, sat across from the restaurant, sipping water. Not exactly the opening Nick had hoped for, but not catastrophic for a Monday, either.

Tad Lichtas, a new hire, approached with a serving tray tucked under his arm. "So, you think things'll pick up?"

Nick forced what he hoped to be an encouraging smile. "They should. We've got ads running on KCJY and WML."

"KCJY? Isn't that like, an AM station? Man, no one listens to them."

"No one under the age of twenty, perhaps. But those who go out to eat—and tip their servers—do."

A tense voice rose from the right side of the restaurant, and Nick turned to see Helen standing at Mrs. Jedlicka's table. The overhead light cast elongated shadows over the old woman's scowling face. Three other women affectionately known as the Lilac Ladies, on account of their obsession with all things purple, accompanied her.

"Excuse me." Nick gave Tad a parting nod and crossed the room. "Good morning, Mrs. Jedlicka. Ladies. Is there something I can help you with?"

Tiny lines fanned from the old woman's compressed lips. "Yes, I believe you can. As I was telling your waitress Helen here, I'd like my normal order of sweet-n-spicy meatloaf, divided onto two plates, and a cup of broccoli-cheese soup."

Helen crossed her arms. "And I told her we don't have meatloaf anymore."

Mrs. Jedlicka's face puckered further, loose skin nearly swallowing her narrowed eyes. "Young lady, I've been coming to this restaurant going on thirty years, well before you were born. Been ordering the same thing all that time."

"Times change." Helen tapped a pen against her order pad and glanced about, as if in a hurry.

"Well, I never." Mrs. Jedlicka grabbed her purse. She faced her friends who looked from her to Nick with wide eyes followed by apologetic smiles. Such sweet ladies. Why they put up with the likes of Mrs. Jedlicka was beyond him.

Nick donned what he hoped to be a warm and accommodating smile. "What Helen meant to say is we have made a few changes with our menu. I'm sorry for any inconvenience this has caused, but I'm sure we can figure something out." If he made concessions for one, soon everyone would come to expect it. But they had the time, and he certainly couldn't afford to turn anyone away, least of all his most frequent and loyal customers. "I'll talk to Chef Rictor."

Returning her barbed gaze to Helen, Mrs. Jedlicka folded her hands and settled back in her seat. "I appreciate that."

Helen huffed and followed Nick into the kitchen. "So what, we serve made-to-order now?" She started to stalk off.

"Wait a minute."

She whirled around and crossed her arms, head cocked.

Nick inhaled and exhaled slowly, waiting until he could speak calmly to continue. "Remember, the customer is always right."

"But she—"

"I don't care if she asked you to bring cow intestines on a silver platter. I expect you to treat her and everyone else who walks in here with kindness and respect. And if you have a problem, you come to me."

She rolled her eyes, "Whatever," and slipped back into the dining room. Most likely to flirt with the bartender, an action that was becoming increasingly frequent.

Leaving a simmering pot on the stove, Rictor wiped his hands on a towel and approached Nick. "When you gonna cut her loose?"

"I thought the extended layoff would take care of that for me." Nick chuckled, watching Marlow, his prep chef, slice tomatoes. "Any chance you can whip up some meatloaf?"

"Let me guess, Mrs. Jedlicka's not too thrilled about our menu changes?"

"Not exactly."

"Might be able to throw something together."

"Thanks." Nick's cell chimed, and his lawyer's number flashed across the screen. "You got things handled?"

Rictor nodded and returned to his sauté pans.

Answering the phone, Nick slipped down the hall to his office. "Mr. Cooper, is something wrong?" He closed the door. "You receive my psych eval back?"

"No. The report won't be sent out until ten days prior to the hearing." He paused. "I just got off the phone with Ms. Hawke's lawyer."

Nick held his breath.

"They've agreed to counseling."

He exhaled, a smile emerging. "That's great."

"There's one slight catch."

Nick huffed. "Of course. Leave it to Marianne to find a way to manipulate things in her favor." With absolutely no concern as to what was best for Jeremy. "What's she want this time?"

"To choose the mental health professional."

"No way. I'm footing the bill, right?"

"I know it's not optimal, but she won't budge."

"Meaning if I don't concede, it won't happen." Nick dropped into his office chair. Regardless of what happened between him and his son, the boy needed counseling. Besides, this was an important first step—the first concession Marianne had made in quite some time.

"Fine. Whatever she wants, just so my boy gets some help dealing with his grief."

Jeremy needed help dealing with all the fallout of Nick and Marianne's divorce as well, but that was a battle for another day. After the courts awarded Nick custody. Unless . . . "This won't come back to bite me, will it?"

"Do you mean, will the counselor testify in Ms. Hawke's behalf?"

"Yeah."

"There's no telling. Would you like me to withdraw our request?"

Nick closed his eyes, rubbed them. What kind of conniving quack would Marianne find? Or try to find. Surely a mental health professional would see past her tactics. Besides, he would be there to counter the lies and show the counselor, contrary to what Marianne led everyone to believe, that he wasn't a monster. He was man who loved his son. "No. It's fine. Tell her that's fine."

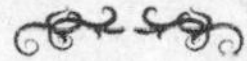

Tammy entered Heartland Donation Services' office complex as Heather was leaving.

Holding the door, the tall brunette flashed a smile. "What're you doing here? I thought you had the day off."

"Ellen called me in."

"Oh, right. The Nory thing."

"What Nory thing?"

"You haven't heard?"

"Heard what?"

Heather stepped back inside and glanced around as if checking for listening ears. "Guess she blew it big time."

"Like how?"

"Not sure, but I do know the attending physician was pretty upset." She glanced at her watch. "Anyway, I better go. I'm doing a community service deal this morning. Good luck."

Tammy's gut knotted as she watched Heather leave, and she fought a sudden urge to follow. Instead, she turned and steeled herself for the thrashing that was sure to come. Dealing with Ellen on a good day was hard enough. But after a hospital complaint, legit or not? Tammy would rather down a mouthful of antiseptic.

She tapped on Ellen's door before easing it open. "You wanted to see me?"

Ellen remained sitting. Frowning, she indicated the chair in front of her.

Crossing the room, Tammy struggled to meet her boss's narrowed gaze.

Relax. This isn't your issue or your fault—it's Nory's.

Tammy perched on the edge of her seat and cupped sweaty palms over her knees.

Her boss most likely would lecture her on dependability and punctuality. Tammy would apologize and assure her it would never happen again—although she still hadn't found reliable childcare. Ellen might hold a grudge for days, but she'd move on eventually.

She steepled her hands under her chin. "What's going on with you?"

Tammy shifted. "I'm . . ." Admitting she was between sitters would only make things worse. "What do you mean?"

"You were on call last Saturday, correct?"

Tammy nodded.

"You knew your schedule well in advance?"

"Yes, ma'am."

"Why did you ask Nory to take the call?"

"I didn't think it'd be a problem, ma'am. I covered for her when she had the flu, and I thought—"

"Your frequent inability to fulfill your responsibilities concerns me."

"I apologize. It won't happen again."

"I should hope not." Ellen leaned forward, paused. "Perhaps you need to consider whether or not you are still capable of doing your job."

Tammy snorted. "You are blowing this way out of proportion." Her temperature rose. She breathed deep in an effort to calm herself. "I had a . . . personal issue but I found a replacement. In a timely fashion. After all the hours I've put in, all the times I've picked up the slack, done your bidding, I'd think you could give me grace this one time."

"Unfortunately, that was not an isolated event but instead, an indication of a larger problem. Tell me about your new boyfriend."

"Boyfriend?"

"Mr. Nick Zimmerman."

Heat seared Tammy's cheeks. "He's not my—that's none of your business."

"It is when you're fraternizing with a donor's father."

"I resent your implication." Her fingers dug into her knees. "Not that I have to explain myself to you, but he's a friend from high school."

"I see." She pressed her lips together and stared at Tammy for a long moment. "I suggest you evaluate whether or not you're cut out for this job, Mrs. Kuhn."

"Great idea." Tammy sprang to her feet and stormed out, slamming the door behind her.

Chapter 38

Office door ajar, Nick sat behind his desk going over a recent sales report. Not the best reopening they could have had. Had the fire—Helen's screeching, the sudden evacuation, the temporary closing—cost him customers? People operated on habit. For years, this fact brought them to the Flaming Mesquite, but now? What if they'd found another restaurant to frequent?

Then he'd need to be diligent about finding new patrons.

He moved a pile of inventories off his desk calendar. The radio ads had gone out all week. Clearly money poorly spent—money he didn't have. A camera crew would be out next week to shoot a commercial. Another waste of much-needed funds?

They needed some kind of hook—some way to stir up a newsworthy buzz.

"Hey, boss?" Rictor poked his head in. "There's some guy here to see you. Name's Sherman Easton. With Sherman Properties and Investments." Rictor frowned. "There something I need to know about?"

Nick straightened the papers in front of him. No sense worrying Rictor over what could amount to nothing. "Send him in." When the time came—*if* the time came—he'd talk to Rictor and all the staff. "How're things out front?"

Rictor shrugged. "Wouldn't exactly call it steady, but we've got a few eaters. Hopefully the dinner rush will be better." He studied Nick for an extended moment, still frowning, then slipped out.

He returned a moment later with a stiff and starched Mr. Easton. The man was dressed in gray from his shoes to his tie. His hair—also a dull gray—resembled a 1950s bowl cut. He carried a leather briefcase.

Nick rose to meet him. "Thank you for coming."

"My pleasure."

Shaking his hand, Nick glanced at Rictor who remained in the doorway, arms extended in a slight Popeye stance. Clearing his throat, Nick excused him with a nod and closed the door.

He faced Mr. Easton. "Can I get you something? A soda? Water?"

"No, no, but thank you." The man surveyed the office. "Have you given my offer more consideration?"

"I have." It'd kept him up for three nights now, his angst increased with every low sales report. And still, the insurance payment hadn't come. He was beginning to think it never would.

"How much are you pulling in, say, over a week?"

"Before or after the fire?" Nick motioned for Mr. Easton to sit.

"Both."

Nick exhaled through tight lips. "We've never been a Green Olive." A five-star restaurant located in the heart of Old Town. "But we've held our own, thanks to our regulars." Most of their clientele were second and third generation customers. Adults who'd grown up eating blackened salmon and sipping the Flaming Mesquite's famous peach mango tea. Although since the fire, this "loyal crew" had dwindled.

Maybe they shouldn't have changed the menu or their slogan. He'd talk to Rictor about that later. Unless this meeting went well. Then there'd be no need.

"How much you in for?"

Nick glanced at a stack of mail—bills sandwiched between junk mail—on his desk. "A chunk of change." He was beginning to sound like a politician, but he had no intention of bearing his woes to this guy.

Mr. Easton nodded, and with elbows propped on Nick's desk, rested his chin on intertwined hands. "How much would it take for you to walk away free and clear?"

Nick ran numbers through his head—unpaid invoices, credit card bills, the mammoth insurance deductible, out-of-pocket expenses he'd covered waiting on his slug-of-an-insurance agent, the remainder of his initial purchase loan.

But what about Safe Haven Ministries—his dad's home base? "I've got an automatic deduction to a nonprofit—an important one. It's tax deductible. Set up by my grandpa. Any chance of negotiating that in the sale's terms?"

"Everything's negotiable." Mr. Easton moved his briefcase to his lap, snapped it open, and sifted through his papers. "I spoke with the board." He pulled out a formal offer printed on fancy paper. "See if these figures aren't more to your liking."

Nick reviewed the latest offer. The guy had gone up $25,000, exceeding the original purchase price by $70,000. 70K that would go a long way toward legal and medical fees, with a bit left over. Could he really sell Grandpa's restaurant? To a developer? The place would be torn down, and all the memories with it.

But what could he do? Each day he stayed open, bankruptcy loomed closer.

Either way, he'd lose the place. Besides, all those memories were based on lies.

"That's a generous offer." Nick studied the page one last time before standing. "I'll get back to you, sir."

"I understand this is a difficult decision, but be advised, the offer expires July 15th."

Nick nodded, the weight of his decision pressing down on him as he showed Mr. Sherman out.

The man had barely left before Rictor appeared, jaw clenched. "What's the deal, Nick? You ditching us or what?"

He didn't have answers or the time to give them. But he did have plenty to ask. Motioning for Rictor to enter, he closed the door, then moved to his desk. "I went to the Safe Haven Ministries."

Rictor stared at him for a long moment before giving a slight nod.

"My dad's been alive all this time, and no one told me. Grandpa, you, Mom, Gloria—God only knows who else was in on Mom's dirty little secret. You lied to me, Rictor. So did Grandpa." That was the hardest one to take—his grandpa, the man who had taught Nick how pray.

Rictor leaned back. "Far's I can see, your mom's the only one that spun a tale. The rest of us were just trying to . . . prevent your mom from jumping ship. All your Grandfather wanted was a chance to see you—to be part of your life. Had to follow your mom's rules in order to make that happen. Not that it helped any."

A lead anchor sank to the pit of Nick's gut as the memory of his junior year—the last time he saw Grandpa—came rushing back. He'd stopped by the restaurant after school, like normal, headed straight for Grandpa's office.

"Don't do this, Vicky." Grandpa's face looked drawn, tired, his eyes sad, almost desperate. He reached for Mom but she raised a hand and widened the distance between them.

"I can't do this anymore. I'm sorry."

"So don't. Tell the boy the truth. He can take it."

Nick stepped into the office. "Truth about what?"

Seeing Nick, Mom's face blanched. Her mouth, agape, trembled, as if struggling for words. Nick looked to Grandpa for answers, but none came.

Mom straightened, eyes narrowing on her father-in-law. "Nick, tell your grandfather good-bye."

"The man loved you." Rictor's voice cut into Nick's thoughts. "Everything he did was because of that."

He stared at Rictor, nerves firing as the past rushed back, memories swirling together—him sitting in Grandpa's office munching on French fries. On his mom's lap, her soft arms wrapped around him, the familiar scent of coconut lotion soothing his young mind. Teaching Payton to ride a bike, to catch a ball, to hit a grounder. And Jeremy . . .

"I've got to go, and you've got a restaurant to manage."

Outside, thick clouds blanketed the afternoon sky, the humidity oppressive. At his car, he paused to inhale a calming breath. Enough restaurant-Dad-Grandpa garbage. He was about to pick up Jeremy, and he refused to let his bitterness from the past spoil their visit.

If only letting things go came that easily. Although he tried to fight it, the trip to Marianne's only heightened his tension. He pulled into the drive, wound tight and expecting the worst.

Lord, keep Marianne in check, please. Let me pick up my boy in peace.

For once.

The garage door was closed, as were the curtains—the entire house shut up like the Pentagon. A deceptively cheery sign toting the values of love stood among tulips and marigolds.

Nick's mood lightened as he moved to the stoop. He had a full day planned with his two favorite people—Jeremy and Tammy. Some hiking followed by a loud and crazy dinner at Jimmy Jo's, an arcade that served the greasiest pizzas this side of the Mississippi.

Smile emerging, he rang the bell, then waited.

The faint sound of voices, or perhaps the television, seeped through the door. No approaching footsteps. He rang again.

After the third ring, Marianne answered wearing a white sundress and sugary smile. Holding the door ajar, she blocked the entryway. "I was about to call you. Jeremy's not feeling well. It'd probably be best to reschedule."

Nick fisted his hands. Craning his neck, he glanced over her shoulder. Jeremy sat on the couch, dressed in shorts and a T-shirt, watching television. Besides his stiff posture—hands in his lap, back erect—he looked fine. "So we'll take it easy. I'll put in a movie."

Marianne's eyes narrowed. "I'll call you when he feels better."

"I'm not buying it." He stepped forward and pressed a hand on the door. "Jeremy, grab your stuff, buddy."

"Good-bye, Nick." She closed the door.

Nick stared at it, hot blood coursing through him.

The manipulative, conniving—

He pulled a notepad from his back pocket and flipped it open. He checked the date and time on his phone then jotted it down.

Went to pick up Jeremy for mutually agreed upon visit. Arrived on time at 11:00. Visitation was denied.

We'll see how well Marianne's manipulative tactics stand up in a court of law.

CHAPTER 38

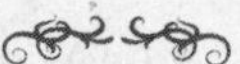

Tammy rinsed off a quart of plump strawberries, then set them on a towel to dry. A picnic basket—packed with quartered sandwiches, vegetable sticks, and homemade spinach dip—waited on the counter. A quart of lemonade and freshly-made Jell-O cake chilled in the fridge.

Tylan milled around her feet. "Can I have a strawberry? A fruit snack? I'm hungry."

Smiling, Tammy poked him in the gut. "No. This is for later." She rubbed a knuckle against her chin, mentally running through a list of items. "Why don't you bring a Frisbee?"

Tylan's face bunched into a cheeky smile. "Are we going to Lander's Park?"

"Maybe, if Nick and Jeremy want to."

"I should bring my mitt and bat. So we can practice." His brow furrowed. "'Cept that might be bad, him being on a different team and all."

Tammy bit back a chuckle and ruffled his hair. The logic and loyalties of a six-year-old. "I'm sure your teammates won't mind in the least."

Tylan's toothy grin returned. "I should bring some jars, too, so we can catch some frogs and tadpoles. Maybe we can make a fishing pole."

This led to a rather lengthy conversation on the proper kinds of sticks and what to use for twine, which soon morphed into an elaborate tale of boy versus wild. Tammy's heart swelled. Was God merging two of her loves—her kids and Nick? And if so, did that mean . . .

Her stomach fluttered. After all these years, all the mess and heartache, might God be offering her and Nick a second chance?

Becky entered wearing Bermuda shorts and a red ball cap, ear-buds dangling around her neck. "Do I have to come? It's going to be so boring."

Tammy studied her daughter—her shiny face free of gaudy makeup, a splattering of freckles dotting her nose, her modest clothing. She'd even participated in morning devotions without a single eye-roll or diva-sigh. She was growing up. Showing signs of maturity, of self-control. But not enough that Tammy felt comfortable leaving her home alone—not all day.

Her phone rang. She glanced at the number. Nick. Suppressing a rather childish giggle, she held a finger to silence chatty Tylan and answered.

"Hi. I was just think—" Heat singed her cheeks as she clamped her mouth shut. "You couldn't have picked a more beautiful day—"

"We're not going to make it." His voice held a definite edge.

"Oh." Her heart sank. "Is something . . . ? Is everything all right?"

"I'll call you later." He hung up.

Tammy stood, jaw slackened, not sure whether to be hurt or angry.

What had just happened?

Tylan scampered into the room, grinning and loaded down with a Frisbee, his mitt, baseball, and bat. He dumped them on the table, then dashed back out, probably to get more gear. Only to be disappointed.

Chapter 39

Nick parked in front of a brick Victorian home with green trim, shaded by towering oaks. Lace curtains hung in the windows and white-blossomed shrubs framed a white, wraparound porch. Spiraling stairs climbed to another porch on the second floor, a hand-shaped sign dangling above the entrance. "Gypsy Palm Reading." According to a shoddy sign stuck in the mulch, Oak Park Health and Wellness occupied the bottom floor.

Shaking his head, he stepped out into the humid late-afternoon air. He stopped, eyeing Marianne's car parked next to an old lamppost. A chill swept over him as he looked at the giant sign shaped as an opened hand, swaying on rusted hinges. What kind of nut had she found? Maybe this wasn't such a good idea.

Straightening his spine, he continued up the cracked walk to the front steps. The place was unlocked and inside was a small sitting room turned lobby. Marianne and Jeremy sat side by side in antique leather chairs, she with spine straight and face puckered, him with shoulders caved, eyes downcast. His tennis shoes dangled a foot from the floor.

"Hey, bud." Nick smiled at Jeremy. He stepped forward. Jeremy pulled back, shrinking into his chair, looking to his mother. Nick tensed, resisting the urge to glare at Marianne.

Facing his son, he forced a smile instead. "How's your summer going?" He sat across from Jeremy and propped his elbows on his thighs.

The boy shrugged.

A door to their right squeaked open and a squat woman with long black hair emerged. Tortoiseshell glasses rested on her bulbous nose.

Nick stood and extended his hand. "I'm Nick Zimmerman. Jeremy's dad."

Marianne sprang to her feet, clamoring forward so fast she nearly tripped on the corner of the coffee table. "I'm Marianne. We spoke on the phone." She weighted her words as if conveying a secret message.

His temperature rose, his nerves going on hyper alert as he watched his son—a boy-turned-pawn in Marianne's obnoxious game—stare at the woman with wide eyes. He sat with his back straight, clutching the armrests on either side of him. His cheeks paled, and he chewed his bottom lip.

Charcoal eyes set in deep sockets made a slow shift as the woman studied each of them in turn before turning to Jeremy with a tight smile. "Hello. And you must be Jeremy."

He nodded, shrinking further in his chair.

"I'm Anita Bowman. Well, then." She motioned toward her office. "Ms. Hawke, Jeremy, shall we?"

A gleam sparked in Marianne's eyes, a slight smile emerging. She touched Jeremy's arm, "Come on, sweetie," watching Nick over her shoulder.

Ignoring her sour expression, Nick followed, but Mrs. Bowman moved in front of him, blocking the entrance to her office.

"It would be best, for Jeremy's sake, if you didn't attend the first visit."

"You're kidding me." He stared from Mrs. Bowman to Jeremy to Marianne, his temperature rising as her smile grew. "You realize I'm the one paying for this little party, right?"

The woman's frown deepened. "Good-bye, Mr. Zimmerman. I'll be in touch."

Right. With a bill.

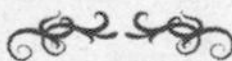

Outside the Kuhn house, a low wind howled like a mournful friend, and branches scraped against the siding. Flashes of lightning lit the inky sky as rain pounded against the roof and windows.

Tammy curled in the corner of the couch, her old high school yearbook opened on her lap. At her feet, Tylan built an elaborate Lego-land structure. Becky was spending the night with friends. Despite the steady drone of the television set, the house felt quiet. Too quiet.

Lonely.

What she wouldn't do for adult conversation—someone to share her day, her fears and concerns with. She missed Vanessa.

And Nick.

She studied the image of her and Nick on the page before her. Thick, wavy hair that never quite behaved, crystal blue eyes filled with mischievous laughter. The crooked tilt of his lips. Standing beside him in her shimmering gown and high tops, she'd tried to act nonchalant. Smiling for the camera, hoping he wouldn't hear the pounding of her heart or see the frequent blush in her cheeks.

And he hadn't. Hadn't a clue how much she'd loved him or how it broke her heart when he left.

Nothing had changed.

She couldn't handle another heartbreak, and that's exactly where this was headed. Nick's last phone call—and the fact he hadn't called since—proved that much. Not that she blamed him. The man had just lost a son. But that didn't give him the right to act like a jerk.

With a heavy sigh, she picked up her phone and glanced at the blank screen.

"What's wrong?"

She looked up to find Tylan watching her.

Tammy smiled. "Nothing, sweetie." Setting her yearbook onto the coffee table, she patted the cushions beside her. "Come here, little man." As extra bait, she held up the remote. "*Mission to Mars* is on."

Tylan glanced from his Legos to her before giving a slight shrug. Grabbing his plastic dinosaur, he climbed onto the couch and nestled into her arms.

Closing her eyes, she rested her chin on his head, the ends of his hair tickling her skin. Her heart ached as a verse from her morning reading came to mind.

"It's not good for mankind to be alone. I will make a helpmate suitable for him."

A helpmate. A friend. Someone who knew the most intimate details about her, who loved her, wrinkles, gray hair, and all—*'til death do us part*.

A siren sounded, swelling then fading with the distant hum of traffic. Tammy glanced at the clock, then settled further into the cushions. She was off this weekend. No scrambling to find childcare, no fighting to catch a few hours of sleep. For once.

Tylan slid to the floor, returning to his Lego creations. Closing her eyes, she let her head drop back against the couch.

Her phone rang, and she sat erect. Vanessa? That girl always knew the precise moment to call.

"Hello?"

"Good evening, it's Rita, from the call center."

Tammy's heart sank. Not tonight. "Yes?"

"I've got a 56-year-old male, suicide, at Riverview Memorial. Name's Troy Stevens."

There was no sense reminding the woman it was her night off. Either another OPC had called in sick or they were all at other hospitals. Since it was a stormy Saturday, it was most likely the latter. Not that it mattered. Tammy was already on Ellen's watch list. She couldn't decline this call.

Only problem—she still hadn't found reliable childcare. Which meant . . . She looked at the church directory, her stomach souring.

Rita continued to relay the patient's information. "He suffered from carbon monoxide poisoning. The daughter found him in the garage with the car running. He's not a registered donor, although he did leave a suicide note asking that his organs be donated. The daughter's already at the hospital. No other next of kin we're aware of."

"Okay. Thanks, Rita." Hanging up, Tammy stood, observing sweet Tylan. He'd stopped playing and watched her with a frown.

"Sorry, sweetie, but Momma's gotta go in."

"Is Stephanie coming over?"

"No. Not this time." She reached for the church directory. "Maybe you can spend the night with Dickson."

Tylan's face brightened. He bobbed his head and jumped to his feet. "I'll bring my new Xbox game."

And if Kelly, Dickson's mom, said no? She'd deal with that when the time came.

Tammy tried Kelly first but got the answering machine.

"Hey, it's Tammy. I . . ." Begging for a sitter was hard enough. Blurting it over an impersonal answering machine? "Call me. Please."

She hung up and tried Carol Hudson.

"Hello?" Voices—laughter and what appeared to be children's squeals—sounded in the background.

"Hi, Carol. It's Tammy. I wondered . . ." She swallowed and traced her finger along a groove in her coffee table. "Listen, I hate to ask, but I got called in to work tonight, and I . . ." The words clogged her throat.

Carol didn't respond right away, and when she did, her tone sounded nasally. "I wish I could help, but we've got company. Sorry. Maybe next time?"

"Sure. I understand."

Tammy dialed the next person on the list, then the next, then the next. She stopped at Constance's number.

How desperate am I?

She glanced at the clock. Pretty desperate.

But there was always Dover.

She sat there for a full minute, her mind vacillating between total humiliation and escape. Well, escape tinged with a bit of parental nagging. But for her kids' sake, for never having to scramble for childcare . . .

Regardless, she couldn't bail tonight—not on such short notice. Someone's life depended on those organs. No. She needed to swallow her pride and call the one person she'd rather avoid—Condemning Constance.

"I'm ready." Tylan bounded out of his room lugging a stuffed duffel bag. A horned dinosaur head poked out from the top.

"I'm sorry, bud, but the Hudson's aren't home."

Tylan heaved a heavy sigh and dropped his bag, flopping beside it. "Isaac?"

"He's got the flu."

"Ronnie? Charles?"

Tammy shook her head as he continued to list the names of every boy in their children's ministry from the third grade up. "Sorry, bud." The clock continued to tick. If she didn't find someone soon, Ellen would make the Dover decision for her.

"Then who?"

Studying her phone, she breathed. "Let me call Constance—"

"No! Not her."

"I don't have a choice."

"What about Dad? He'll take me."

Her heart wrenched. "I'm sorry, sweetie. Just this once. I'll find a sitter for you—"

"Like Joni?"

"Like Joni."

His head drooped, and he pulled his duffel bag closer. While he fished through its contents—probably looking for his favorite video game—she made the dreaded call.

Constance answered on the second ring. "Tammy, are you okay?"

In other words, *Do you realize what time it is?* "Yes, everything's fine. I just . . . I hate to bother you, and I know it's late notice, but . . ."

"You need someone to watch the kids." She sounded like she'd choked down a rotten lemon.

"I know it's a lot to ask. And it's just Tylan. Becky's at a friends'."

As silence stretched across the line, Tammy envisioned Constance sitting in a stuffy, mildew-infested chair, frowning, as she recounted all the mistakes, according to Constance, Tammy had made. In a nutshell, the woman felt Tammy had utterly failed as a wife and mother, as if she was somehow to blame for Brody's infidelity.

Constance's breath, loud and heavy, reverberated through the line. "You will bring proper nightwear? No need to bring his Bible. I have one he can borrow in the morning. He is staying overnight, I presume?"

"Yes, if that's all right."

"Of course. Children need their sleep. Studies suggest many students diagnosed with ADHD really suffer from severe sleep deprivation and stress. Stress! At nine and ten years old." As Constance continued to talk about the downfalls of modern society, Tammy gathered her things and ushered Tylan out the door.

Constance continued her lecture as Tammy pulled out of her neighborhood and down the block.

Glancing into the rearview mirror, she offered a glowering Tylan an apologetic smile. "Listen, Constance, I hate to cut this short, but I'm about to turn onto Falcon and—"

"Oh, my. Talking and driving? I wasn't aware. I'll see you when you get here, then."

With another lecture keyed and ready to go?

Luckily, Constance had run out of energy by the time they arrived.

The woman stood in the doorway wearing a checked housecoat with lace trim. The lights were off, minus the one above the entry and a lamp on a corner end table. A musky scent drifted from the living room.

"Come in." Constance stepped aside and motioned Tammy and Tylan inside.

Tammy checked her watch. "I can't stay."

Clutching his duffel bag with both hands, Tylan shrank back, but Tammy nudged him forward. Squatting to his eye-level, she lifted his chin. "You be good, okay?" She hugged him, pinning his arms to his sides, then stood. "Thanks, Constance. I really appreciate this." She handed her a page of emergency numbers. "Text me if you need me."

"I'm sure everything will be fine."

Tammy nodded and slipped out, casting one last glance at her son.

He stood in the center of Constance's living room, head drooped, looking like he'd lost his best friend.

Chapter 40

Riverview Memorial—a hospital with a large free clinic—operated in a sketchy part of town. Two men dressed in black jeans, heavy boots, and black bandanas gathered on the corner. Across the street, a woman pushed a grocery cart loaded with plastic bags and what appeared to be crushed soda and beer cans. Two men—one lanky, the other large—were dressed in tanks and cut-offs.

Tammy parked beneath the streetlight as close to the entrance as possible, tucked all valuables beneath the seat, and grabbed her computer bag. Slipping out, she locked her car, then, holding her tote bag close, scurried across the lot.

As she neared the entrance, a flash of movement in the shadows caught her eye. She turned to see a man dressed in a grungy ski jacket, large gashes exposing yellowed stuffing. He paced the sidewalk. Long, wiry hair hung below a black ball cap, puffed red lettering etched across the brim.

Nearing her, he paused beneath the overhead lights and lifted a dirty face, intense eyes locking on hers. Those eyes. Those distinct, piercing eyes, almost icy blue—just like . . . Reading the words on his cap, she gasped. Was that the same logo as in the picture Nick had shown her?

She blinked, studying the straight nose, angular jar, thick bottom lip. But it was his eyes—those bright, blue eyes—that struck her most.

Taking her delay as an invitation, the man stepped closer with stiff, jerking motions, plastic cup extended. His gaze shot from her to the ground, then back to her again.

Tammy glanced around before pulling a five dollar bill from her back pocket. She folded it and placed it in the cup, holding her breath against the thick stench of urine and vomit.

What were the chances? Slim to none. This couldn't be, unless God had brought her here, on this night, at this time. But was this what Nick wanted? It was one thing to know his dad was homeless. But to know how broken, how filthy, how utterly destitute? It'd shatter him.

"Sir, what's your name?"

He flinched and stepped back, hugging his torso. Shaking his head, he mumbled something and started to slip back into the shadows.

"I won't hurt you." Tammy lowered her voice as if talking to a fearful child. "I'm . . . Sir, do you know a Nick Zimmerman?"

The man froze, his mouth opening slightly. He stared at her. "Nickie-Nickie-Nick-Nick?" Tears filled his eyes, but then his face hardened and the twitching returned. "Doesn't want you. Leave. Leave us alone." Dropping his cup, he continued to step backward, hands pressed against his ears.

She didn't have time for this, but she couldn't just walk away. Stepping forward, she pulled a business card from her pocket. "My name is Tammy Kuhn, and I'm friends with your son." She held the card out.

Mr. Zimmerman stared at it, shaking his head.

She righted the cup on the ground, returned the money that had spilled, and dropped her card inside. "My number's on this card. Call me. Your son wants to see you. He loves you."

The man stopped shaking and lowered his hands, but made no move to pick up the cup.

Inching backward, she watched him for a moment longer before entering the hospital.

Poor Nick. All these years he'd longed for a father, and now . . . She called him, getting his voicemail. This wasn't information you delivered through a recording, but he'd want to know as soon as possible. "Hey, Nick, call me. I found your dad." She relayed his location. "I'm about to meet with a donor family, but I'll call you tomorrow."

She ended the call and put her phone away. Right now, she needed to focus on her job and whatever open door's God might provide.

Inside the ICU, Tammy didn't recognize the woman seated at the nurses' station. And based on her deep frown lines, this wouldn't be a positive encounter. In fact, the entire staff seemed on edge.

Two scowling doctors stood at the end of the hall, and although Tammy couldn't hear their words, their tense body language indicated an argument. A tall nurse with short hair dashed out of a patient's room looking like she'd swallowed an earthworm. Hopefully she wasn't Troy Stevens' bedside nurse.

Offering her best smile, Tammy approached the brunette at the nurses' station. She noted the woman's nametag. Kisha Chealey.

"Good evening, Ms. Chealey. I'm Tammy Kuhn with Heartland Donation Services." Shaking the woman's hand, she glanced at the monitor to locate patients' names. Troy Stevens, room 456. Bedside nurse—Julie Hutto. Oh good, a sweet Christian lady passionate about donation.

She exhaled, the tension seeping from her neck and shoulders.

Kisha grabbed a red binder from the shelf behind her. "The family coordinator's meeting with the daughter now. Whew-ee. Don't envy you, girl."

"Why? Something happen?"

Kisha shook her head. "That's one bitter woman."

Tammy gazed down the hall. Enraged families didn't bother her because she knew where their anger came from—a deeply wounded heart struggling to say good-bye.

"Thank you, Kisha."

She left in search of Julie Hutto, finding her in room 448 checking a sleeping patient's vitals. Tammy waited patiently in the doorway.

When Julie saw Tammy, the woman's face lit up. She made a few marks on the patient's chart before approaching Tammy. "Hey, girl." She gave Tammy a hug. "Haven't seen you in a while." She scanned the hall, her smile fading when her gaze landed on Dr. Lynch exiting a patient's room. It reemerged, subdued, when she turned back to Tammy. "You're like a breath of sea-mist air on a smoggy day."

"Bad night?"

"More like a bad month." Julie leaned closer and cupped a hand around her mouth. "There's been a few complaints filed . . . on Dr. Lynch. Well, and the hospital in general. We're under investigation, and since Dr. Lynch is on the board—"

"Everyone's on edge."

"To put it mildly. Because it's always everyone else's fault, right?"

Dr. Lynch caught Tammy's gaze with an icy stare, making the hairs on her arms rise. She looked away, turning her back to him. "Could be good, you know."

"If they fire him, you mean?" Julie shrugged. "I'm not holding my breath. That man's like a rabid raccoon, creating all kinds of havoc but always slipping under the radar, leaving someone else to take the blame."

"The truth will come out. It always does."

"Yeah, later rather than sooner. But what do I care? I retire next year."

"You serious? You're too young to retire!"

"I'll be fifty-two in October, although I feel more like eighty-five, thanks to this place. Figured I'm due for a change. Less stress, more glamour." The skin around her eyes crinkled. "Like diaper changing and snotty nose wiping." She laughed. "Gonna spend my golden years doing the grandma-nanny thing, soaking up all kinds of hugs and giggles, while I still have some life in me."

A memory of Tammy's kids nestled on Mom's lap, a picture book spread before them, resurfaced, pricking Tammy's heart. Her children were blessed to have such loving and attentive grandparents, and if she moved to Dover . . .

Julie touched Tammy's elbow. "Everything all right?"

"Huh?" Tammy smiled, her cheeks warming. "Yeah, I'm good." She checked her watch. "Can you take a minute to go over Mr. Stevens' lab work with me?"

"Of course." On the way back to the nurses' station, Julie talked about the patient's history. "His tests—blood and urine cultures, spinal taps—all came back normal." At the monitor, she pulled up the MAR screen first, then clicked to the consult record.

"The daughter's at the bedside now. I believe your coordinator's still with her."

Tammy nodded. "I'll pop in to introduce myself, see if she has any questions. What's her name?"

"Penny Mellor."

"Mellor. So she's married?"

"Don't know. No one's with her, if that's what you're asking." She smoothed her bangs to one side. "Might want to prepare yourself. The girl's pretty upset."

"I heard. Thanks, Julie." Tammy gathered her things. She glanced down the busy hall, mentally preparing herself for what could be a vicious attack.

Lord, give me the words, the wisdom to know when to speak and when to listen. Most of all, help me to treat this precious woman with grace and kindness.

Dr. Lynch approached, staring at his cell phone. Sitting straighter, Julie suddenly focused on a patient's chart in front of her.

Tammy slid her bag—laptop inside—over her shoulder and gave her friend a sideways hug, whispering into her ear. "Hang in there. Dr. Lynch can only bite for so long before he gets quarantined."

Julie chuckled. "I hope you're right."

Making a wide sweep to avoid the angry doctor, Tammy continued down the hall to Mr. Stevens' room. A puffy-eyed woman with long black hair sat at the bedside, a box of tissues on her lap. She held one in her hands, smoothing the edge between her thumb and fingers.

Regina Harlee, a Heartland family coordinator, sat with her, patiently waiting. This process couldn't be rushed. Although lives were on the line—critically ill patients waiting for organs—right now, it was all about the donor's family.

Regina stood. "Penny, this is Tammy Kuhn, the organ procurement coordinator."

Tammy extended her hand, offering the woman a sympathetic smile. "I'm here to answer any questions you may have, to offer support. Whatever you need."

Penny nodded. She stared at her dad with narrowed eyes. "He committed suicide."

Tammy's heart ached for this girl. She pulled up a chair and sat beside her. "I'm very sorry."

She shrugged. "Didn't hurt me any. I haven't spoken to the man in almost thirty years. Ever since he walked out on me and my brothers, leaving my mom to care for three kids under six."

"That must have been very difficult."

"We made it, no thanks to him. For ten years, the man never gave us a second thought. No letters on my birthday, no phone calls. Nothing. Then one day, he shows up asking for forgiveness and saying he wants to start over again." She snorted. "How convenient, huh?" She shook her head and cursed. "I told him to get out."

It was like a dark cloud enveloped Penny—a cloud thicker and darker than grief, as she continued to rant.

She stood, face void of expression, and turned cold eyes toward Tammy. "You do what you want with him. I'm through."

Unable to speak, Tammy watched the woman leave.

"So sad." Regina shook her head. "To see someone so consumed by bitterness. Reminds me of something my momma used to say. 'Bitterness is the worst kind of cancer. It buries its roots deep into one's heart until it strangles everything else.'"

Tammy froze, feeling exposed, like someone had elbowed her in the gut.

After a few hours of sleep, Tammy arrived at Constance's to find a smiling Tylan. His hair was damp and neatly combed, his shirt buttoned, collar down. His shoes were on and tied. The aroma of bacon and buttered toast filled the air. The rabbit-eared television set was turned off. A stack of old books, the covers a faded green, sat on the coffee table in front of him. One lay open, facedown, on the couch cushion beside him.

Constance was wearing a calf-length, tan skirt and a button-up blouse. She smiled, eyes bright. "Please, come in. Can I get you a cup of coffee?" When she glanced at Tylan, the edges in her face softened. "We were reading Aesop's Fables—the story of the wolf who threatens to eat a dog." She looked at Tylan. "Of course, we suspect the wolf will get his due, don't we, Tylan?"

Grinning, he bobbed his head. "Then we're going to make pudding—the real kind. With eggs."

Tammy chuckled. "Are you now?" She grabbed a book that had fallen onto the floor and set it on the coffee table. "I hate to break up the party, but I imagine Ms. Constance has a busy day ahead."

"Not at all." The woman stepped forward, standing between them. "In fact, I have the entire day free."

Tammy studied the woman, suddenly so . . . hospitable, almost pleasant. She didn't quite know how to respond. And Tylan? He seemed perfectly content to remain in the woman's home, on her couch, indefinitely. Someone with good manners would stay, at least for an hour. But Tammy's drooping eyes and the fatigue weighing on her shoulders necessitated sleep.

She placed a few more toys—a wooden train with a frayed pull-string, an old sock monkey that appeared hand sewn, and plastic army man—on the coffee table. "I wish we could, but . . . another time, perhaps?"

Constance's face fell. "Yes, of course." She stiffened and turned to Tylan. "Come now, obey your mother. We can read these another time."

"And make pudding?" Tylan asked.

She nodded. "Absolutely. Perhaps your mother and sister will even join us next time."

Tammy's heart pricked at the almost desperate hope in the woman's eyes. Constance was lonely. She smiled and touched her on the arm. "That sounds lovely."

Chapter 41

Nick swallowed past a dry mouth, struggling to fully grasp what Tammy said.

He watched a droplet of condensation slide down his glass. "I should be happy. Or relieved." He shook his head. "All I ever wanted was a father. Someone to come to my football games, to take me on a college-hunting tour. In high school, I used to stare up at the bleachers, imagining my dad cheering me on."

Tammy placed her hand over his. "I know. I remember."

"Now what?"

Tammy's eyes glistened with unshed tears, her mouth lifting into a sympathetic smile.

The waitress appeared with their food and set matching plates of pancakes and sausage on the table. A lump lodged in his throat as he stared at the steaming links and golden cakes, the butter melting into a creamy puddle. Had his dad eaten today? Real food, or what he scrounged out of a garbage can? Where had he spent the night? Not at the shelter. Not if Tammy saw him at Riverview Memorial.

He looked into her blue eyes, so kind. "You're sure it was him?"

"I'm sure."

Nick straightened and set his jaw. "I need to find him." He stood, dropped a twenty on the table, and started to leave.

"Wait."

He turned.

"I'll go with you."

An overwhelming sense of love swept over him—a love that reached to his very depths. This would be tough. Painful. Letting go of the dad he'd created in his dreams, coming to grips with who his dad really was. Learning to accept—to love—his dad, homeless and insane.

But he wouldn't have to do it alone. God had brought Tammy. Sweet, loving, beautiful Tammy.

"I'd like that." He checked his watch. "Although . . . I don't know how long it'll take."

She smiled. "I've got all day. The kids are spending the day with a dear friend." Her eyes softened, and she reached for his hand. "I figured you might need a friend today."

He looped his fingers through hers and gave a gentle squeeze. "Thanks, Tam. I really appreciate you." He gazed into her eyes, noticing every turquoise speck, every eyelash curl, the soft lines beneath them revealing decades of laughter. So beautiful, inside and out.

After she gathered her things, he led her out of the restaurant and to his car.

Engine idling, he gripped the steering wheel with both hands. His stomach turned, an overwhelming sense of guilt pressing down on him as he thought of all the homeless men and women he'd passed throughout his lifetime. Looking at them with disdain, disgust.

For I was hungry and You gave me nothing to eat, I was thirsty and You gave me nothing to drink.

Dirty, hungry, desperate faces swam through his mind, swirling, merging into one—the face of his father.

His dad.

Lord, I'm so sorry. Please forgive me.

Tammy laid her hand on his arm.

He smiled at her. "I'm glad you're here." His voice grew hoarse. "You always have been—when I've needed you most."

Tears filled Tammy's eyes as she looked into his, and for a moment, it appeared she wanted to say more. But then, with a slight smile, she gave his hand a squeeze and nodded. "Of course."

Nick studied her a moment longer, then checked the time on the dash. 8:15. The Flaming Mesquite would open in under three hours. Lunch rush would hit in four, but nothing Chef Rictor couldn't handle. Especially considering their low numbers of late.

He drove through the heart of downtown, then merged onto the freeway, slipping between two slow moving semis. "Janet from Heartland Donation Services called me."

"Oh? What about?"

"I contacted her. I wanted . . ." He swallowed. "I've been praying for the recipients of my son's organs. Every day. It brings me great comfort to know my son helped to save lives. But it'll bring me even greater comfort to see them in heaven someday. That'd be the greatest blessing. To know that through my son's gift, someone else was given the chance to find eternal life."

He cast Tammy a sideways glance. "I feel like God's been burning a message in my heart, and I asked her if there might be some way to share it. She said there was an organ donation awareness conference coming up. Said maybe I could share my story. And what God showed me through it."

"That's wonderful, Nick."

As they neared Riverview Memorial, high-rises with reflective windows gave way to abandoned lots and dilapidated apartment buildings. On the corner of Farner and Ninth, two kids—neither older than ten—walked along the median. They held squeegees, and a plastic bucket sat between them. Whenever the light turned red, they darted into the street, squeegees raised, moving from car to car.

Nick wanted to give them money, but he was sandwiched in the middle lane, and the light turned green before he had a chance. With a heavy heart, he continued past an old lady, back bowed, shuffling down the sidewalk with a cane.

So many hurting people. How had he never noticed before?

Thank You, Lord, for opening my eyes to the needs all around me. Show me what I can do. How You want to love these people—these moms, dads, sisters, and brothers—through me.

After a three-hour search, he pulled into a parking lot and let his engine idle. "He could be anywhere." He shook his head. "I'm not going to find him, am I?"

"I don't know." Tammy's gaze flicked to the clock on the dash, suggesting perhaps Nick had stretched his search a bit too long.

"Sorry to steal your day."

"You didn't steal it. I'm glad to be here. To walk with you through this, wherever it leads."

His chest warmed—and ached—as he looked into her tender eyes. Warmed by her love but shredded by the wounds this trip had reopened. Wounds that deepened his commitment to gain custody of Jeremy, so his son never had to experience life without a dad. A close-knit family—with Tammy and her kids in it.

But was that what she wanted? His heart swelled at the possibility. She was a great mom, a strong Christian . . . but did she trust him? Enough to unveil her heart? To let him in?

After scanning the street one last time, Nick shifted into reverse. "I better get you back." He looped around and headed east on Sycamore. A corner convenience store caught his attention, and he turned into the lot. An old man with caved in lips, bony shoulders, and a matted beard, rifled through a nearby garage can. He held a plastic bag in one hand and dropped an empty beer can into it.

"But first, I need to do something." Nick parked, leaving the engine running, and got out. He dashed into the store, returning with a liter of water and two hot dogs.

"Excuse me, sir?" He approached the man who continued to dig through the trash. "Sir?"

The man startled and whirled around, eyes wide. His arm instinctively rose to shield his face, as if warding off blows. Nick's heart wrenched as once again an image of his father flashed through his mind.

"You hungry?" He held out the hot dogs.

Squinting, the man stared first at the hot dogs, then at Nick, his wrinkled face scrunched as if trying to determine if he was a threat.

Lowering his shoulders to appear as nonthreatening as possible, Nick raised the hot dogs again. He set them on a napkin on the curb, placing the water bottle beside them. As he rose, he noticed a silver cross dangling from a chain around the man's neck.

For I was hungry and You gave me something to eat.

Taking the food, the man smiled. "God bless you, son."

Nick nodded. "You, too." Tears pricked his eyes as he returned to his car. *Lord, may someone show the same kindness to my dad. And please, help me find him.*

Chapter 42

Standing in the Flaming Mesquite's kitchen, Nick inhaled the rich aroma of sautéed garlic and onions. Fresh mussels steamed in a large pot while red peppers sizzled on the open grill. Allen, his new dishwasher, appeared to be working out well. He was a retired vet suffering from Post Traumatic Stress Disorder, sent by the Safe Haven Ministries. The guy, aged sixty-five, had gone through Safe Haven's rehab and life skills training. He currently lived in a halfway house a few blocks away but hoped to find low-income housing by fall.

"Hey, there, Boss Man." Sauntering over, Rictor tucked a hand towel into his apron belt. "Think we'll get a lunch rush today?"

Nick glanced at his wait staff milling near the food counter, and shrugged. "Hope so, but you know what they say—slow and steady wins when frantic falls apart."

"Not in this business." Rictor glanced at the stainless steel prep table where Julio, also a new hire, sliced tomatoes. In front of him, bins of chopped romaine, boiled egg slices, and other salad fixings sat in ice. "But look at the bright side. You'll have plenty of food to take to the Helping Hands."

"Thanks for the voice of confidence." For the past week, Nick had been taking leftover items to a local soup kitchen. No sense throwing away what someone else desperately needed. But as generous as he strived to be, selling the items would be even better—for everyone. Because if his business failed, there'd be no leftovers to donate.

He frowned, thinking of the sale offer lying on his desk. He'd hate to see this place bulldozed, but what could he do? Things were picking up, but not fast enough. And that high-priced commercial he'd hoped would help? It'd been a major, humiliating flop.

"You good, man?" Rictor studied Nick with a furrowed brow.

"Huh? Yeah, I'm fine. Just thinking."

"You know . . ." Rictor rubbed his chin and gazed past Nick. "What if we did some sort of eating contest? Like those on TV. It'd be a great way to generate buzz. Might even be able to get the local media out here."

"What'd you have in mind?"

"Something like, 'Eat five pounds of ribs and your meal's on us.'"

"And if they can't?"

"Then they gotta pay. At say, forty bucks a pop, we could make a killing."

"Or land even more in debt."

"Nah." Rictor flicked his hand. "We may get a few human garbage disposals, but most folks will bail after the second pound. And they'll bring their burger-munching, soda-slurping friends."

"When can you pull this off?"

"I can place an order today. We should have the ribs by tomorrow afternoon."

"Okay. I'll call the newspapers and local radio station to see if we can't get the media out here."

"Keep your chin up." Rictor fist-nudged Nick's shoulder. "This place survived riots, two tornadoes, three changes of ownership, and a major economic downturn. It'll ride through this little hurdle, no problem." His gaze intensified. "*We'll* ride through this one." He made a sweeping motion with his arm. "All of us. Because we're family. Always have been."

Nick's stomach soured. He couldn't sell this place, destroy his grandpa's legacy, and leave Rictor without a job. He'd find a way to make things work. Somehow.

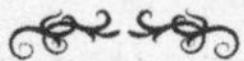

Arriving late, Tammy slowed as she neared Constance's house for her son's welcome-back-to-the-states party. Minus a dented minivan, a Camry, and the pastor's maroon pickup, the street was oddly bare.

Maybe she had the time wrong, and she was actually early? Great. Just what she needed—an extra hour of awkwardness.

She pulled into the driveway and cut her engine. There was a soft click of Tylan's seatbelt unfastening, followed by a flash of movement as he lunged for something on the floor. After a series of grunts and moans, he emerged holding a wrinkled Sunday school paper, his plastic dinosaur, and a storybook called *Jesus Loves You*. Stains dotted the cloth cover, the pages made of thick cardboard, corners chewed.

Tammy turned to face him. "What's that for?"

Tylan beamed. "I found this in my closet. Want to show it to Ms. Constance. She's got a box of books like this and old toys and everything. She likes this kind of stuff." He tilted his head and studied the grungy cover, as if trying to figure out why, then shrugged. "I'm going to give this to her. For her collection."

Tammy's heart warmed. "That's very thoughtful. I'm sure she'll love it."

While she led him up the walk, Tylan chattered about the other "treasures" Constance had in her box. Items she had played with as a child, her children after her. Now stored in a box kept in her attic.

Tammy pressed the doorbell, Tylan practically bouncing beside her. His bouncing would likely escalate less than thirty minutes in. "You brought your DS, right?"

Tylan nodded.

"Good."

The door swung open and Constance greeted them with a smile that widened upon seeing Tylan. "Hello." She placed her hand on his shoulder and glanced past them. "Where's Becky?"

"At a friend's."

"I see. Please," she moved aside, "come in."

Tylan headed for the couch.

Tammy greeted everyone, extending her hand first to the pastor, then to his wife, and picked one of many empty chairs. Constance stood in the center of the room, looking a bit wilted, or perhaps out of place.

"Well." She checked her watch, then glanced out the window. Facing her guests, she pressed her palms together and offered a tight smile. "Brent should be here any moment." The corners of her mouth twitched. "Can I get you a glass of tea, Tammy? Or a cup of coffee?"

Tammy looked at the silver-serving tray on the coffee table. Beside this sat a matching platter filled with deviled eggs, cheese squares, and mini-cucumber sandwiches. Sugar cookies with delicate frosting filled another tray next to tiered, pedestal plates.

Tammy rose. "Everything looks lovely, Constance." Tammy placed some cheese chunks and a sandwich on her tray. Not hungry, she nibbled the crust and watched Tylan from the corner of her eye. He seemed content with his DS game. A blessing and a curse. It made the moment easier, but if his contentment continued, it negated an easy excuse for leaving.

"So . . ." Pastor Broers set his plate down. "How has Brent been? Still doing a lot of traveling?"

Constance looked again to the window. She nodded. "He's working in mergers and acquisitions now. He's been quite busy, as I'm sure you can imagine." She checked her watch, then looked back at the window.

"I can." The pastor shifted and looked around the room before settling on a painting of a golden pitcher set behind a bowl of fruit. "Interesting piece. Do you enjoy art?"

Constance followed his gaze. "My great-grandmother painted that."

"How lovely. I like how . . . the gold contrasts with the pale blue background, don't you, dear?" He looked at his wife.

Dabbing her mouth with her napkin, she nodded. "Oh, yes. It really makes the fruit stand out. In fact, it looks good enough to eat," she chuckled.

Soon everyone returned to staring at their plates.

Twenty minutes later, guests began to politely excuse themselves. Tammy touched her purse, ready to do the same, but the frown on Constance's face stopped her. It was like watching a child—one with wrinkled skin and gray hair—rejected in the lunchroom.

Suppressing a sigh, she settled back into the seat cushions. Staying another ten minutes wouldn't hurt.

After seeing her guests out, Constance returned to the living room. She watched Tylan for a moment before excusing herself. She darted down the hall and returned carrying a wooden crate filled with toys and fairytale books.

Tylan jumped to his feet and held out his book. "I brought this for you."

"Thank you." Constance set her items down and took the book.

Tammy watched them for a while longer, her expression one she'd seen countless times from her mother. Something contentedly maternal.

She sat with her back straight, hands folded in her lap. "I apologize for my son's absence. He is quite busy. And you know how men are with phones and messages." Her smile returned. "Enough about me. How are you?"

"Good. We're good."

"When do you work next?"

Tammy fidgeted. "Tuesday. But I should have . . ." Childcare? Considering she hadn't even scheduled interviews yet, not likely. Because no one had responded to her ad. Where were all those people searching for jobs?

Feeling a bit exposed, she observed the room. Three picture frames decorated the mantel—one of a much younger Constance holding a toddler and an infant. To the right was a photo of a man in a college cap and gown, to the left a blond woman wearing a shin-length jean dress.

"You have a daughter?" Tammy asked.

Constance followed her gaze. "Yes, that's Melanie, my youngest." She stared at her hands, tightly intertwined. "I haven't seen her in ten years."

"Oh. I'm so sorry."

She watched Tylan, the lines etched from her lips to her chin deepening. "I made many mistakes when my children were young. I was a single mom, like you."

Tammy winced, but kept her expression void.

"I spent more time watching television than taking my kids to church. Children need their fathers, and in lieu of biological fathers, they need to see godly men living out their faith. Positive male role models help children recognize predators, and believe me, they're out there, for what they are."

She frowned. "The closest my daughter came to seeing a godly man was from the back pew on Easter and Christmas. Then one day charismatic, well-dressed cult leader Geoffrey Laine started showing her attention, and she fell hard." She studied her nail then, shaking her head, raised sad eyes. "I tried to reason with her, but after years of living like strangers . . ." She shook her head. "It was too little too late."

Years of Constance's comments came rushing back. Words Tammy took as condemnation now clarified in the context of Constance's admonitions. As abrasive as her approach was, she meant no harm. Quite the opposite. She was nothing more than a wounded woman living with a lifetime of regrets, trying to find restitution.

How hard would it be to humor her?

Tammy offered a genuine smile, one that warmed her from the inside out. "In answer to your earlier question, I'm on call Tuesday through Friday. My schedule's pretty unpredictable. I could get called in at any time or not at all."

"Wonderful. Tylan and I will find something to do, I'm sure."

"Thank you. I really appreciate your help." Tammy stood. "We better go. Thank you for having us."

"Ah." Tylan's shoulders slumped, his torso practically flailing forward. "Five more minutes?"

Tammy raised an eyebrow. Interesting. She shook her head. "Sorry, sweetie. Maybe next time."

They said their good-byes, and Constance showed them out. With a hand on Tylan's shoulder, Tammy strolled to her car. At the curb, she paused to glance behind her. Constance stood in the doorway, watching them.

Once again, Tammy's heart pricked. That woman needed them as much as Tammy needed her. Maybe more.

Chapter 43

Nick looked at the address on his sticky-note then checked the rusted modular in front of him. It sat on the edge of a vacant lot sandwiched between a recycling plant and a junkyard. A sagging chain-link fence bordered the property on one side, weeds twining through it. A brick warehouse with boarded windows occupied the opposite side of the street.

He looked in his rearview mirror, tempted to turn around, but he'd made an appointment.

Stepping onto the oil-sheened street, he was accosted by the stench of burnt plastic. He approached the building—a mobile home-like structure with metal siding and yellowed curtains—and climbed the rickety stairs. He paused on the stoop, inhaled, then knocked. Heavy footsteps approached, followed by a screech as the door eased open.

A man who appeared to be in his midforties with a paunch belly and deep scowl lines appeared. He wore his gray-streaked hair in a loose ponytail.

"You Nick?" The man's breath smelled like garlic. With his lips bunched, he scrutinized Nick—from his leather loafers to his collared shirt.

Nick swallowed, nodded, and extended his hand.

They shook.

"I'm Mike Fermin, founder and president of Fathers' Rights United." He moved aside, the floorboards creaking beneath his heavy boots. "Come in." He motioned to a metal folding chair positioned in front of a desk covered in paper, Styrofoam coffee cups, and Chinese take-out containers.

Ducking to avoid a strip of flypaper dangling from the ceiling, Nick followed him across the room and took a seat.

"So." Lowering to his chair with a grunt, Mike leaned back rested his hands on his stomach. "Your ex-wife's giving you grief and you're tired of playing the fool."

"I'm trying to get custody."

"Full?"

Nick nodded. "It's been a long go, but I think we're finally getting somewhere. At least, I hope. They can only drag this thing on so long, right?"

"You'd be surprised. You both undergo a court ordered eval?"

"Yeah, but I didn't get any warm and fuzzies from the psychologist."

He studied Nick for a long moment, his dark eyes narrowed under bushy brows. "It's unlikely the judge will rule in your favor. You know that, right? And they're liable to slam you with her legal fees."

When Nick didn't respond, Mike leaned back and crossed his arms. "Sorry, man. Just telling you like it is. Judges don't like dads. Trust me, I know. Speaking from experience here."

This wasn't the pep talk Nick had been hoping for. But he wouldn't be deterred, no matter what this man said. Jeremy needed a dad. Needed to know his father still loved him—loved him enough to fight for him.

"You got a lawyer, I bet." The man's gravelly voice cut into Nick's thoughts.

Nick nodded.

"Money-sucking leach, am I right? Scheduling then rescheduling court dates, stringing you along on your dime." He leaned forward and propped his elbows on his desk. "That's what they do, you know. Lawyers don't want to go to court, don't want to settle, either. Because then their money stream runs dry. I've been fighting this battle for over ten years. Spent near $100,000 in lawyer fees. You know where it got me?"

Nick shook his head.

"Nowhere, that's where. Nowhere but back in that stupid lawyer's office listening to Mr. Suit and Tie spouting all his legal mumbo jumbo. In the end, it amounted to nothing but bills sent on fancy paper."

"What do you suggest I do?"

"Like I said, judges almost always rule in favor of the mother unless she's abusive or emotionally unfit or something. And even that's hard to prove. You gotta have documentation—a lot of it. And reliable witnesses. Not your momma or nothing. Otherwise it ends up being your word against hers. Still does, half the time."

"But that's changing, right? I read an article—"

The man laughed. "That's why it made the news, man. What's your ex do? She got a job?"

"No."

"So she's a stay-at-home mom."

"Well, yeah, but she's living with a guy—her boyfriend."

"The courts don't care about that—marriage, partners, friends with benefits—as long as the guy's not a predator or anything. But even that's hard to prove."

Nick tensed and looked to the door. This felt like a waste of time. "How can you help me then?"

A gleam flickered in the man's eyes. "I can help you take matters into your own hands. Fight fire with fire. Give her and her swanky lawyer a reason to go to court."

"I've already got a court date."

He waved Nick's comment aside. "They'll postpone it. Unless you force their hand."

"How do you propose I do that?"

"Gotta hit her where it hurts—her pocketbook. You stop sending checks, I guarantee they'll get you in court right quick."

"And in jail. No thanks."

"For an overnight, maybe. Small price to pay to get an audience. A chance to tell your side."

"At the expense of my son?"

"I doubt he even knows you're footing the bills."

"I don't do it for recognition." Nick stood. "I appreciate your time."

Mike pulled a business card from his desk drawer and handed it over. It looked like it had been printed off his computer. "If you change your mind."

"Thanks." Nick tucked the card in his back pocket and moved to the door.

The man followed and stood with his hand on the frame. "I wish you the best. It's a long climb, but playing nice won't help anyone."

"Listen, Mom, can I call you back?" Phone pressed to her ear, Tammy glanced in her rearview mirror. Bags and dark circles shadowed her eyes, thanks to a restless night. The woman from her last OPC call, Penny Mellor, had haunted her dreams. Her hardened face and icy tone, such venom, sitting beside her dying father. But what had bothered Tammy most, wrenching her awake in sweat-dampened clothes, had been when Penny's face morphed into hers.

Inhaling, Tammy smoothed a lock of hair behind her ear. *I'm not like that. I'm angry—at Brody. And I have a right to be. But I'm not a hateful, bitter woman.*

Yet.

"Bitterness is the worst kind of cancer. It buries its roots deep into one's heart, until it strangles everything else."

She shuddered.

"Honey? Are you still there?" Tammy's mom's voice interrupted her thoughts.

"Sorry. What were you saying?" She grabbed a tube of lip gloss from her purse and dabbed it on. She refused to walk into Ellen's office looking like a haggard has-been. If the woman chose to fire her, so be it. Tammy would take the news with dignity.

"You're still spending Labor Day weekend with us? I'd love to take the kids school clothes shopping."

Tammy smiled. "I know you would. And yep, that's the plan. I've got Thursday through Monday off that week." If not longer, depending on the reason behind Ellen's meeting.

"Sounds great."

Tammy hung up, turned her phone on silent, and tucked it into the side pocket of her purse. She stared across the lot at the Heartland Donation Services building.

When she reached Ellen's office, door ajar, Tammy found her boss on the phone.

Ellen glanced up, her glasses falling to the end of her nose. "I've got to let you go. Thank you, Douglas." She motioned Tammy in. "Have a seat."

Tammy crossed the room and perched on the edge of her chair. Her stomach rolled. Despite her desire to the contrary, she forced herself to look her boss in the eye.

Ellen removed her glasses and placed them on her desk. "You've been with Heartland for some time."

Tammy nodded.

"And up until recently, you've done a satisfactory job."

Satisfactory? Tammy had been with Heartland ten years—longer than any other OPC on the team. No complaining, picking up slack when others fell short, dealing with Ellen's emotional outbursts. And the only word Ellen could use was satisfactory?

"I know things have been . . . challenging, since your divorce."

Again, Tammy nodded.

"My sister is going through a very . . . unpleasant divorce right now, so . . . I appreciate how you've managed all your challenges over the past few years."

Tammy's eyes about bugged out of her head. Was that an apology? "Thank you, ma'am."

"I also appreciate your level of compassion and sensitivity to our donor families. And, for the most part, your ability to work well with hospital staff."

Wow, another completely unexpected accolade. What had changed Ellen's perceptions? Tammy had been certain the woman hated her.

Ellen cleared her throat. "We've received a grant for increased community awareness. I want someone familiar with our needs, area hospital staff, and the common concerns voiced by the public, to facilitate this endeavor." Ellen studied Tammy for a moment. "And I don't feel Yvonne is qualified or experienced enough to take on the additional responsibility alone, at least, not yet. I would like her to report directly to you. I'd also like you to help update our training materials and the information packets we distribute to various organizations."

Tammy's jaw went slack. "Are you offering me the position?"

"Temporarily, yes. It will be less pay, but the hours should be . . . more conducive to your current situation."

"How long do you see this new position lasting?"

Ellen tapped a finger on her chin. "A year." She paused. "I'll need an answer by the first." Ellen grabbed the phone receiver and swiveled her chair so that her shoulder faced Tammy.

Was this a gift from God? An answer to prayers? Finding childcare for a nine-to-five would be easy, and with this being a temporary position, she she'd have plenty of time to find someone to watch her kids on an on-call basis, once she resumed her normal duties. Though her direct involvement with donor families would be limited, maybe even nonexistent, this would only be temporary. She wouldn't have to give up her ministry to donor families forever.

And there'd be no need to move to Dover, no need to leave Nick.

But could she afford it?

The following Sunday, she arrived to church early, needing time to pray. To think. The kids were at Brody's for the weekend. As usual, he'd been late picking them up. And this time, Tammy had lost it, initiating a screaming match in front of the kids, hurting them in the process. The words spoken by Regina some time previously played through Tammy's mind, as they had often since their encounter:

"Bitterness is the worst kind of cancer. It buries its roots deep into one's heart, growing like a parasitic vine, until it strangles everything else."

Am I bitter, Lord? Is that why I'm so easily irritated? Why Brody gets me so angry, I could spit? Or scream, as she had Friday evening. *This isn't who I want to be, Lord.*

Slipping into an empty pew, she opened her Bible onto her lap, flipping to the passage she'd read that morning. It was from Luke 6:45. *"A good man brings good things out of the good stored up in his heart, and an evil man brings evil things out of the evil stored up in his heart. For the mouth speaks what the heart is full of."*

Tears pricked her eyes as she read the verse a second time, the ending phrase standing out to her. For the mouth speaks what the heart is full of. She knew she was a child of God. She'd been saved by grace and given everything she needed to live a life that honored Christ. To show the fruits of the Spirit listed in Galatians: love, joy, forbearance. So why didn't she? *Help me to be more patient, Lord.* More loving and joy-filled. Not only for me, but for my kids' sakes.

Closing her Bible, she breathed deeply and straightened against the back of the pew. She startled to find Jenson standing in the aisle beside her, watching with a furrowed brow.

"Is everything all right?" he asked.

She smoothed a stray lock of hair from her forehead and nodded. "I'm good. Just doing a little soul searching this morning." She gave a nervous laugh.

"Oh? Nothing too serious, I hope."

"Don't worry." She waved a hand. "I hid the bodies where no one will find them."

"Good. I was worried about that." He glanced at sliver of seat between Tammy and the armrest. "Mind if I sit here?"

"I . . . uh . . ." Would conceding give him the wrong impression? Make him think she was interested? But then, how could she say no? "Not at all." Tucking her skirt beneath her legs, she scooted over. Well enough over to allow for plenty of room between them.

Jenson sat, closer to her than she liked, and laid his Bible on the other side of him. She scooted again, increasing the distance between them. "So, how's the realty business going?"

"Good. Great actually." He went on to tell her of his latest properties, one under contract and an additional one he expected an offer on sometime this week. Then they transitioned to baseball, little league, and Tammy's kids.

"Tylan's doing great," she said. "His swing has really improved."

"That's fantastic. You know, I'd love to take him to the batting cages sometime."

Tammy bristled. "I appreciate the offer . . ." Surely Jenson wasn't using her kids to get to her? She gave a mental shake of her head, chiding herself for being so distrustful, another negative quality she really needed to work on. *Lord, I'm a mess.* Regardless, this conversation was becoming increasingly uncomfortable.

She looked around. People had begun to meander in, filling in the back rows. The Wyatt family walked by, smiled and waved. The pastor and worship leader stood on the far corner of the stage, talking. Finding no reasonable reason to leave, she opted for the one known to women nationwide.

She stood. "I better use the restroom before service starts." Which was true enough, considering all the coffee she drank that morning.

"Of course." Jenson rose, unfortunately, blocking her way. "Before you go, I was wondering if . . . I mean . . . Would you like to go to dinner? Or lunch? Or maybe coffee?"

Tammy suppressed a sigh. She couldn't dodge this any longer. To do so would be unkind. She sat back down and waited until he'd done the same, then, she swiveled in her seat, facing him. "Listen, Jenson, you're a great guy." The moment she said that, his entire body wilted, as if in anticipation of what was to come. "And I'm flattered by your invitation." How could she say this in a nice way? "I'm not . . . I'm in love with someone else."

"The man I saw you and your kids with at the restaurant?"

She wasn't ready to admit such aloud. "I'm so sorry." She laid her hand over his and offered what she hoped to be a gentle smile. "If you'll excuse me." She stood, stepped around him into the aisle, and walked out of the sanctuary, knowing she'd done the right thing but feeling terrible for doing it.

Chapter 44

Nick parked in front of Marianne's, the tightened tendons in his neck and shoulders ready to snap. Mike's words wouldn't stop replaying through his mind. *"Judges don't like dads."* Especially those who neglected their sons—left them to get killed by hit-and-run drivers.

Advice given by Howie early in Nick's divorce resurfaced, luring him: *"You need to take matters into your own hands. Fight fire with fire."*

No. Regardless of how immature and spiteful Marianne was acting, regardless of how much was stacked against him, he refused to make Jeremy a pawn. Nick's son needed a dad, not a snake. A man who demonstrated what it meant to follow Jesus, even when things got hard or weren't fair. God would rise up in Nick's defense—fight on his behalf.

Wouldn't He?

Nick gazed at the cloudless sky. *Are You there, God?*

No answer. Not that he really expected one. God had spoken to him once—not with words, but with a gnawing uneasiness the night Nick pulled out of Howie's drive—but he hadn't listened, and Payton had been killed because of it.

I'm sorry, Payton. I'm so very sorry.

A cool breeze swept over him, carrying the soft scent of lilacs. Breathing deeply, he stepped onto the sidewalk and continued up the walk. Voices and music rose from Marianne's backyard. Nick peered through the stained glass paneling flanking the front door. The interior was dark, the television off.

He rang the bell and waited.

No answer. He checked his watch and rang again.

Nothing. He descended the steps and continued around the house. The side gate stood open, and in the yard, people gathered in clusters of threes and fours. Wade manned the grill, a buddy on either side of him. Marianne stood a few feet away talking with Victoria, her best friend. They both held what appeared to be martinis, and based on Marianne's large, sweeping arm movements and slight sway, this wasn't her first drink.

He entered the yard and looked for Jeremy. He and another kid, maybe two years younger, hunched over the flowerbed, bug nets in hand. Forcing a chuckle despite his knotted stomach, Nick approached and placed a hand on Jeremy's shoulder.

"Hey, there."

Jeremy spun around, eyes wide.

Nick's heart ached to see the boy who once climbed on his lap, who once rode on his shoulders and wrestled with him on the living room floor, now regarded him with fear and distrust. He offered what he hoped to be an encouraging smile. "You ready to go?"

Jeremy looked past Nick's shoulder, and his face blanched.

"Get off my property, you murderous, conniving—" Staggering toward him, Marianne let out a slew of curses.

"Your word against hers. Unless you have documentation . . ."

Nick faced her and reached into his back pocket for his phone. "Marianne." Pulse quickening, he scrolled through his screen until he got to his voice record app. He hit record.

"Ooooh." She wiggled her fingers in mock fear. "Look at that. Mr. Kid-killer's calling his lawyer." She cursed again, nearly tripping. Her drink splashed over her hand.

Nick stepped forward, creating a barrier between Marianne and his son. "Calm down." He turned to Jeremy. "Go get your bat and mitt, son. I figured we'd hit the batting cages, maybe toss the ball a bit."

"Uh-uh." Marianne wagged a finger. "He's not going anywhere. You've already killed one son." Stepping closer to Jeremy, she bent over so her face was less than an inch from his. "He doesn't care about you. Never did. Can't you see that? All he cares about is that stupid restaurant of his." She gave a hollowed laugh. "And look where that got him. He's just trying to make me miserable. Wasn't enough that he murdered my firstborn, then sold his organs to that petite little girlfriend of his."

"You're drunk." Nick kept his voice low, calm.

Around them, conversations stilled as people gathered, forming a wide horseshoe as if Marianne might turn on them. And she would, if provoked.

She whirled around and stabbed a finger into Nick's chest. "Give it up, already. Jeremy wants nothing to do with you. Can't you get that through your thick skull?" Spittle flew from her mouth. "You disgust me. Get off my property before I call the cops."

Hands fisted, Nick took one breath after the other until he could speak without losing control. He turned to Jeremy and dropped to his eye-level. "I love you, Bud."

Marianne shrieked and clawed at Nick's arm. Her nails sliced through his skin. He jerked away, holding Jeremy's gaze. "Always have, always will." Tears filled the boy's eyes as he looked from Marianne to Nick.

Nick stood. He couldn't bear to see Jeremy like this—terrified and torn between his parents. "I love you, Jer. Never forget that, okay?"

He refused to take part in this vicious tug-of-war.

But he couldn't give up. And hopefully now that he had Marianne's hysterics on tape, he wouldn't have to.

Once outside of the gate, he stopped recording and called his lawyer. The secretary put him through.

"Nick, how are you?"

"I need to meet with you. I've got something you should hear. Something that'll help our case."

"I was just going over your file. I have a few minutes this coming Monday. Can you stop by at 3:10?"

"I'll be there." He knew Marianne would mess up, given enough time.

He grabbed his pocket notebook from his console and added today's event, including place, date, and time. Tonight, he'd convert his recording to an MP3 file, building his case piece-by-piece.

Engaging the engine, he cast a parting glance at Marianne's house and shook his head. It was so sad. She had no idea how much she was hurting their son. How many years of counseling, of patient loving, would it take to undo the damage she'd caused? More than that, what would it take for Marianne to move past the pain of their divorce . . . so Jeremy could have a loving mom? One who baked cookies and read stories, not hurled swear words.

Was that even possible?

As if in answer, an old verse swept through his mind. *"'Not by might nor by power, but by my Spirit,' says the Lord Almighty."*

Nick's heart pricked as an image of Christ on the cross emerged. Blood dripping from his hands and feet, his face twisted in anguish while his tormenters insulted him from below.

His words, spoken shortly before his death, sliced through Nick's soul. *"Father, forgive them, for they do not know what they are doing."*

Nick closed his eyes. "Holy Father, Lord Jesus . . ." The words lodged in his throat, held back by pain and anger.

He swallowed hard. Without Christ, Marianne would never change—would never be the mother Jeremy needed.

"Soften Marianne's heart. Help her to see her need of You."

When he opened his eyes, a weight lifted off his shoulders. Inner resolve strengthened his depths, filling him with determination not to win the case, although that desire remained. But instead, to demonstrate, through this custody battle, the grace and truth of the cross. It wouldn't be easy or pleasant, but for Jeremy's sake, for Christ's honor, he'd do it. With God's help.

In route to his restaurant, he flicked on the radio, humming to praise tunes. He'd left a near-empty dining room with sour spirits but returned to find at least a dozen cars in the lot. Not a major rush, but progress. And he recognized three vehicles belonging to some of his most loyal customers—those he hadn't seen since the fire.

Thank You, Lord, for turning all things to good, for bringing hope out of the mess I've made.

Inside the restaurant, Ella Winston, his new hostess, stood behind the podium talking on the phone. Upon seeing him, she asked the caller to hold, then placed her hand over the receiver. "It's Mr. Myron from Ozark's Angus."

Nick raised an eyebrow. Their ribs were due to arrive tomorrow morning, just in time for the rib-eating contest that afternoon. Was there a problem? "I'll take the call in my office."

On his way, he glanced into the kitchen. Everyone appeared busy, focused—just like before the fire.

Rictor looked up, grinned, and made a thumbs-up sign. Nick smiled back and nodded.

They were going to make it.

As long as they didn't hit any more major speed bumps.

In his office, he settled into his chair, he picked up the phone. "Good afternoon, Mr. Myron. What can I do for you?" The man wasn't one to make social calls.

"I'm sure it's a technical glitch, but the credit card number you gave me has been declined."

His Visa bill. Nick's mouth went dry.

"Is there another card you can give me?" Myron asked.

"Can you give me a minute?" He put the call on hold, then rifled through the papers cluttering his desk until he found his most recent statement. He checked the due date and rubbed his face. Last week. Not having the funds to pay it, he'd put it off, hoping things would turn around. They hadn't. At least, not enough to cover all the expenses that kept piling in.

He pulled out his business ledger. Short by $500, and he still had to cover payroll.

Now what? How much did he have in his personal savings?

Stampeding caterpillars took up residence in his stomach as he returned to his phone conversation. "Listen, Mr. Myron, can I call you back in five minutes?"

The man paused. "Yes, sure."

Nick hung up, turned to his computer, and navigated to his personal checking account. His savings was getting pretty thin, and there was no telling how much this upcoming custody battle would cost. These things could drag on for years. If he drained his savings and their court date got delayed . . .

But they needed those ribs. They'd already placed ads with the local media, had reporters scheduled to come out. He grabbed his office phone and called the kitchen. Rictor answered.

"Yeah, Boss?"

"Those ribs we ordered won't be coming in."

"What? You can't be serious." He paused to control himself, taking a slow breath. "Okay. So what now?"

"I don't know." Nick massaged the back of his neck as if doing so could stimulate his brain cells into finding a solution. Except they were out of options. "Best thing to do now is to cancel."

"All right." Rictor sighed. "I'll call the newspapers."

Just when things were beginning to look up, Nick had hit another barrier.

Lord, are You trying to tell me something? Because right now it feels like I'm climbing up a greased slope.

Chapter 45

When Nick arrived at his attorney's office the following Monday, the secretary sent him right in.

Mr. Cooper sat behind his large cherry desk. Plaques decorated the beige wall behind him. Built-in bookshelves lined with leather-bound editions and black binders, potted trees positioned between them.

The lawyer rose with a smile. "Mr. Zimmerman, come in." He motioned toward a plush leather chair, then returned to his desk. "As I mentioned on the phone, I've been reviewing your case." He flipped open a file, checked the contents, then closed it. "Once again, I would like to stress, I believe you would stand a better chance if we changed our petition from full to joint custody."

"That won't work. Marianne doesn't follow the court rulings."

"Then we can file contempt charges."

"We've done that. It doesn't help. I want full custody. That's the only way I'll get to see Jeremy."

Mr. Cooper studied him for a moment. "You said you had something you wanted to show me?"

"Right." Nick pulled his cell phone from his pocket. "When I went to pick my son up, Marianne lost it. She'd been drinking, and I . . . Well, you can listen for yourself." He hit Play.

Other than an occasional raised eyebrow, Mr. Cooper listened with a placid expression. When the recording ended, he leaned back in his chair. "I understand what you are dealing with, and it is quite unfortunate. Quite unfortunate indeed."

"This shows how unstable she is. How destructive. There's a law against this, right?"

"Against?"

"Parental alienation. When one parent manipulates and trains a child to reject the other parent?"

"There is, but it is very difficult to prove."

Nick grinned. "Unless you have it all on tape."

"Unfortunately, this recording is not admissible in a court of law."

"You can't be serious."

"Sorry. Unless she knew the recording was being made, I doubt the judge will let it in."

Nick sighed and massaged the back of his neck. Once again, just when he thought things were turning around, someone side-kicked him. Mr. Cooper continued to talk about the case, but Nick barely heard him. Didn't have the energy to listen. He wasn't ready to concede defeat, but he was getting close. Hanging on by his last fingernail.

But there was still one more person who needed to hear this recording—Anita Bowman, Jeremy's counselor.

An hour and a half later, he sat in her office and played the recording for her.

She listened with a stoic expression. Not the slightest raised eyebrow or flicker of a frown.

When it ended, she studied him for a long moment, then stood. "Thank you, Mr. Zimmerman." She checked her watch, then crossed to the door. "I have a client waiting."

Nick stared at her. "That's it?"

She opened the door with a stiff smile. "Good day, sir."

Shaking his head, a heavy weight pulling his shoulders to the ground, Nick trudged to his car.

Why did it feel like everything was stacked in Marianne's favor?

Where are You, Lord? Because I could sure use some help here.

Back at the restaurant, he passed through the dining room, his gaze on the floor, and slipped silently into his office. A stack of missed calls sat on his desk, including one from Sherman.

This was a no-win situation. Either he lost the restaurant—forced his staff into unemployment—or he lost his son.

With his luck, he'd lose both.

Ella poked her head in. "There's someone here to see you, sir. A man by the name of Randy Motz."

Nick frowned, trying to place the name. Unable to, he was about to ask Ella to take a message, then changed his mind. He had nothing better to do—other than stew in his mess. "Send him in."

While he waited, he clicked through his emails, mostly spam. There was one from Tammy. He pulled it up, and tears stung his eyes. His son's liver recipient planned to be at the Organ Donation Awareness Conference and wanted to meet him.

Memories of the night he told Payton good-bye stole his breath.

"Sir?"

He glanced up. Ella stood in his office doorway. A tall, black-haired man was with her, one of the men from the mission. Did this man have information about his dad?

Nick lunged to his feet. He rounded his desk, crossed the room, and extended his hand. "I'm Nick Zimmerman."

Dressed in creased slacks and a button down shirt, the man nodded. "I know who you are." He glanced around the office, his expression softening.

Ella looked at Nick and reached for the doorknob.

He nodded. "Thanks."

It clicked closed.

"Please, have a seat." Nick indicated the chair in front of his desk.

The man remained standing.

"Been a mighty long time since I been in this place." He shook his head. "Mighty long." With one arm crossed, he ran his fingers over his mouth and gazed at a picture of Nick's grandpa posted on the far wall. It was taken during one of his many charity events. "Your grandfather was quite the man." He settled into the chair across from Nick, studied him. "You don't remember me, do you?"

Nick shook his head. "Sorry."

Randy leaned forward and pulled a wallet from his back pocket.

He flipped it open, removed a photograph, and dropped it on the desk.

Nick studied the image of a lanky man—no more than twenty—with long, black hair, pimples dotting his pale face. Standing near Flaming Mesquite's dishwasher, he wore his sleeves rolled up, a stained apron tied around his waist.

"That you?"

Randy nodded.

"You knew my grandfather."

"Best man I ever met. Helped me climb out of the gutter. Offered me a job, told me I was worth something. Weaseled me into going into rehab—into making something of myself."

"You know my dad?"

Holding Nick's gaze, Randy nodded.

"You know where he is?"

He shook his head. "Sorry." He looked around the room. "I heard about the fire. That's rough, man."

Nick shrugged.

The man observed him for a moment longer, then flipped his wallet back open. He produced a folded check from the folds and handed it over.

Nick took it. "What's this?"

"My way of saying thanks."

Nick opened the check, stared at the large amount. Enough for him to climb out of the mess he'd landed in. Unable to speak, he looked up.

"It's yours."

"This is too much." Nick shook his head. "I can't." He needed it, every dime, but he couldn't.

The man stood. "Sure you can."

Nick swallowed, thinking back to his desperate prayer offered but moments ago. *Thank You, Lord. Oh, sweet Jesus, thank You.*

Randy ambled to the door.

Nick bolted to his feet. "Wait."

Randy paused, turned.

"I'll pay you back."

With a slight smile, Randy shook his head. "Don't want it. Just pass it on. Find a way to help someone else, when you can."

As soon as Randy left, Nick's cell phone rang.

Mr. Sherman.

"Good evening, Nick. I received your message. Are you ready to make a deal?"

Still holding the check, Nick smiled. "I'm sorry, Mr. Sherman, but I'm going to have to decline. Have a great day."

Chapter 46

"Way to go, slugger!" Tammy gave Tylan a high-five, then wrapped him in a hug.

When she released him, Becky lifted his arm and bent it in a bodybuilder pose.

"Quite the arm you got there, big guy." She dropped his arm and poked him in the ribs. "I say this calls for ice cream." She turned to Tammy with her hands clasped below her chin, her bottom lip poked out.

Tammy looked at Nick. She never had asked him about the day he canceled on her last minute. And he'd never brought it up. Vanessa would tell Tammy to let it go and assume the best in Nick. Vanessa was probably right. "What do you say? Wanna join us?"

He gazed toward the east field where Jeremy's team was just beginning their game. "Sure, ice cream sounds great." The corners of his eyes crinkled.

"What?"

"I might have something worth celebrating as well."

"Oh, really?"

He nodded, then told her about a man from his past who showed up at his restaurant with a large—very large—check.

"Wow, that's amazing. Your grandpa left quite a legacy, didn't he?"

"That he did." Still smiling, he focused once again on the ball field.

"Hey." She nudged his shoulder. "Back to the ice cream. Think maybe Jeremy can join us?"

Nick frowned. Then he sighed and looked away. "Maybe." He breathed deep. "I'll call you when his game's over."

"We'll wait."

Becky rolled her eyes and Tammy tossed her a warning glare. With a dramatic exhale, the girl sank to the ground and started plucking blades of grass. Tylan dove for the chips, then sat beside her, perfectly content to spend the afternoon eating.

Tammy watched Nick. He looked so tired. Defeated. She knew he'd had some bad visits—more like nonexistent. People like Marianne made her ill. What she wouldn't give for her kids to have an involved father—someone who actually showed up for visitation, to baseball games.

She nudged Nick with her shoulder. "Hang in there."

He nodded, and a tendon in his jaw clenched. "Trying to."

They sat in silence for a while, watching the game, cheering on occasion. Tammy stole occasional glances at Nick, wishing she knew what to say. It had to be hard to be kept from his son, especially after having just lost his oldest. It had to be hard on Jeremy, too, not being able to see his dad. She thought of Brody, of his crazy schedule and apparent lack of concern. She knew he loved their kids. She just wished he'd make them more of a priority.

Cheers erupted, and she glanced up to see the crowd on their feet, waving their hands. On the field, Jeremy's team huddled around the coach, pumping fists in the air.

"Yay!" She clapped her hands and turned to Nick. "They won."

He smiled, stood, and wiped his hands on his pants. "I'm going to congratulate him."

She sprang to her feet. "I'll come." She turned to Becky. "Watch your brother, will you?" This generated another eye-roll. Tammy laughed and shook her head. "Teenagers." Twining her fingers with Nick's, she accompanied him down the hill toward the bleachers.

As they drew near, Nick stopped and dropped her hand.

"What is it?" Tammy followed his gaze.

"My ex-in laws." Squaring his shoulders, Nick narrowed his eyes and continued forward. Tammy followed close behind.

Two feet from the dugout, a large woman with long gray hair intercepted them. "The nerve."

Marianne joined her, standing with her hip shoved out, arms crossed.

"Darlene, Marianne." Nick stepped aside and looked past the women toward the field entrance where Jeremy and his teammates spilled through. His face lit up when his son approached. "Jeremy, buddy."

"Haven't you done enough?" Darlene glared. "You're killing your son, can't you see that?"

Nick exhaled. "I just want to see my boy."

Tammy waited a few feet away, wanting to offer support but not wanting to increase tension further.

The woman grabbed Jeremy's hands and thrust them toward Nick. "Look at this." The skin was red, chaffed, like it'd been rubbed with sandpaper.

Nick's face blanched. "What happened?"

The boy's head and shoulders drooped.

"Leave him alone." Marianne rushed forward.

Her mom raised an arm, holding her back. "He's stressed out, that's what happened. He's turning obsessive compulsive, washing his hands a hundred times a day. Talking about wanting to die. Because of you."

Nick flinched.

"Jeremy? Son?" His voice cracked.

Tammy's heart ached.

Marianne wrapped an arm around Jeremy's shoulder. "It wasn't enough to kill one son? You've got to destroy the other, too?" With an eye on Nick, Marianne brought her lips to Jeremy's temple. "Come on, sweetie." She and the others left.

Tammy looked from the receding pack to Nick. Without a word, he turned to go, face angled toward the ground.

She grabbed his hand. "Don't give up."

He jerked his arm away. "I can't do this."

"He needs you, Nick."

"Really?" His face hardened. "Because what I saw said different. I can't win, Tammy. The more I try, the worse she gets. The worse it gets for him."

"So you're just going to walk away?" She snapped her fingers. "Just like that?"

"What else can I do?"

"I'd expect you to stick around, not bail when things get hard. Men. You're all the same." The minute the words flew from her mouth, she regretted it.

Nick blinked, the pain in his eyes slicing at her heart. He shook his head and walked away.

She started to go after him. "Nick?"

Back to her, he raised his hand and kept walking.

Camped on the bank of Raccoon River, Nick watched the flames lick at the kindling stacked in front of him. A thick stream of smoke billowed into the sky, filling his nostrils with the soothing scent of burning wood.

He and Grandpa had spent countless Saturday afternoons here, tossing fishing lines into the currents. Nick never caught anything other than old shoes or tangled branches, but he always left content and relaxed. Like everything in the world would be okay. He'd brought the boys here once—back when they were barely old enough to hold a fishing pole. Always planned to return—do some camping, maybe teach them how to shoot a bow.

Never got a chance, and now it was too late.

Nick grabbed a twig and snapped it between his fingers. If only he hadn't left that night.

He thought of his dad, of his mental illness, his homelessness. Had he asked himself that same question? Was that why he quit coming around? Was his mom right? Would it have hurt Nick had his dad stayed?

Of course not. The man was his dad, and Nick loved him, regardless.

Would Jeremy say the same? But his hands . . . His raw, inflamed hands.

In his effort to help his son, to win custody, was Nick hurting Jeremy?

Releasing the sobs clogging his throat, he cried until his eyes and throat burned and his throat was hoarse. Then wiping his face with the back of his hands, he grabbed his Bible. He wanted to pray, needed to pray, but no words would come.

So instead, he sat, watching the dark shadows of clouds move across the night sky, swallowing then releasing the stars. The fire crackled, the flames lowering to a faint glow.

Payton, I'm so very sorry.

Payton is with Me. God's words swept through him, stealing his breath.

An image of his boy, surrounded by the purest white light, standing on a golden street, arose. Nick reached for the sky, as if he could touch his son.

Payton loves you. He always did.

Sobs wrenched through Nick's body, tears gushing until he could barely breathe. Eventually his sobs lessened to a sniffle. Wiping his face, he stared at the glimmering sky for some time listening to the fire crackle and crickets chirp.

Payton is basking in My love. It is time you do the same.

Nick grabbed his Bible once again and opened. Heart laid bare, he looked at the black letters without really seeing them. *Show me how, Lord. Help me.* A gentle breeze swept over him, turning the pages. A piece of paper slipped from the book and landed on the ground.

Nick picked it up. Notes from a sermon he'd listened to five years ago—six months after his divorce. He turned to the verses referenced on the page.

Galatians 5:1: *"It is for freedom that Christ has set us free. Stand firm, then, and do not let yourselves be burdened again by the yoke of slavery."*

The word *freedom* echoed through his mind, stirred a longing within him. But freedom from what? He reviewed the pastor's message.

"There are many types of slavery—sin, legalism, the inability to forgive—and the worst of all—the one that holds us in bondage and

keeps us from grabbing hold of freedom in Christ—is self-loathing. Let it go, and let God's love in."

Tears blurred Nick's vision, and he dropped the paper.

Give it all to Me—the pain, the shame, walk in My redemption.

With the image of Payton pressing on his mind, Nick closed his eyes and bowed his head. "Help me, Lord. Take away my guilt and shame. Help me to walk in the freedom of Your cross."

The wind rustled the leaves on nearby branches like a soft melody. And amidst the gentle sounds of night came God's words, like the soft tickle of a feather, so softly Nick almost missed them.

Stand firm.

He lifted his head and contemplated the message he sensed deep in his heart. He felt like he had nothing left to give and no strength left, but the Bible said God's strength was made perfect in man's weakness. Maybe because that was when folks leaned hardest on Christ.

That he could do.

Chapter 47

Tammy sat on the couch hugging a throw pillow, feet curled under her. Vanessa, in town for work, sat beside her, nibbling a brownie. The rich aroma of chocolate and fresh brewed coffee filled the house. Tylan and Becky were both in bed, the steady blare of the television now replaced by soft praise music. Music that should have soothed her but only deepened the ache in her heart.

Vanessa set her dessert plate on the coffee table and turned to face her. "So, you going to tell me what's got you all bummed or do I have to guess."

Tammy ran her hand along the leather cushion. "My life, that's what."

Vanessa studied her. "Nick?"

Tammy held Vanessa's gaze, shrugged, then looked away. "Men in general, and my tendency to drive them away."

"What happened?"

She told her about the encounter at the baseball game.

Vanessa listened, bobbing her head. "And then what happened?"

"It's not so much what happened . . ." She hugged her pillow tighter. "I'm through with men, that's all. Through with having my heart ripped out and stomped on."

Vanessa's eyes softened. "He's not Brody."

"I know he's not. But that doesn't mean he'll stick around."

"He moved, Tam. And he was just a kid. You both were. You can't go through life expecting people to leave you. You can't give Nick, or anyone else for that matter, half of your heart and expect them to hang on. It doesn't work that way." She paused. "I know you've been hurt, betrayed. And that stunk. What Brody did wasn't right. But you gotta let that go."

Tammy sighed, blinking back tears. "I'm not sure I can. I can't . . . go through another breakup."

"You gotta forgive him, T."

"I'm not mad at Nick."

"No. Brody."

Tammy tensed.

"That's the only way you'll learn to trust." Vanessa grabbed Tammy's hands in hers and gave a gentle squeeze. "Just let it go."

Tammy inhaled a shuddered breath, her words but a whisper, "I don't know how." A tear slid down her cheek. She wiped it away.

"It won't be easy. The first step's the hardest. And this might be something you have to choose daily, because forgiveness is rarely a one-time thing. It's more like a constant battle, but you gotta fight it. You gotta keep fighting, every day, every moment if you have to. Give it all to God—your anger, your hurt, your fears. He can handle it. And He can heal you, if you'll let Him. Come here." She placed her arm around Tammy and pulled her close.

Tammy rested her head against Vanessa's shoulder and let the tears fall. As she did, a dark cloud began to lift. It still hurt, and she was still afraid—so incredibly afraid—but she glimpsed freedom.

"Let's pray." Vanessa nudged Tammy with her shoulder then bowed her head. "Lord God, help Tammy through this. Help her to release her anger and bitterness. Give her the strength to forgive, to love without fear or self-preservation."

"Thanks, V." Tammy straightened and smoothed her hair from her face. "It's getting late. I should probably head to bed. You know, my couch is still open, if you want to stay here."

"Hm, give up my nice hotel with its queen sized bed and down pillows, paid by my boss, to wake up with a kinked neck." Vanessa was booked at one of the nicer hotels in town. Tammy couldn't blame her for not wanting to stay over.

She laughed. "Well, when you put it that way."

Vanessa stood. "Call me?"

She nodded and walked her to the door. "Thanks for coming over. I've missed you."

Vanessa hugged her. "I've missed you, too."

After she left, Tammy returned to the living room. Her Bible lay on the coffee table, beckoning her. Emotions raw, she fell to her knees. She clutched the leather book to her chest, the edge pressed under her chin.

"Oh, Lord, it hurts so bad. All those lonely nights—the fear, the betrayal." The image of Brody standing at the door—suitcase in hand, eyes cold—flashed through her mind, initiating a fresh surge of bitterness. "I'm so angry! It wasn't fair. He walked out on me. Walked out on us."

As soon as the words left her mouth, a verse from her morning Bible reading came to mind. *"The Lord our God is merciful and forgiving, even though we have rebelled against Him."*

No. It wasn't fair. But neither was Christ's death on the Cross.

She knew what Christ was asking her to do, what He'd been asking her to do for some time, if she was honest. It was past time she obeyed. Closing her eyes, she gripped the Bible tighter. "With your help, I choose to forgive." Hopefully, one day, God would align her feelings to match.

Chapter 48

Nine months later

Nick sat in a stuffy courtroom, sweaty palms spread flat on the table in front of him. Mr. Cooper sat beside him, flipping through a notepad. Next to this was a file filled with legal papers—documentation of the many times they'd been in this very spot.

Stand firm.

He repeated the phrase in his mind again and again, willing his nerves to calm. Lifting his chin, he breathed deep and exhaled slowly. He scanned the courtroom.

A podium with a microphone separated his table from Marianne's. Wearing a pale blue blouse and starched skirt, she sat with her spine erect, looking like the perfect soccer mom. Her lawyer, a brute of a man with bodybuilder shoulders, whispered in her ear.

Behind them sat Marianne's entourage—her mom, glaring at him. Her dad, chewing on a fingernail. And Victoria, Marianne's best friend, sitting with hunched shoulders, face angled downward. Her gaze flicked to Nick before returning to her lap.

So she was here to testify against him. He expected as much.

But the one he worried about most was Anita Bowman, Jeremy's counselor. Dressed in gray, she sat near the back door, shoulders back, head straight. Face void of expression, she stared at the empty judge's stand.

"All rise."

Nick startled at the sound of the bailiff's voice. He stood on numb legs as the judge made her entrance.

"The court is now in session. The honorable Judge Galde presiding."

The judge, the same one who'd presided over their last hearing, sat. She glanced at the papers in front of her.

"You may be seated."

Nick's chest burned, and he released the air he'd been holding. He relaxed his shoulders.

Stand firm. He could do this. God could do this.

The judge glanced from Nick to Marianne. "Good morning. This court is assigned for the petition of custody of the minor child, Jeremy Zimmerman, filed on behalf of the petitioner, a Mr. Nick Zimmerman." She reviewed their case briefly before addressing his lawyer. "Mr. Cooper, are you ready to proceed?"

Nodding, Mr. Cooper stood and launched into his opening argument, relaying Nick's long list of grievances. "My client believes it is in the child's best interest for him to be awarded full custody."

"You may call your first witness."

Mr. Cooper called Nick to the stand, and he testified to all the events that had brought him to this point. Of course, Marianne's lawyer lashed into him, accusing him of negligence.

"Is it true, Mr. Zimmerman," Mr. Dewolf's voice lowered, taking on a booming effect. "That your son, Jeremy Zimmerman, is afraid of you?"

"Because his mother has made him so. She feeds him with so many lies—"

"Objection," Mr. Dewolf said. "Inflammatory."

The judge leaned forward. "Mr. Zimmerman, answer yes or no, please."

Hands fisted, Nick looked at his lawyer. Mr. Cooper nodded.

Nick sighed. "Yes." His stomach cramped. He swallowed past a wave of nausea. There was no way the judge would rule in his favor. In fact, by the time Marianne's lawyer finished, Nick might not receive any visitation at all.

His lawyer questioned him next. "Mr. Zimmerman, when was the last time you received your court ordered visitations with the minor child?"

"Nine months ago, the week Payton died."

"And prior to that time, had you and Ms. Hawke agreed upon what dates the minor children were to remain under your care?"

"We did. We agreed I would have them over their spring break."

"Did they stay for their entire visit?"

"No, they did not." Nick told the court about Marianne's reaction on the night of Payton's death and how she had withheld visits since. He also talked about his efforts to get Jeremy into counseling. "I know losing his brother—seeing him die—was very hard on Jeremy. I wanted to do everything I could to help him get through that."

"In fact, you paid for the counseling sessions, isn't that correct?"

"I did."

"Can you please tell the court about your son Payton's death?"

Tears blurred Nick's vision. Blinking them back, he clenched his jaw, inhaled and nodded. "Yes."

"On the night of the accident, when did the police arrive?"

"Uh . . . Eight. Eight thirty maybe. About the same time as the ambulance."

Mr. Cooper continued to ask Nick questions about that night. How long he'd known Beverly, why he trusted her to supervise the children.

When finished, Nick rose and stepped down. His knees felt ready to buckle as he left the witness stand. Jeremy's counselor, Anita Bowman, was called next.

The judge swore her in, and she took the witness stand, eyes focused straight ahead, chin raised.

Nick swallowed against the urge to vomit. How could he stand firm when the attack kept escalating? Anita was nothing more than a paid puppet—and on his dime! The woman hated him. That much was clear. Even after he'd played the recording documenting Marianne's hysterics, she'd refused to help. Refused to act in the best interest of his child.

Marianne's lawyer stood a little taller. "Mrs. Bowman, can you please tell the court how long you have been counseling the minor child, Jeremy Zimmerman?"

"I have met with the child and his mother on eight separate occasions. I have also met with the child alone, without his mother, on four occasions."

"And how did the child appear to you?"

"Very upset, as I expected."

"And is he frightened of his father?"

The counselor looked at the lawyer for a long moment before responding. "He is very confused."

"I can imagine. Mrs. Bowman, what do you believe is the cause of his confusion?"

"His mother."

Marianne gasped, and Nick's head snapped up. The lawyer's mouth gaped. He stared at Mrs. Bowman as if dumbfounded.

"It is my opinion that Marianne Zimmerman's compromised mental state has been extremely detrimental to the emotional health of the minor child."

"Objection." Mr. Dewolf stood. "Mrs. Bowman is not—"

"Overruled." The judge's eyes narrowed. She turned to Mrs. Bowman. "Please, continue."

"I do not believe it is in the best interest of the child for Marianne Zimmerman to retain full custody."

Nick's jaw went slack. Marianne's lawyer barraged Anita in an obvious attempt to trip her up, but she held her ground, going so far as to say she believed Marianne was emotionally unstable "at this time," and in need of psychiatric help.

Marianne lurched to her feet. "Objection."

The judge frowned. "Ms. Hawke, you cannot object. Mr. Dewolf, please control your client."

Marianne's lawyer reached for her, but she jerked away. "Obviously my loser of an ex-husband has turned the counselor against me."

Her lawyer grabbed her arm.

"Get off me." She lurched away and faced the judge, hands clenched and shaking. "That man," she jabbed her finger toward Nick, "murdered my son."

"Ms. Hawke, sit down!" The judge slammed her gavel.

"He has no right to be a father," Marianne's voice rose to a shriek. "None." She stepped toward Nick, but her lawyer intercepted her. He said something, but Nick couldn't hear what.

Marianne's face blanched, and she stared around the courtroom. Still trembling, she returned to her seat.

Exchanging glances with Mr. Cooper, Nick suppressed a grin. The judge had finally seen the real Marianne.

Mr. Dewolf gave an audible sigh. "I have no further questions for this witness."

"Mr. Cooper," the judge looked at Nick's lawyer. "Do you wish to cross examine Mrs. Bowman?"

The lawyer smiled. "No, your honor."

Mr. Dewolf called Marianne's best friend to the stand next. To Nick's surprise, she gave a similar testimony.

She looked at Marianne with teary eyes. "I'm sorry. I know this has been a hard year for you, but you're hurting Jeremy." She shook her head. "I can't bear to see it anymore."

Marianne's mom testified next, showing the courtroom where Marianne learned her emotional outbursts. Her dad followed, acting like a hostile witness, which seemed to hurt Marianne's case more than all the others.

The hearing lasted two full days—long enough to make Nick squirm. Rictor, Gloria, Bev, and Howie showed up, talking about what a great dad Nick was. But Marianne had her own supporters—a woman from the unity church she attended, the librarian. A few of her "party" friends, who, of course, came cleaned up and looking like model parents.

But after Mrs. Bowman's testimony, surely the judge would rule in his favor.

Wouldn't she? He'd heard crazy stories—of mentally unstable, bitter women receiving full custody. Of fathers, just like him, being stripped of their rights.

Shifting, he glanced around the courtroom then looked at the judge, who appeared to be watching him intently.

She pinched her chin. "I don't see any evidence that Mr. Zimmerman presents any imminent risk of substantial harm to this child. However, I am concerned with what I have heard in regard to Ms. Hawke's behavior. Based on testimonies presented in this hearing and the reports made by Ms. Anita Bowman and the court appointed evaluator, I am awarding sole physical custody to Mr. Zimmerman."

As she continued to read her verdict, Nick stared at her, struggling to make sense of her words. After all this time, all their battles, was this really happening? He was going to get to see Jeremy? Not just see him, but bring him home? For good?

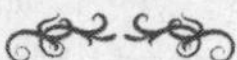

A police officer accompanied Nick to Marianne's, just in case. If there was ever a time for her to get hysterical, it was now. Nick needed to be careful not to do or say anything to make this harder than it had to be. For Jeremy's sake. This was going to be a difficult enough transition as it was.

Standing on Marianne's welcome mat, Nick rang the bell. The police officer stood beside him, arms down, stance stiff.

The soft shuffle of footsteps soon approached, and the door eased open. Marianne stood in the entryway, eyes red and puffy. The end of her nose appeared chafed. She looked from Nick to the policeman and her chin puckered, her lashes fluttering over moist eyes.

With a deep inhale, she turned to Jeremy. He sat on the couch, staring at a blank television screen. "Your dad's here."

She spoke so softly, Nick barely heard her. He worried Jeremy might not have but the boy's head turned. He looked first to Nick, then to Marianne.

Still holding the door, she nodded. He rose and left. He returned a few moments later carrying a duffel bag in one hand and a stuffed lizard in the other.

"Hey, bud." Nick wrapped an arm around his son's shoulder and pulled him close. He looked at Marianne. "Thanks."

Her bottom lip trembled again, and she dropped down to Jeremy's level. "I love you, Jer-bear. You know that, right?"

He nodded, a tear sliding down his cheek. Marianne wiped it away then pulled him into a hug.

Nick's heart ached to see his son torn between the two adults he loved the most. But he'd get through this. With God's help, they all would.

When he looked at Marianne, a compassion so deep it stole his breath swept over him. "You know, I want you in his life. He needs his mom."

More tears spilled over her dark lashes. Palming them away, she nodded.

Nick led Jeremy to the car and dropped his belongings in the trunk. Closing it, he glanced back at Marianne. She stood in the open doorway, hand pressed to her mouth, tears streaming down her face.

He rounded the car and slid behind the wheel. Paint samples were spread across the passenger seat on top of a magazine with tree house building plans. Jeremy sat in the back, watching his mom.

Nick waited until they drove out of the neighborhood before handing Jeremy the magazine. He watched his through the rearview mirror. "Remember that tree house I told you about—the one my grandpa made for me?"

Jeremy nodded.

"Figured it was time you and I make one just like it. Thought maybe you'd like me to paint your room, too. Any color you want. What do you think about that?"

"Any color?"

"Any color."

Jeremy gave a hint of a smile.

Nick reached behind him to squeeze the boy's knee. "Everything's going to be all right. We'll make it through this. I promise. Now, how about a little music?"

Nick pushed a CD into the player and turned up the volume. Casting Crowns drifted through the speakers. *Yeah, we're going to be just fine. Thank You, Jesus.*

Chapter 49

Tammy's stomach knotted as she watched men and women stream into Winchester Manor's banquet room. Not because she was nervous for the event. This was her fifth organ donation awareness conference, and her role was minor. Greet the guest speakers, make sure they had everything they needed, and answer any questions they had. What twisted her stomach was the knowledge that Nick would be here. Marianne had declined Heartland's invitation and all attempts of communication. But Tammy prayed for her. Daily.

She and Nick hadn't talked since their little . . . confrontation. She should have called him. Apologized, if only to save their friendship.

But how could she be friends with the man who held her heart?

She couldn't. It hurt too much.

The Davenport family entered and lingered near the doorway. They glanced about with wide, bright eyes. Rustin, their teenage son and the recipient of Payton's liver, radiated health with his broad shoulders and slightly ruddy complexion. Such a difference from the photo before his transplantation.

Tammy wiped sweaty palms on her pant legs and approached the family with a smile. "Mr. and Mrs. Davenport. Rustin." She shook each hand in turn. "Thank you for coming."

Mrs. Davenport, a slight woman with shoulder length hair curled under at the ends, looked around the room. "Everything's so beautiful."

The room truly was elegant—one of the nicer banquet halls in the town of Oak Park Blossoms. The marble floors glimmered under crystal chandeliers, the light dispersing into miniature rainbows.

Crown molding separated the textured walls from an Italian fresco that arched to the top of the domed ceiling. A man in a tux sat at a grand piano near the far back corner, playing softy.

Rustin was clearly nervous. Standing half a step in front of his parents, he visibly twitched. Cracking his knuckles, he surveyed the room like a timid child and not the determined defensive linebacker Tammy knew he was. The local newspaper called him "The Dominator." Everyone expected him to graduate with a full scholarship. Some said he'd even make it to the NFL. Either way, he was here, breathing, and healthy.

Tammy faced him. "Are you ready for your speech?"

Rustin's eyes widened even further. Fidgeting, he punched his fist into the palm of his hand again and again. "I'm good." A smile flashed, then faded as his gaze intensified. "Is Mr. Zimmerman here?"

Adrenaline spiked through Tammy, sending her stomach on another roller coaster. She glanced at the banquet entrance. "Not yet. But I—" Her breath caught as Nick entered, dressed in a teal shirt that accentuated his muscular frame. Jeremy was with him, holding Nick's hand.

Upon seeing her, Nick froze. Then, as if in slow motion, his eyes shifted ever so slightly to take in the others standing with her.

He looked at Rustin, and for a moment, it seemed as if he struggled to breathe. The two stared at one another. All around them, voices rose, people passed, but in their little sphere, it was as if time had stopped.

A vice squeezed Tammy's heart. She loved this man. Oh, how she loved him.

So tell him!

But this wasn't about her. Besides, what good would that do, except complicate things? Make him feel guilty. He didn't need her and her emotional outbursts, her embittered heart.

Except she'd worked hard to let go of her bitterness and anger. Maybe if she told him, apologized.

She stepped toward him, her stomach roiling. "Nick." She turned to Jeremy and smiled. "Hey, there."

"Hi." Jeremy's gaze flitted to her before making a wide sweep of the room.

"Come on." She touched the boy's shoulder. "There are some folks who want to meet you. To thank you and your dad." Fighting through mixed emotions, she guided them toward the Davenports. "This is Mr. and Mrs. Davenport, and this is their son, Rustin. And this," she motioned to Nick, "is Nick Zimmerman and his son, Jeremy."

Rustin and Nick stared at each other, not speaking for a few moments. Then, without warning, the teen lunged forward and wrapped his muscular arms around Nick. "Thank you. Thank you for giving me the chance to live."

With one arm around his son, Nick hugged Rustin with the other. Jeremy's shoulders shook, his sobs coming out as a soft whimper.

Tammy glanced at Mr. and Mrs. Davenport, fighting tears. Holding hands, they looked from one another to their son with such love, it was as if Christ Himself were in their midst.

And so He was.

Nick stepped back and surveyed the young man standing before him. "You look good. Strong. Healthy."

Jeremy continued to sniffle, wiping his eyes and nose with the back of his hand.

Rustin nodded and flashed a smile. "Made varsity. If I keep it up, work hard, my coach says I may get some scholarship offers."

Nick raised an eyebrow. "Really? Good for you."

"That kid's going to go far." Chest puffed out, Mr. Davenport clamped his hand on Rustin's shoulder. "He'll be the first in the family to go to college." Voice hoarse, he looked at Nick. "Thanks to you. And your son."

Nick's Adam's apple bobbed. He nodded. "Thanks for saying that."

"Good evening." A strong voice came over the loud speaker.

The room quieted as people took their seats. Tammy checked her watch, then addressed Rustin. "You ready?" He was one of the first speakers.

He breathed deep. "Let's do this."

Tammy turned to Nick, her heart breaking.

He held her gaze, his eyes soft, penetrating.

Say something. Tell me to wait, ask to talk to me. Anything.

But he didn't.

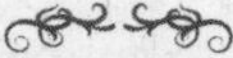

A lump lodged in Nick's throat as he listened to Rustin's testimony—of what it felt like to wait for an organ, fearing he'd die before one came. Of getting the call, prepping for surgery, then waking up, knowing his life would never be the same.

"I think of my donor every day." Rustin's throat turned husky. "Thank God for him. And I vow not to take advantage of the life he gave me. No regrets. I'm going to make it count. Have to." He slowly scanned the audience, then exited the stage.

Applause sounded, and everyone rose. Nick stood on numb legs, thinking of Payton.

But Nick was next, which meant he needed to compose himself. At least enough to give a cohesive speech without breaking down in gasping sobs.

The emcee introduced him, and Nick turned to Jeremy. "You good?"

Jeremy nodded.

Help me, Lord. Nick stood, his speech paper rolled in his sweaty hand. The room went silent as he stepped onto the stage and up to the microphone.

He spread his paper flat on the podium, then gripped the wooden edges. He looked out over the crowd—doctors, nurses, mothers, fathers. Some who'd lost loved ones, others who came to celebrate the gift of life.

"Payton was my firstborn, my bud. I swear he came out of the womb with his fist pumping, ready to take on the world. Found his love—baseball—at age four." Nick chuckled. "He and I spent hours tossing a ball back and forth until I thought my shoulder would come off its hinges."

An image of a four-year-old Payton, hand swallowed by Nick's baseball mitt, came rushing back, nearly buckling his knees. He swallowed and paused to give himself time to regain composure. “What I wouldn’t give to play catch with him one more time.”

He looked at Jeremy who watched him with teary eyes. “I don’t know why God allowed my son to die. That’s something I may never have answers to. But I know he’s in heaven, free of pain. He accepted Christ four years ago at a neighborhood Vacation Bible School.”

He paused to make eye contact with a few of the adults in the room. “Parents, have those conversations with your kids. Help them grasp onto life, but even more important, teach them how to find salvation. Because tomorrow is guaranteed to no one, and this world here?” He pointed his finger to the floor. “Isn’t what it’s about.”

The room went silent, and a few people shifted.

“Payton showed me something—something that drives my every thought. Never waste a moment. Like Rustin said, you gotta live with no regrets.”

He looked at Tammy, sitting at a table to his right, his love.

No regrets.

Opening session concluded, Tammy waited for the guests to mill out of the banquet room to their various breakout sessions. Rustin’s speech replayed through her mind.

“No regrets.”

Her life was full of regrets, the greatest being how she’d blown things with Nick. Was it too late to mend their friendship? To start again?

What must he think of her?

Obviously, not much, otherwise he would’ve called.

And after today, it’d be over for good. She’d have no reason to contact him.

“Tammy?”

She turned to see Nick standing before her, and her pulse quickened. Jeremy sat at a table a few feet away, talking with the Davenports.

“How’ve you been?” His eyes searched hers.

“Good.” *Liar.* “You?”

"Good." He shoved his hands in his pockets.

"You did a great job with your speech."

A heavy silence fell between them as the last few attendees left the room.

This was their good-bye. Nick's version of "let's be friends." Only they couldn't be. Not anymore. Tammy's heart couldn't take it.

"Well." The back of her throat burned as tears welled to the surface. She swallowed them down. "I better go."

She started to leave but Nick grabbed her wrist, his grip sending rippling waves of heat through her arm.

"Wait."

"Yes?" Holding her breath, she turned to face him.

"No regrets. I promised my son—promised myself—not to take life for granted. To hold tight to—to fight for—those I love." He took her hands in his. "Tammy Kuhn, I love you. These last nine months have been miserable without you."

A tear slid down her cheek. He wiped it away, tracing his knuckle down her face to her lip. Following the contours of her mouth with his thumb, he stepped closer, his breath warm on her skin. "I almost lost you once—"

"Twice."

He gave a throaty chuckle. "Twice. But I won't lose you again."

Chapter 50
One year later

Tammy stood in front of the full-length mirror, her veil cascading over her shoulders.

Standing behind her, Mom stepped closer and rested her chin on Tammy's shoulder. "You look beautiful. Simply radiant."

Tammy smiled and ran her hands along the smooth satin. "Thanks, Mom. It's hard to believe."

"What is?" Mom turned to face her. "That you're in love? That you found a man who thinks the world of you? I always knew you would. Of course." She angled her head with a sigh muted by the twinkle in her eyes. "Even though this means you're not moving to Dover."

"Sorry."

"Well, you're only a road trip away."

A knock sounded on the door, and her father poked his head in. His eyes and nose were red. "You ready, pumpkin?" He pulled a handkerchief from his breast pocket and wiped his nose.

"I am." Tammy looped her arm through his.

She waited in a side room outside the foyer for the bridal march to begin. Then the wooden doors opened and her wedding party slipped out one by one.

Tammy's stomach flittered, her legs wobbly, as she walked down the aisle. White carnations decorated the sanctuary pews, and on the stage, lights glimmered among the tulle. Becky and Vanessa, Tammy's maids of honor, stood side-by-side, wearing teal dresses.

Nick and Tammy's boys stood on the other side of the altar dressed in the most adorable tuxedos. All of them grinned so widely, their cheeks had to hurt. But Tammy barely noticed any of that. Her every thought centered on the handsome man waiting for her at the end of the aisle.

Reaching the altar, she turned her head to smile at Nick. The love radiating from his eyes left her breathless.

After the pastor opened and her father officially gave her away, Tammy turned to face Nick who pulled a piece of paper from his inside coat pocket.

"Tammy Kuhn, it scares me how much I love you. I can't imagine living a day without you. And thanks be to God, I don't have to."

He took her hands in his. "Tammy, I promise to love you—every part of you. When you're mad, sad, or laughing yourself into a choking fit. Through wrinkles and gray hairs, college and empty-nesting years. I will honor and cherish you from this day forward, until the day our God takes me home."

Once their vows were spoken and their marriage announced, the moment Tammy had long been waiting for arrived. Holding her gaze, Nick leaned closer and lifted her chin. His breath swept over her, his lips warm on hers.

Still in his tuxedo, Nick helped Rictor load the reception leftovers into the back of a refrigerated truck. Not wanting to waste good food, Nick planned on taking it to one of the local shelters. Standing, he wiped the sweat off his brow, his grin stretching so wide, his cheeks ached. Tammy stood a few feet away, talking with Vanessa. Still in her gown, her skin glowed. Ringlets framed her face, and her eyes glimmered.

My wife. Mrs. Tammy Zimmerman.

"Congrats, man." Rictor clamped a hand on Nick's shoulder. "I always knew you'd find your angel."

"Thanks. You guys did a great job with the meal. I appreciate it."

"Guess we should take up catering, huh?"

"Hardly." Nick's cell phone vibrated in his pocket. He pulled it out and checked the display screen, recognizing the area code but not the number. "Zimmerman."

"Hello. This is Randy from the Safe Haven Ministries."

Nick held his breath.

"Your dad's here. Thought you'd want to know."

Nick hung up the phone and stared numbly ahead.

"You okay, man?" Rictor asked.

Nick turned on stiff legs. He looked at Tammy.

She stopped talking and came to his side. "Hey, everything all right?"

"They found my dad."

"Oh, sweetheart."

He let out a chuckle and engulfed her in a hug, lifting her off her feet. "They found my dad." He pulled away and closed the back door of the van. "Hope they like rotisserie chicken. What do you say, Tam? Wanna take a trip to Safe Haven with me?"

She stared at him. "What about . . . ?"

"Our honeymoon?"

She blushed, nodded.

"Maybe he can come with us." Seeing her eyes widen, he laughed. "Just kidding. But since we're driving to Colorado, I figured we're not in a huge hurry. But I would like to see my dad." A lump lodged in his throat and he cleared it. "Make sure he's all right, and find out how I can see that he gets the care he needs."

She smiled and, stepping closer, grabbed his hands in hers then raised on her tiptoes until their eyes were level. "I love you, Mr. Zimmerman."

"And I love you, Mrs. Zimmerman."

New Hope® Publishers is a division of WMU®, an international organization that challenges Christian believers to understand and be radically involved in God's mission. For more information about WMU, go to wmu.com. More information about New Hope books may be found at NewHopePublishers.com. New Hope books may be purchased at your local bookstore.

Other Books by This Author . . .

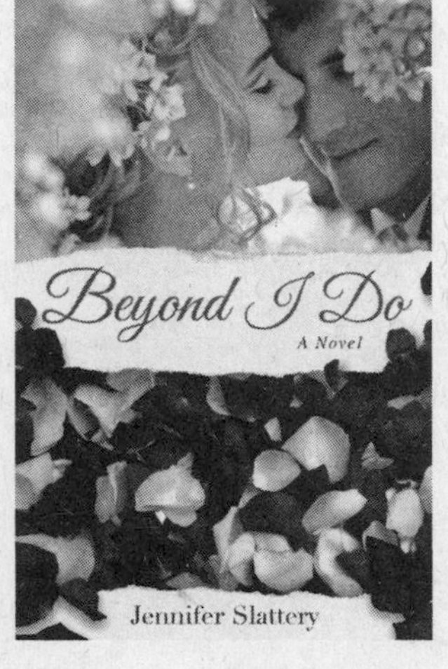

Beyond I Do
978-1-59669-417-0
N144123
$15.99

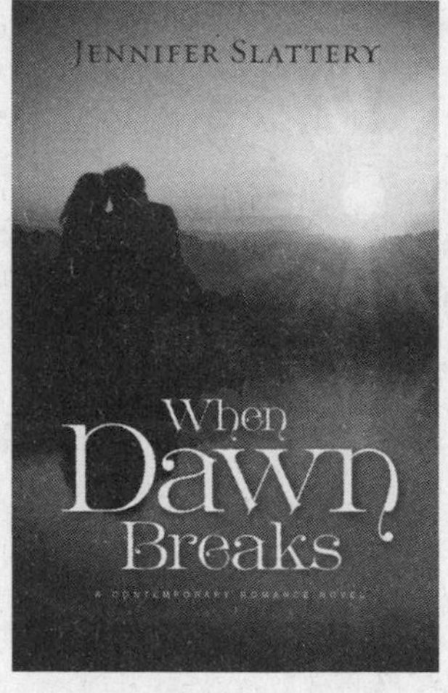

When Dawn Breaks
978-1-59669-423-1
N154102
$15.99